KNOT ALL THAT GLITTERS

DEVYN SINCLAIR

All that is gold does not glitter,
Not all those who wander are lost.

Don't let anyone dim your sparkle, no matter how hard they try.

AUTHOR'S NOTE

Dear Readers,

Knot All That Glitters is not a book that's meant to be dark. However, there are still things which some readers might find objectionable or difficult to read, including gaslighting, discussions of drug use, and the threat of being drugged. While no drug use occurs in this book, those who have had experiences themselves or with family, please use caution. If you feel like this could be a problem for you, please protect yourself. No work of fiction is worth your mental health.

The full list of content warnings is available on my website.

A note about exotic animals:

In *Knot All That Glitters*, you will meet Stormy, a clouded leopard. While Stormy gets lucky in the book and ends up loved in a home that will do everything to care for her, not every exotic animal is so lucky.

The idea of owning an exotic animal as a pet is intriguing. But many are adopted without the adoptees knowing the full scope of care necessary, or the difficulties that come along with the responsibility. Because of this, and the low number of zoos and shelters to take such animals, many exotic pets are abandoned or euthanized.

The situation in the book is specialized, with the Atwood pack both having the financial ability and willingness to take care of Stormy's special needs.

If you are considering adopting an exotic animal, please do your research about the legality, and the *reality* of what it's like and the level of commitment required. And if you feel so inclined, please check out the various conservation efforts of endangered and vulnerable animals like Stormy.

CHAPTER ONE

PETRA

*T*he dress being pulled down over my head reminded me of a flower girl.

I supposed that wasn't entirely fair. The gown was slightly more sophisticated than a dress made for toddlers, but not much.

"Oh, that's lovely." Carmen peeked around the corner and appraised where I stood on the platform for the seamstress.

Forcing a smile at my stepmother in the mirror, I nodded. "It's nice."

And it was nice. A pretty shade of dark green that matched my eyes, with embroidery at the empire waist and neckline. But it felt like a nun's habit because of how much it covered. All the way to the floor, all the way to my neck. I was lucky I convinced the PR team having a dress with no sleeves wouldn't send the press into a frenzy.

Hell, the dresses I wore for recitals when I was younger showed more skin than this.

"I've changed my mind about the shoes," Carmen called from the other alteration room. "You need black ones. No more than two-inch heels. Go find some when she's done."

It was a pity she wasn't an Alpha—she missed her calling as one. My Beta stepmother carried herself with the power of an Alpha, no matter what. She smelled like green apples, and not in the good way. In the sickly, candied way that quickly became too much. Exactly the way it was now.

Pressing my lips together, I just barely kept my eyes from rolling. "Okay."

The seamstress—I thought her name was Helen—smiled at me. "You can go look for them now. You're all set. We don't need to change anything."

I nodded and accepted the hand she offered to step off the pedestal. What a metaphor that was. I needed help to get off a pedestal I didn't want to be on in the first place.

1

"Would you like me to bring you a selection of shoes, Miss Merriton?"

"No." I said the word through gritted teeth. "Thank you."

No matter how hard I tried, no one called me by my full name. They chopped off the first part. Even though I understood why, it still felt like someone poking a sore bruise every time it happened.

But I couldn't be mad at the woman. She was just trying to get through her day like everyone else, and she also had to deal with Carmen at her worst. The least I could do was cut her some slack.

I walked out of the dressing room and onto the main floor of Bergman's fashion department. The high-end department store catered to the wealthy and famous. Naturally, Carmen shopped here and nowhere else. She was on a first name basis with most of the staff, with weekly fittings for her ever evolving wardrobe.

Thank fuck I only had to come here when I needed something for an event. I didn't mind dressing up. The gowns I walked through were stunning, and any number of them would have been amazing to wear. But daughters of politicians didn't get to make those kinds of decisions.

One more night, Petra. That's all that's left.

The shoes were all the way across the sales floor, so I took my time winding between the displays and mannequins, imagining I could wear something that actually showed I had a body.

Like *that* one.

A mannequin on a raised platform showed off a gown I would kill to wear. Black, but shimmering. Every color could be seen shifting in the sparkles, from a gorgeous buttery gold to ocean-deep blue. The sleeves slipped off the mannequin's shoulders and wrapped around them, giving the effortless and sexy illusion the dress was falling down when it wasn't.

Not to mention the slit in the side of the skirt was high enough that whoever wore it wouldn't need underwear. The bright white of the mannequin's plastic hip was bared for all to see. Imagining walking into a room in that dress?

The rush of power was intoxicating.

Sadly, I had no occasion to wear a dress like that, even if I would be permitted to.

"You would look fucking incredible in that."

I jumped, my heart racing, only to find my friend laughing. We both yelled in surprise and greeting, happiness bursting out of me. "You scared the shit out of me."

Eva May Willams grinned at me and pulled me into a hug, enveloping me in the scent of roses and the lighter scent of coffee. Her two hulking bodyguards were only a few feet away, and it was a miracle she wasn't accompanied by a crowd of paparazzi. "That is entirely your fault," she said. "I called your name a couple of times, but you were in your own little dreamland."

I rolled my eyes. "Self-preservation, I promise you."

Eva looked me up and down. "I'm guessing there's no chance you can switch out this dress for that one?"

"My father and stepmother would have a heart attack," I said. "And then dad's campaign manager would have a heart attack. Plus the entire PR team. Basically, if I wore a dress like that, I'd murder around ten people."

She laughed and slung her arm around my shoulder. "Still, you'd look killer in that dress."

"Thank you. I'll keep it in my dreams for the day I actually have a place to wear it." I started walking toward the shoes, and she kept her arm on my shoulder, walking with me. "Why are you here?"

"Same reason as you. Checking to make the dress for tonight fits."

My head whipped around to find her smirking. "You're coming?"

"I am."

"Thank fuck. Sloane will be there, too. Please tell me you'll save me from death by boredom?"

Eva laughed. "Girl, we've got you. Don't worry."

I looked at her. "Don't get me wrong, I'm happy you're going to be there. But why on *earth* are you going to be at a political fundraiser?"

"Ah-ah," she wagged a finger at me. "You know we're not allowed to call it that. It's a charity ball for the children."

I tried to fight my laughter and failed entirely. "I've missed you."

"I've missed you *too*. And to answer your question, I always pick a charity or two every year. I am actually donating to the charity. The other thing... we'll see."

Sighing, I glanced back at her security. Eva and I had been friends for a long time. Our families ran in the same circles. Which was why I knew she was trustworthy. And those being paid sometimes weren't.

"Guys, can you give us some space?"

They didn't question, spreading out in both directions.

"What was that look?"

I drifted toward the shoes once more, watching as the security maintained their distance. "It was nothing." I couldn't risk saying anything real out in the open like this, even without the guards breathing down our necks.

She put her hands on her hips. "That's a lie. But it's okay. I'll have all night to get it out of you. How about these?"

Black heels which would look right at home with the other dress. Black and shimmering gold, with a heel a million miles tall. I shook my head. "Two inches."

"Petra, two inches is never acceptable for anything. High heels, pizza size, and dicks."

I covered my mouth and snorted out a laugh. "Eva."

All she did was raise her eyebrows. "You know I'm right, Bee."

My old nickname, because my scent was a lot like honey. That or 'bumble.' I liked Bee more, but only a few people still used it.

"Oh, I know." I grabbed the first pair of black heels I saw that fit Carmen's requirements. "But there's nothing I can do about it until tomorrow."

"Oooh, something I should know?"

We didn't get to see each other often, given her film schedule and my own... restrictions. Everyone knew Eva May Williams, the wholesome and beautiful Omega movie star who recently began to take on edgier roles and sharpen her image. It matched her personality.

Jealousy sparked in my chest before I could push it down.

4

"I start school next week. The *powers that be* finally agreed an apartment downtown would be more convenient than commuting from home. Though I'm still annoyed I had to fight so hard for an apartment I paid for."

"Oh, *fuck* yes." Her voice echoed across the store, scandalized patrons looking in our direction. "And I do mean that literally. Please find someone to fuck immediately."

"*Eva.*"

"*Bee.* Am I wrong?"

I shot her a look, and she laughed.

"Petra." Carmen stood in the doorway of the fitting room, glaring at me. She was already out of her dress and back in her suit. I lifted the shoes so she could see I was doing as she asked. "Duty calls."

"I should get to my fitting, too. But I'll see you tonight." She hugged me again, whispering. "Maybe we'll find someone for you to fuck."

My face heated with embarrassment. I barely held in the laughter on the way back. Carmen glared with equal intensity in Eva's direction. "I thought you got lost."

"Yes," I said, allowing my sarcasm to drip. "It's completely possible for someone to get lost a few hundred feet from where they left."

Her whole demeanor turned cold.

Or colder than usual.

"I don't appreciate your attitude."

The retort was on my tongue and I bit it back. Instead, I sighed. "Will these work?"

"Put them on and let me see."

Back on the pedestal, I stepped into the shoes and let her circle me. The staff waited too. "No. Maribelle, can you find something matte?"

The shoes on my feet had a bit of shine to them, which I liked. But I closed my mouth and my mind and retreated into the place I went at times like this. What I wanted didn't matter. What I liked didn't matter. Everything was already decided.

I could hang on until tomorrow. Then I would have a taste of freedom. Not much, but it was enough. If I could make it through tonight.

"Petra, *where* is your head right now?" Carmen snapped.

"What?" I looked at her, and she was waiting expectantly. "I'm sorry, I didn't hear you."

"That's crystal clear. Let's hope your head comes back in time for the ball. We need you to make a good impression."

I held Helen's hand and changed into the new shoes so she could see them. "No one will be looking at me, Carmen."

"Yes, they will. If you listened, you would have heard me say there's a pack your father and I would like you to meet tonight."

My whole body froze. "Why?"

"Because they're looking for an Omega, are from a good family, and it seems you might be a good fit. That's much better," she said, looking at Helen. Then she smiled at me. The million dollar megawatt smile she reserved for the cameras, or when she wanted something. "See? You look perfect."

I stepped down off the pedestal, still stunned by what she said. Carmen approached and stood behind me. As a rule, I tried not to stand close. Her sickly sweet scent was a cloud of cloying I loathed. She met my eyes in the mirror. "Your father and I really are proud of you. I'm sure you won't let us down."

"So this pack helps him," I said. "That's what it's about?"

"Of course not. Not everything is about the campaign." It was the most blatant lie I'd ever heard her tell. "One of their members is a media strategist. We heard they were looking and thought they might be a good fit."

"No." I turned and faced her, my hands shaking with sudden adrenaline. 'No' wasn't a word I used around Carmen. She always won.

Always.

"*No?*"

"My pack is my choice," I said. "Mom and Dad agreed a long time ago he wouldn't arrange anything."

Carmen rose to her full height—including the nightmarishly high heels *she* was allowed to wear—and stared down at me. "That was before your mother..." She skipped right over having to say the words. 'Before your mother died.' "It's neither here nor there. I agreed to no such thing."

My hands curled into fists. "That's not what—you don't get a say in this, Carmen."

"We'll see." Her smile sent chills running across my skin. "I have a meeting with Ezra. *Do not* be late tonight."

"I won't."

Carmen left, her gait shifting to her public walk. Strong, tall, with just enough sway in her hips to keep people interested, but not so much she was inviting anything. I used to watch her practice.

"Miss Merriton," Helen held open the curtain for me.

"DeWitt-Merriton," I whispered under my breath.

Helen took the dress from me when I passed it through the curtain, and I put my clothes back on. Clothes Carmen had scoffed at when I arrived. Though the jeans and sweater I wore were perfectly acceptable and cute, she wanted me wearing business casual.

There weren't many lines I got to enforce, and the ones I did were small. Like being able to wear jeans. Hopefully, once school started and I was doing everything they wanted, I could scrape together a little more liberty.

"Is there anything else we can help you with, Miss Merriton?" Helen's face was full of kindness, but also pity. The kinds of looks I got from anyone who knew what Carmen was like, but couldn't do anything about it. I dreaded those looks.

"No, thank you, Helen. Have a good rest of your day."

"You as well."

Fat chance of that. Apparently, I was going to a charity ball to be auctioned off to a pack who would help my father's political career, and I was the bargaining chip.

It hadn't always been this way, but it was now. If my father and Carmen got their way, my whole life would be planned out. I needed to find a way out. But I wasn't about to solve that today.

Folding the dress over my arm, I got into the car waiting for me and leaned back against the seat.

Get through tonight. Just one night, and I could breathe.

CHAPTER TWO

PETRA

"Thank you for coming," I said. "Seriously."

"An excuse to drink for free at The Feldman? In a pretty dress? I'm thanking you. Rehearsals don't start for weeks and I'm bored as shit. All I'm doing is taking class every day." Sloane tipped back the glass of champagne in her hand and emptied it. "Oops. Guess it's time for more."

My best friend knew how to make even the most boring event a party. "Still. You know what I mean."

She grabbed two more flutes of champagne off a tray from a passing waiter and handed one to me. "I do know. Now *please* drink something so you can relax. You're one night away from fucking freedom, and I don't think I've ever seen you this tense."

I sipped the champagne and made a face. Too bitter. "Oh my god," she laughed. "It's wasted on you."

"How do you even drink this?"

"How can you not?" She took my glass from me. "We'll get you something you like."

My life would probably be easier if I liked things like wine and champagne. It would liven up functions like this. "I'm going to need something," I told her. "I'm in this nightmare of a dress, and all I want to do is go home and make sure the last of my stuff is packed."

"It's not that bad," she looked me up and down. "Promise."

I crossed my arms. "Says the woman wearing *that*."

Sloane wore a slinky blue dress with a low back and thin straps. It barely clung to her body, and was a potential wardrobe malfunction waiting to happen, but she looked amazing. In comparison, I looked like her frumpy cousin.

"Incoming," Sloane muttered. "Behind you."

"Petra, you look lovely."

I turned and plastered on a smile. "Hey, Dad."

He hugged me, and I hugged him back, ignoring the quiet

click of cameras around me. The truth was, I missed him. He was away in the capital more often than not, and I rarely got to see him. Not the way I used to.

"How are you?" He asked. "Big day tomorrow."

"You know me. I'm always fine."

Dad's eyes narrowed, but he wouldn't ask me here. Not in front of the cameras. He used to be able to read me better than anyone else. Now? I'd been lying so long I didn't know if he could tell the difference.

"Are you sure?"

"Of course." I managed to find my public smile a second before Carmen slipped her arm through my father's arm.

He turned and kissed her briefly, earning more camera clicks from the well-placed journalists around the room. It wasn't a craze of paparazzi, but there would be just as many pictures in the morning.

"Darling," Carmen said. "I told Petra about the Gidwitz pack. They've just arrived, and she's excited to meet them, so I don't think we should keep them waiting."

"Right." My father looked down at his watch. "We have a couple minutes before the speech. Perfect timing."

I gaped at Carmen. Excitement was the *last* thing I felt about this. "Dad, I—"

"Your father's been worried about you, Petra. After everything. Taking this step is a good one. For all of us. You're finally coming into your independence."

I buried my hands in the folds of my dress to keep from showing the way they were shaking with rage. "I need to use the restroom. I'll be right back."

Not waiting for permission, I turned and fled. Sloane was right behind me. "The *Gidwitz* pack? I don't think there could be a less sexy name if they tried. What the hell is happening?"

There were only a few people in the large lobby outside the ballroom, and they looked at Sloane and me as we burst out of the doors like I was fleeing a fire.

"Hey. There's a grand piano."

Emotion hitched in my chest. I knew where it was in the lobby, and I didn't look. It was in a little alcove surrounded by windows that faced The Feldman's gorgeous and lush courtyard. In the morning, the piano was drenched in sunlight, and playing it felt like being in your own little world. I remembered.

Mom used to love that piano.

"And?"

"You should play."

I shot my best friend a look over my shoulder. Now? That was the distraction she was choosing? I didn't have to say anything for her to know it wasn't the time.

Pushing open the door to the bathroom, I made sure we were alone before I leaned on the sink and blew out a long breath. "My stepmother is a raging bitch. That's what's happening."

"Oh." She laughed. "Well, we already knew that."

"Now I'm stuck."

Sloane opened her purse and reapplied her lipstick. Half of what she had on was left behind on the champagne flutes. "Your dad would never force you into a match you didn't want, Bee. You just have to tell him."

I wasn't so sure about that. My dad was a very different man than he'd been when my mother died. He loved me and I loved him, but the man I grew up with no longer existed. He died and was buried right beside Mom and my other dads. "Maybe. But I can't do it here."

Carmen would make sure it turned into me being petulant or wanting attention. She always did, and despite loving me, I saw the shadows in my father's eyes. He believed her.

"Then later. It's just an introduction."

I sighed. "You're probably right. Better get it over with."

Carmen was waiting to ambush me. "There you are. Come along. They're waiting to meet you."

Words were on my tongue, but she grabbed my arm and pulled me back to the ballroom. I twisted and looked back at Sloane, mouthing the word *help*.

She gave me a thumbs up.

I kept my mouth shut as Carmen guided me across the crowded ballroom. In front of us, I saw where my father was already speaking to a group of men, and I cringed. "No fucking way."

"Watch your mouth," Carmen said. "This is a good pack, and they are well connected. Do you want to see your father succeed?"

I pulled my arm out of her grip. "Stop pretending this has anything to do with him."

"It does have to do with him. Everything matters right now, and a courtship with the right pack could seal the deal." Her snarled words were soft. "We'll discuss it later."

"Like hell."

We were there, and I smiled as dad turned and gestured to a tall man in a suit. "Petra, this is Charles Bower. His son is one of the Alphas of the Gidwitz pack. Gentleman, this is my daughter, Petra—"

"DeWitt-Merriton," I finished for him. If I was being introduced, they were going to know my full fucking name.

One of the men stepped forward. "Nice to meet you. I'm George Bower. Charles's son. This is my pack."

He was handsome enough, but in a bland and unimpressive way. Scent cancellers were strong in the room, but I leaned forward a little to see if I could get a read on him. He smelled like... milk?

I managed to keep my face even. "Nice to meet you."

The next one stepped forward, a Beta, and someone approached my father. "Sir, it's time."

Dad smiled. "Seems like I've got a speech to make."

I was shaking the Beta's hand, trying to remember what he said his name was, when it hit me. The entire world reduced to a single breath, because I knew I'd never have a *first* inhale of that scent again.

Whoa.

It was impossible to describe. Rich and dark at first, a bitterness I actually liked. Shifting through something like salt in the air before turning to sweet caramel deliciousness. Holy shit. It wasn't something that had a name, but I wanted to bury my nose in it and *inhale*.

Someone was shaking my hand. They kept introducing themselves, and I hadn't registered a word of it. The last one took my hand and kissed the back of it. "Umm... thank you."

"Of course. We were happy to hear you're looking for courtship," the first Alpha said. "Since we're looking for an Omega, it seemed like a good—"

"Which one of you smells like caramel?" The question blurted out of me. Carmen was already glaring at me, and I couldn't care. I still smelled it but couldn't pinpoint the source, and I *needed* it.

The fourth man in the pack raised his hand. "Maybe me? Mine is sweet, but I've never heard it described as caramel though."

I stepped forward and sniffed him brazenly. Nope. *Fuck* no. He smelled like an old woman's perfume. Lavender soap and too much powder. Dry, stale, and likely to make you sneeze.

"Bee!" a loud voice called. Eva appeared at my side. "I told you I'd be here."

"You did." I felt dazed. Untethered. What the hell was happening?

At the front of the ballroom, someone clinked a fork against a glass, calling for silence. I needed to get out of here. "Go," I whispered to Eva. "*Go*. It was nice to meet all of you."

I didn't wait for their response, practically pushing Eva through the crowd of people toward where Sloane and Eva's pack were standing. I waved to the guys and yanked Sloane close. "Help."

"I did help, bitch," she said with a laugh. "I sent Eva in to get you."

But Eva stared at me. "I don't think she means that kind of help. Look at her eyes. And smell that?"

"Oh, shit. You're perfuming?"

I was. I really was. This couldn't happen in a room full of people. If Carmen knew I was perfuming? Panic clawed through me. "What do my eyes look like?"

Sloane looked. "Dilated. You kind of look like a shark. Big dead black eyes."

"Thanks." I made a face. "I got hit with something. A scent."

Suddenly Eva was grinning. "Oh, hell yes. I love it when this happens. My sister found her pack like this. R.A.S."

"R.A.S.?" I blinked.

13

"Random act of scenting. What does it smell like? We'll tell you if it's something in the air, in case it's someone who has a really strong scent."

I swallowed. The air was clear here, and I hated it. All I wanted was the scent back again, like a desperate addict who'd had one hit and suddenly needed everything, regardless of whether the clear air was helping the perfume problem. "I need a drink."

"What do you want?" Eva asked. "I'll have one of the guys grab it for you."

"She likes the fruity shit," Sloane said. "The stuff you can't taste alcohol in."

"Got it."

Sloane put her hands on my shoulders. "Talk to me. Tell me what it smelled like."

"I—" Clearing my throat, I shook my head. "I don't know how to describe it, Lo. It has so many notes. Salted caramel with this smoky undertone. *Delicious*. It's sweet but not like a sugar high. Like I could eat an entire bag of that candy and the stomach ache would be worth it."

She started laughing, and I shook my head. "I don't know. But it hit me in the face like I'd been punched, and I feel like I'm going through withdrawal."

She laughed. "Okay. I'll keep an eye out. By the way, I swear if you end up bonding a pack with the name 'Gidwitz,' I'm going to mock you for the rest of our friendship."

"Like you aren't going to do that anyway."

"True."

I looked back at the pack I'd rudely abandoned. They still watched me, and Carmen was smiling and laughing, probably trying to undo whatever damage I'd done. It wasn't them. Every instinct I had told me none of the Alphas and Betas in that pack were the source of the scent.

"I'm so happy all of you could be here with me tonight." My father's voice carried over the crowd. The introduction was over and he was speaking and I couldn't focus on anything because I needed more *caramel*.

"Lo," I said. "I need to get my shit together, or there are going

14

to be pictures of me losing it tomorrow, and those will be the headline, not the charity, or my father."

If I stole my father's thunder, and the money being raised for Slate City Children's, Carmen would kill me. And my father would look at me with that disappointed, distant look I couldn't stand.

"Here." Eva shoved a drink into my hand. A curvy glass with an umbrella. The drink was pink. Strawberry and tropical, which was objectively good. And absolutely not what I wanted. A low whine built in my throat, and everyone in the immediate area looked at me.

"Shit," I whispered. "I need to get out of here."

Lo stepped in front of me, subtly blocking my body with hers so I was hidden from the front of the room. She was an Omega, too. But I'd never seen her react to a scent like this. I hadn't either.

"We need to find them." Eva pulled me backwards into the center of her pack, who were creating walls with their bodies. "If you're reacting like this, then whoever's scent that is? They're fucking losing their minds."

I felt... strange. Like I'd suddenly become loose from reality. Wrapping both hands around the drink to steady myself, I glanced at Eva's pack. They were facing away from me. "Thanks, guys."

One of Eva's Alphas, Jack, turned and smiled. "We know what it's like to be blindsided by a scent you can't get enough of." His eyes fell on Eva, and the air between them went taut. You could *feel* the magnetism drawing them together. If they weren't in the middle of a ballroom, they'd be undressing each other by now. He winked before he turned around.

"Fuck, Eva," I muttered. Their single interaction was everything I ever wanted.

She laughed under her breath. "I know. Just make it through the speech, all right? We'll find him. Or her."

"It's a him." Instinctively, I knew that too.

"We'll find him."

I blew out a breath. My mind was clearing in the absence of

the scent. "Maybe it's better if we don't. Anyone who's here probably isn't someone I want to be with."

Most of the events my father hosted for his campaign were like this. They were for a good cause, but they were also for him. And the people who came to them were the people who cared about appearances. Who they donated to, who they were photographed with, or, like that pack, who they bonded with, were the things which mattered.

There was polite applause around the room, the crowd clapping at something Dad said. "Thank you again for coming. Enjoy the drinks and the food. Let's raise some money and make a difference tonight."

My father raised his glass, and the whole room followed suit. I took a sip of the fruity cocktail and closed my eyes. Ignoring the brain freeze, I sucked what was left of the drink down. It was only one drink, and I needed some kind of buzz. I felt a nameless sense of loss. How could one brief blast of scent do that?

Music started, and in the center of the ballroom, my father and Carmen began to dance. A brief reprieve before she was sure to give me a scathing appraisal of my behavior.

"Maybe it was a fluke," I said. "Some weird combination of scents that hit me just right."

"No fucking way," Sloane said, pushing her way past the barrier of Eva's Alphas, still on guard.

One of them, Liam, turned to Eva. "Dance with me?"

It was strange to see Eva blush. She was one of the most confident people I knew, and yet her Alphas still affected her like they were just meeting.

I wanted that.

They went to the dance floor.

Sloane took me by the shoulders. "It wasn't a fluke. We'll walk around and see if you catch the scent again."

"No need," Eva's Alpha Tyler said.

We both looked at him. "Why?"

He chuckled. "Because I'm pretty sure that's him."

I followed the line of where he pointed. An Alpha in a suit stood near the edge of the room. His tie was slightly askew, and I looked just in time to see him run his hands through his hair—a move which looked desperate and panicked.

He looked around the room, searching like he'd lost something precious.

Before I could say anything, Tyler raised his hand and caught the Alpha's eye. He barely looked at Tyler, eyes skimming past everyone and landing on me like a heat-seeking missile.

My entire body shuddered. It was him.

And he was walking straight toward me.

CHAPTER THREE

___

COLE

I sighed into the mic at my lapel. "You're killing me, you know that?"

Harrison's chuckle came through loud and clear despite the music and the humming cacophony of the crowd. "I'm not killing you. You only have to be on duty until after the speech, then I'm setting you free. Nick will relieve you and you can enjoy yourself."

"Enjoy myself," I muttered. "Yeah. I'm going to enjoy myself."

He sighed. "You might as well try."

"Yeah, fine. Switching over."

I changed the channel on my radio over to the rest of the security team and let them fade into the background. Harrison wasn't wrong. It would likely be my last chance to let loose for a while.

Not that hanging out at a charity ball was my idea of 'letting loose.'

The ballroom of the hotel was decked out with flowers that probably cost as much as the fundraiser would make tonight. High cafe tables circled the wide open space, along with tables full of catered food. A stage had been built at one end, where the speeches on behalf of the children's hospital would be made. Soon, I hoped.

Harrison had mentioned a silent auction too? Maybe that was the other tables across the room. I saw some gift baskets and pieces of paper.

People dressed to the nines filled the space, milling about and mingling. The dancing would start after the speech. One place I would definitely be staying away from.

Everything was running smoothly. I was here mostly to make sure they *kept* going smoothly. Russell Merriton was one of the most popular politicians around, but that kind of fervor could also inspire the opposite.

From what I could tell, he was a decent man. He'd done good things for Slate City, and had good ideas for the rest of the country, too. But no one ever agreed on ideas. Came with the territory.

I doubted someone would try anything at a function *actually* benefiting a good cause, but stranger things had happened.

"Check in," I said.

One by one, the guards under my command reported back. Everything was fine. The crowd—a mix of fans and protestors—were safely and calmly across the street outside. All the entrances were secure, and this party was as boring as it was intended to be.

No matter if it would be a chance to relax, I was going home as soon as the speech was over. Get some sleep, start fresh. Lose myself in whatever new job Harrison lined up. He probably left the files in my office. I'd barely been home to look.

"Mr. Kennedy." The event coordinator's voice spoke in my ear. "We're ready for him."

"Thank you."

Merriton always had wide perimeter security at events like this, but we didn't approach unless it was necessary. And when we did, it was the lead. Me. It cut down on unnecessary mistakes and interruptions.

Searching the room, I found the Senator across the room speaking with a group of men and his wife. Perfect.

I wove through the crowd, keeping awareness around me. This crowd would be plenty drunk before the night was over. Nick was going to have his hands full, and I didn't envy him for a second.

Leaning in, I spoke. "Sir, it's time."

He turned to the group he was speaking with. "Seems like I've got a speech to make." He looked at me on the way past. "Thank you, Cole."

"Of course."

My body went rigid, everything locking in place. Merriton was moving through the crowd and I needed to move with him. But what the *hell* was that?

The scent poured over me like someone dumped a tsunami on my head. *Omega*.

Honey and cinnamon. Painfully sharp sweetness undercut with layers of spice. A thousand different shades and nuances, and I needed more. Right the fuck now.

"Cole?" Nick's voice was in my ear.

Fuck. I needed to move, and it felt like I'd been rooted to the spot. Forcing my body to unlock, I moved stiffly behind the Senator, following him to the stage and looking around.

Omega.

The air was clear over here and the scent was still in my nose. It was branded in my mind. One breath I would never fucking forget it. I needed to find the source. I needed—

There were the stairs. I took my spot beside them and glanced around the room. No one was acting like the entire world had shifted in the last fifteen seconds. But it *had*.

Merriton stood with the woman who was introducing him, and I searched the faces in the crowd, looking for whoever smelled like that. There were scent cancellers in the air. I knew because I saw them place the automated dispensers earlier during the walkthrough. A scent that strong?

I didn't know what the fuck to do.

My hand touched my radio as I turned away from the stage. "Harrison."

It took him a second answer. "Yeah?"

"I'm moving Nick in a few minutes early."

"Are you really that bored?"

"No. I need—fuck, Harrison. On the way to the stage I got hit in the face with this scent. I couldn't move. Nick had to talk to me to break me out of it. It's all I can fucking think about. I need to find—"

"Cole." Harrison's voice cut through mine. My pack mates and I were equals. Still, each of us were able to get through to each other if we needed to. "What are you saying?"

"I have no idea. But I'm not in my right mind. I need to find it or I'm going to go crazy. Put Nick in the lead. I'm signing off."

A long pause. "Tell me when you get home."

Of course I would. Because if this scent was what I thought it was...

No. I couldn't get ahead of myself. Hope was a painful thing when it was destroyed.

I pulled the radio off my belt and ripped the earbud out of my ear, shoving them at the nearest one of our employees I could find.

I started where I'd found the Senator in the crowd. But the same group of people stood there, and there wasn't anything. Traces of the sweetness lingered, but the cancellers were already doing their job. The scent was dissipating, and as much as I wanted to shove my way through everyone in search of it, I couldn't.

Not at all, but especially not during his speech.

Fuck.

I followed the thread of it I could still sense. Just that single, tiny taste was enough to make my eyes roll back in my head and my mouth water.

"I'm so happy all of you could be here with me tonight." The Senator began his speech. The words were nothing but a blur in my ears. I followed the scent through the crowd, winding my way toward the back. She had to be here, right?

It was a woman. An Omega.

The scent evaporated, and I cursed under my breath. A drink. I needed a drink. The banquet table was right there, and I grabbed a glass of water. The last thing I wanted was to be fucked up right now. Unless it was on more of the scent.

Take a breath, Cole.

A laugh burst out of me, drawing a look from an older woman nearby. All I was doing was taking fucking breaths, and the air didn't feel right anymore.

Slowly, I drank the glass of water, trying to get a grip on myself. If they were a guest at the ball they would still be here. And at worst, we had a guest list. Though I doubted Harrison would allow me to call every person on the list and see if they knew an Omega who smelled like cinnamon and honey.

When the glass of water was gone, I loosened my tie. One

look at the appetizers told me I didn't want them. Blake would be horrified by the food.

But I still wished they were all here to do this with me.

The Senator was almost done speaking. Soon the dancing would start. It wouldn't make it easier to find someone with everyone moving around.

Polite applause filled the air, and it felt like it was mocking me. *Congratulations!* You lost what could be the best scent in the entire goddamn world.

I ran my hands through my hair, desperately searching the crowd for any sign of someone who was...

What the hell was I looking for?

A raised hand caught my attention. An Alpha was waving. At me. I focused on him and noticed the way he and two others were standing. Like they were blocking something.

Or someone.

Beyond the Alpha stood a woman. Long dark hair swept up off her neck. Green dress that looked like she was wearing someone else's clothes to hide her body. And she was fucking stunning.

Staring straight at me.

My feet moved before I told them to. Because there was only one resounding thought echoing through me.

Mine.

CHAPTER FOUR

PETRA

Sloane took the drink out of my hand. "Holy shit."

I couldn't say anything. Somehow I'd turned to stone under the gaze of the Alpha headed straight for me.

The scent hit me, and what I already knew was confirmed. That rich, caramel scent I couldn't fully describe. And he was...

Fuck. He was incredible. Tall even across the room, with a jawline Eva's co-stars would kill for and a suit tailored to perfection. At the same time, there was a ruggedness to him that stood apart from most of the people in this room. A raw quality. Just a little less polish and that roughness soothed the sharp edges of fear I had.

Maybe he wasn't from this world after all.

"There you are!" Ezra swooped in out of nowhere and caught me by the arm, pulling me away from the group and from him. "We need some photos of you with your father and Carmen."

"Wait—" I twisted away from him to look back, and he just pulled me faster.

"Quickly. The Senator has too many people to speak with for you to take your time."

The Alpha had reached where I'd been standing, eyes still on me as I was practically dragged across the ballroom. Flower arrangements taller than I was lined the edge of the room. My father and Carmen were there, smiling for the bank of cameras.

"Sorry to pull you away from your friends, sweetheart," Dad said, pulling me into his side. "This will only take a second."

"For god's sake, smile," Carmen hissed at me.

I smiled. But my mind wasn't here. It was a hundred feet to the left. His eyes were on me—I could feel them like a brand.

Holy hell. Was this what happened with Dad's pack and Mom? The way they described it all made sense now. Everything made so much fucking sense.

"Thank you," Ezra said to the photographers. "The Senator

has to move on. We have the mayor and the director of the hospital waiting," he said, guiding my father away.

The cameras weren't pointed at us, but they were still nearby. A blessing in disguise, keeping Carmen from ripping into me in front of half of Slate City. I moved back toward the Alpha. The scent.

"I think I managed to undo some of the damage you did, walking away from the pack like that."

I blinked at her. "What?"

"The Gidwitz pack. I got them to laugh off your rudeness, just saying you were excited to see your friends. But it can't happen again."

"I'm not interested," I said.

"I don't care if you're not interested," she said. "The Gidwitz pack and their families are some of the biggest donors we have. One of their Betas is a media genius, and they need an Omega. I don't care. This is going to happen, Petra."

I rolled my eyes. "I need to go."

"You do need to go. Right here. George, I found who we were looking for." Carmen grabbed my shoulders so fast I was dizzy. "You're not leaving this party until you've come to some kind of agreement. And don't even think about complaining to your father. He knows, and he agrees." She pushed me directly into the arms of the first Alpha from the pack. George. He pulled me onto the dance floor with a grin, and we spun in circles.

My head was fuzzy. I needed to get the fuck away from this man. His scent was so far opposite to what I craved, I was cringing away from him. "I think there's been a misunderstanding," I said.

"Carmen explained everything," he said with a laugh. "I get it. Events like this are a little overwhelming, especially with friends in the mix."

I shook my head, pulling myself together. Fuck it. Carmen was already pissed at me and there wasn't anything I could do to change it, anyway. "No. I'm sorry, but Carmen vastly misrepresented my interest in courtship. I'm sorry if your pack got your hopes up, but she didn't even tell me about meeting you until this afternoon."

26

He paused, our rhythm faltering. Then he closed his eyes. "That actually makes more sense."

"I'm sorry. I really am. You guys seem nice, and I was a bit of an asshole. But trust me when I say this wouldn't work."

He smirked. "I know."

"You *know*?"

"Your scent. It's nice, but a bit sweet for me. The others felt the same. I know scent theory isn't everything, but—"

I wilted in relief. "Oh thank fuck."

We laughed together. "Carmen said you were so eager, and my father also thought it was a good match. So we were willing to give it a try. But you're right."

"I'm sure you'll find someone."

He shrugged. "We're not really looking, and if it happens, we're open to it. But we're also happy as we are."

"Thank you for understanding." Glancing over my shoulder, my entire group of friends was watching me, and the Alpha was gone.

My stomach sank.

Carmen watched us from the side of the dance floor, a smug look on her face. "Dance me over there," I nodded to the opposite corner. "We can both get out of this quickly."

"Deal," he laughed. "Friends?"

I nodded. "If we ever run into each other again."

We made it to the corner, and he released me. "It was nice to meet you."

"You, too."

He walked down the side of the room, back to his pack. I watched for a second as he spoke with a smile, nodding back toward me. The rest of them were smiling too, and George leaned in to kiss one of the Betas. I couldn't remember his name, but I was glad they were happy.

Carmen was moving around the dance floor, coming for me. She waved and smiled. The smile had an edge. "Petra."

"Shit."

I knew her well enough to know she wouldn't let it stand, no matter my feelings. Or George's. When Carmen wanted something, she was a junkyard dog. She grabbed on and didn't let go until you gave her what she wanted, or you were in so much pain you couldn't stop her from taking it.

My father saw none of it.

"What the hell was that?"

"You said I couldn't leave until we came to an agreement. George and I both agreed that this is a bad idea."

Rage built on her face. "Everyone has to make sacrifices for this family, Petra. Your entire life, you haven't made any. Your father needs this."

I took a step back. I hadn't *made any*? "If dad needs this, he can tell me himself."

"Oh my *god*, Carmen. That is a fabulous dress." Eva appeared behind her, distracting her long enough for Sloane to grab my elbow. "Come on."

We nearly ran out the side door into one to the hallways off the ballroom. "She's got a target on your back tonight."

"No kidding. Eva won't be able to stall her for long. Carmen will see through it. She's not going to let me leave."

"Yeah, we gathered. Eva and Liam heard the whole thing when she made you dance. And there's more you need to know. But it can wait. We're going to make you disappear. And when your carriage is ready, we'll get you out of here."

"Disappear?"

"Yup." Sloane sped up, yanking open the door to... a closet? "Get in."

"Sloane—"

"Do you want to go home or not?"

The door down the hall behind us opened, and Sloane pushed me inside the closet and shut the door. The lock clicked from the outside. The handle wouldn't budge. "*Sloane.*"

There was no answer. Only the faint sound of voices as she spoke to someone.

"Oh my god, I'm going to kill her."

A second later, the world tilted on its axis and I was falling through the center of it. Caramel and salt.

I spun, and he was there. His tie was gone, shirt unbuttoned, and his hands were in his pockets like he had no cares in the world.

28

"Your friends seemed to think this was the only way."

His voice made me shudder. Low and deep, as smooth as the caramel he smelled like. But the sharpness of the salt was there too, adding to the rough edge.

Like two magnets clicking into place, we both moved. Collided. He took my face in his hands and kissed me. I was wrong about falling through the world. *Now* that was happening and there was no way to stop it. Hurtling through space, completely unmoored from everything I thought I knew.

Perfume filled the tiny space—I couldn't help it. The instincts that made me who I am were screaming that this Alpha needed to take me and make me his.

My arms were around his neck, and his hands were now in my hair. Gripping. Ruining what was left of my ridiculous hairstyle. My makeup too.

Good. I wanted to be fucking ruined.

I couldn't get enough. The way he smelled and tasted. I wanted to climb all of it and live for an eternity. We slammed against the wall together, not stopping for a single second.

His mouth on mine. Our tongues dancing together. My heart pounding in my ears. The way his body pressed me against the wall. I moaned, the same whine building in my chest. I needed this.

Breaking away, he buried his face in my neck, inhaling like it was his first breath after drowning. "Fuck." The single word was a vow and a prayer. Desperate and raw. And more than words, I needed his lips consuming me again.

I pulled him back to me and kissed him. Breathing no longer kept me alive. He did. Kissing this Alpha was oxygen. I didn't know if I could ever live without it.

The door opened, bathing us in sudden brightness. "Let's go," Sloane said, looking behind her. She had my coat and clutch in her hands. "Quickly."

"I—"

She looked between the two of us. "I know. But if you want a chance of escaping this party, it has to be now."

I looked back at the Alpha, his face still inches from mine. He pulled back, thumb brushing over my lower lip. A single second lasted for an eternity. My lipstick smudged his mouth and his eyes were dark as sin. I wanted to fall into the void and never come out.

Sloane grabbed my hand and yanked me toward her. "Now, Bee."

I couldn't look away from him. His eyes followed me as long as I was in sight. I was a mess. My makeup was smeared, my hair tangled and wrecked, and I was fucking smiling.

My car pulled up to the curb, Sloane pushing through the people and photographers on the sidewalk, getting the door open and pushing me inside before sliding in beside me. I knew why I had to leave, but my mind was still in the closet with him.

"Take me home first, Brian."

"Yes, Miss Glass."

Already I was falling into the need to go back. Let the Alpha pin me to the wall—to the *floor*. "I don't care about Carmen. I need to go back."

Sloane turned to me and brushed my hair off my face. "I know you want to. The perfume coming off you is wild, Bee. But unless you want to be forced into an arranged pack bonding, you can't go back."

I whined, my Omega needing more of what I'd had. I hadn't had enough. "I didn't even get his name."

"We didn't have time for much, but we had time for that." She pulled me in for a hug, giving me physical contact. It didn't sate the need clinging to me, but it took the edge off. "His name is Cole."

I breathed in and out, tasting him on my lips and remembering the scent.

Cole.

CHAPTER FIVE

EMERY

I tied the hood closed around the hawk's neck. "Okay. Going to put you to bed now. You're going to be just fine."

The alarm system beeped, followed by the front door opening and closing, and no sound after.

Lifting the hawk onto my gloved hand, I left the kitchen and stepped out into the hall, where Cole was slumped on the floor. He leaned against the door, hair a mess, suit askew, and was that lipstick on his mouth?

"What the hell happened to you?"

He looked at me, staring like he'd been drugged. Then he looked at my temporary pet. "Is that a hawk?"

"Her name is Grace. She needed overnight observation. Didn't want to stay at the office. None of which explains why you look like you got run over by a train."

He laughed once but didn't move. "It kind of feels that way."

My medical instincts kicked in. "Are you okay? Do you need help?"

"He's not injured." Harrison's voice came from the end of the hall. He came down the stairs, face full of amusement. "Cole got a face full of a scent so good he had to bail on the Senator."

I swiveled back to my crumpled pack mate and stared at him. "What?"

"Get Blake," he said. "He needs to know."

My stomach dropped. Both in terror and anticipation. A scent? Hope flared inside me and I shoved it down.

The door upstairs—which had remained closed for more than a year now—was like a paper cut that wouldn't heal. You were always aware of it, and every time it pressed up against something, it hurt all over again.

"Let me get Grace settled."

Harrison went and helped Cole up off the floor. They went

31

to the kitchen, their low voices echoing down the hall. Heading into my home office, I gently placed Grace on the perch I kept for rare moments like this.

She settled immediately, rearranging her feet and getting comfortable. "Be good," I said.

Her owner, worried Grace wasn't herself or eating enough, brought her in earlier today. The bird was eating fine, but she did seem lethargic. I'd run a few more tests in the morning before the owner came back to rule things out. But all things considered, it was probably nothing. Grace was healthy, and pets had moods and phases just like humans.

Blake was already in the kitchen, and I washed my hands. "Please put us out of our misery," I begged.

"I've never felt *anything* like that," Cole said. He leaned his hands on the kitchen island like it was the only thing keeping him upright. "That scent hijacked me. I couldn't concentrate, couldn't stop until I found her."

Blake chuckled, but the way he was standing revealed he was as on edge as the rest of us. "I'm assuming from the lipstick on your mouth you did find her?"

"I did. I—" he shook his head. "I'm sorry. It's hard to think."

I'd never seen Cole this way.

"Tell us from the beginning," Harrison said.

Cole looked at Blake. "You would have hated the food, but I wish all of you had been there. Because *fuck me*. Yeah, after I handed things off to Nick, I tried to trace her through the room, but there were so many people, plus the scent cancellers, I couldn't. Another Alpha tipped me off. I'm guessing I looked desperate. Right as I was about to get to her, she was swept away."

The next bit of the story was wild. Watching the Omega be taken away and then on the dance floor, seemingly against her will, while her friends schemed and shoved him in a closet. With *her*.

"They took her away almost as fast. I don't know what was happening, but it seemed urgent. They kept talking about getting her out of the party. And I was so out of my mind... I don't know who she is."

Silence hung in the air with the tangible taste of hope.

"What's her scent? What does she look like?" I asked.

Cole dropped his hand into his hands. "She's so fucking beautiful. Dark hair, big green eyes." He shook his head. "Honey and cinnamon. I'll never forget it. And I'm kicking myself now because down to my *bones* I know she's ours, and she's gone."

The grief in his tone...

"You don't know she's ours," I said mildly. "She could only be yours. It's not unheard of."

"No." He fixed his stare on me. "No. I can't explain how or why, but she's *ours*."

Ripping his suit jacket off, he shoved his nose into it. "Fuck, it's fading too much. I wish I could show you. I wish I'd taken a second to ask her name. Because I know you're not going to let me call every person on the guest list." The last was directed at Harrison.

He laughed, but it was strained. After a second, he reached out and put a hand on Cole's shoulder. "No. But we can find her."

"The friends," Cole said. "The ones who threw me in the closet. It was that actress, Eva May Williams, and," He pinched the bridge of his nose. "Ballet dancer I think? I know I've seen her face. Glass?"

"Sloane Glass?"

"Yeah, that's her. They were *fully* on her side. Think they would help us?"

None of the three of us said anything. The ache of that paper cut pain pulsing inside my chest. I wished I could latch onto Cole's excitement and make it my own. I desperately wanted to allow myself hope, but that died a long time ago.

Cole saw the look on my face. "I know. I do. It's not like that."

"Yeah."

A connection like the one he described was my dream. But I'd never had that. Not even close. And being passed over time and time again when we sought out a matchmaker was just another piece of the resistance keeping me from belief.

Cole looked at each of us in turn. "I know you can't believe me, and if I hadn't felt it myself, I wouldn't believe me either. But if I find her, will you meet her?"

"Of course," Harrison said immediately. "I do believe what you felt."

The words were carefully chosen.

"Besides," I said. "We would never stand in the way of your happiness, Cole."

He smiled. In it I saw the dream I wish I still had. "Thank you. And it's not just me. It's not."

He left the room, and none of us spoke. There wasn't anything to say. I couldn't count the number of times we'd laid out everything we wanted and needed.

I couldn't bear to think about it.

But I embraced the pain, anyway. I took the elevator to the top floor. It was too silent. The small entryway to the floor had several doors leading into the empty space that was most of the floor. But there was one door in particular...

I shook my head. Even now, I couldn't look at the nest. I chose another door.

With my hand on the knob, I took a breath before opening it. It wasn't anything. Not really. Just an empty space, waiting to be formed by the Omega it belonged to. But none of us came up here anymore.

Why pour salt in a wound?

I leaned against the door frame and looked at the blank canvas in front of me. It was a dichotomy, everything going on inside. The reason I couldn't let myself get excited was because I wanted it so badly. Someone to love and spoil and take care of together. *All* of us.

Losing it again might break me.

And even though I knew more loss would shatter me, I also knew I hoped Cole was right.

CHAPTER SIX

COLE

I dreamed of honey laced with cinnamon.

Of the moment the closet door closed and suddenly the entire world made sense. I could still taste her when I opened my eyes.

Every motion I made was autopilot. Work was the last thing I wanted to do. What I wanted was to track down the Omega and bring her home. Introduce her to the others and let them see the truth.

The Omega was made for us. There wasn't another explanation, and I knew—I *knew*—it wasn't me alone.

But my dreams nearly made me late. It was mid-afternoon by the time I was ready. I worked out, showered, and ate, all thinking about my mystery Omega. I needed to find her. But I couldn't do that until I was fully free of obligations, like meeting my new client.

Harrison sat in his office on the first floor of our penthouse, dressed in a suit, and typing on his computer. "You look intense."

"Busy day," he said, glancing up at me. "Had a few consultations, and we'll meet your new client here in a minute."

Atwood Security was the best in Slate City, and everyone knew it. After being grunts at other companies and seeing the mistakes they made, Harrison and I started our own. But I was grateful every fucking day Harrison did the management.

Last night notwithstanding, my head was on the operational side. I liked assessing, preparing, and the active headspace it took to make sure someone was safe.

"Where's the client?"

He gave me a look. "You didn't read the file?"

"I was a little distracted."

He smiled. "I'll say. Well, if you'd read the file, you'd know we don't have to move far. The client just moved in downstairs. The twenty-sixth floor."

"Really?"

Harrison stood and buttoned his suit. "Really. At the very least, it will be a short commute home. But if you need a day?"

As much as I wanted to take everything and throw myself into the search for our Omega, this was still our business and my job. As soon as my duties were completed today, I was looking for her.

I couldn't even let myself think about her, or I would lose all my focus. The need to find her still burned under my skin. "I do," I said. "But this comes first."

"If you're sure."

"I am."

He nodded. "Good. The client requested you personally."

I followed him out to the front door. "You're torturing me because I didn't read the file, aren't you?"

Harrison smirked. "A little."

"Okay, I surrender. Who's the client?"

"Senator Merriton."

I blinked. "What?"

"His daughter is starting law school and living here while she does. There have been recent threats made against her, so he wants additional security for her, especially while she's not living at home."

His daughter? "Did we know he had a daughter?"

"Of course. His current wife isn't her mother. Died almost fifteen years ago."

The elevator chimed, and Harrison pushed the button for the twenty-sixth floor. "So, this should be fairly easy? I'll get her schedule and examine the vulnerable places on the route. Wide perimeter when she's out, maybe a detail of three. Keep someone on the door when she's home?"

"That's what I'm thinking. He's meeting us as well, so we'll see what he has in mind."

The layout of the floor was different from ours, as we owned the top four floors of the building. There were only two apartments on this floor, the building split equally in half. Our guys were already on the correct door, indicating the Senator was already here.

Harrison knocked, and I heard voices inside. A pair of heavy footsteps approached, and the door opened. The Senator opened the door. "Mr. Atwood." He reached out and shook his hand before nodding at me. "Mr. Kennedy. Please come in."

Gesturing past him, we stepped inside the spacious entryway. The scent of baking cookies filled the space, making my mouth water. I hadn't eaten anything today.

And a second later I felt like I was falling, overcome with a wave of honey and cinnamon.

It was her.

The Senator's daughter was our Omega.

CHAPTER SEVEN

PETRA

I barely slept. Between trying to get my head around what happened in the fucking closet and trying to make sure everything was ready, sleep just wasn't in the cards.

First thing in the morning, I left. I only had a few bags of things to take with me to the new apartment, and the rest of my clothes I could come back for. The bigger things I wanted had already been moved last week.

The building was absolutely nuts. With top-notch security, its own gym and pool, plus an arcade *and* a bowling alley. I frankly wasn't sure what strings Dad pulled to get my application approved, but I wasn't complaining. Though I was glad it was my place. Entirely. Mom left me plenty of money, and both Levi and Garrett left me some as well. The apartment was mine outright, and it felt amazing to stand on my own two feet.

Even if law school was last on my list of priorities, it was too late to stop that particular train. At least I had a place I could retreat. If I still had to live with Carmen *and* go to law school? I didn't know if I could handle it.

Since dad and Carmen stayed overnight at the hotel, I didn't have to deal with whatever she was going to do and say when she saw me again.

I was going to make sure we saw each other as little as possible.

It took a few hours to put everything away, and a sense of peace came over me. As soon as I knew I would be here, I chose things. I helped with the decorations and furniture and made it a place I could really live. It wasn't perfect, but getting away from home was more important.

School didn't start until next week, and I had nothing to do except remember Cole and his lips on mine. The way he smelled and the way his body pressed me into the wall. It was only mid-afternoon, and if I didn't find something to occupy my mind, I would end up in my bedroom with my vibrator and never come out.

Before I could question it, I found myself in the kitchen pulling out ingredients and mixing together chocolate chip cookies. I probably needed a nap and an orgasm, but who needed sleep when you could make cookies?

A nap was only going to make me dream about him.

I would call Sloane and see if she wanted to come over and break in the new place with movies, cookies, and some good old-fashioned drinks. But that needed to wait until she was out of dance class in a couple of hours.

The knock on the door startled me. I slipped the first round of cookies into the oven before answering. I wasn't expecting anyone. Who was here on my first day in the apartment?

Looking through the peephole, I sighed. My father stood there, flanked by his security. Thankfully, Carmen was nowhere in sight.

I open the door. "Hey, Dad."

He opened his arms and walked in for a hug. "Hey, sweetheart. I wanted to see how you were in the new place. And I thought I should knock instead of using the key card."

"Well, I've only been here a few hours, but yeah, it's great."

"Are you baking?"

I let the door shut behind me. His security stayed outside. "Yeah. Gotta christen the kitchen."

"You should be studying," he said. "Have to get ready for those classes."

"School doesn't start till next week. I'm savoring my freedom."

He leaned on the counter in the kitchen, and it reminded me of my old dad. Or who I thought of as my old dad. The man he was before we lost everything and had to start over.

Baking cookies was something we *all* used to do.

"It's good to see you in your own space," he said. "I know I was skeptical, but it's good."

"Thanks."

Tension grew in my gut. It had been a long time since Dad and I had really been able to talk. We were both very different people now, and I still couldn't bear to see him in pain. He'd been through enough.

"I missed you toward the end of the fundraiser."

I cleared my throat. "Yeah. I had to leave quickly. Sorry."

"Everything okay?"

Fixing my gaze on one spot on the counter, I made a face. I polished the spot with my finger because it was easier than looking at him. "Carmen—"

He sighed. "Petra, she's doing her best."

"She was... very insistent about me meeting that pack. Neither they nor I are interested, but she told me I couldn't leave until we came to an arrangement. Because you needed them as allies. So I left."

"I'm sure that's not what she meant," he said with a chuckle. "Don't get me wrong, we'd both be happy to see you settled with a good pack. And the Gidwitz pack are excellent candidates. But you know how she is."

"Yes. I do." I stared my father down. He knew I wasn't a fan of Carmen, and he always did his best to mediate peace between us. But peace was never what Carmen wanted.

He sighed. "I'll talk to her."

"You don't have to. It's not going to happen."

"All right," he laughed and glanced at the clock. "I admit I *did* want to see how you were doing here, but there's something else, too."

Of course there was. I closed my eyes and turned away, checking the cookies in the oven. They were doing well. A few more minutes. Shame on me for being disappointed. How long had it been since Dad had sought me out just to chat?

I missed him. But every time I told him that, he got teary and apologized, reminding us both of everything we lost and reminding him of why he stayed away.

Because I looked exactly like my mother. Something he didn't remember saying to me. But I did. All the time.

My father loved me. There was no doubt. But he also couldn't look at me without feeling like his soul was being ripped out. It was also why I put up with Carmen. After everything, he deserved some happiness. Even if his happiness seemed hellbent on making my life miserable.

"What's the real reason?"

He cleared his throat. "Since you're not living at home, I want you to have protection."

"What?"

"A bodyguard."

My head whipped around, and I expected him to be smiling, like I was in on the joke with him. But he wasn't. If anything, he looked more serious. "Why?"

Now he smiled, but it was his political smile. "I can't want you safe?"

"You always want me safe, but I've been just fine without a bodyguard for years. What changed?"

"It's nothing. Your old man is nervous about you being out on your own. Anything can happen."

"Dad." I stared at him until he hung his head. "What aren't you telling me?"

Crossing the room, he looked out the windows over downtown, and notably, not at me. "A threat was made against you."

Chills crawled over my skin. "What kind of threat?"

"Nothing I'm going to repeat to you. But I don't want you walking around Slate City alone right now."

I leaned on the counter heavily. "I don't understand. This has never been a problem before."

"I've gotten plenty of threats over the years. Even when—" His voice changed and he swallowed. "Even when your mother was alive, I got threats. Sometimes she did too. Comes with the territory. Especially now, when everything is so public."

The timer startled me. The first batch of cookies was finished. I took them out and started moving them to the cooling rack, then spreading out new balls of dough.

My stomach was in knots. A bodyguard?

It was fucked up that I was more upset by the idea of a bodyguard than someone threatening me. But this place—this apartment—was supposed to be freedom. Finally. Not an extension of where I'd been trapped.

"I don't want a bodyguard," I said quietly. "This is the most secure building in Slate City. My driver is going to take me to and from class. There's nothing to worry about."

Dad turned around from the windows and sighed again. "Sorry, sweetheart. This isn't a negotiation. Until we're sure the threat is either fake or not credible, you're getting protection."

I opened my mouth to protest, and he stopped me. "They're the best of the best, and they protect me. You'll barely notice they're there."

"Dad."

A new knock at the door drew my gaze.

"There they are now."

"You can't be serious."

He didn't answer, instead opening the door.

Fuck.

I put the next batch of cookies in. Not even a day in the new place and it was already being invaded by people I didn't know.

"Mr. Atwood. Mr. Kennedy. Please come in."

"Thank you."

Holy balls. The man now standing in my living room was hot. Tall and built, I didn't know why he was in security. He could be in modeling. The barest hint of silver hair brushed his temples, but it did nothing to touch the strength of his features or the way his body was clearly straining against the suit he wore. "This is Harrison Atwood," my father said. "He runs Atwood security. They have an office here in the building, and will be responsible for your security. And this is who will be protecting you."

Every hair in my body stood on end. Caramel and salt and a bitter thread of darkness. I knew who it was before I saw who still lingered in my entryway.

His eyes were fixed on me, body rigid with the same shock. Everything in me wanted to run to him. If I didn't get a hold of myself, I was going to start perfuming in front of my father and that absolutely could not happen.

"Cole Kennedy," he said, coming forward to take my hand. "Nice to meet you."

"Nice to meet you," I murmured.

And Cole's scent wasn't the only one distracting me. The

43

scent rolling off Harrison was enough to put me into a coma. It hit just as hard as Cole's did. Whiskey and cedar with a hint of frost. He smelled like waking up in a cabin in the middle of winter, and it made my mouth water.

Fuck, what was happening to me?

I cleared my throat to cover the whine building in my chest.

"My daughter is a reluctant customer," Dad said, looking at me. "But it will be fine. They'll explain how it works and get you started."

"You're leaving?" I gaped at him. "Now?"

Glancing at his watch, he grinned and hugged me. "I have a rally I need to get to, and it's about an hour outside the city. I'm leaving you in the safest hands I know."

My father kissed my cheek and shook hands with Cole. "Take care of her."

Cole's eyes were only on me when he said, "I will." The darkness in his tone sent a thrill down my spine. He didn't mean it the way my father did.

My dad shut the door, and I listened to the retreat of his footsteps along with his guards. The ding of the elevator. And still I held my breath for a few more seconds before I dared to move.

Just like last night, Cole and I snapped. He gathered me up and held me against his body. One hand tangled in my hair. He was holding me like I was the only thing in the world, and I was holding him just as tightly. "I didn't know if I'd be able to find you," he whispered.

"Surprise?"

He laughed, and loosened his hold, but he didn't let me go. When I turned to look at Harrison, he was staring at me with a look I couldn't decipher. His gaze shifted to Cole behind me, and then back to me. "Fuck." The man broke, sinking into a crouch. "You weren't kidding."

"I was not kidding."

My mind was a whirlwind of scent. I was perfuming like crazy, confused, and I liked Cole's hands on me. But I couldn't take my eyes off the man on the floor. "What's going on?"

"Harrison is my pack mate," Cole said quietly, turning me back to him.

"You told him about me?"

"I told all of them about you."

A blush rose to my cheeks. "I have no idea what's happening. Just that I've never felt anything like running into a scent like yours. Or his."

"Mine?" Harrison asked. His own hope betrayed him.

Cole did let me go then, and I went to Harrison. The sensual softness of cedar and the sharp punch of whiskey curled around me like a physical embrace. It soaked through my mind, erasing any and all thought. If it had been his scent last night, things would have played out in the same way. "Yours."

The Alpha stood from where he crouched, towering over me. This close, I needed to crane my neck to look at him. But it was the awe in his eyes that struck me. "You're not what I expected, Miss Merriton."

"DeWitt-Merriton," I said automatically. "But given the circumstances, I think you should call me Petra."

"Petra," he said. So softly I barely heard it, and yet it grazed my body like he'd drawn his fingers over my skin.

The timer made all three of us jump. I ran over to the oven and took out the cookies before I turned it off. The rest of the cookies were going to have to wait, because what the actual hell was happening right now?

I looked between the two men, dizzy with sight and scent, mind spinning out visions of being caught between them. Knotted and held, mouths on my neck—

"Petra," Cole said with a smile. "Last night I couldn't even breathe. When I realized I'd forgotten to ask your name, I was devastated."

"I'm sorry I had to go like that. My stepmother, she... is very insistent about some things." The connection with these Alphas was so pure and so strong I wanted to tell them everything. To curl up in their arms and let them take away every pain and fear. But I still didn't know them yet.

Cole came around the counter into the kitchen. "When I got home last night, I couldn't stop thinking about you. I dreamed of the way you taste, and as soon as I was finished with my duties for the day, I was going to pull every string I had to find you."

"Really?"

"*Yes.*" I was in his arms again, and he pressed his forehead to mine. "Please meet the rest of my pack. If you react to them like you react to us?"

He didn't need to say more. I knew exactly what a scent-sympathetic pack looked like. I grew up seeing that kind of love every fucking day. I witnessed how powerful and how perfect it could be. It was what made seeing things like Eva and her Alphas both beautiful and painful.

"I know this is fast," he breathed the words into my air. "And confusing. Trust me, it's throwing me on my ass. But please don't make me let you go again."

I didn't want him to let me go. All of it was terrifying, and it was fast. But this was how it happened, right?

Mom went for a walk in the park. Dad and his pack had been playing a game of flag football. They caught each other's scent, and it was the end. It sounded so simple. She went home with them and never left.

I wanted it more than I wanted to keep breathing. And I was so fucking terrified I couldn't draw my next breath. I'd seen how beautiful it could be, and I'd also seen the aftermath. Somehow, I'd mostly been able to come through it. My dad?

Get it together, girl.

Was I really about to talk myself out of this?

No fucking way.

"I don't think you're allowed to let me go," I said. "You're my bodyguard, right?"

He tipped his head back and laughed. The rich sound filled the room, and I wanted to burrow into it and *live there*.

Harrison still stood where he'd been, staring at me. I pulled away from Cole gently, savoring the way his fingers squeezed my hips before letting me slip by.

When I stood in front of Harrison again, I reached out to touch him and stopped. It felt so fucking natural to touch. He caught my hand before I pulled it back. "Yes."

I wrapped my arms around him, and he *sank* into the embrace. It felt like he was everywhere, curved around me from

46

every direction so all I could feel was him. "Why were you looking at me like I'm not real?"

"Because I'm not sure you are."

Harrison moved, pulling back to look me in the eye and tilting my chin up with one finger. "We didn't believe him," he said gently. "Cole, when he told us. We didn't believe it could be real, because we've *tried*. It never happened, and we finally decided to learn to be happy as a pack. Until you, little Omega."

He kissed my forehead, and tears blurred my eyes. There was so much emotion in the kiss, and his scent, the way he felt against me... I was barely holding back from devouring him, yet I wanted to stay here forever.

"You don't know if the rest of your pack will like me."

"They will," Cole said. "I know they will."

Smiling, I looked at him over my shoulder. "Maybe I won't like them."

"Does that mean you'll meet them?"

I nodded. "I—" Breaking away from Harrison's embrace, I dropped my face in my hands. "This is not what I expected when I woke up this morning. It's overwhelming."

"Yeah," Harrison laughed. "No kidding."

"When can I meet them?" I was suddenly eager. I wanted to know if the others smelled as divine. If I would perfume for them too.

"Blake is upstairs," Cole said. "And Emery?"

"He'll come home for this," Harrison said.

I looked between the two of them. "Home? Wait, here?"

"Home sweet home," Cole said. "We own the penthouse. So if you want to meet them, you can. Right now."

I blinked. Whoa.

Something settled in my gut. This was right. And now, was perfect. "Should I bring the cookies?"

CHAPTER EIGHT

———

PETRA

I clutched the box of cookies in my hands, suddenly nervous as we rode the elevator up to the top floor.

Absently, I noted going to strange Alphas' houses immediately after meeting them was usually a bad idea. Except for the fact that these Alphas were already being paid to keep me safe.

The elevator chimed, doors opening. "This isn't the top floor."

Harrison put his arm out to block the doors from closing and grinned at me. "No, it's not. The penthouse is four floors."

I had to pick my jaw up off the ground. Four floors? Holy shit. There was a small hallway between the elevator and the front door. I heard the lock click open as we approached.

A luxurious foyer rolled out in front of me, with hardwood floors ending in a stairway in front of a wall of windows. To the left, there was *another* elevator. This one was only for them.

"Wow."

"Good reaction," Cole said, gesturing me to the right, where a *giant* kitchen opened. A door opened beyond it to a dining room, and another room on the other side, but I was still stuck on the kitchen, because even though it was warm and gorgeous, it was *intense*. Ovens I only ever saw in restaurants and a fridge that was easily double the size of mine.

"Blake, who you're going to meet shortly, is a chef," Cole said.

"More like a restauranteur," a voice said from the door behind us. "I rarely get to cook in any of my restaurants now. Too much business to take care of."

I turned and looked at the Alpha standing there. Sandy blonde hair which was casually messy. A pair of jeans and a dark t-shirt which showed off lean muscles and forearms I desperately wanted to watch knead some bread.

The smile he had on his face faltered, and he froze. My scent hit him, but I couldn't catch his yet—not in the center of his pack mates. Lifting a hand, I waved. "Hi."

He crossed the distance between us and yanked me into his arms. Someone took the cookies from me. I didn't care who. I was submerged in the scent of citrus and bubbly sharpness. He smelled like a mimosa, and I wanted to drink him.

A purr sprung to life in his chest, my body melting in response. "Holy shit, I'm sorry," he said, releasing me and stepping back. "I should ask if this is okay. I—"

"It's okay," I breathed. "More than okay."

"Cole, remind me never to doubt anything you say ever again."

Laughter surrounded me, and Blake drew me back in. For the first time, this felt... real. It wasn't a fluke. This pack and I were connected on the deepest of levels.

Scent-sympathy didn't guarantee compatibility. This wasn't a sure thing. I didn't fucking care.

Blake's purr rumbled under my ear, and his hand was rubbing my back, instinctually soothing anxiety I hadn't known was there. A tiny knot between my shoulders disappeared.

"I didn't know you were a chef," I said. "I'm not sure I want you to try my cookies now."

The way his laugh wrapped around me, I was pretty sure my perfume exploded through the room. "I'm a chef, not a baker."

"Don't let him fool you," Harrison said. "He bakes just as well."

Slipping out of his arms, I went for the box of cookies now sitting on the bar. Cole got there first, lifting them out of reach. "Having just smelled these in your apartment, I'm pretty sure they're amazing."

"I thought you couldn't smell anything but me?" I raised an eyebrow.

"It was about five seconds when I first walked in the door. And they smelled incredible." He leaned closer. "*You* smell fucking edible."

I shivered, watching his eyes go dark and both of us remembering what had been interrupted last night.

"Let's try these before the two of you end up naked on the countertop," Harrison said, stealing the box and opening it.

"I'm not a baker," I said quickly. "It's just something I do for fun and I wanted to use the kitchen."

The other guys each took a cookie and bit into them. An embarrassed flush was already covering my face and neck. It was okay. One batch of sub-par cookies wouldn't ruin this.

Blake groaned. "Fuck me. You *should* be a baker. That's spectacular."

"You're just saying that."

Cole held a fist up to his face, laughing with a mouth full of cookie. He was still laughing when he finally swallowed. "No, he's not. One thing you'll learn about Blake? He never lies about food. He'll make it gentler if he likes you, but he'll never lie."

Harrison slipped his phone back into his jacket pocket. "Emery is on his way."

"You're sure you're not a baker?" Blake stole another cookie.

"No. I'm not really anything."

Cole's eyes cut to me. "You're going to law school?"

They would know, given what they were hired for. I shrugged. "Yeah." All three of their gazes were on me now, like they could see there was more to the story.

"I don't want to talk about that right now."

They took their cue. "I'm going to need the recipe for these. And for you to show me how you make them."

I tilted my head. "The recipe wouldn't be enough?"

"Nope. A recipe is one thing, but a hundred people can make the same recipe, and each result will be a little different."

That made sense. We fell into silence, and I wasn't sure what to do. We were here, our scents matched... what came next?

Most people assumed because my father was well known I'd had some kind of miraculous and exotic life. In reality, it was kind of the opposite. After mom, I didn't do anything. Dad made sure I was protected. Until college I had tutors at home, and I still lived at home even after that. This was the first time I was truly on my own.

Harrison sensed I was at a loss. "Would you like a tour?"

"Sure." I pressed my lips together. "That would be nice."

"What's your favorite kind of food?" Blake asked.

"Oh, you don't need to cook for me."

He smirked. "I'm very, *very* sure I will cook for you. But tonight? I'll have one of my employees bring us some food."

I took the chance to smirk right back. "You're so sure I'm staying that long?"

His face shut down. "Oh. Right. I'm sorry, I should have thought of that."

"Wait," I reached out for him instinctually. "I'm sorry. I was teasing you. I'm not going to pretend this isn't strange, or that I know what I'm doing, but I'm not leaving."

Harrison told me they tried and gave up. These Alphas bore scars in the same way I did. I hated whoever had made them, but it also drew me closer. I understood what it meant to have pain you couldn't control. There were things people said—wholly innocent—that made it feel like my world was crashing down.

I never wanted to do it to someone else on purpose.

"I'm sorry," I said again.

Blake took my hand where it was outstretched. "If we seem too eager, it's because we are," he said.

The way I felt, I understood, but it still seemed impossible. "You just met me."

"Does that matter?"

It didn't, and it did. I shook my head. "I don't know. Yes? No. It's like being caught in a really... *really* great smelling whirlwind."

Blake broke into a smile and laughed. "Yeah, that's about right." His eyes met mine in question, and I nodded. He pulled me closer. "Now tell me what kind of food you like."

The Alpha command in his tone was subtle. I wasn't compelled, but I was *safe*. Those two things weren't equivalent, yet they made sense to me. That was all that mattered. "I like Italian. I mean, I like a lot of things, but that's my number one."

"Any favorite dishes?"

I shook my head. There was too much good food to choose a single one. "No. But I'm not a fan of seafood."

"Good to know. I'll take care of it."

Cole gestured to the hall as Blake released me. "We'll start down here. Through there is the dining room, and we all have offices on this floor. Pretty boring, typical offices. That room is actually where we eat most of the time."

The room he referred to split off from the kitchen and was in the corner of the building. Double walls of windows gave an incredible view of the city, along with a casual table and a couple of couches. It felt like a breakfast nook on steroids. I could see them sitting and drinking coffee in the morning, or even with a casual dinner.

"This is beautiful."

"Thank you." Harrison's hand brushed my shoulder before he pulled it away.

I turned and projected my voice so Blake could hear me as well. "You can touch me." I flushed, having to say it. "I like it. Everything else, we'll figure out. But I don't like the feeling of dancing around each other. It's already kind of weird as it is."

Harrison's hand met my shoulder again. "It is weird, isn't it?" He pulled my back against his chest.

"God, yes. Not in a bad way, but—"

"No, it's good to acknowledge it," he said. "So we all *know* it's weird, and try to figure it out."

"And so I don't make you feel bad by being sassy," I murmured.

"We like sassy," he said quietly, curling himself around me so his lips were at my ear. "*I* love it. It's going to take time to learn each other. Blake is fine, and we all want you here."

I blew out a breath. "Okay."

He was so *big*, I felt tiny next to him. This close, with all these scents? Perfume was spreading through the room. My body was fully on board and way ahead of me.

There was a door to the hall from the breakfast room that let out right by the stairs. He guided me up to the second floor. "This side of the building on this floor is our living area."

The fucking ginormous space was comfortable. Couches and a big TV, more walls of windows and, at the other end, a big fireplace with bookshelves and a few comfy armchairs. There was so much *space*, and yet it didn't feel empty.

"The other side is our private gym and pool."

I went to the other door, taking in the divided space between gym and pool. "You have a pool?"

"The building has one too, and a gym. But we took advantage of the kitchen and dining room having lower ceilings."

"I guess being a bodyguard means you use it a lot."

Cole's mouth tipped into a smirk. "A fair amount."

The way they all looked? I didn't doubt it.

A new wave of salted caramel crashed into me. I had to close my eyes, desire racing through me so quickly I couldn't hold it back. "I'm not much of a gym person, you can probably tell by looking at me."

Cole's hand snaked around my ribs. God, I couldn't get enough of them touching me. It threw into sharp contrast how little anyone touched me in my life.

"I'm not sure if you meant it to be a dig at yourself, but there's nothing wrong with your body. Trust me."

My heart skipped a beat. "I'm not sure how you could tell through that awful dress."

He laughed, breath tickling my ear. "I knew you didn't pick that."

"Nope."

"But your dress wasn't the main thing on my mind."

"What's next?" I asked. Because this was quickly heading in a direction we couldn't turn back from. And I was all for it, but with the last pack member on the way, I didn't want them to walk in on me being fucked into oblivion.

"Our bedrooms," Harrison said. "But I'm not sure that's the best idea."

"Yeah, probably not. You said you had four floors?"

"We do."

The hesitance in Harrison's voice made me look at him. "Is that where you keep the bodies?"

They both laughed, and Cole squeezed me. "No." He took a slow breath. "The fourth floor is our Omega floor."

"You have an entire *floor*?"

I saw the sadness in Harrison's eyes. "Like I told you. We tried."

"What's up there?"

54

Cole walked me into the living room. "Honestly? Nothing. It's a blank space, the nest and the bedroom. We, uh... don't go up there very often. Do you want to see it?"

My heart ached for them. They clearly wanted an Omega, but something had stopped it. "Maybe in a little while. Can I ask what happened?"

I chose a spot on one of the couches, leaving room on either side of me, and Blake slid in beside me, grinning.

"Stealthy," I said.

"More like I took the elevator," he chuckled. "But to answer your question, it just didn't happen. We tried matchmaking. A couple of times, actually, and it never worked out. It didn't feel right for them or for us."

"After a couple of years," Harrison sat in an arm chair across from us, "we stopped. It was too painful to keep putting ourselves out there and getting our hopes up."

"Maybe this was why," Cole said, brushing a piece of hair behind my ear.

"What were—are—you looking for?"

Harrison leaned forward, elbows on his knees, staring at me. "We're happy as friends and as a pack, but we're not lovers. It's just never been who we are. And it's hard to explain the rest—like an itch under your skin, wanting *more*. Someone to be the center of our wheel."

"Someone we can take care of, and spoil," Blake added.

There was no explanation for what brought packs together any more than there was an explanation for what made my Omega react to their scents like this. It was deeper than our consciousness could sense. A resonance and similar desire. Like the pack Carmen tried to force me on. They were happy. They were *together*. They didn't feel the urge to bring in an Omega the way these men did.

Exactly the same way I craved being in a pack like the one I'd grown up in. My mom was so fucking happy. There wasn't a day when there wasn't a smile on her face, and I was used to the displays of affection that came with it.

"I want that too," I whispered.

The door behind us burst open, and I turned to look. An

Alpha in blue scrubs, panting like he'd been running. This was their fourth member. His eyes locked on me, gaze so intense, I couldn't tell if it was desire or hatred.

My instincts got me this far, and they were screaming at me to move. To go to the Alpha. Right now.

I stood, and the world seemed to hold its breath. Moving around the couch, I got a little closer. "Hey," I said. "I'm Petra."

Emery glanced briefly at his pack before his eyes came back to me, still staring. I watched him inhale, and then breathe in again. The room was soaked in my perfume, and I watched his gaze grow dark with near-feral desire.

And my Omega responded.

Releasing the door handle, he slowly came to me, never looking away. His scent slammed into me far faster than he was moving. Rich coffee with whispers of chocolate running through it. Oh, *fuck*. The scent rippled through me and woke whatever was left after the others. It was everything.

My hands went to my stomach, the intensity so great I had to curl around myself. To keep myself still. I *wanted*.

Emery stood in front of me now. His eyes were so blue, I could get lost in them. I could twist my hands into his dark hair. I could fall into his arms and never surface again.

His eyes dropped to my lips and returned. There was something physical between us. True and pure. I knew what he wanted, and he knew I said *yes*.

With a sigh that sounded like the weight of the world falling off his shoulders, Emery slipped a hand behind my neck and kissed me.

CHAPTER NINE

PETRA

*E*mery kissed me like the world was ending and he was ready to burn. One hand sank into my hair and gripped it, his mouth plundering mine as he gathered me up.

I was lost in him. Just like last night in the closet with Cole, I couldn't get enough of the feeling. The taste. The sense of *right* in my chest. That feeling echoed so strongly and so deeply it brought tears to my eyes.

We broke apart, breathless, and I smiled through the tears blurring my vision. "Hi."

He laughed with me, leaning his forehead against mine. "It's nice to meet you, Petra."

"I guess you're Emery."

Crushing me against him, I couldn't breathe in his embrace and I didn't care as long as I could stay here. "When Cole came home last night, he collapsed on the floor and didn't get up for a while. I get it now."

"He didn't tell me that."

Laughter sparked behind me. "Bring her back over here, Em."

I cleared my throat. "Could I use the restroom?"

Harrison nodded his head in the direction it was. "Down the hall."

"Thank you."

I needed a fucking second. This was so much and so overwhelming, and I needed to breathe as much as they needed a chance to talk to each other without me in the room.

In the mirror, I glowed. My cheeks were pink, my eyes were shining, and I looked *happy*.

How long had it been since I looked at myself and felt that way? My life wasn't sad. I worked hard to make sure I was fine. But that's what it was. Most days I was fine. Just coasting along and living. But there were few lows, and even fewer highs.

Amazing how you missed the roller coaster once you realized the road you were on was flat.

I pulled my phone out of my pocket and sent Sloane a frantic text telling her what happened and that I would call her later with details. She was going to absolutely lose her mind.

Running my hands through my hair quickly, I took a few deep breaths before I went back out. Nerves jangled in my stomach. It blew my mind that this could just happen out of nowhere. Yesterday, when I was in Bergman's making sure the dress fit, I'd just been looking for a way out of the monotony before I started a different kind of monotony with school.

Now I had my own place, I found them, and the world was full of new possibilities that were beautiful and terrifying and *daunting*.

I rubbed my hands on my jeans before I cracked the door open again. Four heads turned to look at me. I flushed with the sudden attention and returned to my seat on the couch. Emery now leaned against one of the windows, silhouetted against the sky.

Harrison cleared his throat. "Petra, I don't think it will come as a shock, but we would like to court you."

My heart squeezed in my chest and tears pricked my eyes. I pulled my knees up to my chest, curling up between them, vulnerability slamming down on me.

Blake curled an arm around my shoulder. "Too much too fast?"

I shook my head. "No," I managed to whisper. "Not at all. I want that. It's just—" Swallowing, I stretched myself back out and breathed him in. Citrus and delicious. "It's a little heavy for right now."

"If we're in this," he said. "There is nothing too heavy."

"Not today," I said. "I want to enjoy this."

He kissed the top of my head, and a soft whine came out of me. I ached for tenderness like this. Everything felt so impossibly right.

"What does courting mean for you?" I finally asked.

Cole leaned forward and grabbed one of my shoes, slipping it off my foot, and then the other, before pulling my feet into his lap so I was stretched between them. "Getting to know you," he said. "Spending time with you, doing *this*." His thumb dug into the arch of my foot, and I groaned. "Figuring out everything, because we know being scent matched is only one part of it."

Again, my mind flashed backward, and I pushed it away. Today, of all days, I didn't want to dwell on a past I'd left behind, no matter the similarities between then and now.

"Taking you out," Harrison said. "Though that may have to wait until the threat has been resolved."

I turned in Blake's arms so I was more on my side and could see him properly. "Are you going to tell me what it is? My father wouldn't."

Blake tensed beneath me, and I sat up, wincing. "I guess we didn't get to that part." I looked between Blake and Emery. "My full name is Petra DeWitt-Merriton. I'm Russell Merriton's daughter."

Emery scrubbed a hand over his face. "Well, that explains last night." Then he laughed. "And they're protecting you?"

"I don't know from what."

Harrison folded his hands together, still leaning on his knees, like he was deciding whether to tell me.

"I deserve to know."

"Of course you do," he said immediately. "It's not that. It's... the actual content of the message was graphic. But it was a death threat. Whoever sent it wants your father to stop his campaign and drop out."

"He'll never do that." I shook my head. "He always says, if they're angry—"

"You're doing something right," Harrison finished with a smile. "He said exactly that when he called to ask Cole to protect you. And we *will* protect you." The confidence in his voice was absolute. "We would have, no matter what. But especially now."

A shiver of fear ran over my skin. "Do you have any idea who sent it?"

"We're working on that, but my guess is it's someone whose anger is misplaced and has no real intentions of harming you. But the Senator is right. You never dismiss a death threat."

"No one is going to touch you," Cole growled.

I believed him.

Blake's phone chimed. "That's the food. I'll bring it up."

Standing to help, he gently pushed me back into Cole's arms. "Stay here. We got this."

"But—"

Cole's arms wrapped around my center and pulled me back. "Remember what we said about spoiling?"

"I can help carry some food."

"Not tonight," he said, echoing my own words.

Blake disappeared, and Emery took his place on the couch. He still looked at me like I wasn't quite real. I was going to have to get used to that.

"Can I ask you something?" Cole placed his chin on my shoulder, and already I loved the small familiarity of the movement.

"Of course."

"Last night, when your friend was pulling you away from me, she called you 'Bee.'"

I blushed. "Yeah. There aren't a lot of nicknames for Petra. So when I was younger, because I smell like honey, everyone called me Bee. Or Bumble. Sloane still does, and Eva. A few other friends, too."

"Bee," Emery said. "I like that. And you do smell like honey. I'm going to get a sugar high from your scent."

My mind asked the next question. If my scent gave him a sugar high, what would tasting me do to him?

My perfume had settled before I had that thought. Now it exploded all over again, and the three of them knew exactly where my thoughts had gone. The purring that filled the air told me how much they liked it.

"I hope you meant it when you said you liked everything," Blake called, carrying in a few large bags of food. "Because I had them bring pretty much the whole menu."

"That smells amazing."

"I'm not sure I can say that about anything ever again, now that I've smelled you," Emery said.

Soft music surrounded us from invisible speakers, and I just caught Harrison slipping his phone back into his pocket. The melody was pretty, a cello and other strings weaving back and forth. I fell into it for a single, glorious moment before I released it like I might drop a hot poker.

Danger here. My whole being recoiled from it.

Harrison was watching me when I opened my eyes.

Blake laid everything out on the coffee table. He hadn't lied. There was every pasta dish imaginable. Fresh focaccia bread with rosemary, and a variety of sauces from marinara to alfredo to bolognese.

"Holy shit." I looked at all of it. "That is *so* much food."

"We'll eat all of it, don't worry," Blake said. "If not today, then we'll have leftovers."

Emery laughed and grabbed a plate. "Blake's leftovers are *very* popular at the clinic. We won't have trouble getting rid of whatever's left."

"The clinic?" He was in scrubs, but I didn't know what kind of doctor.

He grinned. "I'm a vet. Mainly for exotic animals."

"I came home last night, and he was standing there with a fucking hawk on his hand like it's normal," Cole said.

Emery rolled his eyes. "Would you rather I have slept at the clinic to watch Grace?"

"A hawk named Grace?"

"She's a sweet bird, as far as hawks go. Some of them can be real dicks."

A vision playing out in my head that stole my breath. This is what it could be like. The five of us enjoying a meal and each other's company. No awkwardness, only familiar comfort.

I couldn't choose just one thing from the display in front of me. I took a little of everything, and it was utterly unbelievable. The sounds coming out of me were not sounds usually associated with food.

We all knew it, too.

"Baby, if you keep making sounds like that over my food, we're not going to make it to dessert."

I raised an eyebrow. "There's dessert?"

He scoffed. "Of course there's dessert. What kind of host—or chef—would I be if I didn't offer you some?"

I decided to tease him again and see if I could make up for earlier in the kitchen. "Does that apply to drinks, too?"

Blake looked around. "Shit. We've got some wine downstairs. I'll grab it."

I caught his hand before he could take a full step. His gaze snapped to where our bodies connected, and heat bloomed. I forced myself to swallow and focus. "I'm so sorry to have to tell you this as a chef, because I know it could be a deal breaker, but I don't like wine."

"Really?" His eyebrows rose into his hairline.

"Yeah." I sighed. "I wish I did, but it's all too bitter for me."

Harrison laughed softly. "Given how sweet you smell, it doesn't surprise me at all."

Blake was still watching me. "Is this the kind of thing where it's a done deal? Or if I were to look for a wine sweet enough you'd try it?"

"I'll try anything once. Within reason," I said quickly, and they laughed. "But yeah, Lo makes fun of me for it. Last night I had a sip of the champagne." My body shuddered. "Nope. But it's funny, because you smell like a mimosa and I love it."

"You're giving me all kinds of ideas."

I pretended I didn't feel those words in every inch of my body. "So what's for dessert?"

"Tiramisu and cannoli."

"Oh my god, I'm going to be nothing but a marble you can roll by the time I leave. But it's worth it."

Outside, the sun was starting to turn the sky shades of orange and gold, all laid out in front of us like a shining mural. "You have this view every day."

"Your apartment has the same view," Cole pointed out.

I nodded. "True, but it's different when it's an entire wall of windows. It's like a panoramic picture."

My phone buzzed in my pocket, and it didn't stop buzzing. I pulled it out and glanced at the screen. Mostly capital letters and exclamation points from Sloane. In the middle of typing a reply, it started to ring. "I'll be right back," I said. "It's Sloane. The girl who pulled me away," I said to Cole.

I slipped out into the hall and answered. "Hello?"

"*WHAT THE ACTUAL HELL I'M SO HAPPY FOR YOU!*"

Holding the phone away from my ear, I couldn't stop laughing. "I think you broke my eardrum."

"I'll break more than that if you don't give me some details."

"Those details will have to be tomorrow. I'm still here. We're eating dinner."

I could imagine my best friend's face perfectly. "You're eating dinner? Or they're eating *you* for dinner?"

"Lo."

"Bee."

Laughing, I shook my head. "The first one. The second one isn't happening tonight."

"Oh, come on, live a little. You were about to *climb* that man last night."

Lowering my voice, I looked back at the living room. "I'm ready to climb *all* of them right the fuck now. But I want to keep my head clear for at least a day. They want to court me."

The squeal that came through the phone could be heard for a thousand miles. "Okay, can you do lunch tomorrow?"

"Bet your ass," I said.

"Good. Now go back in there and get some... dinner. I guess."

I laughed. "You *really* wanted to say dick, didn't you?"

"God, you have no idea."

"I'll talk to you later."

"Love you," she sang the words before the call ended.

Walking back into a room full of their scents was like walking into a buffet full of your favorite foods. Or a candle store.

"Everything okay?" Harrison asked.

I smirked. "She wants details."

"About?"

"Everything that's happening here. The five of us. She's a terrible influence."

"I don't know," Cole said. "She's the one that shoved me in the closet last night, and I've never been so grateful to be locked in a room before."

The music changed around us, and I froze. It was the beginning of a track I knew like the back of my hand and the inside of my heart. The quieting of applause before delicate piano started, echoing through an invisible concert hall.

Grief slammed into me before I pulled it back. It didn't matter how much I loved this recording, it still hurt. A pulsing ache beneath my skin that never *really* went away, no matter how much time passed. Complicated, tangled, and so woven into me it was never going to come out.

"Petra?" Emery's voice reached me. I opened my eyes. "What happened?"

I cleared my throat. "What do you mean?"

"I mean the cinnamon in your scent just darkened and it smells *burnt*." He reached out and stroked a hand down my arm until he held my hand. "What happened?"

How did I tell them this?

"Oh my god," Blake murmured, scrubbing his hand over his face before he looked at me, face full of pain and sympathy. "DeWitt. You're Mallory DeWitt's daughter?"

I smiled, but it wasn't convincing. "I told you it was heavy."

"I'm so sorry," Emery said. "I don't know who she is."

Taking a deep breath, I squeezed his hand. "She's the one playing this song. After this concert, she, two of her bonded Alphas, and me, were in a car accident. They died. I didn't."

The room went deadly silent, Mom's music the only thing playing in the background. It was so beautiful. "I was..." I cleared my throat. "My father had some kind of meeting and couldn't go. But he'd seen her perform so many times... anyway, I've always wanted the kind of pack I grew up in. I'm Russell's daughter, but they were my dads too. So while I'm so fucking *happy*," my voice cracked. "That I'm here and this is even a possibility. It's sad too."

Emery hauled me across the small distance on the couch and into his arms. He arranged me to sit across his lap, and I leaned into him, sinking into the rich scent of coffee and the sweet swirl and bite of chocolate.

"They met in a park. She went home with them and never left."

"I'm sorry for your loss," Cole said quietly.

"It was a long time ago."

"Time doesn't mean anything when it comes to grief," Harrison said. "And given the information your father gave me, I should have known this."

"No." I shook my head. "He does his best to minimize it. For him, it's better to pretend nothing ever happened."

"At least now I understand his added motivation to give you security," Harrison said. "Beyond the threat."

I looked between him and Cole. "We may be courting now, but I'm going to be annoying as fuck to protect. You should know that now."

Cole's mouth turned up into a smirk. "Oh, I'm looking forward to it."

Heat rose deep in my core, and as perfume swirled through the room, I had to remind myself what I'd told Sloane. No sex. Not tonight. I needed at least one night with a clear head. A clear-*ish* head. Before I got sucked in what was sure to be incredible sex.

"You can thank Sloane tomorrow," I said. "We're having lunch."

"Good," Harrison nodded and met my gaze. "I can use that time to install your security system."

"There's like three layers of security between the front door and mine. You really think I need more?"

"I think that until I prove someone's *not* trying to kill you, I want to keep you in a bubble and behind bulletproof glass. But since I can't do that, yes, I would like your apartment to have some extra security. But we'll keep it simple. I'll make sure it deactivates automatically with the key card."

I sighed and snuggled down into Emery. Really, if I was trying not to fuck them, I should move. Because the closer I got to his scent and the more I felt of his body, the more I wanted to.

"Okay," I finally said. "But you're right, I'm not going to be kept in a bubble."

Blake chuckled. "Something tells me you'd pop it even if we tried."

"Here's the other thing." I looked at Cole. "Last night, when you first found me, and I was swept away."

His eyes darkened. "I remember."

"My stepmother wants me to bond with a pack who was

65

there last night. Neither of us is interested, but when she gets an idea in her head, she won't let it go. My dad's going to talk to her, but you need to know because," I winced. "I think it's better if we keep this quiet."

The guys looked at each other.

"It's not because I don't want to be seen with you or anything like that," I said quickly. "I just know what happens when you get on the wrong side of something with Carmen. Or politics in general. If someone's already targeting me, we *really* don't want to add my stepmother to the list."

All of them laughed, and Cole stood, pulling me up off Emery's lap. "You not wanting to be seen with us was the last thing on my mind, honeybee."

"Honeybee?"

"Thought I'd try it out. Yes? No?"

I thought about it, distracted by his hands on me. "I don't know yet. Keep trying."

"And no," he said, dropping his lips to brush across mine. "I agree with not telling anyone. Because I don't care, I'm going to be the one protecting you when you leave this building. Or Harrison. No one else."

The quick possession should scare me, but it didn't. I liked it. But I also liked the look in their eyes when I pushed them. It was fun, and I felt powerful. Only a few hours, and we were already learning to play with each other.

"You sure you should be the one? If you can't take your eyes off me, you won't be able to protect me."

A growl ripped out of both Cole and Harrison, making my hair stand on end. He wove his hand into my hair and guided my gaze to his. "*No one* is fucking touching you."

"Except you," I breathed.

"Except us."

He grinned and kissed me quickly. "Now, what do you say we start courting you? Right now."

CHAPTER TEN

BLAKE

I needed to get my body under control.

Watching this little Omega snuggle with Emery like she was already ours, melt into Cole's arms and tease us? I'd been hard since I scented her walking into the kitchen, and careful not to show it.

Not that she didn't already know. Petra's perfume swirled around us, and every time a new wave hit us, I wondered what had crossed her mind. What kind of dirty thoughts did our Omega have going through her head? I wanted to know all of them and I wanted to recreate every single one.

By the same token, I'd never wanted to mix food and sex. That was my job, and they didn't mix. Until my Alpha scented her, and now my mind was filled with ideas of how to drizzle her with honey and compare the taste to her scent. Compare the taste with *hers*.

I shifted, easing the pressure of my jeans on my cock. At this rate, I was going to have a zipper imprint when I took them off.

Worth it.

If she said she wanted us, we were one hundred percent with her. But I sensed she wasn't there yet. Not that I blamed her. This was overwhelming on every level already. Sex could push it too far. We would get there, but tonight I was happy basking in her presence and scent.

Cole kissed her, a wave of perfume rippling outward as he did so. "Now, what do you say we start courting you? Right now."

"What did you have in mind?" Her voice was dreamy.

"Well," Cole looked around at the rest of us. "I'm thinking the arcade could be fun."

Petra smiled. "The arcade?"

"I don't know about the rest of you, but I do *not* have the focus for bowling right now."

"God no," I said. "But I'm fully prepared to take you down in some good old-fashioned Pacman, Omega."

A wickedly vicious grin took over her face. "You sure about that, Alpha? I think I can take you."

Every remaining bit of blood I had went south. "You can take me any time you want."

Pink rushed to her cheeks, and that sweet as sin perfume washed over me. "Fuck, baby. We better get down to the arcade with you smelling like that."

Her face only turned more pink. "I'm sorry."

"Don't ever say sorry for smelling like you." I stole her from Cole, desperately needing to touch her. Feel her beneath my fingers. "I don't ever want to breathe anything else. But I want to take it at your pace."

I watched her throat move as she swallowed, fighting the thoughts that would have me tugging her down to the couch and sitting her on my face.

"Yeah," she whispered. "We should go to the arcade. Because I want to fall into bed with all four of you, and I don't think that's a good idea."

"I wouldn't say it's a *bad* idea," Harrison said with a chuckle. "But I understand what you mean."

"Let me change out of my scrubs," Emery said. "And we can go."

"Do you need anything from your apartment?" Cole asked Petra.

"Quarters, if we're going to the arcade. Or cash."

"I don't think so," Harrison said. "You won't need that."

"But—"

"No," he said. The word was firm, but he still smiled. "We're courting you. You don't need money—especially not for the arcade."

"You're sure?"

"Very," Cole said. "I'd tell you to save your quarters for laundry if I didn't already know you had laundry in your apartment."

Petra laughed and looked back at me, chest rising and falling.

This Omega was breathing me in as much as I was breathing in her.

I couldn't stop myself. I dropped my face to her neck, inhaling at the point of her pulse. Honey, shining in the sun and making everything sweeter. Cinnamon on toast, mixed in with the rich flavor of her sugar. It wasn't a combination I'd ever done anything with, but I sure as hell would now.

My lips brushed her throat before I pulled back. "I need to let you go now, baby."

"Okay."

But neither of us moved.

Harrison pulled her back from me, raising an eyebrow at me. "Do I need to lock you away?"

He was kidding, but he would do it if I needed him to. But I wasn't close to rut. More like I was drunk on honey. Not a thought I ever thought I'd have. "I'm good."

"Actually," Cole said. "If you don't mind, Petra, I'll change too. Harrison, ditch the suit."

"Of course. I want you to be comfortable."

Cole pointed at me. "Be good."

Petra and I laughed as they retreated. I slid my hands in my pockets. "I know exactly what you mean, by the way."

"About what?"

"It not being a good idea and the best idea all at the same time."

She shook her head and wrapped her arms around herself. "It's so much."

"Too much?" I asked lightly, ignoring the pulsing tension in my gut. Despite this intangible, invisible thing spinning between all of us, history held me back.

"No," she whispered. "I just don't know how to handle it. If I seem a little lost, I'm sorry. This is so far from what I imagined would happen. It's like I've lived an entire life in a few hours."

I held out a hand and resisted the urge to pull her into me all over again. "We get it. Believe me, we feel it too. Whatever you need, tell us. We don't want to fuck this up."

Petra frowned and came toward me, and I took a step back. "Harrison is right," I said. "It's better if I don't touch you."

"Are you telling me not to?"

"Fuck no."

She reached up and took my face in her hands, her voice gentle. "Please hear me when I say this. I don't expect any of you to be perfect. I sure as fuck am not. Hell," she smiled, "I already messed up when we were in the kitchen. This is new and weird, and we're all going to have to trust that we're doing our best.

"I mean, I'd prefer it if no one fucked up on *purpose*." We both laughed, our breath turning short together. "But I don't want you to be afraid to fuck up. We *are* going to. That's not a way to start a relationship, and you can't fuck up being you."

She saw the truth of my words deeper than I had. It hadn't even crossed my mind to think of it that way. I just didn't want to lose a beautiful thing before it started. But she was right.

Our past experiences had made us nervous, and we wouldn't be able to turn it off at will. Still, we were all human, and fucking up was a part of life. Promising to understand all of us were human was the best thing I could ask for.

"I promise," I whispered. "I'm not going to drag you into a sex lair, but I really need to kiss you."

"You have a sex lair?"

"I mean—"

Petra laughed, the bright, shining sound echoing through the room before she twisted herself up to kiss me. The way she wrapped herself around me, I was the building, and she was the ivy. One wasn't the same without the other.

I pulled her into me, devouring her. She tasted so fucking sweet, felt so soft. I purred without even realizing it. Not once in my life had I ever felt so close to out of control, and yet I knew in my bones I was fine. I would never hurt this stunning, precious woman in my arms. Because as soon as I walked into the kitchen, she became the center of everything.

"I thought I told you to be good," Cole said.

Petra's eyes were glassy and dazed. "I don't know, I think that was pretty good."

Satisfaction rolled through me. "And that was only the beginning."

The look she sent over her shoulder had me reciting the

recipe for the Béarnaise sauce I was perfecting. A variation on a classic. Egg yolks, shallots, black pepper, tarragon—

I took a breath, and then another.

Butter, salt, lemon juice, white wine vinegar.

Following Cole and Petra, we went downstairs and waited for the others. The air was clearer here, and it was easier to think.

"You okay?" Emery appeared beside me, saying the words under his breath. "Your Alpha seems close to the surface."

I looked at him and he started laughing. "Like yours isn't?"

"Oh, it is," he said. "Her scent is still on my skin. Something I'll happily get used to."

He headed for them, and I stayed back for one more breath. I couldn't agree more. Petra was all I ever wanted to be used to.

CHAPTER ELEVEN

PETRA

*E*mery looked incredible in scrubs. But in jeans and a shirt like that? Holy hell, if I hadn't already been about to pass out because of Blake, this would have sent me over the edge.

The blue was a muted version of his eyes; the sleeves pushed up to show off incredible forearms and *tattoos*. They'd been hidden under the long sleeves beneath his scrubs. The shirt itself stretched over his chest like it was barely on the right side of being too small.

"Petra?"

"What?"

Emery smirked. "I asked if you were ready? Harrison just got a call. He's going to meet us there."

"Oh." I flushed. Clearly, my attention was elsewhere. "I'm ready."

He reached out and took my hand. Butterflies took flight in my stomach. Such a simple little gesture, and something I'd never really had.

Relationships weren't easy when you were the daughter of a senator, and even less easy when your pack died in the middle of high school. No one wanted to deal with it, and I understood.

I hadn't wanted to deal with it either.

The elevator doors closed the four of us in. I noticed I was at the center of the three of them, like a triangle. Cole was in front, already protecting me. I slipped a finger into the loop of his belt. "I'm going to have a hard time not touching you when you're protecting me."

A sound somewhere between a growl and a moan came out of him. "Same, honeybee."

I pushed my face into the back of his shirt, inhaling caramel and what was currently a much deeper flavor of salt.

When I came to check out Starling Tower, I looked in at the arcade, but I hadn't gone inside it. The elevator doors opened to the hallway, which split the arcade and the absolutely absurd indoor pool. It was so large you could probably fit a boat in it.

But they already *had* a pool.

I shook my head. This was wild. I was never going to fucking sleep tonight.

"After you." Cole let me go first out of the elevator.

Through the windows, I didn't see anyone in the arcade. "Is it always empty?"

"No," Blake said. "But it is a weeknight, so not surprising."

"No, this is great." With no one here, we didn't have to worry about bothering anyone. There were so many games. "You told me you'd beat me at Pacman. So that's the first thing, and no going easy on me. I want to win fair and square."

Blake stretched his arms behind his head, distracting me with a strip of toned stomach as his shirt rode up. "Baby, I'm a chef. We're some of the most competitive fuckers out there."

"Meaning?"

"Meaning I don't care how *fucking incredible* you smell or taste, I'll never *let* you win."

I stared at him. "Prove it."

He turned, heading to the quarter machine, and I looked at the other two Alphas. "This is probably a bad time to tell him I went to arcades a lot as a kid, right?"

Emery covered his mouth to hide his laughter. "Tell him after you kick his ass."

"What else do you want to play?"

"I don't know. Let's do Pacman first. Then we'll see."

Blake came back with a fistful of quarters. "You want to go first?"

I shook my head. "No. By all means, I want to stand back and watch the glory that is your skill first."

"I sense you mocking me, Omega."

"Going to do something about it?"

"Not at the moment," he muttered.

Blake went to the Pacman machine, trying to hide the way he adjusted himself. I smiled. I liked this. I liked teasing them. I never got to be light and easy like this with anyone but Sloane. And Eva, on the rare occasion I saw her.

Chocolate and coffee wrapped around me, along with Emery's arms. He walked us over to where Blake was setting up the machine. I looked down where his arms locked around my ribs and examined the tattoos more closely. "You were hiding these."

"Even being a vet for exotic animals, some people still take you more seriously without them."

I'd never seen tattoos like this. They were an entrancing mixture of curves and edges. Delicate lines created frames for things like a sword and a statue. An incredibly rendered woman's eye that was filled with tears.

"I'm still working on them."

"They mean things?"

He kissed the side of my hair. "They do. I'll tell you all of them sometime."

I had a vision of us lying tangled together, bathed in morning sunlight while I pointed to each tattoo and he told me the story. The vision made me *crave* it even as a wave of desperate grief spiraled through my chest.

If Mom were alive, I'd be able to ask her if this was what it was like. Was it normal to see a future so strongly after a few hours? Was I out of my mind to feel this way? Were my instincts spot on? Could I trust them?

I had so many questions.

Blake began the game. He was good. He jammed the old school stick controller in the four directions it could go, chasing the dots and fleeing the ghosts, and catching the occasional piece of fruit.

He got through four levels before he finally succumbed to the ghosts overwhelming him.

"Not bad," I told him.

"Thank you." A small bow. "Now do your worst."

Taking the quarter from his hand, I smiled. "Don't worry. I will."

Behind me, I heard Emery speak. "You're about to get absolutely shit on. You know that, right?"

I barely kept in my laughter. It was true, but I didn't need to rub it in his face. Putting the quarters into the slot, I sank into the zone. There was only me, the dots, and those little shitty ghosts trying to track me down and suck the life out of me.

The rhythm of the dots lulled me, and six levels later, three ghosts cornered me and there was no way to break free. "Shit," I said with a laugh. "I was hoping to get a little farther."

"Well, you kicked my ass," Blake said. "I've been put in my place."

I turned and took a little bow before smiling. "I went to arcades a lot when I was younger. They're one thing that's *the same* wherever you go, so when we would travel for Dad's work or Mom's shows, we would find an arcade. It was one of the things that drew me to the building in the first place."

The door behind us opened and Harrison walked in. He was now in Jeans and a t-shirt, and it wasn't fair how good they looked. The suit was one thing, but something about seeing Alphas who wore suits in casual attire made me feral.

He had a tattoo too, peeking out from under his sleeve on his bicep. His eyes locked on me, and a small smile appeared. I couldn't quite get a read on Harrison yet. I knew he was exactly where I was, but he was reserved. "Sorry about that."

"Everything okay?"

"Yeah. Just one of our guys verifying something."

"Oh," I said, relaxing. "Good. I was worried it was an emergency. Running a security company, you have to get a lot of those, right?"

Cole slipped past us to try his hand at Pacman, and Harrison took his place. "Actually, if we're doing our jobs, there shouldn't be emergencies. We always hope there aren't any. But if there are any, you'd know."

"Is it ever dangerous?"

He searched my face, like he knew what drove the question even though I hadn't said it. "Sometimes it is, yes."

Lifting a hand, he cupped my cheek and stroked it with his thumb. One little motion shouldn't send my heart and stomach tumbling into free fall, but here I was. "We never go anywhere alone, and all our men are trained as the best. Along with that, we take every precaution to make sure there *isn't* an emergency."

"So you're not going to walk out the door one day and not come back?"

The air around us went tight and breathless. With one glance from Harrison, Blake and Emery drifted away, leaving us alone. He stepped in, hand still holding my face, guiding my gaze to his. "I can't make you that promise. No one should, even if they don't work in a field like mine. Anything can happen. You already know that too well."

I did, and that was why it scared me. These weren't thoughts I normally had. All of this... I'd left it behind. Or so I thought. But hearing Mom play, and being so fucking happy, it was all coming up.

"What I can promise you," he said, "is that I will always do everything in my power to keep myself and anyone I'm responsible for safe. My pack and the people I employ." Harrison's lips brushed my forehead. "That now includes you, little one."

A whine slipped out of me, eyes closing. I was clinging to his shirt, not quite remembering how I grabbed him or how his other arm was now around me. A low, rumbling purr came to life in his chest. If I hadn't already been a puddle in his arms, this would have sealed the deal.

Safety.

My whole life I'd been safe. Dad kept me home after the accident, making sure I never drove anywhere alone and was always inside the secure net he created. This was different.

Being inside a bubble to make sure I didn't die wasn't the same as someone offering to keep me safe. Harrison wasn't just talking about my body, though, given the threat against me, that was part of it. What Harrison offered was more. My mind and my soul.

I hoped my heart, too.

Harrison lowered his head to kiss me. Softly. Deeply. Everything in me ached, the tenderness of his mouth on mine calling up things I wasn't nearly ready to face. And yet I wanted so much more. The rich scent of whiskey and cedar permeated my senses. I needed a distilled version of all of their scents with me at all times.

"Don't let me keep you from enjoying the arcade," he said.

"I'd say I'm enjoying it," I mumbled, and he chuckled. The

sound *did* things to my insides. Pressing my legs together, I leaned my head on his chest. Harrison was still purring, though it was softer now.

I sneaked a look up at him. "I want to play something with you."

"Anything you want." He kissed my forehead again.

"Anything?" It was hard to keep the grin off my face. Because he'd walked into a trap, and he fucking knew it.

He fought a smile. "I suppose I have to stand by that now."

"Yes, you do." Grabbing his hand, I pulled him over to a machine covered in neon lights. "I want you to dance with me."

This wasn't the kind of machine with four arrows you had to stick to. It had one big platform that glowed, shifting through rainbows and patterns, and as you danced, it tracked your steps. It was more about rhythm than direction.

"I deserve this for saying I'd do anything, don't I?"

"Yup." I let the p in the word pop loudly. "But I'll let you choose the song."

"Gracious of you."

"I know." I flipped my hair over my shoulder. "I'm a saint."

Emery now stood behind us. "You got him to say yes?"

"He said he'd do anything."

"A lesson in the importance of word choice," Harrison said, tapping the screen through the music options.

Blake watched us and Cole at the same time. Cole was clearly struggling, frantically moving the joystick around like he was seconds away from being murdered by ghosts.

"This one." A rock song from a few years ago blared out of the speakers. Everyone knew it, and it got seriously intense at the end between a nearly electric beat and screaming guitar solos. The difficulty on the screen said *hard*.

"Are you sure?"

"I said I'd do anything, and I meant it. Not going to cop out by doing short and easy."

I stepped onto the stage with him. "Sure, but I thought you'd pick something survivable."

He put in the money and stretched. "Doubting me already?"

"Not at all," I lied. The screen made two dancers appear side by side, and the lines we were meant to follow came speeding toward us from the 3D distance.

We danced.

I'd played a lot of these dance games in my life, and I wasn't bad, but *fuck* Harrison chose a hard song. A minute in I was breathing hard. Two minutes? My lungs *burned*. There was still a minute and a half left, and I honestly didn't think I would make it. I pushed, forcing myself through the third minute when I stumbled, losing my balance.

Cole caught me before I could fall, lifting me off the platform and out of Harrison's way as he *danced*. He kept going, taking over the center of the platform and not missing a single fucking step.

Perfect. Perfect. Perfect. The combination of steps kept adding up, score rising. Harrison was barely phased. He moved easily, like he did this all the time.

"Did you know he could do that?" I whispered.

Cole shook his head. "I had no idea."

The song kept getting faster, and Harrison went with it, traveling across the small stage with now exaggerated flair. He was showing off. A crescendo of sound came through the speakers for the climax of the song, and Harrison planted his feet on the final step.

One last *Perfect*.

I stared at him as he spun to face me, mouth open in shock. "You come down here and practice on weekends."

"As fun as that would be, I usually don't have that kind of time."

"But you just..." I gestured. "You can just *do that*?"

"Surprise." He was grinning like the fucking Cheshire Cat, and I was the version of Alice who was foolish enough to believe him. "Hope you're not too disappointed."

Completely the opposite. Watching him dance, confident even though it wasn't something he chose, was one of the hottest things I'd ever seen. "Uh-uh."

"Good."

"Okay," Cole said. "What other games are you able to kick our asses at? Or try?"

I turned and pointed. "That one."

A game with guns and aliens I'd always been amazing at. It wasn't anything close to shooting a real gun, and I didn't care. All I knew was I could absolutely *shred* the aliens in the game and it made me feel powerful. I was out of practice. Pacman I'd revisited a couple of times. This one I hadn't.

"You're on," Cole said, heading over to the machine.

I lost. Looking over at Cole and the intensity on his face, the way he held the fake gun and stared down our enemies, I got a glimpse of Cole the bodyguard. Which did nothing for the growing desperation in my gut for them to take me back upstairs and have their way with me.

There were games I wasn't good at but enjoyed playing. Air hockey. Asteroid. The game where overly buff characters kicked each other in the face repeatedly until one of them passed out.

While I was losing so badly it was *sad*, they stole my phone and put all their numbers in. And each of them—except for Harrison—used a name that wasn't really theirs. I hadn't found all of their names yet, but I would.

But mostly, it was easy. Touches that felt natural and teasing that built heat under my skin. Scents I was getting used to and never wanted to leave behind. And temptation was growing too far.

Emery had me pinned against the air hockey table with his hips, kissing me slowly. He bet me a kiss I couldn't beat him at the fighting game, and he won.

Even if I'd been capable of winning—which I wasn't—I might have considered losing on purpose.

"I need to go back to my apartment," I whispered, trying to catch my breath between kisses.

"Why?"

"Because if we keep going like this, I'm going to end up in your beds, and we agreed not to."

He kissed me one more time. "Things change."

"I know."

Stepping back, his blue eyes no longer looked like the summer sky. They looked stormy and dark, ready to unleash power I wanted to be caught in. "You're right," he said. "Though I don't pretend it's going to be easy to let you go."

"Believe me, I understand," I laughed. "But I feel it. It's right."

The four of them surrounded me as we left the arcade and aimed for the elevator. This time we ended at twenty-six. Cole's phone was at his ear. "It's Cole. The client is ready for you."

I looked at him. "What was that?"

"That was Nick. He's going to be outside your door tonight."

Looking at the floor, I winced. "We're still sure it's necessary?"

"Until we find out the truth? Yes, little one."

Harrison calling me that made something unlock in my brain. Of the four of them, he was the tallest and broadest. Compared to him I *was* little, and I loved the way it felt.

I unlocked the door with my key card, and they followed me inside. "If there are people other than Cole guarding me, it's going to get back to my father."

"All of our employees sign non-disclosure agreements," Cole said, stroking one hand down my arm. "They understand that outside the client trying to harm themselves or committing a crime, what they do is their business."

"Even when it involves courting their bosses?"

"Especially then." He leaned in and kissed my cheek, stopping to inhale me deeply. "When do you need to meet Sloane?"

"Noon."

"Then I'll see you in the morning."

I didn't quite want to let him go. Him, or any of them.

Blake caught me around the waist and spun me around before placing his cheek against mine. "I hope I'll be seeing you tomorrow, too."

"I would like that."

We could pretend all we wanted, but there was no way we *weren't* seeing each other tomorrow. It didn't feel like a choice.

Emery wrapped me in his arms, and I fit there perfectly, my head under his chin. There didn't need to be any words. I felt the

81

same kind of awe and desperation as when he walked into the living room and scented me for the first time.

And finally, Harrison held me. "Sleep well," he said. "And if you need anything, you know where we are."

"I do."

He gently pulled away and winked before heading to the door.

"Night." I bit my lip to keep from asking them to come back. One night. We needed one night to bask in the connection.

I closed the door and leaned against it. Cole stayed outside my door until the guy who must be Nick arrived. They shook hands, and I couldn't hear what he said to the man, but he spoke to him for a while before leaving.

"Wow."

Blowing out a breath, I turned back to my apartment. Empty. It was beautiful, and I loved it. But in the absence of all their warmth and scents, it now felt incredibly open and spacious. Too big. I needed darkness and cozy blankets.

The air still smelled faintly of cookies.

I grabbed a couple of the ones I hadn't taken upstairs and went to my bedroom. This place was better. Changing into my pajamas, I burrowed myself into my blankets and turned on a movie to fall asleep to. But I could barely let myself relax enough to sleep.

Four Alphas kept slipping into my head, and I wanted them to stay there. I wanted to dream of them. I wanted more than I ever knew there was to want.

And I couldn't wait for tomorrow.

CHAPTER TWELVE

PETRA

$\mathcal{C}$ole sat across from me in the car on the way to The Saffron Market. Sloane suggested it, and I agreed. It was a place we went when we needed to spend some time without pressure to leave right away. Loud enough to be private, with little stalls of different kinds of food you could order from. The waitstaff kept circling with menus for you to choose, and there was an hourly fee.

I guessed we would be staying a couple of hours as I told her everything that had happened in the last day. In detail.

But at the moment, Cole and I were staring at each other, desperately trying not to touch. Brian wasn't employed by Atwood Security, and he had no reason not to report my actions to my father.

I hoped Dad wouldn't care if I were courting a pack. He'd probably be happy. But given what Carmen wanted, I wasn't so sure. Regardless, I didn't want to put Cole and Harrison in that position yet. Because right now it looked strange. One day protecting me and we were courting?

Of all the people in the world, he would get it.

But everything would come back for him. I knew from experience his grief was only ever a breath below the surface. It never went away, and it never lessened. For years after the accident, he was a shell of himself, doing work and everything else on autopilot. He was a ghost in his own life.

Until Carmen came in and brightened things for Dad as much as she clouded them for me. She was the main reason I wanted to keep things quiet. For the first time in forever, I was living away from her. I sure as fuck wasn't giving her a reason to seek me out.

Brian pulled up to the curb, and Cole got out first, scanning our surroundings before holding out his hand to help me out of the car. "You're eating here?" He asked.

"Yeah, Lo and I like it. Why?"

He shrugged. "It's one of Blake's restaurants."

"You're shitting me."

"I am very much not shitting you." Holding out an arm, I stepped in front of him, leading the way into the restaurant. We had a reservation, and Lo was already sitting at the table tapping away on her phone.

"Petra," Cole said, catching my arm. "I'll be here near the door. If you need me, or anything looks strange, I can be there in seconds."

I looked up at him. "Cole, how serious is this threat?"

He tried to cover his reaction and failed, wincing. "I looked over everything last night after we left you. It's... Harrison is right. Until we know the truth of it, I'm taking no chances."

"Okay." My voice sounded small.

"Nothing is going to happen to you. We're not going to let it." He looked around quickly before dropping a kiss on my cheek. "Have fun and say hello for me. Oh, and tell her thank you."

I smirked. "I'm sure she'll be over the moon to know you're happy about her throwing you in a closet."

His laughter followed me to the table. Sloane looked up when I was almost there and leapt out of her seat. "Oh my god, *hi*." She yanked me into a hug and froze. "You brought him with you?"

"Girl," I shook my head and sat down. "I have so much to tell you. Starting with, Cole is my bodyguard, and he wants to thank you for the stunt you pulled with the closet."

"What the fuck?"

"I know."

She signaled for the nearby waitress. "First, what the hell? Second, why on earth do you need a bodyguard?"

"Hold on to your toe shoes. Cause it's gonna take a minute."

We ordered food, and I told her everything. I wasn't wrong—it took a *while* to get through it all.

"Fuck me," Sloane said. "Or rather, fuck you. In every conceivable way. Because I'm jealous and I also need *someone* in this friendship to get railed. God knows I've got nothing."

I choked on my drink. "Lo, give me some warning next time."

"You should know this about me by now."

"I really should."

"So?" She picked up some noodles off her plate with a pair of chopsticks. "Are you going back to them for some delirious, scent-soaked sex? Please tell me yes, because I don't think I'll survive hearing about you going to bed with *cookies* instead of *cock* a second time."

A laugh burst out of me so suddenly, I nearly spit out my drink. "Honestly, I don't know if I'd be able to resist it. It's like... being dunked in a vat of ice cream and being told you can't eat it."

Sloane rolled her eyes. "You can't complain when you voluntarily abstained."

"It was the right thing to do."

"Bullshit," she muttered.

I held out a hand across the table. "Remember that time when you went out with that Alpha... what was his name?"

"Craig?"

"Craig." I shuddered. "Yeah. Him. You went out with him and called me from the bathroom cause you weren't sure about going back to his place, and you decided to wait until date number two? It's like that."

She took my hand. "Bee, choosing not to fuck an Alpha because you're not sure if you want to take it further isn't the same as resisting a scent-sympathetic pack and you know it. Just admit that you're scared, please."

"What?"

Pushing her plate to the end of the table, she sighed and held out her other hand. I put mine in hers so she was holding both of them. "You're going to say you're not scared, but I need you to hear me out. You don't talk about it ever, but as much as you love this—and you do, I can see it in your eyes—it fucking *terrifies* you."

"Why would it terrify me?"

My best friend gave me a look which told me she wasn't going to put up with my shit today. "Because it's too similar to your mom and your other dads. Being swept up by a pack and loved immediately? It's too familiar. You're scared to be happy, because in your head, that kind of happiness only leads to pain."

"I—"

"And I know," she cut me off. "That you're aware of the comparison. I don't think you're doing it on purpose. Hell, you talked about it with them. But this is deep. And I have bad news. It's not going away."

I made a face. "You're really shit at pep talks, you know that?"

"Not a pep talk, my love. This is an intervention. If what you say is true, and it is, because I don't think I've ever smelled anything as intense as that closet."

I blushed, but she kept going.

"Then you're only hurting yourself by holding back."

"What if it hurts, anyway?"

Harrison's words echoed in my head. *Anything can happen.*

Sloane shrugged. "Then it hurts. Pretty much the way life goes."

She wasn't wrong, but it still wasn't an easy thing to hear or believe. "I wish I could talk to her. Find out what the hell *normal* is supposed to be in all of this. I feel like I'm a hundred miles out at sea and have no idea what to do."

Finally, Sloane released my hands. "I know it's not the same, but talk to Eva. It's the way she found her pack. Her sister too. It won't compare with talking to your mom, but at least you could get an idea of how things might go."

"Yeah." My throat was dry. "Anyway. Let's talk about you for a bit."

"Do we have to?" She asked. "I'm boring."

"No, you're not."

"Right now I am. I get up, go to class, sometimes twice, ice my feet, and go to sleep. If by some miracle I'm still awake, I'll watch some trash TV."

I laughed. Sloane was a dancer with the Slate City Ballet, but their rehearsal season didn't start for a few more weeks.

"Enjoy the boring then. Because next month you're going to beg me to kill you because you're so exhausted."

"It's true. I'm a multitude of contradictions." She sighed,

shoulders slumping. "But speaking of my job, I have a meeting with the company director I'm really not looking forward to."

"When?"

She tapped the screen on her phone. "Like half an hour."

"Shit, you need to get going."

"But this is more fun."

I glared at her in the way only best friends could get away with. "I'm not going to be responsible for you being late to meet your boss." Lifting a hand, I summoned the waitress for the bill and also drew the attention of an Alpha I was pretty sure had been staring at me the whole time.

Cole made his way through the tables and ended up at ours. "It's nice to meet you, Sloane," he said. "Under less frantic circumstances."

"Cole." She stuck out a hand for him to shake. "It is good to meet you. Please pass on to your pack that if you hurt my best friend, I know a lot of people with very strong legs who will happily follow me to kick your ass all the way across Slate City."

He looked at me and grinned. "I like her."

"*She* is going to be late if she doesn't leave."

"I still need to pay."

"Actually you don't," Cole said. "It's on the house."

Sloane looked at me, and I still looked at Cole. "Did you call him?"

"Bet your ass I did."

"Wait." Sloane held up a hand for us to pause. "What am I missing?"

My whole face and chest were red. "This restaurant is Blake's. I was going to pay."

"Why should you have to?" Cole asked, subtly taking my hand under the table.

"Oh my god, you guys are so cute I'm going to vomit." Sloane hopped up from the table and half hugged me. "I'll see you later, okay?"

"Okay."

She drew eyes as she left the restaurant. Sloane drew eyes wherever she went, tall and graceful as she was.

Cole still held my hand out of sight. "Where to now?"

I yawned. "Actually, I didn't sleep that well, thanks to these four guys. Don't know if you would like them. Wouldn't leave me alone all night. Kept making me have these dreams."

A low growl skittered across my skin. "Careful, Omega," he warned. "I'm this close to kidnapping you myself and taking you back to our place."

My words had the effect they wanted, and I grinned. "I don't doubt I'll end up there tonight. But since I didn't actually sleep that well, I thought I might take a nap until everyone's done with work."

"We can do that." He pulled out his phone and sent a text. I assumed to Brian.

"Now I'm the one who's boring. Guarding someone who goes to lunch and home."

Cole looked around the restaurant a final time before leading the way to the doors. "Trust me, honeybee, guarding you will never be boring. I feel like I've been electrified."

"Really?"

"Really."

A minute later, Brian pulled up with the car again, and Cole and I pretended there wasn't a magnet pulling us together like our lives depended on it. All the way home.

CHAPTER THIRTEEN

PETRA

I woke up fuzzy.

It was still light outside, and my phone told me it had only been a few hours. But *fuck* I did not feel well. Pain pulsed low in my gut, and my chest burned. Shit.

Did I get food poisoning?

Blake was going to be really pissed about that if it happened at his restaurant.

The wave of pain subsided, and I breathed out. Well, that put a damper on my plans for the evening. I wasn't going to spend the night with them if there was a chance I would throw up on them.

Not the way I wanted to start a courtship.

I called Sloane. She picked up on the third ring. "Hello?"

"Hey." My voice croaked. "How did the meeting go?"

"It went..." she hesitated, and in that silence, I knew there was far more than she was going to say. At least over the phone. "It went fine. Why do you sound like you're dying?"

I groaned. "Because I am. I think I have food poisoning. Wanted to warn you, since we ate the same things."

Sloane started laughing. Full, loud laughter. "Oh my god."

"Well, first, rude of you to laugh at my pain. Second, what the fuck is so funny?"

She had to get all the giggles out of her system before she could find her voice long enough to tell me. "I have bad news for you, Bee. I feel fine."

"What do you mean?"

"I mean, you're right. We ate all the same things, and I feel fantastic. You, however, spent a good portion of the last day with Alphas who make you perfume more than the Bergman's scent department."

Another low pulse of pain in my gut, and it clicked into place. "Fuck."

"Oh yeah."

"No. Sloane, it can't happen like this."

She snickered. "How exactly is it supposed to happen, then? Your body is letting you know, in no uncertain terms, what it wants. I think you should listen."

"Of course you do."

I closed my eyes and rolled onto my back. When was the last time I had a heat? It was a while ago, and I stayed in my room at the mansion with knotting toys and enough food to last me through it.

There wasn't a way for a politician's daughter to pick up someone random to fuck her through a heat. So I fucked myself. It worked well enough.

In college, I tried having someone help me through my very first heat, and it felt wrong. Everything felt wrong. The dorm room was too big and echoey, and the Alpha, who was an acquaintance from my classes, smelled wrong.

He didn't smell *bad*, just wrong. My Omega had said 'fuck this,' and asked him to leave. Thankfully, he was a good sport about it. The next time I bought knotting dildos, the strongest vibrator I could find, and waterproof sheets.

What happened *after* the heat wasn't something I ever wanted to remember.

"I don't know what's going to happen," I told her. "But if you don't hear from me for a few days, you know where to find me."

"At what point do I put out the 'I think Petra has been murdered by her Alphas' call?"

"Considering my father is *literally* paying them to keep me safe, I think we're fine. But I'll have my phone, and I'll text you Cole's number. Check in after two days and we'll see how it goes."

"So you're going to let them help you?"

Yes.

My whole body shuddered. The idea of staying away from them during a heat was just as wrong as the college Alpha. I couldn't. I needed them. My Omega needed them. And I was about to fuck up whatever plans they had for the next few days.

"I'm not sure I have a choice."

"Of course you do," Sloane said. "If they don't let you have a choice, I don't care who they are. I will *fuck them up*."

I laughed through a wave of pain. "No, that's not what I meant. I just mean anything else would feel wrong, and I don't think I could do it."

"Oh. Yeah. That makes sense."

"If I told them to leave me alone, they would. But it would break them as much as it would break me. So I guess this courtship is getting shoved into high gear. Check in the day after tomorrow?"

"Done." She said. "I will celebrate on your behalf. Now go tell your pack so they can, lovingly, fuck the shit out of you."

"Oh my god."

She made a sound I knew too well as her sticking her tongue out. "You love me."

"I do."

"Make sure you hydrate. You know, for all the cock you're about to consume."

"*Goodbye*, Sloane."

She laughed as I ended the call. Any humor was short-lived. Throbbing pain took over my stomach for a long moment. God, this sucked. The beginnings of a heat were always the worst, and mine lasted forever. Every Omega was a little different. Some heats came on within hours, and some took a couple days.

Who knew, maybe being around them would make my heat come on faster, but I had at least twelve hours of this pain ahead of me. Even with the industrial strength painkillers I kept for this reason.

I got myself up and took them before I could think too hard about it. No matter what was about to happen, I needed to be able to function.

Quickly, I changed my clothes. During the nap I sweat through mine. The fever was already kicking in, though it was low.

Slumping down on my couch, I started scrolling through my contacts and added Harrison to the chat first. The next one I found was Cole, listed under *Badass Bodyguard*. I sent Sloane his number before adding him to the chat.

Blake put himself in under *Petra's Personal Chef*, and Emery was *Mr. Exotic (animals)*. I snorted a laugh. These Alphas were dorks, and I loved that. They got put into the group chat, too.

It was around the time when I thought they might be home.

> Hey, it's Petra.

> Are any of you guys home?

> Petra's Personal Chef: We all are. Emery just got here.

> Can you come down?

> Mr. Exotic (animals): Are you okay?

That was a tricky question. Was I okay? Physically, yes. There wasn't anything wrong with having a heat. It was part of life as an Omega. But I was nervous and overwhelmed on top of the pain. Last night now made more sense. The apartment felt empty, and all I wanted was closeness and comfort.

Tears pricked my eyes.

Fuck.

Already my emotions were at the surface. This was the way it was.

> I'm okay.

I didn't want to tell them I was going into heat over text message.

> Badass Bodyguard: We'll be right there.

Getting myself up off the couch, I ran a hand through my hair. I didn't look my best right now, and I instinctively chose clothing which made me feel good. Which in this case was a hoodie three sizes too large for me, stolen from Sloane when the ballet company was getting rid of old gift shop merch, and leggings that were lined with fabric so soft it felt like velvet.

There was a guard standing outside my door, and exactly like they said, he didn't bat an eye when all four Alphas approached my door and I opened it for them.

The way they looked at me, they were wary. I shut the door and leaned against the wall. Emery was closest to me, and he looked like he was holding back panic. "Are you sure you're okay? You don't seem okay."

I smiled, but it was weak. "Well, when I woke up from my nap I thought I had food poisoning." Blake went rigid, and I shook my head. "I don't. Sloane is fine and everything was incredible. But... umm." My cheeks were on fire.

Why was this so hard to tell them? It wasn't like sex wasn't going to happen between us. But somehow, it felt like too much to drag them suddenly out of their lives because my body reacted like this.

"You're going into heat?" Emery asked quietly.

Someone else saying it out loud relieved me. "Yeah."

Cole stepped in and wrapped his arms around me. "Were you nervous to tell us?"

I nodded into his shirt.

"Why?"

"It's a lot. It's so fast. I don't want to force you into anything."

"Jane?" Emery's voice came from behind me, and I turned my head to see him on the phone. "Cancel my appointments for the next four days and be on standby to cancel more if needed. Call in Sandra and Dean to take care of emergencies. Make calling me a last resort, but my phone will be on." He hesitated, listening to the person on the other end of the line, but his eyes were on me. "Don't give a reason unless they ask. But I'll be on heat leave. Thanks."

He ended the call, and I closed my eyes. "I'm pulling you out of your lives."

"This is what it means to be in a pack," Emery said. "I know we're not one yet, but it doesn't matter."

"You want to help me?" I knew they did, but I needed to hear them say it. My Omega needed to feel that connection.

A quickly smothered growl came from Harrison. "Did you think there was a question about it?"

Cole tightened his arms around me, his scent strengthening. Between him and Emery, I desperately needed a caramel latte. "No," I mumbled.

"But?" Blake asked.

"But I never want to assume anything. And heats make me... less secure." The only way I could say how much I *needed*. Admitting it out loud was terrifying.

Cole transferred me to Blake's arms, and nothing about it felt strange. "I think I speak for all of us when I say please assume, baby. And if you can't, I'm more than happy to tell you."

"Thank you." My words were muffled by his sleeve.

"How long do we have?" Cole asked.

I straightened, but didn't pull away. "Probably like twelve hours, but I don't know if being around you will make it come faster."

"It probably will," Emery said. "But that's okay. The question is if you need to see the nest before we go."

Turning, I looked at him. "Go where?"

"To get everything to make your nest," Blake said.

My nest.

My heart twisted in hope. "I thought we would just use my room."

"Is that what you want?" Harrison asked carefully, and when I hesitated, he stepped closer and tilted my chin up exactly like he had last night. "Tell the truth, little one."

I shook my head. My previous heats had been in my bedroom, and it wasn't what I really needed. I'd thought about getting a bigger apartment to make myself a permanent nest, but it seemed impractical for a single Omega. So I didn't. "No," I whispered.

"Good girl," he whispered back.

My whole body went still, soaking in the little drop of praise like a flower that hadn't been watered in years. I melted further into Blake's arms.

Pain rolled through me, contracting all my muscles and forcing a wave of heat over my skin. "God, this part sucks."

"Do you need to see the nest first?" Cole asked.

"It's okay," I said, wincing. "Less movement is good."

"Come here," Harrison said. Blake released me and Harrison swept my feet out from underneath me, lifting me easily. "Let's go."

I leaned my head on his shoulder, another rolling pain flowing through me. Pain like this made me feel weak, and I hated that. "I took medicine, but it hasn't been very long."

Cole opened the door for us and touched the guard on the shoulder. "Stay here."

"Yes, Sir."

"Soon you won't need the medicine," Harrison said quietly. "We're going to make sure you feel good."

He carried me into the elevator. Blake pressed the button to take us up, and inside their apartment, we took the elevator again to the fourth floor. This was the first time, and it smelled like... nothing. Unlike the rest of their penthouse, which held their scents, this was absent of almost everything.

"Over there. That's the entrance to the bedroom."

"It looks like it's the entire floor."

"It is," he confirmed. "Mostly. The bathroom connects the bedroom and the nest, which is over here."

Emery opened the door into a cozy space. It was big enough to fit all of us, but small enough to feel *right*. The ceiling was low and painted black, so it already felt shorter. The rest of the place was pretty blank, my mind already decorating it in my head, instincts telling me where things needed to go.

Harrison nudged my temple with his nose. "What do you think?"

"I like it," my voice was quiet. Awed.

"Are you sure?"

"Yes." I didn't sound excited, and I knew it. How did I explain? My emotions were everywhere and Sloane was fucking right. "I'm sorry."

There was a low wall right in front of us, so the nest could have a curved, padded shape. Harrison turned and sat on it, the

95

others surrounding us. The rumbling purr in his chest made me feel safe, but I was still a mess.

"Why are you sorry?"

"I get really emotional during my heats."

Emery took my hand and held it between the two of his. "That's fine and normal, and not why you're apologizing."

I swallowed. My heart pounded in my chest, and I wished I didn't feel so fucking terrified to admit that I *was* terrified.

Harrison's lips brushed my ear, volume low enough only for me. "Trust us, little one. Tell us what's going on."

"I'm scared of this. Not of you," I said quickly. "Of this. Sloane called me out on it earlier today, and she's right. I'm fucking terrified of this. Because what if it works?"

Blake tilted his head. "If we work?"

"What if we work, and we're happy, and—" I cut off.

My entire world flipped upside down in one night. I wasn't just a kid in high school anymore. I was the daughter of a dead woman. The daughter of a dead pack. The poor girl. The one people were afraid to talk about their families around because they didn't want to remind her that hers was *dead*. Before Dad pulled me back and had tutors come to me at home.

The one thing he'd done.

I'd watched him become a different person and never come back. In a way, he'd died too. I'd become the adult. I was the one who got us through things when he couldn't. My entire life was a witness to the kind of grief love could cause. And it was spine chilling to think about losing myself if something happened to any of us.

Understanding shone on Blake's face. "What if we work, and we're happy, and something happens to us?"

My voice cracked. "Yeah."

Emery lifted the hand he held and kissed it. I saw grief in his eyes too, though I didn't know the source. He'd known pain. Maybe they all had and hadn't had a chance to tell me yet.

"It's okay to be scared," Blake crouched so he was closer to my level. "It's so fucking okay, baby. Do you trust us to take care of you, anyway?"

Of course I did. I nodded.

"Brave little Omega," Harrison whispered.

"We're scared too," Emery said, squeezing my hand. "I know I am. We can be scared together, and no matter what happens, we're still taking this one day at a time. We're still courting you, heat or no heat."

Something loosened in my chest, the depth of fear and emotion releasing the claws wrapped around my lungs.

"There she is," Cole said with a soft smile.

I leaned my head on Harrison's shoulder. "Sorry."

"Don't apologize, sweetheart. You didn't do anything wrong. And if I could let you into my mind, I'd show you how much I like you being in my arms and taking care of you."

My stomach flipped. If this really did go well, I might see into their minds at some point. Feel what they felt. The enormity of that...

"What do you say we go get things to build you a nest?" Blake was grinning so wide it didn't seem real.

I looked at each of them. "Is this the kind of thing where, even if I protest and tell you it's fine, you're going to insist?"

"Yes." Harrison's voice carried power just short of a bark.

"And you're sure?"

Cole chuckled. "Are we sure? Honeybee, we've been waiting to do this forever. Whatever you want or need to make this nest yours before the heat starts? You've got it."

"Will there be cameras?" I asked. "I wish I didn't have to ask."

Harrison kissed my temple. "We'll be careful," he said. "If we see a camera, Cole and I know exactly what to do."

Pressing my lips together, I looked at each of them one more time. My nerves were still there, along with my fear. But I trusted them, I wanted them, and telling them the truth allowed me to let it go. With each passing second, my need grew. This was going to happen. Excitement began to tingle in my mind, and I took a deep breath, smiling. "Let's go."

CHAPTER FOURTEEN

PETRA

*T*he last time I was in Nest Inc. was years ago. It was different now, and somehow, it seemed bigger. The medicine kicked in while we drove, so I felt better. But Emery was right. It was moving faster being near them. I still had time, but not nearly the twelve hours I was used to.

"Where do we start?" I asked.

Harrison's hand brushed my lower back. "I'll see if they have a recommendation. Start looking."

"Okay."

Blake grabbed a giant cart and headed straight into the section on the first floor. Which wasn't nesting materials, it was everything but. Fuzzy robes and bath bombs you could customize with your own scents. Comfy socks and eye masks. This was the section of the store meant for pampering Omegas.

"Is there anything you *don't* like?" Blake asked.

I stared at him. "Umm, I don't like floral scents, and I don't like the color brown."

"Anything else?"

My eyes narrowed. "Why?"

"Remember when you asked us what we wanted, and I told you we wanted someone to spoil? This is part of that." He hauled me into his arms. "We are going to spoil the *shit* out of you."

I shivered. "It's so weird."

"Why?"

"I'm just not used to it. I know people probably think I'm already spoiled, being who I am, from my family, but I'm not. Privileged, yes. But... not like this."

Since I'd taken care of myself for the last fifteen years, I didn't tend to do anything overly extravagant. My apartment was the one concession I made because it was *mine*. And even that was restrained. It wasn't that I didn't like gifts, they just didn't feel the same when they came from yourself.

"Get used to it, baby. I'm going to figure out your favorites, and once I do, it's all over."

A flush rose to my cheeks, and he grinned before kissing me. "Start picking things and don't limit yourself."

I did. A set of pretty nail polishes. Some big, fluffy towels and a robe. Soft socks and lotion that smelled blissfully like nothing and made my skin soft as suede.

Emery and Cole were off in one corner looking at something, and Blake was gleefully throwing things in the cart. There was so much more here than I chose, and I laughed. "You're going to buy the whole store."

"Probably."

I pressed my hands to my stomach. The medicine only did so much. "How many restaurants do you have?"

"Five."

"Holy shit. The food today was incredible, by the way."

"I'm glad." He lowered a purple loofah into the cart. "And you don't even know how happy I am that it wasn't food poisoning."

I laughed. "Yeah, that wouldn't have been fun. But tell me this. Do any of your restaurants have dessert?"

"All of them do. Did you want something?"

"For probably obvious reasons, I'm craving caramel, chocolate, and coffee. Preferably all at the same time."

He pulled out his phone. "I can make that happen."

Harrison approached, a tablet in his hand. "They have a checklist to make sure you know about everything. Starting with colors."

I blinked. "Wow."

"You have anything in mind?"

"Maybe." An image formed in my head. Heat spiked through me and made me dizzy. "Whoa."

Harrison caught my hand and guided me to the elevators. "They'll catch up," he said when I looked behind us. "I want to make sure we get you what you need."

It was an ocean of choices in front of us. Cushions and fabrics and textures. If I thought about it, I was overwhelmed. So I let my instincts do the choosing.

Who knew if I was being influenced by the heat or the fact that everyone seemed to want me in colors like green and blue, but I wanted fiery colors. The colors in my apartment were warmer neutrals, with shades of reds and golds in my bedroom.

I wanted the same for my nest. A deep crimson for the cushions, with fabric so soft I literally could not wait to lie on it naked. No matter how weird that sounded.

Oranges and yellows of every flavor for pillows and blankets. There was even some metallic gold I couldn't resist. It was so fucking *pretty*.

The final touch was a big, utterly soft blanket in the palest blue-purple. Like the hottest part of a flame. It felt right, and Harrison's eyes warmed when I put it on the list.

It was enough. I felt good. Settled. "How will we get it all back?"

We went down the escalator at the other end of the store. Blake, Emery, and Cole were still on the first level, and the cart was piled higher than I'd seen it before. "They're going to do it for us," Harrison said. "They've gotten used to it now, people needing to outfit nests in a short amount of time. So they have a team. By the time you're ready, the nest will be too."

"I might need one more thing," I said, pressing into his side. He was so warm. Or maybe I was warm. The pain flowing through me was less of an ache and more of a spark now. It still hurt, but it wasn't a full fledged flame.

"What's that?"

"Can I have things that smell like you? I don't know, like a shirt?"

Harrison picked me up again, handing off the tablet to a nearby employee. Cole saw us, waved, and took the cart, brimming with candles and other goodies, over to the same employee. "Little one, I will bury you in my shirts if it makes you happy."

Leaning up, I kissed his neck. I liked the feeling of his skin under mine. Needed it closer. "I think we should go home," he said quietly.

"Yes, please."

Emery appeared next to us. "How'd it go?"

"You guys didn't have to stay away."

"We know." His smirk was mischievous. "But we had ideas."

"What ideas?"

He shook his head. "No ruining the surprise."

Emery's scent hit me with him standing so close, and all I could think about was licking him. He was wearing a shirt. I didn't like that. But if he took it off and gave it to me...

"Can I have your shirt?"

The words blurted out of my mouth before I could stop them. My Alpha laughed, the sound filling the room. "As soon as we get home, yes, you can have my shirt."

"Or a hoodie," I said. "Like this one. But smelling like you guys."

"Cole," Harrison said. "Get the car. Quickly please."

Emery stepped into my space. So close I was squeezed between the two of them. Yes. Just like that. More of that, please. "I like being an Omega sandwich."

He was desperately trying not to laugh. "I'm just going to take your temperature, okay?" His lips brushed my forehead. That little kiss echoed through every part of me. It was on fire. I was on fire.

And oh, how I wanted to burn.

They were candles and I was the wax melting because they were so *fucking hot.*

"I got really lucky," I said. "You know why?"

"Why?" Harrison asked, shifting me so my legs wrapped around his hips, holding me up with his hands on my ass. This showed me exactly what he felt right now, and it did approximately nothing to cool the heat under my skin. Harrison was big, and so was whatever he was packing under his clothes.

"Petra?"

"Huh?" I blinked.

He kissed my cheek, eyes filled with humor. The way his fingers gripped me told me everything I needed to know. He was amused, but he was also holding back everything I fucking needed. "Why did you get lucky?" He asked.

Blake opened the door, and Harrison carried me out to the car, not bothering to put me down before he slid into the back seat.

"I got lucky because all of you are hot as shit. And you have too many clothes on." I reached between us for the hem of his shirt before he stopped me.

"Not yet, little one."

I whined, fire building under my skin. This was so much faster than usual. There was still a little time before the pure fire snapped in, but arousal held me in its grip like a spotlight on a dark stage. It was all I could see, and everything else was darkness.

"Don't worry," Blake said. "You're going to get everything you need, baby."

Leaning over, I kissed him. Still straddling Harrison's lap, his hands on my hips, being stretched between them was only a preview of what was to come.

Blake kissed me back, drawing his tongue along mine. I moaned before he pulled away. Dizzy. Drenched between my legs. Savoring the taste of him.

There would probably be a wet spot on Harrison's jeans when we stood up.

Hot. I was too hot. I needed cooler air on my skin. But there were hands on my wrists keeping me from pulling my shirt over my head. "I'm too hot. I need it off."

"You're doing so good, little one." Harrison's words sounded close, but he was still holding my wrists, keeping me hostage.

"It's never this fast," I told them. "I usually have so much time. Just hours and hours of pain."

A hand stroked down my spine. Emery's hand, as he turned from the front seat. "You're responding to us, Petra. It's not a bad thing. Promise."

"Breathe, Omega," Harrison commanded, pulling me harder down on his lap. I squirmed, and he held me still. Underneath me, he was hard as a rock, and I wanted more of the feeling.

One hand came up into my hair, pulling my head back and exposing my neck. His teeth closed over the point of my pulse, just hard enough to make me freeze and go limp. "We're almost home," someone said. "They're going to build your nest, and we're going to get you settled."

Harrison's tongue ran over my skin as he released the bite, sucking instead. Fuck, that was so good and was both helping and not helping at the same time. I moved my hands, and he growled, keeping my Omega in check.

"Here we are."

Carried. I was carried and moved. My entire world had shrunk to the single point of contact where Harrison's mouth met my skin. There were windows showing off the city at sunset —a fiery view which matched the fire in my mind and body. A blanket on the floor, and suddenly I was looking up at the ceiling, with my Alpha looking down at me.

"All right, little one." He was the one straddling *my* hips now. I arched my hips, and I savored the delicious power of watching his gaze deepen and darken. He wanted this, too. I needed it. "They're putting together your nest, and we need to talk about some things. Blake brought you the dessert you wanted, so I'm going to help you out of the sweatshirt, and then you're going to eat it while we talk."

I pushed up against him, only to find my wrists pinned under his hands. God, it was so hot. And not just my temperature. All we needed was our clothes to disappear and for him to be inside me. "I don't want to talk. I want you to *fuck me*."

He laughed, low and deep. "There's nothing that's going to stop that now, Omega. We're going to fuck you so long and so hard, you're not going to forget it. But as much as I want to drive myself into this sweet pussy right this fucking second, we still have some things to talk about before the heat fully takes you. If you understand, say 'yes, Alpha.'"

I understood. I didn't like it, but I understood. "Yes, Alpha."

"Good girl." The word combined with a purr, and my leggings were soaked. It was only going to get more intense.

Harrison lifted the hem of my sweatshirt and helped me pull it up and over my head. I was only in a bra underneath. A plain black one. When I put on the clothes I hadn't been thinking about sex appeal. But the look in his eyes told me it didn't matter.

"Here," Emery said. A piece of fabric touched my hand. His *shirt*. I grabbed it and inhaled. Chocolate and coffee and Alpha. Harrison lifted himself off me, and I sat up. Emery slid in behind me, pulling me between his legs. My heated skin met his bare chest, and I whined.

I needed so much more than this.

"Here you go," Blake said, holding out a plastic cup with a straw.

"What is it?"

He smirked. "Try it."

Cold coffee splashed across my tongue. Chocolate and caramel mixed in. It was a fucking *smoothie*. The icy sips cooled me just enough to take off the edge. "Whoa. That's really good."

"I'm glad, baby. Now talk to us."

I took another sip, holding the drink in one hand and Emery's shirt in the other. "About?"

Emery's hand crept across my bare stomach and pulled me back into him. His cock was a rock hard pole in his jeans, trapped between us. "Limits," he said. "Is there anything you don't want us to do? Anything we need to know?"

I couldn't think of anything they might do I wouldn't want. All my mind could think about was being pinned beneath them, knotted and helpless. Breathless. Pleasured.

"I can't think," I said, taking a sip of coffee.

"Do you want more than one of us at a time?" Emery asked. "Is there anywhere we can't touch or fuck?"

"Yes," I breathed out the word. "I want all of you. And no, I don't care. Take me everywhere. I've never done this, and I need everything."

Emery tensed for a second before he leaned in, kissing the side of my neck. "What do you mean you've never done this?"

"My first heat, in college, I tried with an Alpha I knew. Felt wrong. Smelled wrong." Fuck, this drink was delicious. It was disappearing too fast. I wanted another one. They asked me a question? Right. Heats. "I used toys after that. And vibrators. They're in my apartment. Oh, and some fuckin' *serious* water-proof sheets. We should have gotten some of those for the nest."

Cole chuckled from across the room. Why was he so far away? Why was he—

He didn't have a shirt on anymore. His body was every inch the body you expected a bodyguard to have. Muscles and abs thrown into sharper relief because of the setting sun. "He really uses that gym downstairs, huh?"

Emery laughed into my skin. "We all do, sweetheart."

"What kind of toys did you use?" Blake asked.

I looked at him and sucked more coffee-chocolate-caramel-fucking-amazing through the straw. His gaze dropped to my mouth, and neither of us had to say anything to know what the other was thinking about. "Big ones."

"You'll have to show me sometime."

I smirked. "Afraid you can't compare, Alpha?"

"Oh, baby, no. You'll have to show me so you can remember what it was like before you had a real Alpha."

"Prove it." I was taunting him, trying to get him to snap. If he made the first move, I couldn't be held responsible for what I did.

Blake shook his head. "Nice try. Just a little longer. They're almost done."

Cole looked through a door I couldn't see through. "He's too far away."

Harrison put his hand on my ankle. "He's watching them finish your nest so we know when they're done."

Emery ran his hands up the side of my body, squeezing my ribs. "If there's anything else you can think of, you need to tell us, okay?"

"I gave Sloane Cole's number so she can check on me."

"Good idea," he said gently.

The straw hit empty air, making a slurping sound. The smoothie was gone. "Can I have another one sometime?"

"Absolutely."

"I need one that tastes like you too," I told Blake. "But without alcohol." Then I looked at Harrison. "I love the way you smell but I don't think it would make a good smoothie."

He laughed. I fucking loved the sound of it, rich, vibrating through the air. I swore I felt it. "No, I don't think so, little one. But here." Stripping the shirt over his head, he handed it to me. Now I had two shirts, one in each hand.

I shoved my face into them.

Impossibly, the combination was incredible. "I stand corrected. Maybe mocha and cedar whiskey is something I need to taste."

"You will," Emery whispered. Every hair on my body stood on end. "Because you're going to taste us very soon."

"Fuck." My head lolled back on his shoulder, the temperature inside me rising to a fever pitch.

Lips touched the back of my neck. "How close are they?"

"Very," Cole called.

"Good," Emery said. "Because our little Omega is about to turn into a phoenix."

Correct. My skin was on fire. Or at least I was pretty sure I was burning. And not just with flames. With need. I moved, trying to turn and tackle Emery to the ground, but he held me between his legs. "Easy, Omega."

There was no easy anymore. Not when I *felt like this*.

"I need to ask you one more time, Petra," Emery said. He was moving his hands on my bare skin, soothing me along with the sound of his purr. "We're about to get you naked. Are you okay with that? And with everything that's going to come after? You can always say no, but I need to hear yes."

I managed to turn in his arms and bury my face in his neck. Yes, yes, yes. More. Now. Every place his skin touched echoed beneath my skin and grew. Only one thing could make it go away. A knot. More than one knot. Lips and hands and tongues and cocks.

"I need to hear you say it, sunshine."

The sound that came out of me was needy. Desperate. I liked sunshine. Was living sunshine. The sunshine inside me was scorching me alive. "Yes."

The door clicked shut, and I whirled. Cole was gone. Why was he gone? Where did he go? Panic clawed at my throat, and my voice was somewhere between a whine and a wail. What if he didn't come back? "Where is he?"

Hands held my face, and I met steely blue eyes. "Breathe, Petra." Harrison's command shuddered through me and offered relief. Oxygen flooded my lungs. "He's showing the team from Nest Inc. out of the house and coming right back. He didn't leave you, sweetheart."

"I need him." All four of them had to be here with me or it didn't feel right, didn't feel right, *didn't feel right*.

Harrison lifted me. "I know. And he'll be here. Let's go see your nest."

My nest. I held the shirts in my hands up to my nose and breathed. The bathroom we walked through was fucking ginormous. A big tub I wanted to roll around inside of and a shower. It was pretty, and I twisted around in his arms to see, utterly distracted.

But the light dimmed, and we stepped into the nest. The ambience went quiet, all the fabric consuming the noise. I stared. Rich red velvet was everywhere, blending into the dark ceiling and creating the dark, cozy cave I wanted.

Stacks of blankets and pillows were around the floor, all the ones I'd chosen, ready for me to put them where they went.

Harrison put me down, my toes squishing into the softness of the fabric. The orange, frilled pillow needed to go over there, and the shirt in my hand had went next to it. "Can I fix it?"

"Make it yours, sweetheart."

I gave in to the frenzy in my brain and dove straight in.

CHAPTER FIFTEEN

PETRA

I pulled the metallic blanket out of the pile and spread it where it went, overlapping with some of the pillows. Harrison's shirt went there too. But I needed another one. "Shirt," I said. "I need a shirt."

One appeared in my hand. It smelled like Blake. I inhaled his citrusy mimosa scent before tucking it into a crevice. The pale blue blanket I tossed to the edge of the nest, over the low wall. That was for later.

My Alphas stood at the edge of the nest, watching me, and in my frenzied arrangement of blankets and pillows and shirts, I hadn't noticed all of them were now naked.

Oh, *fuck*.

When Emery held me, I'd been so close to him I hadn't noticed his tattoos spread all the way up his arms and across his chest. Harrison's tattoo was more reserved. Cole was here again, and my Omega settled, knowing he was safe and *mine*.

So much skin. Overwhelming skin and muscles and... everything else I could now see.

Like my body had been waiting for the nest to be complete, something cracked inside me. Pain, pure and real—need which couldn't be denied—snapped through me. A knife in the gut only solved by *them*.

I still had clothes on. The fabric was wrong and itchy. Too tight. But I couldn't move to take them off. I *needed* and I no longer knew what that meant. My nest was ready, and everything else—

Anxiety built in my chest, and I looked at them. "Help."

Cole reached me first, salted caramel swirling around me. His hands on my skin calmed my mind, not my body. I needed more. More. More.

Everything was lava. In a second, I was going to spontaneously combust. "I'm sorry you missed me," he said, sliding the straps of my bra off my shoulders. "I'm here now."

Jumping, he caught me. I slammed my mouth against his, falling into a place of only instinct. He was *mine*. "No more leaving."

"No more, honeybee."

Fingers brushed my back, undoing the bra. I didn't care where it disappeared to.

The last time I'd tried, that other Alpha... I shuddered. He'd waited for direction on everything, and I'd been so tired. I was tired already, the fever making everything shaky. I needed them.

"I don't want to think," I said. "Don't let me think."

My back hit the pillows, Cole only pulling away from me long enough to tear my leggings down the middle—right at the seam. The fabric was soaked through with my slick and I was still dripping. He ripped the pieces off my legs and I was free. Only for a second before he fit himself against me and plunged *deep*.

His mouth came down on mine, claiming my voice and the sounds I made. Claiming all of me. Every piece of me shattered with light and heat, coming apart with pleasure that was too much and not enough.

How long had it been since I was filled like this? Since I'd had anyone at all?

Nothing but frantic couplings in the back of clubs Sloane took me to. With Alphas and Betas drunk enough they wouldn't remember who I was. Sloppy and barely enough to take the edge off.

Cole was none of those things.

Long and straight, he filled me up so perfectly I couldn't breathe, and whatever air I had left, he stole kissing me. It was like we never left that fucking closet. I needed him everywhere, and he *was* everywhere. Driving his cock into me with relentless force. Taking the brunt of my need and unlocking that final piece of myself that needed to let go.

"Don't hold back," I begged him. "Don't hold back."

Bracing himself on his arms above me, Cole *fucked*. I was already too far gone, arousal having built with every touch of softness and every word they spoke. Every heated glance and time they told me to wait a little longer.

Lightning flashed behind my eyes, pleasure like steaming rain exploding outward. I arched off the pillows, Cole matching every movement, fucking through this nova of an orgasm. It was only the beginning. This was the fuse to the bomb, and I was already ticking.

"Fuck," I choked on the word, unable to stop my body from tensing and shaking. "Fuck."

Cole slowed his pace, rolling his hips and kissing me gently. "There you go. You needed that first one. Now I can take my time."

"No you fucking can't," I growled.

Another thrust had me gasping, his thumb rubbing over my clit, using my own slick to tease me. "Don't let me think," he whispered, reflecting my words back at me. His lips brushed my cheek lightly, raising chills across my skin as he moved in slow motion, teasing me with his cock. "Tell me what you want, Petra. Do you want control? Or do you want us to take care of you?"

I whimpered, and he brushed his thumb over my clit again. "If you let go, honeybee, I promise we'll give you *exactly* what you need. Even if you don't know why."

"I—"

"You're in heat." He dragged his tongue up my neck, and I saw white. "So you forget we have instincts too. And those include exactly how to fuck this honey-soaked cunt until you scream."

A bright flare of pleasure peaked behind my eyes. "You," I breathed. "I choose you."

"Good girl." The words came from elsewhere in the nest. I suddenly needed more of them like I needed water in a drought. Feverishly and furiously.

Hands touched my ribs and shoulders, Cole still moving too slowly. So fucking slow, and yet every movement drew out the aftermath of my first glorious orgasm.

Finally releasing what remained of my control was like a key in a lock. No more fear and anxiety, no more worry. Cole pulled back and Emery's face appeared above mine, upside down. "Hey, sunshine." He kissed me before I could say anything. "Remember when I said you would taste me?"

I moaned. "Yes."

"Good."

He disappeared only for a moment before I was treated to the delicious sight of his body over mine. Straight up abs and pecs to where he gazed down, gaze all lust. His cock brushed my lips, and I opened, arching back for him. God, he tasted good.

Exactly like he smelled. Chocolate and coffee. If he weren't guiding the curve of his shaft deeper, I might have laughed at the idea of a mocha flavored cock. But there was nothing funny about this. Just the air brushing past my skin aroused me. My nipples were so hard they hurt, and I was trapped between two Alphas hell-bent on driving me out of my mind.

"Fuck, Petra," Emery's voice growled low.

I swallowed him deeper. There was nothing I wanted more than them. I could take all of it. Down my throat. Farther.

He grabbed my hands and laced our fingers together, connecting us and holding me down. I closed my eyes, and my two Alphas drove into me together. Hard and easy. Cole's fingers dug into my hips, pulling me onto his cock, and he hit a place inside me that made everything feel like *glitter*.

Emery still had my hands, but another one slid around my throat. "Look at you, baby." Blake's voice was soft near my ear. "Taking all of him down your throat like a good Omega." He squeezed gently, emphasizing the feeling of friction, and I groaned along with Emery. "So deep, you could take his knot, too."

My back arched off the cushions, pleasure spiraling together, weaving from everywhere into a wave about to push me over the edge. It was so close—right there all over again.

"That's it," Blake said, releasing my throat and sliding his hand down my body. "Listen to my voice, feel everything they're giving you. Our little Omega, stuffed full of cock and ready to come."

The calm, casual nature of his words, as if I weren't being fucked ruthlessly from both ends, broke me open. I shuddered, arching and writhing, at once trying to get closer and get away from all the sensations. Too much. Too fucking much.

Pleasure crashed down on me in a second wave. I soaked Cole's cock, allowing him to thrust that much faster. Harder. Impossibly deeper. Every ripple dragged me down into a haze of pleasure and heat, and I realized I couldn't breathe.

Emery plunged into my throat and held himself there, depriving me of air for one more second before he dragged himself out and away. The world surged back into color, another wave of shimmering fire twirling through my mind.

Cole braced himself over me again, burying himself to the hilt. Over, and over, and over. "*Fuck.*"

I needed to speak, to beg him for more, and I couldn't. I was a creature of light and stardust, made of voiceless pleasure and fractured fire. His mouth fell to my neck, and he drove into me again a final time, his own heat spilling inside me as his knot swelled, locking us together.

The *knot*.

It pressed up against all the places I needed it to, creating little fireworks and sparks every time either of us moved, and I couldn't seem to stop moving. Reaching. Touching. Pulling him closer. Somewhere, my voice found its way back to me. "This is so much better than a toy."

"Damn right it is." Cole kissed along the line of my jaw. "You feel so good, honeybee, squeezing my knot like that."

I did it again, and he moaned into my neck. "Just wait until it releases."

"Threatening me with more orgasms?" *Please* threaten me with that. I needed it. They needed to hold me down and fuck me until I was full of every last drop of their cum and it was leaking out onto the cushions.

No risk there. My baby maker was locked up tight thanks to the Omega implant. Nuclear powered exactly for reasons like this —where I wanted to be railed within an inch of my life without getting pregnant.

"Let me have a taste," Blake said.

Cole leaned back on his knees, exposing where we were locked together. "Blake," I choked out his name. His tongue slid over my clit, slick meeting slick and sending pleasure into overdrive.

Sealing his mouth over me, so close to where I was knotted, he sucked deep. I was too close. Another orgasm washed up and over me, and he laughed. "Baby, you taste just as good as your scent. You don't have any idea the things I want to do with that flavor."

One more lick, circling my aching clit, and he crawled up to me. "Should I tell you?"

Cole rocked against me, knot pressing into the places in my body that made me see stars. "Yes." The word was a sigh and a prayer.

"Your cum is so fucking sweet I want to drink it," he whispered. Blake's fingers replaced his tongue, teasing. "Or I could sweeten my morning tea with *you*."

"I—" I gasped, going blind with the tiny motions of his fingers. My whole body shook, overloaded. "You can't."

"No?" His laugh skittered over my skin. "I think I could. Put you on the counter in the kitchen every morning and ravage your cunt with my tongue until you come all over it. Or maybe I'd use my fingers. Tie you to a chair and tease you until you sweeten all our coffee and tea."

He was kidding. He had to be kidding. And yet the images played out in my head, and I saw myself writhing and helpless under his attention, coming over and over again until he chose to release me.

"I'm going to make a whole line of desserts, baby. They'll be honey and cinnamon, and no one will know but us that they're based on how fucking deep and sweet you taste. But *actually* tasting you?" He lifted his fingers to my mouth and painted my lips with my own wetness before kissing me and moaning with pleasure. "That's just for us."

Blake licked his lips, cleaning every bit of me off them before he cleaned his fingers. "I think you're going to be my favorite dessert."

Cole's knot eased enough to release me, and we fell apart. It was so much faster during the heat, driven by the Omega's need to have knot after knot, and the Alpha's need to give them.

Emery took his place, rolling me onto my stomach before plunging deep. He pulled me onto my knees and curled around me. "This won't take long, sunshine. Your throat almost did me in."

The way his cock curved, I already saw stars. Every thrust broke my words apart. "You didn't. Let me. Taste you."

A breathy laugh turned into a groan in my ear. "If I'd come down your throat, my knot would have been in your mouth. And you're not ready for that. But you will be."

Emery unleashed himself. I dug my fingers into the cushions, holding on, savoring the sounds of his hips slapping against mine, grunts of effort every time he bottomed out inside me, and the growing bursts of delicious, carnal brightness.

Power and heat built in my core, taking every layer of pleasure which came before and amplifying it. Unifying it. Until it was just me and a star of golden ecstasy exploding outward. Nothing to see, nothing to hear, nothing to do except fall into it. I think I screamed. I knew I collapsed beneath Emery, all of his strength now used to pin me to the floor of the nest and fuck me.

I came around his cock, slipping into a fog made of sunlight and bliss. Lips brushed my spine. My name hovered in the air.

Emery came.

His knot locked inside me.

Deeply.

Differently.

Perfectly.

My body sagged on the cushions, and Emery moved slowly. Easing us onto our sides together, his arms around me. The fire inside me was quenched and banked. It would come back, but now it needed to rest. I just needed to close my eyes.

It would come back.

"Don't leave," I begged. "Don't leave me."

Fingers combed through my hair, brushing it off my heated skin. "We're all here, sunshine."

"Good."

Emery's arms locked around me as tightly as his knot. I couldn't stay with them. Warm darkness pulled me down, something deep allowing me to finally *breathe*.

CHAPTER SIXTEEN

HARRISON

*P*etra went limp in Emery's arms, and we all blew out a breath. The beautiful Omega was nearly shining with pleasure, face finally at peace.

Blake looked between us. "Do you think she meant no leaving the apartment or leaving the nest? I'd like to go make her some food that's not a frozen coffee."

I weighed the possibilities. "This round let's not risk it," I said. "She *panicked* when Cole left the room before. I'd rather her know where you are and see you leave than her wake up and find you gone."

"Good point," he whispered.

Cole was still catching his breath. "We'll tell her when she wakes up. That we're not leaving the apartment, but we might have to go get her things from the kitchen."

Running a hand through my hair, I leaned back against the low wall that ran along the section of nest near the door. The last few hours were a whirlwind. Leaning out of the nest, I retrieved my phone from my pants pocket.

"What the hell are you doing?" Cole laughed.

"I haven't had a chance to cancel everything," I said. "The trains still need to run on time, even if the top two people at the company are occupied."

Emery stroked his knuckles down Petra's cheek, and she snuggled deeper into his embrace. He smiled in response. "We've been telling you to hire a secretary for years," he said when he could take his eyes off her. "This is just one of the many reasons why."

I laughed softly. "I think it's a little late this time around. But there aren't many moving pieces that need management at the moment, and we both have our phones for emergencies."

Whatever forces in the universe brought Petra directly into our path, I begged them not to let any emergencies interrupt this heat. Her admission broke my heart. And yet, it made sense. When your life was turned upside down by something as horrible as losing half your family, it shaped you.

"Do you need to take care of anything, Blake?"

"I'm good. I'll just make sure General Managers know not to bother me for the next few days."

I finally focused on what she'd done around the nest. The colors she chose were gorgeous and fit her perfectly. Pillows lined the smaller interior of the nest, patchwork by blankets and our shirts. We needed to ask her if she wanted more. Hell, if she asked me to move my entire closet in here, I wasn't sure I'd be able to say no.

"Is there anything we should know?" Emery asked, his eyes locked on mine. "About this guy who's coming after her?"

I forced the anger in my chest down. Petra needed all the rest she could get right now, and my growling wasn't going to help that. The first threat we received was pretty run of the mill. A simple threat saying if Russell didn't do what was demanded, Petra wouldn't make it.

The follow up threat was the one which made my skin crawl. Details of exactly what they would do to Petra should their demands not be met. "They, uh..." I cleared my throat. "They made it clear they want her death to make a splash, so regardless of whether she lives or dies, they get their way. Make it a 'public' execution. There were plenty of examples given, none I feel like repeating."

There was a reason the Senator hadn't told Petra the details. I didn't ever want her to know. We weren't going to let the fucker anywhere near her. She didn't need to know someone imagined murdering her so vividly. It was enough that Cole and I knew.

"And it's real?" Blake asked.

"Until we know for sure it isn't, we always treat death threats as real. But in general, threats which detail a plan are real."

All of us stiffened. The idea that anyone could threaten Petra was horrifying by itself, apart from our attachment to her. She was beautiful, kind, and sassy. It wasn't her fault she was born to a man who chose politics, and his campaigns had nothing to do with her.

Unfortunately, family rarely worked that way. So I would protect her. With my life if necessary.

"I know she's only downstairs," Cole said. "But even there, it's not as secure as she would be here."

I nodded. "Yes. But we can't push that."

"Why not? Us leaving already makes her nervous. If she were here, she'd have even less to worry about."

Blake sighed and scrubbed a hand over his face. "Because trauma is a bitch, and it's not only about that."

We all looked at him and waited.

"She's nervous about us leaving, or losing us, because of what she's lost. But the repetition of history with us also scares her. Scent-sympathetic matching was how her parents met. And as amazing as it is for all of us, diving straight in with us feels like, for her, putting herself on the path to losing everything."

"Fuck," Emery muttered, curling around her further. They weren't connected anymore, so he turned her to face his chest, stealing one of the blankets from the nest lining to keep her warm next to him.

I stood and went to the nest thermostat on the wall and turned the heat up. It would regulate once sex resumed and everything was fiery, but my Omega wouldn't be cold. Not while I was around.

"You held back," Cole said to me. "Everything all right?"

Smirking, I sank back onto the cushions. "With the amount of sex we're about to have, there will be plenty to go around. I'm just letting the ebb and flow move naturally."

The scent of her had me hard, and I had been since we came to the nest. I wanted to feel the way her body hugged my knot. See her lips stretched around me on her knees. Hear her voice cry out as I took her ass, or fucked her along with one of my fellow Alphas. Taste her skin and the flavor of her cum on my tongue. Bathe in her scent so it fucking never came out of my nose.

Petra stretched and sighed under the blanket, head falling against Emery's chest. She looked so at peace now, I almost wished she could remain in that state of bliss forever, free from her pain and her fear.

But no matter how many times it surfaced, we would address

it. Soothing Omegas was part of Alpha instinct. Every Omega, but even more so ones like Petra. Ones we were connected with so deeply we couldn't explain it. And Omegas needed Alphas to feel safe, calm, and protected.

Walking into her apartment for the first time? I hadn't needed Cole to tell me it was her. I knew immediately. It was like being hit in the chest with a battering ram. A line which carved through your life and divided it into *before* and *after*.

"I meant to ask." I aimed my statement at Blake. "How did you know? About Mallory DeWitt?"

He smiled. "My own mother was a fan. She was broken up about it. So I just... knew about it. One of those odd facts you file away. It was big news at the time, just because an accident like that is always big news. But I think only people in the music world would really remember now."

"She was in the car," I said. "That night."

Emery wrapped his arm around her back, instinct driving him to protect her even though she was already in his arms. We could have lost her before we even knew her.

Cole stared over at her and rubbed his chest. "I understand why she's terrified. How can this happen so fast? Like, I get it. I *want* it. But it's still... daunting to think two days ago we had nothing, and now we have her."

Daunting was certainly the word. Because it felt like every tether to my life had loosened itself and reattached to the beautiful, sleeping woman in front of me.

I was the oldest member of the pack. Not old, though the others teased me about the bit of gray in my hair. But old enough I'd thought it was over. This floor would remain empty forever, and we'd have a good, fulfilling life as a pack.

Thank fuck I was wrong.

The deepest part of me acknowledged the fear we all had—that we'd go all the way, and she wouldn't choose us. But I knew without a shadow of doubt I would still do this. Any time with her was worth it, regardless of the outcome.

I hoped she chose us.

I sure as fuck had already chosen her.

"Speaking of food," I said. "Are we set?"

Blake laughed. "No. Not even close. But I'll have Martin set up a delivery of more meals tomorrow. Tonight, we'll be fine."

Emery laughed. "Your managers are going to get tired of sending us food."

Sometimes we used Blake's restaurants, but most of the time we fended for ourselves, or he cooked because it wasn't something he got to do as often now that he had so many places to manage.

"Tough," Blake said. "They can deal. I never use my owner's perks. If they complain because I'm using them on the woman I hope will be our Omega, they can work somewhere else."

My heart squeezed in my chest.

Our Omega.

I felt it in the air—the desire between the four of us to make it true. Make her ours forever.

We barely knew her, and yet I knew *all* of her. I couldn't wait to spend every moment of this heat and every moment afterward knowing each and every piece of her. From the things she cherished, to the still broken edges of her grief.

My eyes traced her form beneath the blanket and the small bits I could see. Just looking at her pulled at my Alpha. She was mine. Ours.

Our Omega.

CHAPTER SEVENTEEN

PETRA

*T*he vibration of a purr was the first thing I felt. The fire of heat was banked in my gut. Rising again, but not quite at the surface. But I was still stretched against a warm body and wrapped in softness.

I opened my eyes and saw ink on skin. A feather curled in front of my nose. Reaching up, I traced it with my finger. The purring stopped for a second before starting again, stronger and louder. "Welcome back, sunshine."

Emery pulled away from me just enough to let me look up at his face. "How do you feel?"

"Good," I said, twisting to look around my nest. The soft lights on the ceiling warmed us, the light from the room's sole window gone. The sun had set.

The three other Alphas were still here, and my Omega breathed out in relief. "Hi."

"Hello." Blake grinned and crawled across the pillows to get to me. "I wanted to wait until you woke up. But you need some food, baby."

My stomach growled like it heard him and agreed. "Food sounds nice."

"But that means I have to go down to the kitchen. I'm not leaving the apartment—none of us are. But I wanted you to know where I was, so you don't worry."

The anxiety I felt when Cole was gone rose. My conscious mind understood he wasn't going anywhere. But my heat mind and my instinctual Omega brain didn't want him to leave.

He didn't leave. I tried to soothe the fears which seemed so much closer to the surface right now. All the hormones flooding my brain, I couldn't stop the way I felt. "How long will you be gone?"

"Not long. Just enough to get you some food and some water." He slid the palm of his hand behind my neck and kissed me. "You can't go your whole heat without eating. Tomorrow I'm going to have food delivered, but tonight I need to make it."

"Okay." It still made me uncomfortable, but there wasn't any way to get around it. There wasn't any way for five people to stay in a room for days without leaving, unless you were torturing them or something.

"I'll be as fast as I can." He pulled me to him and kissed my forehead. "You'll be okay."

"I'm sorry," I whispered.

"Look at me." My eyes had slid away from his. His voice was gentle. "You don't have anything to be sorry for, baby. I know it makes you nervous. They're going to distract you while I'm gone."

One more kiss and he stood, slipping out the door into the hallway. I whined even though I tried not to. He wasn't going anywhere, and yet I couldn't get rid of the awful hollow feeling in my gut.

Emery shifted behind me, moving so I was leaning against him like I had before we came into the nest. His purr never stopped while Blake spoke to me, and I tried to relax into the sound and the feeling. Wrapping his arms around me, he leaned down and whispered in my ear. "You're okay, sweet girl. We're going to make you feel good."

Harrison knelt in front of me and ran his hands down my legs. "I think it's time I had a taste of you." One corner of his mouth tipped up. "If Blake is going to make a whole line of desserts based on this, I need to experience it firsthand."

Emery held me fast, and Harrison pushed my knees apart, not hesitating to dive straight into my pussy. His moan brought the heat closer to the surface. "Mmm, Blake is right. Those deserts are going to be bestsellers."

"You can't," I managed, breathless and writhing. "You can't base that on me."

"Oh, he can," Cole said. He knelt a few feet away, watching Harrison's mouth between my legs and stroking his cock.

Harrison pulled back, turning to bite my thigh. Hard. I gasped, unsure whether it was pleasure or pain as he soothed the sting with his tongue. He bit my other leg, higher this time. "Harrison."

One long lick up the center of me. "Just seeing what my Omega likes. I like those little gasps you make. They tell me I did something right."

"I—"

Harrison bit me again, scraping the soft skin where my leg met my body. So close to where I was curious what his teeth would feel like, and yet didn't want to know. Wetness gathered, and he saw it. Tasted it. "Does my Omega like a little pain?"

"I already know she likes to be held down," Emery said. "I wonder what happens when we give her both?"

"I do?"

"You do." His breath brushed the shell of my ear, words so soft I was the only one hearing them. "I'm holding you still right now. So Harrison can eat your pretty pussy to his heart's content and you can't do anything about it."

A burst of slick made me so wet, drawing up arousal so quickly I felt dizzy.

"Fuck," Harrison laughed. "Whatever you said, Emery, don't stop. She's fucking soaked."

The tip of his tongue brushed my clit, and that's it. Followed by a barely there feathering kiss. Not enough. Not nearly enough. I lifted my hips, trying to make him touch me, and he simply smiled.

Emery held me when I tried to pull away, and exactly like he said, I was suddenly so fucking wet it was spreading down my thighs.

"Each of us is different." He still spoke softly into my ear, Harrison kissing my thighs and brushing slightly harder kisses against my clit. "Me? I like a bit of everything. I can give you slow and sensuous or hard and dirty. But after the heat? When you're in *my* bed? I want a night where you do exactly what I tell you to, when I tell you to, with no hesitation. Because I think there's a part of you that likes to *obey*."

I shuddered, gasping at the first *real* stroke of Harrison's tongue curling into me. He moved so slowly, it was delicious agony.

"Isn't that right, sweet girl?"

My mind blanked out, body straining toward pleasure and mind spinning with images of Emery telling me to *obey*.

"Yes," I answered. "Yes."

"Not all the time," he said. "You're too sassy for that. But we're going to have fun, sunshine."

Harrison's hands now spanned my thighs, hands so big it felt like he was touching me everywhere. He sealed his mouth over me, sucking deep, and I broke apart, pleasure flaring behind my eyes and growing stronger because neither of them let me move.

"Please," I begged. What the hell was I asking for?

Harrison dragged his teeth over my skin, sending shakes through me and pulling me back to the edge again.

I opened my eyes and saw Cole still watching us, hand moving furiously up and down his shaft, eyes dark with lust.

"Cole," Emery said. Nothing else. But my caramel Alpha stood and approached, standing over my body, stroking his cock. Harrison released a thigh and slipped two fingers into me, thrusting hard and fast into the small, rough spot that made everything shine.

I cried out, and Cole slid into my mouth. He already tasted of rich caramel and the thread of salt which made it deeper. Better. He stroked himself, groaning as he stared down at me.

"Suck his cock," Emery whispered, tightening his arms around me further. "Suck his cock while Harrison sucks *you*."

I obeyed, drawing the tip of Cole's cock deeper, swirling my tongue around the head and savoring the sweetness he offered. But I could barely focus on Cole when Harrison's fingers were inside me, not letting me rest for a single moment. Pleasure hovered just out of reach, slightly beyond where his fingers fucked and pressed, coaxing my body to drown in sensation.

Moaning, I gave in. I let the sensations take me. The feeling of Cole's cock thrusting over my tongue, and Harrison's tongue circling my clit. Over and over and over again.

"Fuck, honeybee," Cole ground out the words through a clenched jaw, head thrown back as he stroked harder. Faster. Coming with a groan that left my pussy *soaking*.

My whole world revolved around the sounds he made and the

candy now coating my mouth. I understood now why Blake said he could drink me. Cole was the solution to every sweet tooth. And I'd barely done anything. He'd made himself come, watching *me* struggle to suck him.

Harrison scraped his teeth over me again, biting down on my clit hard enough for the burst of pain to flash through me and combine with the sweet flavor Cole pumped down my throat. Not hard enough to do anything but make me come.

I swallowed, my voice coming in moans and gasps, every nerve on fire with pleasure. My body bucked against arms and mouth and cock, unable to escape any of them and not wanting to.

Harrison licked me slowly, bringing me down from pleasure, and Cole looked down at me. I remembered that look. It was the same one he gave me before I was pulled away from him by Sloane. Right before he ran his thumb over my bottom lip.

Exactly like he did right now, catching a few drops of his cum which had spilled. "Open."

I did.

"Stick out your tongue, Omega. Show me you swallowed it all."

I had swallowed it all, and loved it. He painted my tongue with what I'd missed. "Can't let anything go to waste, can we?"

My whole body shook, wholly at the mercy of arousal I couldn't control. I wanted more. Needed more. I would drink them dry if they let me and didn't care what anyone thought about it.

Closing my lips around his thumb, I savored the last of his sweetness, marveling that I could have more whenever I wanted. Before this heat was over, this taste would be a part of me. Imprinted in my mind and memory. And even knowing that, it wasn't good enough. The only thing which would satisfy the craving was tasting them. Another thing I needed to ask mated Omegas.

Was it... normal to crave Alpha cum like you were an addict in need of a fix?

Even if it wasn't, I didn't know that I would care. They were too delicious.

The door to the nest opened, and Blake came in with a large tray covered in food. Emery squeezed me one last time. "Was that a good distraction, sunshine?"

"Yeah." My voice sounded hoarse. "I'd say so."

Blake laughed, setting the tray at the edge of the nest. "I guess I missed a bit."

My nose got the better of me, scenting *comfort* food. Mashed potatoes and gravy, corn, and what looked like turkey. "It's like Thanksgiving food," I murmured.

"Kind of," Blake admitted. "But more like it was things which were quick and easy to make."

"Turkey is quick?"

"Already cooked, baby."

"Oh."

A blanket draped around my shoulders, covering me and keeping me warm—not that it would be a problem for long.

Harrison passed me one of the loaded plates and a bottle of water. "Drink something too, please."

As soon as the water hit my lips, I realized how thirsty I was. Heat meant *literal* heat, and they'd already burned up all the water inside me. The bottle of water was gone in about thirty seconds, and then I started on the food.

"Fuck," I mumbled. "This is really good."

"Glad you think so," Blake said.

Fluffy mashed potatoes with brown gravy that hit *just* right. The corn and turkey were good too, but I could probably dive into a giant tub of those mashed potatoes and consume them all. The portions on our plates weren't huge, and I knew better than to ask for more. More would come later. But you didn't want to eat too much at a time during a heat, because fucking while you were too full was fun for no one.

Even if you were the one fucking yourself.

Another bottle of water appeared in my hands after the food was gone, and I sipped it. I didn't have much time. They woke the fire inside me when they pinned me down and made me orgasm.

I shrugged the blanket off my shoulders, my skin becoming

too hot for it to stay there. Another sip of water. The others were eating, too. They needed to eat just as much as I did.

The writhing, rising dragon of arousal inside me didn't care about that.

Forcing myself back onto the pillows, I closed my eyes. "You okay, baby?" Blake's voice reached me.

"I'm trying to let you eat," I whispered. New energy raged through me now that I'd fueled myself, my mind slipping away into that place where instinct warred with reality.

It was incredible to be here, floating, with no cares in the world except for what felt good. But it wasn't a very considerate place. And yet, fire crashed down on me in a way I wasn't able to resist. They were doing everything for me. This could wait a few minutes.

A warm body slid in next to me, lips on my neck. "I ate while I cooked," Blake said. "Use me, baby."

My brain turned *off*.

I pounced, rolling onto him, and Blake was ready, catching me with a grin before he slid me down onto his waiting cock. He was a little shorter, a little thicker, and had a different kind of curve than Emery. They all hit different places inside me, and none of them were bad.

Dropping down, I kissed him, tasting that nameless combination that was him and whatever minty thing he'd eaten to make sure he could do this. "I feel weird," I said.

"Why?"

"Fucking while people eat."

He thrust up into me, dissolving any thoughts I had left in my brain. "Trust me," he said, words strained with the force of his hips. "Nothing is more important than you right now."

The needy sound I made drove him both harder and faster. Blake's hands on my ribs steadied me and held me still while he fucked, and I held on. The orgasm was heading toward me at the speed of a train, and I was helpless.

"I like watching you come apart on my cock almost as much as I like tasting you."

One hand slid between us, finding my still-swollen clit. A five minute food break did nothing to ease that pleasure. Rolling his hips, Blake gave me everything, and I took what I needed. Rocking back into him, fucking him just as hard, finding the exact pace that sent starbursts flaring across my vision.

I drenched his cock, moaning into Blake's neck. Every orgasm was exquisite, and yet it was a black hole. The pleasure gave me what I craved and was sucked away, needing more almost immediately.

It took me long moments to realize Blake wasn't knotted inside me. He hadn't come. The look on his face told me he was incredibly aware. His eyes shifted away from mine a second before a hand stroked down my spine. "Remember how we asked you if you wanted more than one of us?" It was Cole.

"Yes," I breathed the word. Both a confirmation and an answer to his unspoken question.

This, I had never done. The desire was there, but I wasn't brave enough to try a toy in my ass by myself. It was enough fucking myself into exhaustion during a heat, no chance I needed help with *that* if I got it stuck.

Cole's mouth followed the path his hand had taken, kissing down my spine until he reached my ass. "Mmm," He bit down on one cheek.

I squeezed down on Blake in response, causing him to curse. The chain reaction turned me on. "Please," I looked over my shoulder at Cole. "Please."

"How can I argue with that?"

He was there. I felt him. And he was too fucking big. "God, I'm never going to fit you."

Cole pulled me up off Blake's body, suspending me between them. "Yes, you will." His voice dripped with confidence, and he was right. Omegas could take almost anything, and right now I wanted *everything*. "Brace yourself on Blake's chest and relax."

How could I relax? He was—

"*Ohhhh*." The sound came out of me as he pushed in. Suddenly, everything got tighter and brighter. Full. I was full, and it was barely the tip. Blake's thumb rolled over my clit, newly sensitive, and watched my face.

"You like getting fucked in the ass, baby?"

"I don't know," I moaned. He hadn't fucked me yet.

Inch after inch, Cole pushed in. Never stopping, steadily filling me up until I could barely breathe. Oh fuck. I wouldn't survive the two of them. It was too much. Too good. I wasn't quiet, every move Cole made dragging my voice out of me.

"There," he finally said, and I felt his hips flush against me. "All the way in, honeybee. How do you feel?"

I couldn't speak. All my words were gone, replaced with moaning. They laughed together, Blake thrusting up as Cole pulled back out, and they let loose.

One and then the other, the rhythm just different enough for them to fuck together for brief moments before they split apart. I wasn't even quite over the last orgasm—this one blended in. A rolling tide of golden light carrying me away into oblivion. Riding the tide, riding them, riding through the scorching heat that burned inside me.

"Look at me." The words broke through the haze of pleasure with Blake's hands on my face. "That's right, Omega. Look at me while your Alphas fuck you."

I could barely keep my eyes open, the need to sink into every sensation dragging me down. But he didn't let me. My face brushed his. "You're already full of us," he ground the words out, clearly close and holding on. "Gonna fill you up even more with our cum and knot it so deep inside you it'll never come out."

God, his mouth. The filth he painted in my mind made me pant with need. It was just for me. Just for this. To create fantasies we could play with and drown in. He spoke against my lips. "I'll watch whatever's left drip out of you and paint you with it. So you don't doubt whose Omega you are."

Light fractured behind my eyes. I shattered on a cry, convulsing on both their cocks, moving between them like a woman possessed, dragging out every moment of pleasure as long as I possibly could.

They didn't stop. Having given me what I needed, they took what *they* needed, fucking me like they needed my body to draw their next breath.

I didn't know who came first. It was all blazing light and moans and breath. One knot filling me and then the other, the friction of them pressed together sending me over the edge again.

My body was limp across Blake's chest, lungs heaving. We all caught our breath together. I managed to find what was left of my voice. "You have a dirty mouth."

"And you like it."

Couldn't argue that point. Even fucking myself, I'd never come so hard, so many times so close together.

Cole kissed my shoulder, moving across my back. I was once again an Omega sandwich. With the opposite Alphas. Speaking of which. I turned and looked. My other two Alphas watched with undisguised interest.

And one of them hadn't fucked me yet.

The knots inside me were easing, and I needed the Alpha who was watching me with heated amusement.

I slipped out from between Cole and Blake, crawling across the nest to Harrison. He sat against one wall, and the same way he'd dove between my legs, I dove between his and wrapped my lips around him, groaning. His thickness and the heat of his skin. The intoxicating scent swirling around me. The way his hand came down on my hair, doing nothing but touching me. Like he was praising me without words.

"Don't let go," he said, rising. I kept his cock in my mouth while he stood, taking more of him.

Harrison was so fucking tall. He towered over me on my knees. And the look in his eyes told me he liked me down here. I didn't think it was possible for him to get any harder, but I felt it.

The hand on my head sank into my hair, guiding me deeper. Harrison's eyes never left mine, and every inch of me was *aware* of him. I reached between my legs, body needing more even now. He saw the movement, and one corner of his mouth moved. A barely there smile to tell me he saw it and liked it.

But he wasn't going to do anything about it while I was on my knees for him.

White-hot arousal poured over me from head to toe like I'd been anointed with it. Releasing him from my mouth, I licked down his shaft. All the way. Until my tongue found his balls, and I moaned again, savoring the feeling of them on my tongue.

"Petra." My name on his lips made me suck harder. I wanted

to drive him crazy. I wanted him to lose that stoic control he seemed to have. I wanted the animal I knew was inside him.

I wrapped my lips around the tip of his cock and drew my tongue around him slowly. Harrison was my lollipop. My fingers between my legs found the motion I liked, nearly forgotten in the frenzy of heat, and I forced my mouth deeper. I fucked myself while I fucked him.

He swore, using the hand in my hair to pull me off his cock. In less than a second I was off my knees and pinned against the soft wall of the nest, knees pressed to my chest as Harrison buried himself inside me.

His cock was the biggest. I knew, and then I *knew*. Every delicious inch dragged against me, and I lost myself. I was clawing at him to bring him closer, crying out every time he slammed into me. Harder. Deeper. He would imprint himself on my body so I would never forget.

"Alpha." I whimpered the word.

Harrison tossed my legs over his shoulders, grabbing my wrists and pinning them to the cushions along my body. Everything was him. He was keeping me in the air, keeping the pleasure coursing through my body, and he was still holding back.

I squeezed my pussy down on him, and he growled in warning. "Omega."

So I did it again.

My Alpha swore, shouting the word and unleashing himself. I yielded. He was made to give, and I was made to take. I came around him, crying out and going limp where he held me. But he didn't stop, thrusting with punishing force.

I came again, slick soaking both of us, and he wasn't done. My Omega sensed his Alpha and the pure, singular focus to make me submit. I fucking did. My head tilted to the side, practically daring him to bite me and make me his. Right now I didn't fucking care. I wanted his teeth on me and to feel the intensity I saw in his eyes.

He fucked another orgasm out of me.

This one was jagged and on the edge of pain. It tore me open in the best way and laid me bare. Nothing left. Just him and me.

Lunging for my neck, Harrison's tongue dragged over the spot I wanted him to bite. And he didn't.

He slammed deep and held himself there, knot thickening to lock us together finally. The difference between it felt like running for miles and being unable to stop. I was dizzy, the feeling of his knot soothing me down into comfort.

Pulling back, he heaved in lungfuls of air, staring at me like I was the one thing he wanted, and yet somehow, the one thing he couldn't have.

"You're holding back," I whispered. He released one hand when I moved it, bringing us down the wall together and onto the pillows. I traced his cheekbones and jaw, dazed and awed. Sated. "Why?"

All he did was smile. "What makes you say that?"

"I feel it."

Harrison leaned forward and kissed me. Long and slow, tongues sliding against each other in a dance that was flint to the sparks of my heat.

"Here." Emery passed me my half-drunk bottle of water. "You'll need it."

"Why?"

"Because," Harrison kissed me again, knot loosening between us. "We can feel things too, little one. Like the fact that you're just getting started."

Emery sank down beside me. "And I've decided I haven't tasted enough of your skin."

His mouth closed around my nipple, and I arched into his touch. Harrison was right. I was barely getting started.

CHAPTER EIGHTEEN

PETRA

*E*mery held my breasts together and shoved his cock between them, fucking so close to my mouth I could almost taste him, and he wasn't fucking close enough.

Blake's tongue moved between my legs, slow and soft because he liked teasing me. And they all together liked contrasts. If one of them took me hard, the other went slow. And Blake was contrasting with the Alpha fucking my tits.

"Right there," Emery growled. "Right fucking there."

The smooth friction of his cock against my skin was an entirely new kind of pleasure. My own wetness covered my breasts, making it easy for him to take me like this.

I never imagined it would be so fucking hot.

Lust radiated from him. Dominance which made me melt. And finally, a darkness I craved. It lived under the surface in all of them, bringing that edge we all needed. These Alphas were soft and gentle. Until they weren't.

After that, all bets were off, taking me exactly where I needed to go.

Emery closed his eyes, thrusting hard and fast, riding my tits like he would die if he didn't. He threw his head back. "God, yes. *Fuck*, Petra."

One more driving plunge and he erupted. Cum splashed on my skin, mingling with the rest of my slick covering me.

Dragging one finger between my breasts, Emery used it to paint me. Covering my nipples and drawing lines lower on my stomach. He leaned over me, every inch the savage Alpha he looked like. "I like seeing you covered in me, sunshine." A nip at my lips and a growl. "Smell like sunshine and taste like sin."

Blake sealed his mouth over me, my body arching up into Emery. His hand came around my throat, the other one still lazily painting me with his seed. "I don't think I'll ever have enough of you."

His mouth consumed mine, tongue fucking my mouth the way Blake's fucked my pussy.

"You won't have enough," Cole confirmed, sliding an arm underneath me and pulling me away from the two of them. "But neither will the rest of us."

Cole flipped me over like it was nothing, dropping me onto his cock. I collapsed on his chest. It had been three days. At least three days. I wasn't completely sure between bouts of them fucking me and feeding me. They took me to the shower at one point. Which only turned into me seeing them soaking wet and soapy and sending me into another frenzy.

I kissed his chest, exhausted and unable to stop. "Using toys wasn't this tiring."

"I would hope not." Cole laughed before gripping my hips and beginning to take me. "Don't get me wrong, I'm all for toys. But there's something special about an Omega wrecked because of you."

I pushed up, eyes narrowed, fierce territorial instincts rising. Jealousy like nothing I'd ever felt for this mysterious woman. "An Omega?"

He smiled and pulled me back down to him, kissing me until I had no breath left and no mind left to question. "You, honey-bee. We've never done this with anyone but you."

Instantly, my doubts fell through, and my question didn't bother him. All our instincts were close to the surface. Reacting first was natural.

"Now that I've had it with you," he growled the words, "I don't want it with anyone else."

Hands skimmed down my ribs, followed by a searing kiss on my neck. "I'm sure we can prove to this little one the only Omega we're thinking about is her," Harrison said, fitting his cock against my ass.

He hadn't been there yet, and as he was the biggest physically of the four of them, his cock was... proportional.

Fine. Proportional my ass—the same one he was about to fuck—the man's cock was fucking huge.

And somehow it fit. He slid into me all the way, my heat-primed body taking every delicious inch. I came just from the feeling of the two of them inside me together.

This felt different. An inferno built in my gut—something bigger than the ones before it. I was swiftly losing my hold on myself, exactly like the beginning of the heat.

"More," I begged.

Emery's fingers wove into my hair, gripping firmly and guiding my mouth to Blake's cock. Down his shaft, until I was pressing my lips against his stomach, and Emery was the one holding me there.

Full. Every hole taken and filled, exactly like I was meant to be. Emery called me a phoenix when I began the heat, and I felt it now. I burned alive, from the inside out.

And none of them had moved a muscle.

An invisible wave swept through all of us, and they moved as one. My vision went white.

Pleasure slammed down on me like the sky itself fell down and wrapped itself around my body. I screamed—or tried to scream—around Blake's cock. All they heard was a muffled, desperate moan.

Hand tightening again, Emery pulled me off Blake and fit himself against my lips, pushing in to the hilt. And again. Back and forth between them. He moved me where he wanted me, the two of them sharing my throat.

I still tried to suck every time they slipped in, savoring the flavors bursting over my tongue. I was drunk on them. High on them. Out of my Omega mind.

A cock so far down my throat I couldn't breathe, covered in slick and cum, Alphas in every hole...

I was the happiest I'd ever been.

Cole and Harrison took me without mercy, never stopping, never slowing. I didn't come again. I simply never stopped. Wave upon wave of glittering, shimmering pleasure took me, drenching my mind and overwhelming my body.

They took me and made me into a being made of light and bliss. Nothing but a vessel for all this fucking *heat*. Reduced to only my senses. Delicious friction and flavors. Both my scent and theirs, blending together into a true perfume I didn't ever want to forget. The fierce, wet sounds of them fucking me combined with their voices telling me how good it felt and how much they wanted me.

Harrison's mouth found my shoulder. "You have no idea how much I want to bite you, little one."

My only response was somewhere between a whine and a sob. I had no voice left. Fire and pleasure stole that too, another sharp slice of pleasure cutting through me. It felt so good it *hurt*.

"Just a taste," he whispered, his mouth drifting to my shoulder. Harrison bit down. Not hard enough to break the skin, yet enough to mark me. This wasn't him biting my thighs. This was a small fraction of the Alpha he held back. Pain flared and swirled, combining with everything else in one final explosion.

No breath.

No movement.

The firestorm ripped through me. Sheer, savage pleasure with fangs and claws, I wanted to beg for more. This time I screamed, unable to hold back, and somewhere in the fog, they came too, knots locking me between them.

Emery and Blake filled my mouth, one after the other. Yes. Yes. *Yes.*

My orgasm evaporated all at once. It felt like being dropped on the ground after being underwater too long. I heaved air into my lungs, curling my head on Cole's chest. Like the air after a rainstorm, things were cool inside me.

My heat was over.

"It's done," I swallowed thickly, barely able to speak. "It's done."

Harrison leaned over me, pinning me between himself and Cole. "You were incredible, little one." His mouth brushed over the place he'd bitten—there would be a bruise, and I found I didn't mind in the slightest. "Good girl," he whispered into my skin. "Brave Omega."

I closed my eyes against the rush of emotions. The end of the heat was as disorienting as the beginning of one. The hormones that drove you into madness all leaving you at once left you vulnerable and sometimes a bit sad. Harrison's words helped, and their warmth.

"I'm so tired," I murmured. It was frustrating, considering a heat was nothing but sex and sleep. It was still a marathon.

"We're not kicking you out," Cole laughed, purr springing to life beneath me. "No one's going anywhere until you're ready."

Harrison's purr joined Cole's. I melted in between them. "That's not fair."

"We never promised fair, baby." Blake sat a few feet away against one of the padded walls.

The knot in my ass eased first, allowing Harrison to pull away. I felt empty without them inside me. Hot tears pressed against my eyes. This was normal, but I didn't like it. I didn't like feeling sad. The entire heat was incredible. I didn't want my own brain to ruin it.

Cole's knot finally eased, and he turned us on our sides, cuddling me into him. The richness of his scent surrounded me. "What do you need, Petra?"

"I don't know."

"That's okay." A hand swept down my spine. "What did you do before?"

I tucked my face deeper into his skin. "Slept until I didn't feel sad."

"Are you sad now?" His purr hadn't stopped, but it grew louder now. More intense.

"I'm always sad when it's over. Just the way it is. I'm fine."

Cole drew my face out from its hiding spot and looked at me before kissing me, long and slow. "How about this?" The others were listening too. "We'll stay here until you're ready, and then we'll all go shower. Separately. As much as I want to be in there with you, you know what happened last time."

I nodded.

"Then once we're all clean, we'll have some food and take it from there."

"Yeah."

He pressed a kiss to my forehead, and I relaxed.

They were still courting me. They wanted me. My heart warmed inside my chest. It thawed a little of the ice. One downside of nature. When you went so far in one direction, you had to bounce back in the other one to equalize. At least the post-heat sadness didn't last for days.

"I need to go back to my apartment after the shower," I whispered. "Not forever. I just don't have clothes. And you ripped my leggings off me."

"Damn right I did." Cole was unapologetic. "And of course. As soon as you're done, we'll go down. We bought you a robe at the store. It will be good enough, even if I'll want to poke the eyes out of whoever is guarding your door."

I laughed. "Really?"

Snarls sounded around the nest, and it only made me smile more.

"Yes, really," Harrison said. "I have a trench coat you can borrow."

Twisting around in Cole's arms, I saw he was completely serious. "I think a trench coat in your size would probably drown me."

"That's the idea. I could wrap you up enough to be covered."

I just smiled. Their wanting me to be covered was completely different from Carmen or my father. They wanted me to cover up so there wasn't any bad press, or so no one could give my father a hard time about his willful daughter.

God forbid anyone saw us at Nest Inc. She would have a fit.

"Okay," I breathed out. "I'm ready."

Cole kissed me one more time before letting me up, and Harrison caught me, kissing me soundly. Blake spun me in his arms and took his kiss before Emery was last, drawing me deeper. Pure, natural arousal flooded me. "Go shower," Emery said, smirking. "Before we end up in here for a few more hours."

When he released me I was unsteady on my feet. But I was calm. Some of the things they bought me were laid out in the bathroom, including the robe they mentioned. It was gorgeous, a deep red which shimmered with gold. Just like the nest.

My phone was on the counter too, plugged in. I had a million and one notifications. From everyone. Dad, Carmen, Sloane, Eva. I ignored everyone except Sloane. Her texts consisted of dirty, teasing innuendos and her wishing me well on my journey to get railed. And a confirmation she spoke with Cole.

I texted her.

> Finished heat. Exhausted. About to shower off everything and then probably go back in for snuggle seconds.

To my surprise, it was early in the morning. Time ceased to have any meaning in a heat. Sloane probably wasn't even awake yet, so I didn't wait for her response.

I just stood under the hot water in the shower until I felt more like a person. Bottles of shampoo and body wash lined one of the shelves, all new from our shopping trip. Taking my time, I searched for one that felt right. I didn't want to wash their scents off me completely, but I also didn't want to mask them with any other scent. It felt wrong.

Giving in, I washed myself and my hair with a scent cleanser, knowing full well I was going to have their scents all over me again soon enough.

Now away from the intensity of the heat, I felt the aches and pains of spending three solid days fucking. It wasn't bad, but I was still exhausted. God, what day was it?

Toweling off my hair and body, I wrapped myself in the robe, savoring the softness. Fuck. My phone informed me it was Friday, which meant school started on Monday. So much for the sadness not lasting for days. It was probably going to last for months once I started.

But Sloane had responded.

> FUCK YES, BITCH.

Then,

> Seriously though. Really happy for you. Call me when you can, though. Got some stuff to fill you in on.

Uh-oh.

I slipped out into the hallway and crept down the stairs to the third floor. This was where all their bedrooms were, but I didn't know which was which.

Yet, my mind said, and I blushed.

Rolling my eyes, I sat down on one of the steps. The fact that I was even capable of blushing after everything we did together was ridiculous.

"Ready, honeybee?"

Cole stepped out of the room farthest down the hall on the left. His hair was wet, some of the same dampness making the t-shirt he wore stick to his skin. Barefoot in low-slung jeans, I was ready for a whole lot of something.

"Yeah. I think I need coffee too. Or tea. Something with caffeine."

"Pretty sure Blake is way ahead of you," he said, taking my hand and tugging me down the stairs.

"You know, it's just down the elevator. I can go by myself."

"You can. But I'd rather you didn't. And I'm not saying that because I don't want Sean to get an eyeful of your perfect legs. It's still my job to protect you, and now that the heat is over, we're diving headlong into figuring out who this guy is."

It seemed strange that anyone would care enough about me to want to kill me, even in the context of Dad's position. But I also wasn't foolish enough not to take it seriously.

We rode down to my floor in comfortable silence, and to his credit, Sean didn't bat an eye as we let ourselves into my apartment. Cole backed me against the wall, pressing his body into mine. "Take your time. Call me when you want to come back up."

"Or maybe I'll surprise you and just knock on the door."

A low growl had me smiling. I liked the possessive responses I could get out of them. Pushing and pulling and sass. They liked it too, even if they pretended they didn't.

"I'll add your prints to the locks as soon as you come back.

You're never going to wait outside the front door like a salesman. But Petra," he tilted my face up and anchored me more firmly to the wall. "Someone is trying to kill you, honeybee. I know you're joking, and this building is likely safe. But please don't tease us about this. Call me."

I swallowed down the fear. Cole was too serious now, and it was him taking it so seriously that frightened me. "I'll call you," I promised.

"Thank you. I'll be back whenever you're ready."

Watching him close the door behind him was harder than I expected. One deep breath in, and one deep breath out. I armed the security system Harrison had installed and headed to my bedroom. Time to find some clothes.

CHAPTER NINETEEN

EMERY

I laid on my bed, staring at the ceiling.

Wow.

Petra was right. Heats were exhausting.

In the best fucking way, but still, my body felt like I'd spent three straight days in the gym. I think all of us could slack off in that department for the next few days.

Now clean and dressed, there came a kind of restless energy. We'd been going so hard, stopping felt strange.

But I was more sure than ever, Petra was our Omega. The way she responded to each of us—what we liked, how we fucked —was in sync.

Walking into the living room and scenting her was now the defining moment of my life. I would do whatever it took to show her we wanted her, and that she was already ours. On the deepest level, she knew it too.

Omegas needed Alphas the same way we needed them. They took comfort and safety, and we got to protect them and soothe them. An impossible thing to describe to anyone who hadn't experienced it.

I already missed her scent. And her body.

Being knotted inside Petra was like being given a slice of heaven. Her body hugged mine like nothing I'd ever felt. Snug and perfect. Sharing her was amazing, but I wanted her to myself, too. That night I'd promised her where I'd take control. And many more nights with everything else.

Too many ideas swirled in my head for just *one* night.

No chance of going to the clinic today, but I checked in with Jane, anyway. Thankfully, no emergencies had occurred. Not even anything out of the ordinary.

"Well, I guess that's not exactly true."

"Uh-oh," I laughed. "What's up?"

She sighed. "We got a call about an exotic animal. Seems its owner passed and they want to know if there's a way to place it somewhere. As soon as possible."

"What kind of animal?"

Typing sounds came through the phone. "A clouded leopard."

My eyebrows rose. That was a beautiful animal. And stranger, they weren't a client. There weren't many other vets who treated the kinds of animals I did. "Yeah, have them bring it in. I'll definitely take a look at her and we'll see what we can do."

"Sounds good. Should I take appointments for Monday?"

"Yeah, I'll be in."

She laughed knowingly. Jane was an older Omega with a pack of her own. She knew exactly what had been happening. "Sounds good, boss."

I heard voices in the hall and followed Harrison and Blake down to the kitchen. The scent of coffee hovered in the air. "You put coffee on before showering? You're my hero."

Blake chuckled. "Figured we'd all need it."

The front door opened, and Cole came back. "We need to add her to the locks."

"I don't want her coming up here alone," Harrison's voice was firm.

"Which is exactly what I told her. But if you or I aren't available and she's with one of the guys, I don't want her standing outside."

Harrison conceded the point.

"What's next?" Blake asked. "Maybe I'm just wrung out from the last couple of days, but I'm not sure where we go from here as far as courting."

"Dates." I shrugged. "Getting to know her and letting her get to know us."

We knew far more about our little Omega than the reverse. There was nothing to hide, but learning someone took time.

"If I had it my way, I'd bond her tomorrow," Cole said under his breath.

No one disagreed with him.

"Once she comes back upstairs, we give her the gifts,"

Harrison said, groaning on his first sip of coffee. "Fuck, that's good."

Blake raised his mug. "Only the best."

Harrison scrolled on his phone, eyes glued to whatever was in front of him.

"Anything new?" I asked.

"Yes and no," he said. "No press coverage that I can see of us at Nest."

Good. I didn't want to hide our relationship with Petra, but I knew why it was wise to do so. With the pressures of her family and the press, she didn't need anything added to it. But more than that, if this man—I assumed it was a man—who was threatening her, saw her involved with a pack, would he escalate?

"Are we sure this has to do with the Senator?" I asked.

The three of them looked at me, Harrison's eyes alight with particular interest. "Why?"

"If it were really focused on him, why not just threaten him?"

Blake shook his head. "Because it hurts more. Look at Petra. Her whole life has a giant hole in the middle of it because she lost loved ones."

That was true. "Have there been any threats against the Senator's wife?"

"None that we know of."

I braced myself on the counter. "It's not my field."

"That doesn't matter," Harrison said. "Tell me what you're thinking."

Grinding my teeth together, I sorted out my thoughts. "It could be nothing. But I just wondered if there's more to it than her father. I was grateful there were no photos of us together, because what if he makes a move because he sees her with us? What if there's another reason he's settled on her?"

"It's worth some thought," Cole said.

"The only press she's had in the last few days is close to us, but not quite. A few of the tabloids picked up on tension between Petra and the stepmother. But nothing huge." Harrison looked between us. "For now, let's keep it that way. We're not hiding. If someone asks us directly, don't lie. But keep it as quiet as possible for her sake."

I couldn't help the next question out of my mouth. "Would bonding make her safer?"

The energy in the room changed. We all wanted it so deeply it hung in the air.

"I don't know. Possibly. But it creates a whole other set of problems for her. Let's cross that bridge after we've had more than a week of courting."

We all laughed.

"I need to go grab my gift."

Cole and I pretty much bought out the entire store. Her bathroom was stocked with everything she needed. Hell, more than she needed. But our scent-sympathy gave us an idea. Everyone had a gift, but mine was a set of bottles. Four of them. One for each Alpha. The formula inside took your scent once you touched it, designed to replicate. And she would have all of our scents on demand.

Of course, I would prefer her to get my scent directly from me. But while she was living a few floors down, I wanted her to have it. She could spray any clothes she needed to, and I'd still give her one of my hoodies to live in.

Who were any of us kidding?

We'd give her everything.

Our Omega had us wrapped around her finger, and all of us wanted to be there.

I sorted through the bags in the big blank room. There were cozy socks and bath bombs and nail polish. It was like a cliché sleepover exploded all over the room. I grinned. She would love it.

How would she decorate this place?

I found the set of bottles and grabbed a marker from my office before ending up in the living room. My bottle was all set. "You guys do your scents whenever you're ready."

Cole did his, capping it again as his phone buzzed on the table. He looked startled and answered it. "Yeah?"

He shot to his feet. "What?"

The rest of us were on our feet too.

"I'll be right there."

"What's going on?" I asked.

Cole was already moving. "That was Sean. Carmen came to

Petra's and basically forced her way in. He says there's a lot of yelling."

"Do we all go?" Blake asked.

"No," Harrison said. "If it's Carmen, it has to be me. I'm the head of the company. If she has any issues with the security, I'll deal with it."

My entire body tensed with the need to *go*, *claim*, and *protect*. She wasn't in danger. It was only her stepmother. But I still wanted to make sure she was okay.

I forced myself to hand Blake his blank bottle. "Here."

He stood just as stiffly.

"I know. He'll bring her back."

Finally, Blake took the bottle from me, and the three of us returned to tense silence. It was only about five seconds later when Cole stood. "Fuck it."

"Yup."

We walked toward the elevator together.

CHAPTER TWENTY

PETRA

*D*ressing myself was harder than it should be.

What did you wear for courting? The first day had been an accident, and the ruins of my leggings were probably still somewhere in the nest. I'd have to see if the hoodie could be recovered.

I finally settled on comfort. We weren't going anywhere today, that was for sure. Soft pants and a camisole. I planned on stealing a sweatshirt from one of them. Which Alpha, I hadn't decided yet. Maybe I'd rotate through them.

Banging startled me. Loud, obnoxious banging coming from the living room. "What the hell?"

It was the front door. Someone was yelling in the hallway, and Sean was yelling right back. More banging.

"Petra, *open this door.*"

I rolled my eyes. Carmen. Peeking through the hole, I saw her, face red with fury and Sean's body blocking her from coming any closer.

With a sigh, I opened the door. Letting her get whatever tantrum was about to happen out of her system was easier. She'd just keep coming back otherwise. "It's okay, Sean. Thank you."

Carmen pushed past him, roughly knocking him with her shoulder as she came inside. I winced. But he didn't look upset. He looked concerned.

I shut the door behind Carmen. "You could knock like a normal person instead of screaming at my security."

"If you would answer your fucking phone, Petra, maybe I wouldn't have to scream at some random man. Where the hell have you been?"

My phone sat on the kitchen counter. Now that she was here, I was grateful I'd showered with the scent canceller. I couldn't imagine what she would have done had she walked in on me drowning in the scent of my Alphas.

"I've been unavailable."

"Yeah, no shit." She tossed a stack of newspapers on the counter next to my phone. I grabbed it and looked at everything I hadn't bothered to before my shower.

Scrolling quickly through her messages, I saw she'd been trying to get a hold of me constantly. Her last message was yesterday when she threatened to come over here if I didn't respond.

Oops.

"This is exactly what I was afraid of," she pointed at the papers.

I took a deep breath and sighed, mentally preparing myself for whatever she'd latched onto this time. The headlines were fairly benign, but they all featured one thing.

Me and her.

We showed tension. There was strife in the Senator's household. Showdown between stepmother and stepdaughter. What is the stepdaughter hiding? What's the real story? Does Petra Merriton's stepmother actually love her stepdaughter?

I laughed internally at the last one.

"So?" I looked at her. "They don't have anything. It's all speculation."

She scoffed. "Don't be naïve, Petra. You know speculation is all it takes to make a story. How have we not made it clear enough by now? No. Bad. Press. Ever. We can't afford it. Not after last time, and not if you don't want to kill your father's campaign before it even gets started."

"What do you want, Carmen?" I let the papers fall back through my fingers. "I wear what you want me to wear at events. I keep out of the press ninety-nine percent of the time, and when I don't, it's nonsense stories like this. I'm starting law school at the best school in the country on Monday. *Can I help you?*"

Carmen stalked toward me, and the fiery pain registered first before I realized she'd slapped me so hard I stumbled. "Yes, you can help me. You know damn well that running for office is the only thing your father has left. And since you didn't have the courtesy to die with your mother and give him even more of a sympathy vote, the least you can do is be the kind of daughter he needs now."

Pain that had nothing to do with the slap cut through me. This wasn't the first time Carmen had said something along those lines, but it hit differently this time. Facing brutal similarities between my mother's life and mine had brought rage and grief to the surface. Because of the Alphas upstairs, I'd been able to breathe through it. But now?

I blinked, cooling my voice down to ice. "Excuse me?"

"Your father's poll numbers are mediocre at best. Because he has policies that are actually good for people, and bad for the people who actually decide things. Good people don't win elections. But good impressions do. Which is why we'll be announcing your engagement next week. A bonding ceremony right before he announces the run will solidify things. We've run the numbers."

Rage built in my chest. "Get out of my apartment."

"Did you think I was kidding when I said your father needed this?" She hissed at me, not moving. "He does, and he loves you too much to ask for it."

"What about the part where he told me he was going to tell you to *fuck off* when it comes to my love life? I'll go along with your bullshit for stuff like the charity ball, Carmen. Hell, I'll even go into a profession I hate because it makes Dad happy and he can still look me in the eye when I say I want to be a lawyer. But you do *not* get a say in who my pack is. End of story." My voice rose. "Now *get the fuck out*."

"You know what Russell actually said to me after your little conversation? He said he's worried about you. He wants you settled down. What he won't say is that he needs you out of the way, so there's no chance of you fucking this up. Not like last time."

I rolled my eyes. "It's been what, eight years? Nobody even remembers that, and you and I both know it wasn't what everyone said."

My stepmother smiled like I just walked into her trap. Out of the bag on her arm, she pulled more papers. "These are from yesterday. You're telling me nobody remembers?"

She tossed them on top of the others on the counter.

Does the Political Party Princess Need Another Intervention?

The picture was of the two of us at the fundraiser. It was right after I parted ways with George. My face was flushed, and she looked irate. Whichever photographer took this deserved an award, because this had to be literal seconds before Eva and Sloane put their rescue plan into action.

Underneath, the next paper had another photo. This one I knew too well. It was of college-aged me, looking like I was drugged out of my mind. Next to it was a different photo from the charity ball, but this time it was Sloane getting me in the car. I looked *wrecked* because of my time in the closet with Cole.

Petra the Partier Strikes Again? What's she hiding?

These weren't good. But they were tabloids. "These are gossip magazines. They live off lies."

"Of course they are, and of course they do. And it doesn't matter to anyone but us. The real news will sense a story and go digging into you and suddenly we're dealing with all this *shit* all over again." She took a step toward me and I stood my ground. "God knows whatever the hell you were doing to make you look like that picture, but it's going to stop. I don't care what you want. I'm not letting you torpedo your father's dreams because you're selfish."

I couldn't look at her. If I did, I wasn't sure if I would burst into tears or go into a screaming fit or rage. Maybe both. I was already doing everything I could, and them dragging up bad history wasn't my fault. I was already giving them *everything*.

Like hell was I giving up the one good thing in my life.

"Get out," I said again.

"Not until you tell me you agree."

"Get. The fuck. Out."

She sighed. "Next week, we'll do an interview—"

"*GET THE FUCK OUT*," I screamed at her. "I swear to god,

154

Carmen, I will have you removed from this building if you don't get your ass, and its implants, out of my apartment."

"Petra—"

I did what she'd done to Sean, knocking her with my shoulder on the way to the door and yanking it open. "Now."

The sharp click of her high heels stalked toward me, and I still didn't look at her. "You want to be a brat? That's fine. It changes nothing. You're here because of your choices, Petra. If you hadn't fucked up, maybe you could be trusted to choose your own pack. As it is, this is happening."

"Go to hell."

She left, her heels moving down the hall. I heard the ding of the elevator.

Sean turned to me. "I'm sorry, Miss—"

I held up a hand. "I let her in because I knew she wouldn't stop. You were right to keep her out. I'd prefer if she weren't allowed in the building without my permission either, but we can't have everything."

"Yes, you can." Harrison strode down the hall from the direction of the stairs. "I'll be deactivating her key card as soon as I get back to my office. Senator Merriton requested they both be issued one, but this is my home and your home. She doesn't need to be here."

I nodded. "Thank you, Sean."

The other three were right behind him, and Harrison looked exasperated. Whatever was about to happen, I couldn't do it in the hallway, so I retreated.

Harrison waited until everyone was inside before closing the door behind him. "Sean called Cole when he heard the yelling," he said.

A sharp intake of breath drew my gaze to Cole. "Did she hit you?"

My cheek was still warm from the power of her slap. It was probably red. "It's fine," I said quietly. "You guys don't have to deal with this. I was about to call Cole anyway to bring me back up. We can... watch a movie or something."

My arms were wrapped around myself, and at the moment, they felt like the only thing keeping me from falling apart. I couldn't even process everything that happened in that short space of time. But I knew I wanted to time travel backwards to where I was tucked away in the nest with them, safe and happy.

"If it's fine, then why aren't you looking at us?" Harrison asked.

Because looking at them would unlock everything, and I couldn't do it. But I didn't say the words.

He appeared in front of me, and I kept staring right through his chest. "Petra, look at me."

"I can't." My voice was tight, barely there because I was holding so much back.

His hands skimmed down my shoulders and arms before he wrapped them around me. "Look at me, little one. Please."

I lifted my eyes to his, and my heart cracked. The only things in his eyes were concern and understanding. My face crumpled, and I let it come, hating every fucking second. I didn't cry.

Teared up? Sure.

But I didn't cry.

I was crying now. My hands found their way into Harrison's shirt, clinging to him. One of his hands cradled the back of my head, holding it to his chest like he could protect me from all of this.

Every emotion poured over like a fountain, and I couldn't keep them out. This was why I didn't do this. Because if I started I couldn't stop, and I hated *feeling like this*.

Harrison purred, but the knot in my gut didn't ease. I was just one person, and it felt like I was stuck. No matter what I did, I couldn't find a path that made everyone happy, and I paid the price every time.

Cole's voice came along with the sound of paper. "Harrison."

I felt him turn and look at the papers on the counter, but I was still lost in my own world of misery, tucked against him.

Another body pressed against my back, adding another purr vibrating through me. Blake.

Somehow, feeling another one of them near me only made me cry harder. My chest *ached* and it was hard to breathe. This hurt and I couldn't fucking explain it. There was too much of it and too many layers to go through. After it was all out in the open, they probably wouldn't want me either.

"You're breaking my heart right now, little one." Harrison held me a little tighter. "Whatever you're thinking that made your beautiful scent drop down into pain and fear, I promise it isn't true."

He couldn't know that.

"Now you don't have to say anything, but you let me know. Do you want to stay here or go upstairs? One tap with your fingers for here, two for upstairs."

I released his shirt enough to tap twice.

"Cole has your phone. Do you need anything else to take with you? One for yes, two for no."

No. Two taps. I only wanted them.

"Good girl," he said, bending to kiss the top of my head. "Let Blake take you, okay? I need to speak to Sean, and I'm going to revoke Carmen's key card when we get upstairs."

I nodded, allowing Blake to replace Harrison. He did more than that, scooping me up. Turning my face into his shoulder, I hid. "You're gonna be okay, baby," he whispered.

Right now, I wasn't so sure.

My face was still hidden, but I still closed my eyes. I didn't even want the chance of seeing what Sean thought of me being carried out of the apartment sobbing.

I didn't open my eyes until I heard the door of the penthouse opening.

"Cole," Blake said. "Ice pack is in the freezer."

"Got it."

"I need to grab something real quick," Emery said.

The second elevator took us up, but not to the nest floor. Blake carried me into the living room and to one of the huge, comfy couches. My tears were slowing now, the huge gush of emotions passing. Even not coming down off of heat hormones, it would have been intense.

Blake laid me down on the couch, quickly arranging a pillow under my head before he crouched in front of me. Reaching out, he brushed away some of the tears. Not like he was dismissing them, but acknowledging them.

"Someone's coming in to clean the nest." I whined at that, but he kept going. "Not our scents. Just the mess we made. It'll be ready a little later and we can go back there."

"Ice pack," Cole said, handing it to Blake.

"I'm fine." My voice croaked.

Blake pinned me with a stare before pulling his shirt over his head and wrapping the ice pack so there was a thin layer of fabric around it. "You are very much not fine," he said gently. "I can almost see the imprint of her hand on your cheek."

I hissed when the cold met my skin. It felt good. Maybe she hit me harder than I thought. Of all the things that hurt, the slap was the least part of it. And there was no ice pack for my heart.

"Sit up for a second, sunshine." Blake helped me to sit up, and Emery appeared. "Arms up."

He tugged the sweatshirt over my head and helped my arms through it. It was warm, and it smelled like him. Another wave of tears flooded my eyes.

"You said you wanted one before the heat."

"Thank you."

I laid back down, cheek on the ice pack.

Surrounded by his warmth and scent, the truth of safety began to sink in. Emery sat with me and pulled my feet into his lap. Blake sat in front of me, holding one hand in his, drawing soothing circles in the center of my palm. Cole was nearby.

They all purred.

"We can talk later," Blake said, standing. He and Emery moved me, rearranging all of us so my head was pillowed in Blake's lap. "You had a good idea, baby. Let's watch a movie."

Yeah. That was good. Movies meant I didn't have to think. And the last thing I wanted to do right now was think.

CHAPTER TWENTY-ONE

HARRISON

*R*age burned in the center of my chest. A glowing coal eating through me, urging me to do *something*. I watched my pack carry Petra to the elevator and turned to Sean. "What happened?"

"She came and tried to pass by me. Started banging on the door and demanding Miss Merriton answer her. I did my best to get her to stop, but she wouldn't, so I had to physically move her away from the door and put myself in front of it. That was when Miss Merriton opened the door and she went inside.

"I couldn't hear what they were saying, but when they started yelling, that's when I called Mr. Kennedy."

"We appreciate it," I said.

"On the way out, Mrs. Merriton said some pretty harsh things. I don't doubt that was tame in comparison to what was said inside."

My hands curled into fists. "Thank you. When you're relieved later, please make the standard report."

"I will." I turned, and he cleared his throat. "Mr. Atwood?"

I looked back.

"Should yourself and your pack coming to retrieve Miss Merriton be part of my report?"

It was a carefully worded question. He was on thin ice, and he knew it. I knew it too. Getting involved with a client was a no-go. And if it were anything other than the wild situation we were in, I couldn't say I would approve. As it was, I needed to speak to the people who'd already seen us. For Petra's sake, this had to be under the radar.

"No," I said. "Don't include it."

"It's just that—"

"I know." I sighed. "I know. This wasn't planned. We're scent-sympathetic and courting. But because of the threats against her, it's in all of our best interests to keep it quiet."

Understanding flared in his eyes. "I understand."

Finding a scent match wasn't rare, but it was still uncommon enough that when it happened, everyone understood the rules changed.

"Thank you."

All my people were trustworthy. Even without speaking to them, it was the expectation anything and everything private they saw while on a job was confidential. I'd only ever had to fire someone once because of it, and no one had ever toed near the line again.

But even I understood the allure and temptation of talking about the boss breaking the rules.

I went straight to my office.

Until I spoke to Petra, I wouldn't say anything to the Senator about his wife putting hands on his daughter, but like hell would that woman ever set foot in the building again without express permission.

I logged into our system and revoked her access, quickly adding her name and picture to the list of people who needed either permission directly from me or from whomever they were related to in order to enter.

The Senator had requested that he and his wife both have key cards, and I hadn't seen an issue since it was a common practice for families who visited often. Now, I would be declining any similar requests.

I was fully prepared to deactivate her father's card too, if Petra wanted it.

Closing my eyes, I leaned my elbows on the desk for a moment. It would be a long time before I forgot the sight of Petra collapsing into sobs. I never wanted to hear her make those sounds ever again.

In my entire life, I'd never heard such broken sadness.

And when her scent shifted...

It was clear she was upset and heartbroken. But the note of cinnamon had dropped down so low it smelled burnt. Not just burnt—nearly rancid. I needed to know what kind of thoughts took her there, as much as I was afraid of what they were.

I stood, unable to stay away from her any longer. My Omega needed me, and I needed to be there with her.

The television sounded low when I reached the second floor. I didn't see Petra, but the way Emery and Blake sat told me everything I needed to know about where she was. Cole sat nearby, watching. I caught his eye.

He stepped out into the hall to meet me, pulling the door nearly closed. "Sean's okay?"

"Yeah. We're going to have to address this with our employees who see us with her. He had questions. Polite ones, but I don't blame him."

"Yeah." Cole glanced over his shoulder. "You saw the papers?"

I shook my head. "No, I didn't get a close look."

He shrugged. "Tabloid headlines. The ones you mentioned, but also more we hadn't seen. Clearly trying to make something out of nothing. A lot of the pictures are from the night we met, including one of her... after we were in the closet. There's one other picture, but knowing Petra—even as little as we do—I don't think that's what did this."

"It might be part of it," I said.

"Maybe, but my gut tells me it's way more than a few crappy headlines."

I sighed. "Can't say I disagree. Why the movie?"

"Because she's not even close to being ready to talk," Cole said. "If she didn't need us, I'd be in the gym pummeling something into dust."

"That can come later." The exact same instinct was in my gut as well. I wanted to make something *hurt* the same way Petra was hurting.

"She'll notice if we're gone too long," he said.

We both entered the living room, and I barely noticed whatever movie they'd put on. My eyes were only on the little Omega curled on her side, buried in one of Emery's hoodies.

I sat down between them in front of the couch, laying an arm over her before slipping my hand beneath the sweatshirt so I could touch her skin. She needed the visceral kind of comfort.

Petra didn't seem to react, but I felt the slight relaxation in her muscles. Cole grabbed a chair and put it behind the couch. She was surrounded by scents on all sides. It was good we had nothing planned, because there was no way any of us were leaving our Omega's side.

CHAPTER TWENTY-TWO

PETRA

*S*lowly, I settled. I think at some point I fell asleep for a while, hypnotized by Harrison's fingers on my spine. But when the credits rolled on the movie they played, I felt clearer. Not *good*, but a little better.

Harrison turned off the movie and turned to me. "Time to talk, little one."

"Do we have to?"

He smiled. "We could pretend there's not something happening, but I don't think it will make any of us feel better."

I sat up, stiff from laying in the same position for a couple of hours. "Yeah."

The one problem was I had no fucking idea where to start. Clearing my throat, I crossed my arms. "So my stepmom's a bitch."

Harrison was clearly trying not to laugh at that. "So I see."

All the emotions came rushing back, and I was going to cry again. *Fuck.*

I covered my face with my hands. "I hate this. I don't cry."

Fingers circled my wrists, firmly pulling my hands away from my face. "Do you feel safe with us?" Harrison asked.

"Of course."

He smiled, sadness infinite in that gaze. "It's not a given, sweetheart. Trusting us with your body is one thing. We all know trusting with your mind and heart is a different beast."

I looked down at my hands in my lap. "I don't know where to start."

"How about I start," Emery said.

"What?" I remembered the pain I'd seen when I admitted I was scared of the heat and everything working out.

He reached out and tugged on his sweatshirt before moving me so I was cradled on his lap—far closer than I'd been for the

163

movie. "I lost my pack too," he said softly. "Not the same way, but they're gone all the same."

My heart hurt for the both of us. "How did it happen?"

"When I was young," his voice was as soft as the way his hand stroked down my side. "They left me at a shelter. Not in Slate City, but I never saw them again. I like to think it was a hard decision, but I have no way of knowing."

I curled more tightly into him. "Did you ever look for them?"

"I did. They passed."

"I'm sorry." A choked whisper.

Emery lifted me, bringing me up so he could kiss my forehead. "I'm all right. But it does affect you, and it's okay that it does. It's one of the reasons I chose to take care of exotic animals. There are many, many exotic animals who are abandoned because their owners don't realize how difficult it is to take care of them. And I know how that feels.

"I'm telling you this right now so you know it's okay to experience pain, even when it's from people who are supposed to love you."

"Carmen never loved me."

"No," Cole said. "But your father does. I saw it at the ball and the day we officially met."

I pushed off Emery and returned to the center of the couch. I wanted warmth and comfort, but I also needed to have my head fully with me, and touching them made me fog up in the best way.

"I guess you saw the papers," I said.

A hand brushed my shoulder from behind, and Cole came around the couch. He had the papers with him. "I did."

I gestured for the others to look. Not like they were a secret when they were for sale everywhere, or had been in the last week. The stories were all online too, no doubt. "None of it's true," I said. "Well, I guess the tension between Carmen and I is. But not the drugs. I've never had or needed an intervention, I promise."

Harrison's hand came to rest on my ankle. "Were you worried we wouldn't believe you?"

That same burst of fear momentarily took root in my gut. "Yes."

He inhaled. "That was what turned your scent."

"I can explain the picture."

"Given the fact that the second one is because of me, you don't have to, Petra."

I sighed. "Yes, I do. Because it has to do with everything else. I told you I'd tried a heat with an Alpha in college. My first heat. Liked him well enough, but something didn't feel right. He didn't take charge the way I needed him to. Every little thing I had to tell him. Plus, he smelled different and wrong, so I asked him to leave and I... figured out the rest myself."

A growl built beside me before Blake smothered it. "Why do I think I'm not going to like this?"

"Because you're not. That picture," I pointed to the blurry one where it very much did look like I was wasted, "was taken during that heat. I still don't know who took it. But it turned out the reason he felt wrong and was acting so very un-Alpha-like was because he was high. When I kicked him out, he left the drugs in my room. So someone took the picture and found his drugs after it came out in the press. I had no idea they were there. And suddenly I was the cliché politician's daughter getting into trouble."

Snarls shredded the air, but Cole was on his feet. "What's his name?"

"It doesn't matter," I said. "He's not the one who took the picture. And yes, I'm very sure."

"I still want to know it," he said through his teeth, hands curling into fists.

"Anyway, the story was everywhere, and it really fucked things up for my dad. He managed to turn it around once I'd pulled out of school and gone to 'rehab.' But now, I can't have any bad press. Every time I do, they drag it back up. And Carmen is... so fucking aware of it. So all of this pissed her off, along with the fact that I have no interest in the pack she's shoving at me. But it doesn't seem to matter."

"What do you mean?"

I pressed my lips together. "She claims that the only way to combat this, and the only way to help my father's campaign, is to give him something really good, and something to root for. So an

165

engagement and bonding ceremony right before he announces...
That was about the time I told her to get the fuck out of my apartment."

The air was tense around us. "She thinks it's your responsibility to make sure his campaign goes well?" Emery asked.

"Yes."

"Why?"

All I did was look at the papers on the coffee table. "Because I fucked up once and almost destroyed his career. And her other personal opinion."

"Which is?" Harrison pressed.

"That I should have died with my mom and other dads."

Every bit of breath in the room evaporated, and Cole's voice was so cold it could crack. "What did you just say?"

"If I'd hadn't made it that night, I would be out of the way. I wouldn't be a... problem. But I survived. And then I made everything worse with that, and it keeps going because no one will fucking *forget about it*. So I owe it to him. I do want him to be happy." I blew out a breath. "It's why I'm starting school on Monday. You should have seen his face when I told him I was starting law school. I don't think I've seen him that happy since before the accident."

Now that the words were flowing, it didn't feel like I could stop. "He changed when they died. It was like... he died too. I had to make sure everything still happened for a while. His soul left him. Carmen was the first person who brought any kind of life back into him. He deserves to be happy, so I'll deal with her bullshit for him."

Harrison turned to face the couch fully. "You also deserve to be happy. And it is *not* your responsibility to take care of your father's campaign. Not because of one mistake, which *wasn't* a mistake. It was a violation of your privacy so deep I want to tear whoever did it limb from limb."

That made me smile. "I'd enjoy that. But it doesn't fix anything."

"Like hell it wouldn't," Cole growled.

"I'm going to talk to my dad," I said. "He's been away so much these past couple of years at the capital, we haven't really been connecting. He agreed with me that my pack is my choice. I just need to talk to him. But the whole thing with Carmen... because of the heat, everything's so close to the surface. So what she said about my mom hit harder than usual."

"Than usual? She's said those things before?"

"Oh." They hadn't realized it was a regular thing. "Yeah."

The look on Harrison's face gave me shivers. "I should go a step beyond the key card and putting her on the 'no admittance without permission' list. I should ban her from the fucking building."

"You could do that?"

"Yes. I could. Atwood Security is in charge of security for the all of Starling Tower, on top of being one of its biggest patrons. We don't own the building, but I can certainly ban one woman from the premises if I want to."

I leaned forward and wrapped my arms around his neck, kissing him. He didn't waste a moment, arms closing around me and deepening the kiss until we were both breathless and I was perfuming like we hadn't just fucked for three days straight.

"Thank you."

He laughed. "Don't thank me for that. It will be my pleasure."

"Why did she hit you?" Emery asked.

"Because I pointed out all the things I already do to make sure I stay under the radar, and she didn't like it. But thank goodness I washed your scents off. She would have lost her mind."

"Speaking of scents," Emery leaned forward and picked up a bottle sitting on the coffee table. There were four of them, and I hadn't paid much attention to them before. "This is my heat gift, sunshine. Or it will be, once the rest of these idiots do their bottles."

I took the small glass container from him. In black marker, *Emery* was scrawled across the white label. "Wait," I gasped. "Are these you?" As soon as I uncapped it, the familiar chocolate and coffee scent wafted from the bottle.

"So you can always have us."

His hoodie surrounded me, and I still wanted to keep my

nose at the small sprayer, inhaling everything. "That's amazing. But you didn't have to get me a gift."

"I beg to differ," he said. "And you're going to get more than one. Prepare yourself."

I laughed, my chest still tight with emotion. All of it needed to come out, but it didn't mean I was happy it had. Blake slipped an arm around my shoulder and pulled me over to lean on his shoulder. "Thank you for telling us."

"I don't like crying."

"I don't think anybody *likes* crying. But you don't have to be afraid of it with us."

My body relaxed against his. This was what I wanted. Safety and peace. Recovery after all of that and my heat. Though it had been one way to purge the post-heat sadness.

"Any other plans for the day?" Emery asked. "Anything you want to do?"

"What were we going to do before all of this?"

Cole smiled. "This, but with fewer tears. And more gifts."

"Then let's do that," I said. "I want normal."

Blake kissed my cheek. "We can do normal, baby."

I snuggled down next to him and breathed him in. Hopefully, once I got everything out into the open with Dad, this would be my new normal.

CHAPTER TWENTY-THREE

EMERY

I didn't usually come into the clinic on Sundays. Neither did Jane. But this call was one I had to answer. Jane sat behind the desk in casual clothes. "Hey, boss."

"I'm sorry you had to come in for this," I told her.

"I'm not," she said. "And you won't be either. Promise. They're in room three."

I took the clipboard she held out to me. Scrubs hadn't been on the agenda today, so I wasn't in full doctor mode. Hopefully, this particular client wouldn't mind.

Knocking softly on the door of room three, a voice told me to come in. An elderly Alpha sat in the chair, cane leaning against the wall.

"You must be Dennis," I said, holding out a hand.

He shook it, grip still strong despite his age. "I am."

The large carrier by his feet was silent. "My assistant told me you're looking to re-home your pet."

"Yes." The man took a shaky breath. "I don't want to. I love her more than anything. But she's not happy."

"Let's take a look." I set the clipboard down and sank to the floor cross-legged in front of the carrier. In the shadows I saw a large paw, and the tip of a pink nose. "What's her name?"

"Stormy. She's only a year old."

Slowly, I opened the cage, and Stormy looked out at me. She was beautiful. Most clouded leopards were. "Hey girl," I used the tone of voice I'd developed over time. It made animals more comfortable. "Feel like coming out and saying hello?"

She raised her head a little and stared at me. God, I knew that look. It was eerily similar to the look Petra had after she came back from her confrontation with her stepmother. Pure pain. Only in animals there was nothing to disguise it, and they couldn't fully understand why they were hurting.

I turned and reached behind me, opening a low cupboard

169

where I stored treats for exactly this reason. The rustle of the bag got her attention. "Oh, you're interested, huh?" Scooting back from the carrier, I gave her room. "Come say hello."

Holding the treats out on the palm of my hand, she watched me carefully. Then, slowly, she unfolded herself and crept out of the carrier. Her looks around the strange room were quick, her stance low so she could retreat if she needed to. But she made it all the way to my hand and licked the treats off my palm.

When they were gone, she sniffed my hand gently and rubbed her head against it before rubbing her side against Dennis's leg. I stroked my hand down her back, the animal now comfortable because she knew I wasn't going to hurt her. "She seems to like you."

"Oh, she does." Dennis sighed. "My pack was small. Only three of us and our Omega. They passed first, and it was just Ivy and me. She'd always wanted one, and I thought, 'what the hell.' Stormy here bonded with her so fast. It was beautiful. But—" The Alpha's voice choked off, and he cleared his throat. "My Ivy passed two weeks ago. And Stormy doesn't understand. She keeps crying and looking for her, and I don't know how to tell her she's not coming back."

Standing up, I put my hand on the man's shoulder. "I'm sorry for your loss."

"Thank you." He sighed heavily. "Stormy is a beautiful animal. Sweeter than can be. But in our empty home, she's devastated. I would love to keep her, but I'm afraid if I do, she'll waste away looking for Ivy. She hasn't been eating as much."

"I know this must be hard." I crouched down next to the cat and stroked behind her ears. "Thank you for trying to find a place for her instead of just releasing her."

"I would never do that."

I smiled at his tone. If only everyone could stay the same.

"The only thing—" I looked away and gave the man some privacy as his eyes teared up. "I'm not delusional. I know I'm old and probably don't have long left. But I hoped wherever you place her, I might be able to see her from time to time. Until I'm gone."

Fuck. Now he had my heart aching. This was a look into a

possible future for myself and the rest of the pack. The result of a long and fulfilling life. Worth every second, but still resulting in pain. Love always ended in grief for someone. It was a testament to its power that we threw ourselves headlong into it anyway, knowing what would happen.

I'd already made the decision when I said. "Of course. That will be just fine."

"How do you know?"

Stroking down Stormy's back, she rolled onto her side and allowed me to pet her belly. "You're a very sweet girl," I told her. "You're going to be very happy, I promise."

Then I looked at Dennis, and I let the truth of my words seep into the bit of Alpha dominance I allowed out. He needed the reassurance as much as I did. "I've just met my Omega. Me and my pack. We're not bonded yet, but if we have it our way, we will be. I think Stormy would be very happy with us in our home. And it would be an honor for you to come see her whenever you want to."

He looked shocked. "You're going to take her?"

"Yes."

It wasn't a conscious decision, it just *was*. I knew Stormy was coming home with me the same way I knew Harrison was my pack when I first met him. Guarding some celebrity bringing in their capuchin monkey, who was having a rough go of it.

We knew, and he'd handed me his card before he left.

Stormy was ours, too. We had more than enough room, and Petra would love her. I was very sure Stormy would love my little sunshine just as much. I nearly chuckled. Sunshine and storms.

"She'll be well loved with us. I promise."

"Thank you." His voice shook, and Stormy noticed. She turned and rubbed his leg, looking up at him with big, sad eyes. "It's going to be okay, girl. You're going to be so much happier than with me. I'll come and visit you."

I looked at him. "Will you be all right? On your own?"

A grim smile. "What choice do I have?"

"Hold on just a second." I stepped out of the exam room and went to my office, scribbling a note on the back of one of my business cards. "Here's my phone number," I told Dennis.

"Whenever you want to see Stormy, call me. We'll make it happen. And if you need anything else, let me know."

He chuckled as he stood. "You don't have to take care of me, son. There's an entire pack that needs your attention more than I do."

"My pack will agree with me when I say 'bullshit.'"

Dennis laughed once. "Very well." He grabbed his cane from the wall and leaned down to pet Stormy one last time. "Forgive me, okay? I want you to be happy."

We shook hands, and he took his leave, Stormy watching him go with what seemed like confusion and sadness. After a few beats, she turned and went back into her carrier, curling up like she'd been when I arrived.

Poor thing.

I reached inside and stroked her nose. "We're going to get to know each other really well, you and I. And you're going to love your new home."

She didn't respond, but that would take time. Carefully, I closed the carrier and pulled out my phone to call Blake.

"Hello?"

"I need a favor."

My pack mate laughed. "All right. What's up?"

"I need you to get a bunch of raw meat."

CHAPTER TWENTY-FOUR

PETRA

*T*his restaurant didn't belong to Blake.

Thank goodness, because Aurelia's wasn't my favorite place. It was too uptight and pristine for my taste, but my father and Carmen loved it, so that's where we were eating.

Thankfully, without Carmen.

"It's going to be fine, honeybee," Cole said from across the car.

His words were low enough for Brian not to hear them, and that annoyed me. I understood exactly why we were keeping this quiet, and going into a dinner with my father I couldn't smell like a male. But that didn't mean I was happy about him being so far away from me. He couldn't even purr without Brian hearing.

I pulled out my phone and texted him.

> What are the odds you and Harrison can make up a reason for me to use one of your drivers so I can actually sit next to you?

The phone screen lit up his face, and he smirked.

> We don't have to make anything up. It's better for you to use our cars anyway, as they're under Atwood Security surveillance 24/7, and these cars aren't.

> Oh my god, please do it. You sitting over there is going to make me lose it.

Cole raised an eyebrow.

> You want to go into this conversation smelling like me?

> I don't care if I have to start carrying around industrial strength scent neutralizer. I don't like hiding.

> None of us do. It's going to be okay.

My lips pressed into a flat line. He didn't know if it would be okay. He was just trying to make me feel better. And it did.

A little.

I'd barely been away from them this weekend. We all slept in the freshly cleaned nest, and though it wasn't as frantic, they made it very, *very* clear that even though the heat was over, nothing else between us was.

Which had me floating on cloud nine until my father called and asked me to go to dinner. I had no idea what Carmen said to him, if anything, but I was terrified. Which was why I wanted to be in Cole's arms right now and not sitting by myself in the middle of a leather seat.

The car pulled up at Aurelia's, and Cole got out first, taking my hand and helping me out after he looked around and made sure things were okay.

Brian didn't wait, driving the car away. He'd come back when we needed him. "I don't want to be here," I said quietly. There were people with cameras milling around. It made sense, given Aurelia's was a popular destination for celebrities of all types. No doubt some of them followed my father here.

They hadn't noticed me yet, which was good. But I couldn't lean into Cole the way I needed to.

"I know you don't," he said. "But you do *need* to be here. You and your father have to talk about this sometime."

"We do," I said. "But it won't happen. My father loves me, and he loves Carmen. To him, that means keeping the peace and nothing more. I doubt tonight is going to make a difference."

Cole glanced around us again. "Well, I am your security. I work for you. If you want to leave, tell me and we'll go."

"Okay."

I braced myself and went for the doors. Cameras clicked, and I did my best to ignore them. My outfit was perfect. A shiny silver

174

top and sleek black slacks. The top probably wasn't as conserva-tive as my father and his campaign might want, but there was nothing in this outfit to give the press ammunition.

The maître d' looked up and smiled. "Miss Merriton. Your father has already arrived. Please follow me."

A low growl came from Cole, and I held out a hand low. Correcting my name wasn't worth the argument for people who didn't see me regularly.

She led us back through the restaurant to where the private rooms were. Or alcoves, rather. Shrouded with curtains, they offered privacy to those who needed it, but because it was only fabric surrounding the space, there couldn't be any yelling matches.

Which was why it was a good thing Carmen wasn't here.

"Right this way," the woman said, gesturing to the curtain.

"Thank you."

She did exactly what I hoped and left, not bothering to make sure whether I made it inside or not. But I needed a second.

I glanced around. Where we stood, no one could see us. "Can you kiss me without touching me?" I asked quietly.

"I can kiss you without touching you *much*." He grinned. "We just rode in a car together. It won't be noticeable." Then he added, "And remember that no one else is as aware of my scent as you are."

Slipping one hand behind my neck, he kissed me softly. A gentle purr sprung up in his chest, instantly relaxing me.

"I want him to meet you," I said.

Cole chuckled. "Your father is very familiar with me. And Harrison."

"But as security. Not as his daughter's Alpha."

"Is that what I am?" He teased. "Stop stalling, honeybee. The sooner you go in there, the sooner I can take you home."

I hated that he was right. "Fine."

He kissed my temple. "If you need me, I'm here."

Pushing through the curtain, my father looked up from where he was typing on his phone. "Hey, sweetie."

Standing up to hug me, I worried he would scent Cole on me, but he didn't react at all. "Hey, Dad."

"Glad you could make it on such short notice."

"I'm not really busy until tomorrow."

Dad grinned. "You must be so excited."

Absolutely fucking not. "I'm ready."

We sat down, and he reached over, putting his hand over mine. "I'm really proud of you, Petra. This is going to be so good for you."

"But that's not why you asked me to come to dinner."

He sighed. "No, it's not. The press about you this week isn't good."

Picking up the menu, I glanced over it. I didn't really need to. I'd been here more than enough times, and the choices never changed. "It's just gossip."

"If you need help, Petra, you need to tell me."

I closed my eyes and steadied myself. "Dad? I'm fine. You know as well as I do everything the first time around was a misunderstanding."

The silence was telling.

"Listen, Petra, Carmen and I think—"

"What did she say to you?" I asked.

Dad carefully set his menu to the side. "She said you had a disagreement."

"Is that what she called it?"

He sighed, and the sound was familiar. My stomach already felt sick. "I know things have gotten worse between the two of you. Maybe that's my fault. I haven't been around much to help you guys get to know each other."

I laced my fingers together in my lap. "You've been married for ten years. I think Carmen and I know each other as much as we're going to. And we're never going to see eye to eye on things. Like whether she has a say in who I bond with."

A waiter came in, and we paused the conversation while we ordered. I ordered a salad for no other reason than it was small and quick to eat. I loved my father. I really did. But I didn't want to stay in this conversation the whole night.

We handed over our menus and he poured wine before leaving us alone again.

"I brought this for you," Dad said. He leaned down to the

side of his chair where his briefcase sat and pulled out a slim folder and handed it to me.

"What is it?"

I opened the folder, and dread sloshed in my stomach. George, the Alpha from the charity ball, stared back at me. It was an entire profile on who he was, what he did. A quick glance confirmed the rest of the papers were the other members of the pack.

"Thank you. I'm not interested." I handed him the folder, and he refused to take it.

"Petra."

"What part of this is so hard to comprehend?" I asked. "I met them. Carmen practically stripped me down and *threw* me at George. We both agreed it wasn't a match. So what is this?"

"Take a look at the last page for me."

I flipped through the folder and found the page he was talking about. On one side was my name, and information about me. Medical information. On the other was the info for all the pack members in the folder. At the bottom was an assessment.

Compatibility: 94%

"Okay," I said. "And?"

"And you're not going to find a lot of matches like that. Bonding a pack like this will be amazing, Petra. Especially once you get to know them. Not only for the compatibility, but it will protect you."

I glared at him. "From what?"

"I know your bodyguard is here," he said. "There's still a reason you have one. Alone, you're vulnerable. Bonded, you're much safer."

Picking up my glass of wine, I downed it in one go, hating every single swallow. At this point, I didn't care. I needed it. "What are you really saying, dad? Because it sounds a lot like what Carmen said, which is that an engagement announcement will significantly help your campaign."

"That's not what I'm concerned about. I'm only thinking

about you. And everything this week... and before. I think having a pack would be a good steadying influence on you."

"I know you and I haven't been as close the last few years, Dad, but I'm good. I'm happy. Everything is going well."

He took a sip of his own drink and stared at me. "I disagree. I've set up a meeting with them next week."

I looked around the room. "Should I use my invisibility to haunt people or fight crime?"

"What?"

"I must have turned invisible because you are *not hearing me*."

"No, Petra," Dad said. "You are not hearing me. I'm your father, and it's my job to make sure you're taken care of. There are many, *many* packs who started as arranged matches and are the happiest packs in the world.

"And with everything this week... I know it's gossip. But gossip starts somewhere. I know you don't like being in the press, but bonding will take you off the table. George's father Charles owns a portion of at least half the media outlets in the country. They won't go after his daughter-in-law."

I stared at him, not recognizing the person in front of me. "Are you telling me you expect me to go through with this? Regardless of how I feel about it?"

He had the grace to look uncomfortable. "I don't like doing that."

"Good, because I'm not."

"I need you to think about it. Please. For me."

Emotion flooded my system. "You promised." The words came out as a hiss because I was suddenly close to crying. "The minute my designation hit, you and Mom *promised* you'd never force me into anything."

"Don't bring your mother into this."

"Why not?"

"Because *she's not here*." His voice thundered through the room, and I didn't doubt people heard him in the restaurant. He cleared his throat and straightened his tie. "She's not here, and that was a long time ago."

"After how you met, how can you expect me to do this?"

"Don't you see?" Dad leaned over, and there was fire in his eyes. "It's so much better this way. I loved your mother more than anything in this world, and losing her broke me. If I hadn't loved her like that, it would have been hard. But it would have been better. You can be happy this way. Take it."

"*No.*"

"People are starting to talk, Petra. There are whispers that I'm keeping you single so you can stir up drama like this bullshit with the press and I can come to the rescue in order keep my name in the papers."

Sarcasm slathered my tone. "No publicity is bad publicity."

"I can't have people thinking I'm manipulating my own daughter like that."

"Oh, but you can force her to bond with people she has no desire to? Can't imagine that will play well in the press."

Dad ran a hand through his hair, messing up the perfect style his team made for him. A sure sign he was stressed. Good. I was stressed too.

"You're too old to be pulling stunts like this, Petra. In college was one thing. But you're an adult now. You're going to law school. I'm sorry my career puts you in the spotlight, but it does, and you need to take responsibility for that. I am *trying* to protect you. Being happy with a pack you can get to know will make you far happier in the long run than flitting around and making headlines for attention."

Someone had snuck up behind me and dumped a bucket of ice water on my head. Or that was what it felt like. So many things clicked into place. "You don't believe me," I said.

"I don't know what you mean."

"You don't believe what happened in college was a misunderstanding. You think I was actually high? You think I'm going after all these headlines on purpose? That was why you were so resistant to me moving out. That's why you did everything you could to keep me at home. So you could make sure I stayed *out of sight*?"

Carmen was the one who got me into the 'rehab' program. She was the one who made sure everything was taken care of with the school because Dad was busy in the capital. Everything blew over so easily, I thought he knew.

I thought he believed me.

This was his version of an intervention.

"I wasn't high," I told him. "That never happened."

"We all make mistakes."

Anger replaced my grief, and suddenly I was molten. "What happened to you? How can you sit here and look at me, listen to me telling you the truth and you still not believe me?"

Now he was angry too. "I'll believe you when you start telling me the truth about everything."

"When have I lied to you? When have I *ever* lied to you?" Even now, with my new suitors, I hadn't lied to him. He didn't know yet, but I never lied.

He took a sip of wine. "You will be at the meeting with the Gidwitz pack next week. End of story. You are going to meet them appropriately and give them a chance. You are going to think about this, and you are going to consider all the options before you throw away what could be incredible."

"Dad—"

"Sweetie, please." He closed his eyes, and his voice filled with pain. "Don't make this harder than it has to be. I don't like bringing you down, but your actions speak for themselves."

"The next time you want a report of my actions, talk to me and not the papers."

"I asked Carmen. She said you were erratic at the fundraiser. That your pupils were blown out. You were jumpy and rude. I saw it too. You think I'm being unfair, but I'm not."

I sat back heavily in my chair. They'd seen the effects of Cole's scent on me and thought I was high. Fuck.

Tears flooded my eyes. He didn't believe me.

"I just want you to be happy, sweetie."

"You have a hell of a way of showing it."

Dad blew out a breath. "When you're my age and your daughter is making the choices you have, you'll understand."

I stood, pushing back my chair. After that, I wasn't staying.

"Where are you going?"

"Home," I said over my shoulder. "So I can think about my

actions and mourn the fact that my father thinks I'm an out of control junkie who needs to be sold into an arranged marriage to be saved from herself."

Another sigh. "That's not what I'm doing, Petra."

"It's exactly what you're doing. Carmen might tell you it's not so you can feel better, but it is."

I turned, and he spoke just as I reached the curtain. "Good luck tomorrow."

Pausing, I tried to find anything to say, and there was nothing. I pushed my way through the curtain and found Cole's eyes on me. "I want to go home."

He didn't say anything, but his eyes told me enough. He'd heard some, if not all, of that. And I couldn't talk about it here without losing my shit. So I simply followed him out of the restaurant to wait for the car.

Maybe I was right. Maybe Dad did die that day even though he wasn't in the car. Because that man was my father, but I didn't recognize him.

CHAPTER TWENTY-FIVE

———

PETRA

I said nothing in the car on the ride home, and Cole didn't either. But as we got out, I said quietly. "Please take care of the car thing. I can't do it like this."

"I will."

Placing his hand on my lower back, he ushered me inside our building and upstairs. The door to the penthouse shut behind us, and he pulled me into his arms. I shuddered, letting myself relax for the first time. "How much did you hear?"

"How much did you want me to hear?"

"Cole."

His lips brushed my forehead. "Not everything. But enough to know it didn't go well."

"Understatement of the fucking century."

"Want to talk about it?"

I shook my head. "Not really. Not yet, anyway."

"Okay. Let me go talk to Harrison about the cars, and it sounds like Blake is in the kitchen."

Cole let me go, but not before he tilted my face up and kissed me. Simple, soft, and perfect. If Dad saw us together, would he realize why I didn't want any of it?

Probably not. Because of what happened. Did he regret loving Mom? Garret and Levi? I hoped not. The idea that he regretted my whole life wasn't something I could examine closely. Because I would fall apart if I did.

I wandered into the kitchen. Blake faced away from me, chopping something on the countertop. Walking up behind him, I slipped my hands around his waist and tucked my face against his spine.

"Hey, baby," he said. "You okay?"

I shook my head into his shirt.

Leaning over, he rinsed his hands in the sink and wiped them off before turning in my arms so he could hold me. "What happened?"

No words came. How could they? I didn't know how to talk about this. There wasn't anything I could do to fix it, either. Because now that I knew the truth, even introducing Dad to this pack with the intention of telling him I wanted them would only look like, to him, me trying to get out of something.

They were going to ask me about it, but I didn't want to relive it over and over. I would tell them all at once.

One of Blake's hands rubbed up and down my spine. "You weren't gone very long."

"No."

"You want some tea while you tell us about it?"

I huffed a breath. "You're so sure I'm going to tell you."

Blake rested his chin on the top of my head. "Part of the deal, baby. Part of being a pack. You share everything, even if it's uncomfortable and even if it hurts. Because it hurts more if you don't." Then he sighed. "But I think you've been by yourself for a while now, haven't you."

Not a question.

"Yeah." We were still for a moment more. "I'll take the tea."

"Coming right up." He released me to put on the water, and I caught a glimpse of what he'd been working on before I came in.

"Um, Blake?" My eyebrows rose as I looked at him. "That's a lot of meat."

He laughed. "About that—"

"Stormy, wait." Emery's voice called from the hallway before a blur shot past me on the floor, sliding on the tile floor between Blake and me. Too startled to move, I stared as the blob resolved itself into... a cat?

That was one big fucking cat.

"She's so fast," Emery said, catching his breath in the doorway to the kitchen. "I'm getting the idea her last house wasn't this big."

I looked up at Blake and found him grinning. "We have a new pet," he said.

184

Emery tugged me away from the counter and kissed my cheek. "My emergency appointment didn't go as planned."

"I can see that." My eyes were still on the cat, who was now sitting and looking at everything with big, curious eyes. "What is she?"

"A clouded leopard. The Omega she was bonded to died recently, and the Alpha who brought her in was worried for her. He didn't want to let her go, but she was suffering trying to find her person. I knew as soon as I saw her that I couldn't let her go anywhere else."

"She's friendly?"

He brushed another kiss on my skin, this time on my neck. "She's almost as sweet as your scent."

I crouched down and held out a hand to her. She didn't move right away, but came slowly, curious. Her pink nose touched my fingers, and she sniffed my hand before pushing her head into my palm. "Hi there," I said quietly. "Her name is Stormy?"

"Yeah."

"Hi, Stormy."

Like she understood, she stepped in closer, suddenly rubbing her body against mine and knocking me on my ass. A rough sound came from her chest. Not quite a purr and not quite a growl. It was a happy sound as she turned, continually pushing her body into mine.

"She likes you," Emery said.

"I like her."

Stormy turned in another circle before sitting down across my legs. She was heavy, but I didn't mind. "I didn't think leopards were meant to be pets."

Emery sighed, crouching down beside me and scratching her head. She lolled on my lap, rolling to show her belly and let us pet her. Her fur was soft, and I pushed my fingers into it.

"They're not. Wild ones aren't friendly. But because these are so cute, people often capture them to be pets. Or breed them. Though she has some teeth on her, Stormy isn't any more ferocious than a normal house cat. But no, in general, they're not supposed to be pets. Another reason I want to keep her. I know how to take care of her."

"So that's what the meat is for."

"Yup," Blake said, stepping back to where the counter was full of it. "Just cutting it up into portions so we have some ready for the next few days."

I looked over at Emery. "What was Harrison's face like?"

"I like to think my face was reasonable." He stepped into the kitchen and came over to me, leaning down to kiss the top of my head. "I could never resist something as cute as her. Or you," he added softly. "She's clearly already making herself at home."

Stormy rolled back over, rubbing against me one more time before going to explore. She walked over to the breakfast room, looking at everything.

"You should have seen her in the office," Emery said. "She was so sad. Already this is much better for her. I told her Alpha he can come visit whenever he likes."

"Of course." Harrison tucked his hands under my arms and lifted me to my feet. "Did you get to eat dinner, little one?"

For the brief moments I'd been thinking about Stormy, things were better. Now I was back to reality. "No," I said. "But I'm not very hungry."

The kettle on the stove whistled. "We'll see how you feel after tea," Blake said. "But we're all here now. So talk to us, baby."

"Where's Cole?"

"I'm here." He leaned against the kitchen wall behind me. "We're taking an Atwood car tomorrow, so you can kiss me as much as you want."

His tone told me he was teasing, but my heart was still heavy. "Thank you."

"All right," Harrison said. "Up."

He lifted me and sat me on the kitchen island, pushing to stand between my knees. Even sitting up here, I wasn't as tall as he was. The others I was at least close to looking in the eye.

Stormy came back and curled her way through Harrison's legs, looking up at me with big eyes that felt so hopeful she lifted my spirits.

"Here, girl." Blake set down a plate of the cubed meat, and Stormy went immediately, her tail curling around her feet as she ate.

Harrison's hands came down on either side of my hips, putting him firmly in my space. "Tell us what happened."

I pressed my lips together. Already I'd told them so much. About everything. Sharing stuff with people who weren't Sloane wasn't easy for me. And we weren't bonded yet. They didn't need to deal with the awful drama that was my life.

Especially when it was getting worse.

"I'm sure I'm not the only one who has problems," I said. "Emery had to deal with this today, and both you and Blake are running businesses. Cole has to deal with assholes all day. I'm fine."

Harrison reached down and removed my shoes one at a time and tossed them aside before slowly massaging them. "The worst thing I've had to deal with in the last month is banning your step-mother from the building. People come to me because they're scared, so generally they're pretty nice to me. Blake chooses his general managers well, so any drama rarely makes it to him. Emery has seen some pretentious assholes at his clinic, but at the end of the day, they get in line for the sake of their animals. And Cole can handle whatever comes his way."

"His point being, we have plenty of space on our plates to help you. Not only do we have the space, but we *want* to. And when something happens with one of us, you'll be here," Cole said.

Blake set the teacup down beside me on the island and kissed my shoulder. "Told you. What it means to be part of a pack."

I swallowed. "My dad thinks I'm out of control. He thinks what people said about what happened in college was real, though I didn't know that until now. It occurred to me that Carmen was the one who managed all of it. And on top of that, she made it sound like what happened at the ball was me on drugs and not... what it was. Blown out pupils. Erratic. Jumpy."

I shook my head. "He thinks it's all for attention and wants me to meet that other pack. Gave me this folder claiming we were so fucking compatible and wants me to be bonded and out of the way, so I'm not in the press and protected from whoever's coming after me. I don't know why he doesn't believe me. He kept saying all this stuff too about how something arranged is better because you won't get hurt if someone dies, and now I can't even introduce you guys to him as a pack cause all he'll think is that I'm trying to rebel against what they want me to do. And—"

Harrison took my face in his hands and kissed me. My mind went blank, and he pulled back, looking at me. His thumb gently stroked my cheek. "Take a breath for me, little one."

All of it had come out in one burst, like a water balloon being popped.

"That's what he said?" Cole asked. "That you were on drugs at the charity ball?"

"He didn't say those exact words, no. But Carmen told him how I was behaving, and since he apparently thinks I was using in college too... so much makes sense now." I slowly picked up the mug of tea and took a sip.

"Thank you for telling us," Harrison said.

"I don't want it to only be about me. You guys have lives too, and if we're courting, I want to know about them."

"You will," Cole said. "Promise."

Stormy made a little sound somewhere between a meow and a huff. She stared at me, seemingly unhappy I was up on the counter. "What was that sound?"

"A chuff," Emery said. "It's a happy noise."

"Man, she has big teeth," I said. Stormy's canines were long. Not saber-tooth tiger long, but *long*.

Harrison helped support me as I slid down off the island, and Stormy was immediately tangled in my feet. "I think she's adopted you," Blake said.

"That's a good sign, right?"

Emery nodded. "A very good sign."

I wrapped my arms around myself. "What am I going to do? If my father doesn't believe me, I have no power."

"He can't do anything to you, sunshine."

I closed my eyes. "I know what you're saying, but we also both know it's not true. He's running for chancellor. His word will always overrule mine. And if they decide something, they will make it happen. Right now, they've decided I need to meet with this pack. Thankfully, he stopped just short of ordering me to bond with them. But I will meet with them, because I don't care what my father or Carmen says, they're just as *not interested* as I am."

"Hopefully it won't even get that far," Cole said.

My phone buzzed in my pocket, and I pulled it out to glance at it. An unknown number. Probably spam. I flicked the screen on to delete the message and froze.

They were photos. Of me. From tonight. At a bit of a distance, but it was still clearly me and Cole right after we got out of the car. And another one when I left the restaurant, Cole right by my side.

The message was clear and simple.

Guards won't stop me.

My hands suddenly shook, and I set down the mug before I spilled it.

"Petra?"

I held out my phone to them. A growl so fierce it had me curling in on myself and Stormy cowering behind me.

"Harrison," Cole snapped before putting an arm around me and taking the phone from me.

Harrison stalked away into the breakfast room, entire body rigid. Cole was stiff too, but he was silent, staring down at the screen.

"What is it?" Emery asked.

I sank out of Cole's arms and down to the floor again, guiding Stormy into my lap. She put her chin on my shoulder, nearly hugging me. "It's okay," I whispered. "He's not mad at you."

Cole showed them the phone.

"How close would he have to be to take that?" Blake asked.

"Depends on what he's using," Cole said. "It's elevated, so if he's got a zoom lens, it doesn't need to be close. But the fact that he was there at all..."

I tried to feel something about it. Anything. But I couldn't. Someone coming after me like this almost felt abstract in comparison to the betrayal I felt from tonight's dinner.

Cole went over to where Harrison stood, looking out the windows, and I heard him speaking. "Don't go back in there if you can't keep it together."

"You don't think I fucking know that?" It took a couple of minutes before he could return. "I'm sorry, Petra."

"I know it wasn't at me. I understand."

"Can I borrow your phone?" He asked. "I want to get what I can from the photos and the message. The faster we can find this asshole, the faster you're safe."

I nodded, enjoying the warm heaviness of Stormy on my lap. "No arguments from me."

He took the phone and exited the kitchen.

"Cole?"

"Yeah, honeybee."

"What does this mean for me?"

Sinking down on the floor, he sat with me, sliding both Stormy and I between his legs, so we were all leaning against the kitchen island. "It means we're going to be careful," he said. "I'm not going to let anything happen to you."

"None of us are," Emery said. He sounded every bit as fierce as Cole.

"You guys are probably tired of sleeping in the nest," I said. "But I don't really want to go home."

"Dibs on you wearing my clothes as pajamas," Blake said.

Cole's hands found their way around my waist. "We're not tired of it. I'll never be tired of it. Because if we're all sleeping in the nest, then I know you're safe. And we're not going to stop protecting our girl." He laughed. "Though I guess it's our girls now, isn't it?"

He began to purr, and I relaxed against him, hoping he was right. And deciding to take what comfort I was allowed while I could.

CHAPTER TWENTY-SIX

PETRA

"*H*oly shit," Sloane said. "Yeah, I don't blame you for not calling me back right away. I don't think you could have *designed* a week both as incredible and awful as what you just described."

"No kidding." I took a sip of the overpriced water bottle I bought from the cafeteria. Sloane agreed to come have lunch, and I had maybe twenty minutes before I had to be in the law school orientation. After that, a whirlwind of syllabus classes before I could go home and pretend this nightmare wasn't happening.

"If they're going to make you do this," Sloane said, meaning the Gidwitz pack, "I wish you'd tell your dad to fuck off about law school."

"I wish I could tell him to fuck off about a lot of things."

Sloane looked at me like she was about to say something and changed her mind.

"What?"

"You're not going to like it."

I rolled my eyes. "Sloane, you've been my best friend for years. If there was a chance I was going to dump you over something, it would have happened already."

She snorted. "Fine. Why *don't* you tell him to go fuck himself?"

"About?"

"About everything, Bee. When the accident happened, he abandoned you. Don't tell me he didn't, because I was there. I saw what you had to do to keep everything going. Now you, one of the most talented musicians *in the world* besides your mother, have given up a career in music to do something you hate to make him happy. And on top of that, he expects you to just bond with some pack because he doesn't know what the hell he's talking about?

"If he won't listen, you need to tell your father to fuck off, regardless of whether he's running for chancellor. This is your life. He can't *make* you do anything. So do what you want."

"I can't." My voice cracked. "I can't."

"Why not?" Sloane's voice was firm. She wasn't just throwing the question back at me—she wanted an answer. And after watching me struggle for so long, she deserved one.

I crunched up the wrapper from the epically sub-par sandwich I bought. Blake would turn over in his future grave if he knew that had been anywhere near my mouth. "Two reasons. The first is, no, Dad can't legally force me to do anything. He can't *sell me* into bonding and he can't force me to go into law school. But it doesn't matter that he can't legally force my hand. He doesn't have to. The media will do it for him. They're already making me out to be this... Omega with a massive problem. If I suddenly start doing everything I want, then they'll be all over me."

"And? So what?"

"So think about it, Lo. Let's say I drop out of law school. Suddenly, I have reporters knocking down my door asking if I'm dropping out of school for a drug problem. They won't leave me alone, and they'll keep going, and the longer I don't say anything, the bigger the story will get. Until I have to make a statement, or the campaign has to make a statement, and by that time, in order to salvage anything, I'll either have to come back here or just hide under a rock for the rest of my life.

"And if it gets that far, my father's chances of winning are gone. Because if he can't control his one Omega daughter, how can he possibly control the legislative assembly or the government? And it will all be my fault. And that's *only* dropping out of school."

I stood, and Lo came with me to throw away my trash. Cole shadowed me at the edge of the room. I felt his eyes on me.

"Okay, I hear you," she said. "But I have another question."

"Shoot."

"Does it matter? I don't mean to be flippant about it, but you're not responsible for your father's career, no matter what that bitch Carmen says. You deserve to be happy, Petra."

Waiting for Cole to meet us at the doors, I looked at my friend. "That brings us to the second reason."

"Which is?"

"He's all I have left of them."

I swallowed thickly. There was no way to deny it anymore. My relationship with my father had been shattering slowly for years, held together with smiles and hugs and desperation to hold on to what we had. If it were gone, the last piece of my mom and dads would be gone. That thought had my chest ready to crack in two.

"Yeah," Sloane said, pulling me into a hug. "I get that."

"How can I just destroy his career over nothing?"

"It's *not* nothing." She growled the words as much as an Omega could growl them. "Your life isn't fucking nothing. And you could easily spin it the other way, Bee. He's destroying your life for his career."

"I should just change my name." It was an attempt to make things feel lighter again, but it didn't land.

Sloane's phone chimed, and she smiled. "It's Eva. Did you still want to talk to her about pack stuff?"

"Yeah. But I don't know if I can now that I'm on lockdown."

"Let's find out. Hey, lover boy."

Cole appeared at my side, and I gave her a look. "Sloane."

She ignored me. "Would a trip to the Nautilus tattoo studio later this week be out of the question, security wise?"

"Are you getting a tattoo?" Cole asked. The heat in his eyes said he wasn't opposed to the idea, or the idea of watching it happen.

"No. Eva will be there, and I wanted to talk to her about a couple of things."

He nodded. "It will probably be fine. Emery got some of his tattoos there. What day?"

"Wednesday."

"I'll see what I can do," Cole said.

I looked at my best friend and let the sarcasm drip. "Thank you so much for arranging that all for me."

"You're welcome." She blew me a kiss. "And seriously? Think about the other thing. Please."

"I'll... try."

"Okay. Love you. I'll text you about Wednesday." She disappeared around the corner before I could tell her thinking about it was a waste of time.

Cole turned so he could see the entire open room behind me, ever the bodyguard. "What was that about?"

"Same as usual. My fucked up life." He frowned, and I looked away. "Bet if you knew it would be like this, you never would have gone into the closet."

"*Petra*." My name was low and swift, delivered with power straight to the heart of my Omega. I looked up at Cole and shuddered. He looked at me with such openness and acceptance, it stripped everything away. "There is absolutely nothing that would have stopped me from going into that closet," he said. "And there's nothing about your life which will keep me away from you now. Don't push us away because you're hurting. We want to be here for you, and we want to help."

"I know."

He gestured with his head out of the door to the cafeteria, and I followed him. The auditorium where orientation took place was just down the hall.

"Come here." Cole grabbed my hand and tugged me into a small alcove that had a water fountain in it. "Nick," he said under his breath into his earpiece.

"Cole—"

"Nick will be standing in front of that entrance in ten seconds." He reached down onto his belt and flicked off his comms.

I blinked. "There's other security here with you?"

He smirked, but it didn't reach his eyes. "You thought we'd leave you with only one guard?"

"I don't know."

A man stepped into the entrance of the alcove, facing away from us and making sure we were hidden. Cole stepped into my space, gently pressing me against the wall. "I know you have orientation. This won't take long. But I want to make something very clear. Whatever is happening in your life? I don't fucking care. Nor do the others. We'll tell you as much as you need to hear it, but that only works if you start to believe it, honeybee."

My breath caught in my throat. Everything felt too close and too confused right now. All I could think about were my father's words and wondering if he regretted everything. Would I regret everything too?

"Don't cry," Cole said softly, curling his hands around my face and tilting it up to meet his. "The last thing I want to do is make you cry."

"Two weeks ago my life was steady," I said. "Now it feels like it's being ripped apart by a tornado. And I'm confused."

"About us?"

"*No.*" The word snapped out quickly enough for him to smile and press one soft kiss to my lips. "But I'm still scared. And I don't know what I'm doing. My head is spinning."

"And I'm telling you. Whatever it is? We'll figure it out. Together, if that's what you want. But I hate seeing pain in your eyes."

"I don't particularly like it being there. But this can't be all about me." I reached up and grabbed the lapels of his suit before he could cut me off. "And I don't mean discounting what's happening. I mean that *we're* courting. I need to learn about you guys at the same time."

Cole thought for a moment, and there was a sparkle in his eye. "I'll tell you one thing right now."

Something about the way he said it made my body sit up and say *hello*. "Tell me."

"Before I was a bodyguard," he leaned in and whispered it in my ear. "I was a competitive gymnast."

"*What?*"

He stepped back and shrugged. "Time to go."

"You can't leave me with that and then expect me to go sit through an orientation that's going to be so boring I turn to stone."

This time the smirk reached his eyes. "Something for you to look forward to later." He exited the alcove, and I saw the flick of his hand that told me his comms were back on. I glared at him as I walked back into the hallway, and he just smiled.

More people were walking by now, flooding toward the auditorium. Many of them were happy and smiling, like this was the best day of their lives. For most of them, it probably was.

A tall woman stood near the doors, watching us enter. An Alpha. I recognized her picture as the dean of the law school. And her eyes locked on me like a hawk as I approached. "Miss Merriton."

She reached to shake my hand, and I met her halfway. "It's DeWitt-Merriton, actually."

"My apologies, Miss DeWitt-Merriton. I'm very glad to have you with us."

"Thank you."

I passed her and sat in the back, already dreading it. Another five minutes and the woman herself took the stage and observed a hush fall over the assembled new students. "Welcome to Slate University Law School."

We walked through one of the buildings to where the car would pick us up. Cole, Harrison, and the rest of the Atwood team had assessed the university and figured out the best routes and locations to keep me safe. Nick was in front of me, and Cole behind. Almost there.

"Stay here with Nick," Cole said, touching my arm. "I need to check the car and outside."

"Okay."

I wasn't familiar with the building we were in. This wasn't part of the law school. Wandering down the hallway, I looked into one of the classrooms and stopped. A grand piano stood in the center of the small room, raised, amphitheater seating rising on three sides. "Nick, is this a music building?"

"It is."

"Is anything bad going to happen if I go in this room?"

He glanced toward where Cole had disappeared. "Let me check it first."

He went inside and checked the corners before giving me the all clear. Sloane would kill me if she knew I was doing this without her, but honestly, it was the first I'd had the urge to play in a long time.

The piano was beautiful. Glossy black with warm wood on the inside. The lid was propped up, exposing the strings and hammers.

Letting my bag slide to the floor beside the bench, I sat and lifted the cover off the keys. It felt like the last time I sat down was yesterday and not... however long it had really been. I tried not to think about it.

There were some songs I would never forget, and neither would my fingers. I placed my hands and began to play.

Slow, isolated notes in a high register. The key of F sharp. A simple and aching melody which played in my dreams. The beginning of the same song that played on recording the first night in the penthouse.

The melody picked up slightly, becoming more rhythmic as a bottom line was added. In my head, I heard the vocals meant to accompany the song. The world around me disappeared, and I sank into the music the way I always used to.

Down into the lower registers, the melody crept lower, taking on a life of its own before coming back to itself and joining together once more. It wasn't a long song, and I didn't want to stop. My fingers found their way through a transition that echoed mournfully on a suspended chord until I resolved it, shifting into a song in E minor with an off-kilter rhythm I'd always liked. The beat and style said it should be something jovial, but the notes said otherwise, holding melancholy you couldn't explain.

My song morphed again, this time into a lilting dance tune which still had a touch of sadness, but brighter in the key of G.

Having keys under my hands felt like taking the first breath after holding it for a century. Like diving too deep and not knowing if you were going to make it back to the surface.

I raced through the last bits of melody, the notes flying up into the empty space, filling the room like a living thing. This felt *good*. I saw the ending, coming to a graceful conclusion that let the last haunting chords linger in the air for long moments before I released the pedal and lifted my hands from the keys.

When my eyes opened, I realized I'd had them closed for most of the time I played. I didn't need to see the keyboard in front of me. Blindfold me and sit me down in front of a full size piano, and I'd have no problem.

Cole was probably ready by now, and I felt worlds better. When we got back to the penthouse, I was going to make him tell me about his days as a gymnast. Because as fit as Cole was, I couldn't see him wearing those one piece jumpsuits they made male gymnasts wear.

I grabbed my bag and stopped short. Cole stood in the door, his hand on it like he'd pulled it open and frozen. The look on his face was pure awe.

He came across the space slowly, never taking his eyes off mine. "Petra. That was incredible."

"Thank you."

"This is why you don't want to go to law school?"

"I—"

Cole's head snapped toward the door, and he was already moving. His body covered mine, slamming us together into the floor.

Nick shouted the word "*DOWN*."

We smashed into the ground, pain ricocheting through my body. A flash brighter than the sun blinded me, and the scent of smoke filled the air.

"Stay down, Petra," Cole's voice came from somewhere. I felt him against me, but I was dizzy. My head ached.

"Wow." The word felt heavy in my mouth.

Someone was trying to kill me, and for the first time, I actually believed it.

CHAPTER TWENTY-SEVEN

COLE

*T*he concussive force hit me straight in the back, pushing me further into Petra's body. Every sense I had was on alert, fighting through my ringing ears. Thank fuck I hadn't been looking in the direction of the flash. The shrieking fire alarms burned my ears.

"Sean," I said, hoping my earpiece was still functional. "Go to the backup rendezvous *now*. Nick, clear the hallway and call the authorities, both city and university."

"Got it," Nick said.

Sean's voice crackled. "Moving. What happened?"

"Later." My voice ground out. "Do not stop for anyone that's not me or the protectee."

"Yes, Sir."

I pushed up on my hands and drew my gun, scanning the room quickly. It was empty, Nick having cleared it. Smoke hung in the dim air. "Petra," I said, looking down at my Omega. She was conscious, but her gaze was unfocused. I'd taken her down hard. Too hard. Fuck.

"Come on, honeybee, we need to get you out of here."

"Cole?"

"Let's go, sweetheart. Nick, as soon as it's clear, I need you with me. The protectee is disoriented and needs assistance." I flicked my comm over to the private channel while I holstered my gun and lifted Petra off the ground. "Harrison, please be close enough to hear."

It took a few seconds, but he clicked in. "What's going on?" We all knew each other well enough to know when something was wrong.

"We're going to the backup plan. Someone threw a flash bang at us. Petra is out of it, but I think she's okay. I need you to get medical to her apartment. Nick's alerting the authorities, but I want to move fast to keep her out of the stories."

199

"Got it. See you when you get here."

"Harrison. Keep Blake and Em away for now, in case the campaign forces their way in."

"Fuck." The word was under his breath. "Yeah. Get her back here."

I flipped the comms back, making sure I had her bag. "Are we clear?"

"Yeah," Nick said. "Go."

We moved together, back the way we'd come and toward the other rendezvous, which would be burned after today. They'd been following her. Where was Nick standing that they'd been able to get past him and me? I couldn't think about that right now. We needed to get to the car.

Terror gripped my chest like a vise. And for the first time, I truly understood why we didn't allow our employees to have relationships with their protectees. If I hadn't been so fucking enamored of her, I might have known sooner.

Harrison's voice echoed in my head, telling me that I knew in time. I protected her, but it didn't feel that way. It was too close. What if I hadn't noticed the scent or heard the footsteps that set off my instincts? What would have happened if the person followed up with more than a flashbang?

Almost there. "Sean?"

"Around the corner."

"Get ready, Nick. Moving stop."

A maneuver we practiced in training. Our clients never knew how much training each of our employees went through or how insistent we were on keeping the skills sharp. It was why we were as successful as we were.

The black sedan came around the corner, stopping neatly in front of us right as Nick made it to the curb and opened the door. I slid in with Petra, and he shut the door behind us. Sean hit the gas, and we were gone.

"Nick, you're okay to handle cleanup?"

"Yeah, I got it."

"Okay. Sean, get us back to Starling Tower. Going off comms for a minute."

I didn't wait to hear his response, pulling the earpiece out of my ear. Petra was limp in my lap. "Hey, honeybee, you in there?" My voice sounded calm, but I was anything but.

"Yeah," she said. "My head hurts."

"Did you hit it when I pushed you down?"

She swallowed, drawing my eyes to the movement of her throat. "I don't know. What happened?"

"I don't know everything yet. But someone threw a very bright explosive at us. It's used to disorient and blind people. We're going home right now and we're going to get you checked out, okay?"

"Okay."

Everything in me wanted to touch her. Explore her body with my hands to find out if she was injured. I held myself back. If she *were* injured, I wouldn't be helping her and might make it worse. Harrison would have medical staff at her apartment by the time we got there. "Does anything else hurt? Other than your head?"

"I think I'm fine. My ears are ringing."

"That's normal."

Fucking hell. Nothing about this was normal. *Normal* people didn't experience what it was like to have a grenade thrown at them.

As soon as Nick and the authorities found whatever remains of the device were there, it would be good. What monsters like this used could tell you a hell of a lot about who they were. And I was more determined than ever to find this fucker.

Curling my arm further underneath her, I tried to be gentle when all I wanted was to crush her against my chest.

"Could that have hurt me?" She asked. "Actually?"

I lifted her higher so I could feel more of her body against mine and take in the honey scent drifting from her hair. "It wasn't a bomb. It would be very difficult to kill you that way, but it could hurt you, yes." Pressing my lips to her temple, I closed my eyes and breathed her in.

She was here. She was safe. She was in my arms. It was all that mattered right now. "We're almost home."

"I feel better. You don't have to carry me."

Smothering the growl building in my chest, I turned it into a purr. "If it's all right, I need to hold you right now."

Petra looked up at me, those green eyes so close and so big she made me forget everything for long seconds. "Are *you* okay?"

"Yeah," I whispered. "And I'll be even better once you're inside and getting checked out."

She lifted her hand to my face. "You're not hurt?"

I shook my head. "No."

The way she searched my face made me wonder if she believed me. I wasn't injured, but the truth was I was too focused on her to care, even if I was.

"You still need to tell me about being a gymnast," she said.

I huffed a laugh. "I will. Promise."

We pulled up to the front of the building, and I slipped my earpiece back in. Harrison was on the main frequency. "Take the car straight back to the garage, Sean."

"Harrison?"

"Come straight in."

One of our guys was already walking toward the car, opening the door so I could step out with Petra. We drew looks from people on the sidewalk, but I didn't care. Harrison opened the main door for us, his eyes drinking in Petra. He felt the same way I did.

In less than a minute we were in the elevator together, Harrison pressed up against her other side. "Petra, look at me?"

She obeyed, looking up at him. "Hi."

I saw the emotions war on his face before he broke, leaning down to kiss her quickly. A soft moan escaped our Omega, and it told me everything I needed to know about my state of mind when it didn't instantly make me hard. Her safety was all that mattered, and I was teetering. Harrison saw it. This wasn't rut. It was an entirely different kind of instinct.

The doors opened on the twenty-sixth floor, and voices flooded toward us. The hallway was filled with our people outside Petra's door. The medical team and the guard assigned to her door.

"Make room," Harrison's voice had them moving to the side.

We stepped up to the door. "We need your keycard, hon— Petra." The endearment was so easy to use, and I needed to be more careful in front of everyone, our team included. Non-disclosures could only go so far.

Harrison retrieved her card from her bag, and I carried her inside.

"Who are they?"

"The medical team. They're going to make sure you're okay."

"I am."

"They're going to make sure." I didn't leave any room in my voice for argument. Setting her down on the couch, I knelt in front of her. "Please let them look at you. I'll be over in the kitchen with Harrison."

"But—"

I glanced behind me. They weren't inside yet. I kissed her, hard and fast. "As soon as they're done, it's just you and us. Promise. We have to do things the right way."

She looked at me, and she was still dazed. Even though she felt fine, I wondered if she really was. Had I been the one to hurt her?

The team filed in behind me. Betas. I scented the three members of the team, relieved Harrison had called the all-Beta team. I wasn't sure how my Alpha instincts would tolerate another Alpha near her at the moment. I squeezed her hand and stepped back, allowing the team closer, though she was still looking at me.

"Hi there, Miss Petra. I'm Rosie. I'm going to take your blood pressure first."

I nodded, and she refocused on the Beta in front of her. Taking the moment, I retreated to the kitchen. Harrison was already there, waiting for me. "What happened?"

"I don't even know. It was so fast. Nick needs to get the remains of whatever was thrown so we can trace it."

"First, I need you to tell me what the fuck happened, Cole. You're not a rookie. Keep it together."

Shoving my hands through my hair, I crouched down on the floor and took a couple of long breaths. I wasn't a rookie, but it sure as hell felt that way right now. "She was playing the piano," I said. "I went to clear the area for Sean. Petra stayed with Nick. I heard her ask to go in a room, and he cleared it for her. There was a piano in there, and when I came back, she was playing. It was *incredible*. Nick was at the door, doing his job, and I fucking stared at her.

"When she finished, I went to her, and I scented something wrong at the same time Nick did. I took her to the floor right before whatever was thrown hit. I shouldn't have let myself get distracted. Should have sent Nick all the way back into the hall." I stood, the panic I'd kept at bay suddenly roaring up like an angry lion. "She seems disoriented. What if I'm the one who hurt her because I took her down too quickly? What if I hadn't noticed in time?"

Looking back over my shoulder, the male Beta shone a small flashlight in Petra's eyes. "Fuck, Harrison."

"Take a breath," he said. His eyes betrayed the same fear I had, but he was holding it down because one of us had to. "You did what you needed to. You kept her safe, and you got her out of there as fast as possible."

"It could have gone a different way."

"But it didn't." His mouth formed a line. "Switching gears for a moment, I need to ask you something as a co-owner."

"Now?" I blinked.

"Now. Because I want to stop taking payment from Senator Merriton."

My whole body stilled. "You want to stop protecting her?"

Harrison's growl was low and fierce, calling to and challenging my Alpha. "Of course not. But right now it's my job to go back upstairs and call him and tell him what happened. Which means he'll probably come here and see her. And given what she just went through with him? I don't want to report anything about her to him. While he's paying for her protection, I have to."

I hadn't even thought about it, which was why Harrison was the one who dealt with that side of the business. "What are you going to say when he asks why you're not taking his money?"

"I wasn't planning on telling him. I was just going to mark the invoice as paid. So we have a little breathing room to figure this out."

I swallowed. "Is this going to backfire?"

"I hope not. But I also don't care." Harrison's face was grim, but I understood the meaning beneath the words. The instant we scented Petra and knew she was ours, she became the priority. More than a company that could be rebuilt if necessary. More than money. More than our own lives. Whatever it took to protect her—even if it was from her own father—he would do it.

And I would do it too.

"Yeah. I approve."

"As soon as they're finished, I'll call him."

Shaking my head, I crossed my arms and stared at the floor. "Try to make sure he doesn't come here. She might be fine, but him being here wouldn't help things." I paused, everything spinning through me. "Maybe I shouldn't be the one guarding her."

"Stop it," he said, voice low and harsh. "Yes, you should. There's no one with more motivation to keep her safe."

"But I *didn't*." How did I describe the gnawing hole of failure inside my chest? One more second and she could have been blinded. Or worse.

Harrison was wise enough not to talk me out of the spiral. It wasn't something to be talked out of. I had to get through it myself, and it was too soon. But another question was now plaguing me. "It was a flash bang. Why?"

"I'm wondering the same thing," he said, keeping his voice low. "I'm thinking the goal was to take her. But we don't know if any other threats were sent yet."

"The school needs to know, and they need to keep the details as simple as possible. A media frenzy around Petra, more than there already is, will make keeping her safe that much harder."

"Yes."

I turned and watched as the team finished their checks. They listened to her lungs, and Rosie, with gloved hands, gently felt the back of her skull. She winced, and that bolt of pain went straight to my gut. I hurt her.

"Alonso," Harrison spoke into his cell. "Please put the building on high alert. No unauthorized entry. Everyone is double cleared until I say otherwise. And pull Richard and send him to twenty-six, please."

"I'm staying with her," I said.

"No, you're not. You're the right one to protect her," Harrison put a hand on my shoulder. "But you're not okay either. Take the breathing room and make sure you've got your head on straight. She's not going to be alone."

My teeth ground together. I didn't like that he was fucking right.

Rosie smiled and stood, coming over to us. "She's all right. A little dazed, and she's got a nasty bump on the back of her head, but she's not showing signs of a concussion. All the same, keep someone with her to keep an eye on things for the next few hours just to make sure."

Harrison reached out his hand for her to shake. "We will, thank you."

They left, and Richard took his place outside. Harrison made sure before he closed the door with only the three of us inside. I knelt in front of Petra, pulling her close and being so fucking careful with her head.

"Told you I was fine," she said.

"They still want to make sure. Emery's going to come and stay with you for a while."

I moved to sit beside her so Harrison could take my place in front of her. For the first time, Petra sounded like any of this was affecting her. Her voice shook and it fucking killed me. "I can't come upstairs?"

Pulling her to the edge of the couch, Harrison let her wrap herself around him like a koala. She was practically off the cushions. His fingers dug into the back of her shirt, and he buried his face in her neck. No matter how much he was able to hide it, he was on the edge too. "Not yet, little one. Because if your family insists on seeing you, I didn't think you would want the questions."

"There will still be questions if Emery is here."

Harrison chuckled. "Stick him in a closet. He won't mind."

I didn't voice the concern that being in the closet wouldn't mask his scent. It wasn't the most important thing right now.

"I'm grateful you're safe," Harrison said quietly. "And please believe me when I say walking away from you right now is the last thing I want to do."

206

"Then don't."

He kissed her neck. "I have to. Talk to the police, the Senator, see what we can use to track this fucker down."

"It didn't seem real, you know? Even with the pictures, it didn't feel like someone was trying to hurt me."

A pounding on the door startled Petra. She jumped in Harrison's arms. I checked the peephole before opening and found Emery standing there in front of Richard. He pushed past me as soon as I opened the door, Harrison moving just in time.

Emery was gentle, and he ran his hands over her arms. "Hey, sunshine."

He was a doctor for animals, but that made him more qualified than the rest of us to keep an eye on her.

"You're leaving too?" She asked me.

"I'm sorry," I said. "I need to help them with things to find this guy." And get my head on fucking straight.

Her face fell, tearing another piece of my heart open. "It's not for long," I promised. "Okay?"

"Yeah."

Emery glanced at me. He saw too fucking much. I leaned down and kissed my Omega again, wishing I could stay right here with her for the rest of the night.

But if I wanted to stay with her *every* night? We needed to make sure this asshole never got near her again. Harrison said his goodbye, and we closed the door behind us. Every step away from her door was like walking with knives in my shoes.

And each stab was more motivation to get this done.

CHAPTER TWENTY-EIGHT

_____

PETRA

*T*he door shut behind them, and I felt empty.

"Sorry you have to babysit me."

Emery smiled and moved. He curled himself around me and stretched both of us out on the couch. "The only disappointing bit about it is that Stormy isn't here. Pretty sure she's been looking for you all day. But there's never any hardship spending time with you."

I turned over in his arms, finally allowing myself to breathe deeply. Chocolate and coffee. Mocha. Heavy sweetness that wrapped around me just as tightly as his arms. "Something's wrong," I whispered. "Cole doesn't feel right."

"Mmm." He hummed the sound, purring softly. "He's scared."

"Why?"

"The same reason we all are. The same reason Blake is pissed that he can't be down here and Harrison is keeping it together by a thread. Because someone coming so close to you, intending to hurt you, makes us lose our fucking minds."

They all seemed pretty calm. Even now, Emery was steady. "You all seem fine."

"Because the last thing you need right now is four feral Alphas making it worse."

My heart skipped a beat and anticipation heated low in my gut. The connection between all of us was real, but I wanted to see it. I wanted to *feel* it. After today, I didn't want them to pretend to feel anything less than they did.

"Show me."

"Show you what?"

"How you're really feeling," I murmured. "I don't want to guess. I want to know."

We weren't lying side by side anymore. Emery flipped me on my back, a low, possessive growl shredding the air around us. It didn't scare me. His body pressed mine down, the hardness between his legs clear as he moved his hips. If we weren't dressed, he would be fucking me.

"Is this what you want?" His voice was no longer gentle. "Because this is what every piece of Alpha in me wants. To pin you down and take you hard so that everyone, including you, knows that you're mine. To knot you so deep you can't go anywhere, because if you're locked on my cock, you're safe."

He pulled the neckline of my shirt over, exposing all of my neck and shoulder before he inhaled my pulse. "Do you have any idea how much I want to bite you, sweet girl?" The words were low and soft, a contrast to the power humming through him. "So I can feel every reaction you have. Know exactly what gets you off and leaves you a quivering mess. Know when you're happy and sad and everything else about you."

"Emery."

"Say my name like that again and I won't be held responsible for what I do, sunshine. I can watch you for symptoms with my cock inside you just as easily."

"What if someone comes to visit?" I asked. Harrison had to make calls, and my father—

My heart steeled. This was my home. I owned it outright. I didn't have to let in anyone I didn't want to, even family. And right now I didn't want to let anyone in. I wanted Emery to unleash himself on me so I didn't have to think or question anything—just submerge myself in pleasure.

"Emery." I said his name on purpose.

He hauled me up with him as he stood, carrying me to my bedroom. "We still have to be a touch careful," he said. "You're in the clear, but I can't fuck you into the headboard."

"Another time for that, then."

Placing me on the bed, he stood back and looked at me. He seemed taller, Alpha presence dominating the space. It made me want to turn over and present for him, allowing him full access to all of me.

Hell, why wouldn't I do that?

"Do you remember the heat?" Emery asked. "What I said?"

There was no way to forget.

I want a night where you do exactly what I tell you to, when I tell you to, with no hesitation. Because I think there's a part of you that likes to obey.

"Yes."

Emery stepped closer, hand cupping my jaw. He made me look at him. The sparkle of mischief in his eyes caught my desire and made it grow. "Tell me what you want, sweet girl. Because I'll give it to you. I don't need to be in control, but I have no problem taking it, and I'll fucking enjoy it while I do."

"Take it," I whispered, and Emery smiled.

The smile had my stomach tumbling through the floor. We'd all been sleeping in the nest together, and there were definite advantages to that. But I wanted them alone too. The bump on the back of my head throbbed a little, but not enough to make me want to stop this. I wanted it.

With everything going on, I wanted to let go.

"Hmmm, let's see." Emery took the belt off his jeans. "This might work."

"For what?"

He tossed it on the bed and reached for me. "For making sure you get what you need."

"I don't know if I'm ready to get spanked with a belt."

Emery kissed me, teasing my mouth open with lips and tongue until I melted against him. He lifted my shirt up over my head and tossed it to the side. My bra followed. "That wasn't my plan, sunshine. Just keeping your hands out of the way. But I don't need a belt to do this."

There was a challenge in his voice. My skin tingled, head light with anticipation. If he wanted to challenge me, I would rise to it. "No belt then," I taunted, "if you don't need it."

Emery gripped my chin and kissed me again. Power flowed through him and into me. *Alpha*. I whined without meaning to, and he laughed. "You might regret that later, Omega. But let's do it. There's just two things you need to remember."

"What's that, *Alpha*?" I made sure the word was a taunt because I loved the fire building in his eyes.

He turned me so my back pressed against his chest, arms caging me in. "The first is that if you want to stop any time, then we stop. The second is that, until we are finished, you asked me to take control. So I expect your obedience."

The word *obedience* shivered across my skin. My nipples hardened and heat built in my gut. This wasn't a game I usually played, but it felt so fucking right in this moment, I could barely breathe.

"Now take the rest of your clothes off."

I did, and I heard the sound of his clothes hitting the floor behind me. His hands skimmed up my ribs, pulling me against his body again, skin on skin. Emery's purr radiated from his chest, soothing every worry and crease from my mind. Something about the heat of skin and the sound of a purr short-circuited the Omega brain. Even more with people like us, attuned to each other.

Struggling to find my voice, I put my hands over his. "Is this where you order me onto the bed and not let me come until I'm begging you for it?"

A kiss just below my ear. "Where's the fun in that?"

"Not your style?" I couldn't breathe the way he was touching me, lazily exploring my body with his hands and his mouth.

"It could be," he admitted. "Not today."

"What's your plan for today?"

He laughed. "My Omega is nervous about obeying."

I opened my mouth and closed it. I hadn't thought about it that way, but yeah. I was. "A little."

Turning me to face him, Emery searched my face. He was seeing if I was still okay—I felt it. Up close, the tattoos covering his chest were gorgeous. Still following the geometric patterns on his arms, but with triangles and slanted shapes instead of rectangles and squares. Trees and flowers grew out of one shape and rain fell from another. The face of a tiger, fierce and snarling over his heart. Each piece of the tattoo meant something to him. I would ask him later.

Whatever he looked for in my face, he found it. "On the bed. Hands above your head, legs spread."

I shuddered involuntarily. So much *need* shot through my body I couldn't contain it. Backing onto the bed, I did exactly as he asked. "So you're not going to put me through hours of denial?"

Emery followed me onto the bed, settling his knees on either side of my hips. His cock lay between us, hot and hard, and those bright blue eyes pinned me to the bed so completely he might as well have tied me up.

"Denial?" He asked. "There's so much more to control than taking something away from someone." Leaning down, he kissed the skin between my breasts and upward until he reached my jaw. "And you, sweet girl," those words were a moan into my skin that had me squeezing my legs together. Disobeying him because I needed to ease some of the building pressure. "You'll wish denial was what I'd chosen by the time I'm done with you."

"Before the heat," I gasped. "I never would have said this was you."

His mouth quirked upward, revealing the smirk which made a whole new wave of perfume and wetness leave me. "That a bad thing?"

I shook my head. "Uh-uh."

"Good. Now, where are those toys you told us about?"

—

CHAPTER TWENTY-NINE

EMERY

*P*etra's mouth formed a tiny 'o' as she stared up at me, hair spread wantonly across her comforter like I'd already fucked her into mindless bliss. Not yet, but we would get there.

"They're uh…" She swallowed and licked her lips. "They're in the top drawer of my dresser."

"And if I use them on you?"

Her cheeks turned a gorgeous shade of pink. I wanted to turn my sweet Omega into a boneless mess of pleasure, but I wasn't about to do anything she didn't want.

Petra was an enigma when it came to things like this. She was a bit of a brat when she teased me and challenged me. But then she looked at me like she was looking right now, so desperate to be taken out of her own head I could almost hear her thoughts screaming it.

I would happily oblige.

"Yeah," she finally said. "I'm good with it."

"Don't move," I told her, lightly slapping the inside of her thighs so she spread her legs again.

Denial was one thing, and it made sense that her head would go there, but it had never been *my* thing. It was a tool I liked to use occasionally, but I liked the opposite. And it was something I'd barely gotten to experience. Because things like this you didn't share with people you didn't care about. At least *I* didn't, because it wove bonds which weren't easy to dissolve.

I opened the top drawer of her dresser, and my eyebrows rose. Our Omega wasn't kidding when she said she had toys. Every shape and size. This was going to be fun. "Which one is your favorite?"

"Um… the suction." Embarrassment was clear in her voice, but she'd see soon enough I wasn't about to judge her for any of these. Toys were friends, not enemies. Especially for women like Petra, who had a million things going on and weren't in heat. Her mind needed to be overloaded, and these would help.

I grabbed a pink toy which ended in a little hole for suction, the wand you plugged into the wall, and a dildo made of glass. We'd see about that last one.

Her eyes went wide when she saw it. "I almost never use that one."

"Just keeping my options open."

Petra's pussy glistened where her legs were spread, already wet and ready for me. I needed to taste her first. I dropped the toys on the bed beside her before I dropped to my knees and pulled her to the edge of the bed so I could feast.

Fuck, she was so sweet. Blake's idea of using her to sweeten tea and coffee wasn't entirely off the mark. I let her hear my pleasure, pushing her knees wider and curling my tongue inside her before working her clit in slow, deliberate circles.

She was already close, anticipation driving through her and giving her a small, sweet orgasm when I sealed my mouth over her clit and sucked. Honey and cinnamon flooded across my tongue. I could spend every day on my knees drinking this woman in and still not have enough of her flavor.

That small orgasm was only the beginning. I glanced up and saw her hands beginning to drift down. "Keep your hands above your head," I said.

Mental restraints were so much harder to use, because you had to remind yourself to obey. But that was the edge Petra needed—not her hands being tied. But the knowledge she wasn't in charge and didn't have to be. It made everything sharper and brighter. Certainly made my cock harder.

I grabbed the little pink toy and turned it on the lowest setting, allowing the suction to hook onto her clit. "Oh my god."

Laughing, I bent down to fuck her with my tongue. This was nothing. I wasn't going to count her orgasms, but she was going to come over and over and over again until either she or I couldn't take it anymore.

"Do you like it low?" I licked her slowly, gently pulling on the toy so it pulsed and pulled on her clit. "Or high?"

"Depends on the day." She pretended to not be affected, her voice normal and light. The way the muscles in her thighs jumped told me she was anything but calm right now.

I pressed the toy harder against her. "Right this second?"

"Low," she moaned.

"Low it is." I kept the toy where it was, creating a rhythm with pulses and circles, but never allowing the suction to release. She grew wetter and wetter, that needy bundle of nerves swelling under the attention. I fucked her as deep as I could reach with my tongue, savoring what remained of the cum from her first orgasm and looking forward to the second.

Petra squirmed, her hips lifting against the toy and pushing into my mouth. "Remember," I whispered, "come whenever you want to."

"Emery," she breathed. "I'm not in heat."

"Oh, I know, sunshine. Why should you have to wait for heat to have plenty of orgasms?" I removed the toy and used my mouth on her instead.

She gasped, newly sensitive. "Fuck. Fuck. I—"

"Keep your hands where I put them," I told her, adding an edge of power to my voice when they slipped. The toy covered her clit, and she came, shuddering and groaning. One more with this, and I would switch over to the tool I really wanted. But first.

"Why don't you use this?" I asked, picking up the glass dildo and wetting it with her own cum.

Petra laughed, breathless. "It takes work, and other toys work faster. Plus, it's not the most comfortable. I mean... I like it, but it's just not in the starting line up."

"Hmm." I turned it, pushing it gently inside her. "But you like it?"

"Yes."

I turned up the suction toy and captured her clit again, watching her hips rise off the bed and her legs start to come together. "Keep your legs open, Omega. Or I'll find something to tie them open."

"*Fuck.*"

She couldn't see the smile on my face. Watching her writhe in pleasure under my command? Perfection. She was so fucking gorgeous she stole my breath.

One more orgasm. She was so wet there was no resistance against the thick glass of the toy. It wasn't as big as any of us, but the lack of give in the material more than made up for it. Petra's hands dug into the comforter above her head, holding on, trying to hold on and keep herself still and steady. "Don't hold it in, sunshine. Let it go."

"I can't. It's too much."

I clicked the suction vibrator up two more notches, working her body with the glass. "I want this orgasm, Petra. You're going to give it to me."

Hard, steady, and fast, I fucked her with the dildo, keeping the pressure on her clit until her back arched off the bed, body thrashing as she succumbed to pleasure. She wasn't quite screaming, her moans something completely unintelligible.

"That's it," I told her, kissing the inside of her thigh. "Let it happen. Let the pleasure fill you up until you can't take it, knowing you still need a knot to really satisfy you."

"Emery, *please*."

"Please what?"

"I don't *know*."

Her body shook as I turned off the little suction vibe and put it to the side. I waited until I was standing again to pull the glass slowly from her body, so she could see when I ran my tongue over it, tasting her cum. But I wasn't the only one who needed a taste.

"Open." I climbed up her body, and she obeyed, opening that sinful mouth. Watching her take the glass dildo between her lips and taste her own orgasm was almost enough for me to abandon my plan entirely and just fuck her. But no. We both needed this.

"Next time we do this, one of your other Alphas will fuck your mouth while I take my time making you come."

I removed the dildo and her eyes were glazed. "Next time?"

"Absolutely." I bent over her for a kiss. "Now be good and don't move."

"There's more?" Her words were half a sob and half a prayer.

I found the power outlet closest to the bed and plugged in the wand before I arranged her, moving her up so I could kneel between her spread legs, pussy open to me like a fucking gift.

Turning the wand on, I pressed it against her clit and saw her face fill with understanding. "Oh, sweet girl. We are just getting started."

CHAPTER THIRTY

PETRA

I couldn't come again. There was no way. Not in heat? Three orgasms was a lot back to back, but Emery had coaxed them from my body like a conductor in front of an orchestra.

He looked down at me like a king or a god, observing everything he owned and considering what he was going to do with it.

The vibrations against my clit were low, but I knew how high the monster in his hand could go. It was almost as good as—

"I have one more toy," I admitted to him. "It's in the closet."

Emery's eyes blazed with interest. "Tell me."

"You sit on it," I said. "And it... does its thing."

A wicked smile curled over his mouth. "Good to know. But this will do for now."

I shook my head. "There's no way."

He raised an eyebrow. "Are you telling me to stop?"

"No."

"Then there's a way."

One notch up on the vibrator. Already, I felt the pleasure building impossibly. My body felt ragged from what he'd dragged out of me, and I wondered if I'd survive the rest of this.

"Now, you seem to have some trouble keeping your hands where I want them," he said. "This should help."

He stretched over me, gathering my wrists in one hand and pinning them to the mattress. His other hand still controlled the wand, and now it was pressed between our bodies, though he wasn't inside me.

Emery rocked his hips, which moved the vibrator, rocking it up into my clit. *Holy fucking stars and diamonds* it felt so good.

His face watched mine, noting every shake and every whimper. The fact that he barely looked affected turned me on. I knew how hard he was, and I knew how badly he wanted me. But he was holding back and examining my pleasure like a clinical thing. "That's interesting," he said. "You like that?"

He rocked his hips again, forcing the vibrator to move into the position that made me fly to the fucking moon, and I groaned, trying to move. But now I *couldn't*. My wrists were pinned beneath his hand and his knees between my legs kept me open and vulnerable to whatever pleasure he chose to give me.

Oh my god, he wasn't kidding when he said he didn't need the belt.

The orgasm hit me with the force of a storm, pleasure so sharp it tore through me, building on the ones that came before it. I arched off the bed, not remotely in charge of my body. It thrashed and shook, fighting the pleasure as much as reveling in it. Fuck me, I didn't know I could come like that outside of heat.

I was a soft mess of an Omega as I came down, everything limp, weak, and sated. It took me a beat to realize the vibrator was still going. "Emery."

He grinned. "Petra."

It wasn't his hips now. He moved the wand up and down, circling my clit and pushing it against me like he was fucking me with it. "I can't," I told him, even as I felt everything tightening all over again. "I can't."

"Can't you?"

The wand flicked off, and I sighed in relief, and also disappointment.

"Look at me, sunshine."

I didn't realize I wasn't. Opening my eyes, Emery was right there, still stretched out over me, still pinning me to the bed. Nothing soft about Emery now. Every muscle strained like he was holding himself back, and his gaze burned with more intensity than all those orgasms combined. "Do you need to be done?"

"Done?" Did I need to be done? I didn't know, because he proved me wrong every time I came. I didn't think it was possible, and yet it still happened. "I don't know."

Emery grinned and closed the distance between us to kiss me. His words melted between my lips, spoken hushed and reverent between kisses. "Here's what's going to happen, Petra. Until you say the words 'I'm done,' I'm going to wring every orgasm I can from your body. Tell me you can't, tell me to fuck off, tell me it's not possible, but I'm not going to stop until you say those magic words. And until then? You and this gorgeous pussy get no mercy from me. Understand?"

"Yes." Oh, *fuck* did I understand him. What I *didn't* understand was why Emery telling me he wasn't going to have mercy on me was so fucking hot.

"Good. Now come for me."

The wand blazed to life, Emery resuming the brutal, delicious onslaught of pure pleasure.

My words could stop him any time I wanted. Or I could fall into this head first and not come out until I was delirious.

I chose the second.

And I let everything go.

This kind of pleasure had fangs and claws. It waited for me to fall, springing up to tear me apart and piece me back together. My breath came in ragged gasps around the moans and unintelligible words.

Emery held me down and used my own toy to make me come. Over and over again. Every time he pushed me over the edge, the next orgasm was somehow both easier and harder. Easier to get there, harder to get through, every nerve burning and overloaded. But I didn't want him to stop. I wasn't thinking, and that was incredible.

I lost track of the orgasms. All I knew was the pleasure caged me in, just like Emery's arms and body. Impossible to escape and impossible to deny.

My bedding was soaked, every orgasm another gush, and I didn't fucking care.

When he finally pulled the wand away and lined his cock up with my entrance, I was too far gone. The first driving plunge made me come. I couldn't see or breathe. Every cell in my body was overloaded, craving a knot to finish this inferno.

He didn't give it to me. Yet.

The wand came back, pressed just where I needed it while he fucked me slow and deep, rolling his hips and bringing forward new pleasure that rose from within. "You're going to kill me," I told him. "You're going to kill me." And I came again.

"You know what to do to make me stop," Emery growled the words, thrusting harder and turning up the wand once more. It couldn't go any higher, and I was nearly numb. But my body didn't know that.

I bowed off the bed, everything constricting and releasing, ravaging me before the orgasm dumped me back into my own body.

The wand hit the floor next to the bed, and Emery was there, burying himself deep into me. He didn't need the wand any more than he needed the fucking belt.

His hand came around my throat, reminding me who I was obeying while he fucked me.

"I can't, Emery. It's too much," I panted. "I. Can't."

"You can." The words were hot in my ear. "One more, sweet girl. Come all over my cock, and I'll knot this magnificent cunt so deep you'll never get me out."

My pussy clenched down on him, wanting the knot and ready to take him and never let him go. His voice was raw. On the edge of his own pleasure, and I surrendered, giving him everything.

I came. It was fire and pain. Pleasure and glitter. A building firework I was helpless against. All I could do was watch and feel.

Emery slammed home, coming deep, moaning into the same throat he held captive. His knot locked in place, and the firework soared higher. Too much. It was all too much, and I would never have enough.

Taking a deep breath felt like coming out of a coma. I opened my eyes and found blue ones looking back at me. "Welcome to the world of the living," he said with a chuckle before stealing a kiss.

"I don't think I am living," I said. "I think you killed me. Too many orgasms."

"I did tell you that you were going to wish I denied you."

My cheeks flushed. I don't think I did wish that, because holy *shit*. Emery was wrapped around me, one of my legs slung over his hip. He was still inside me, though no longer knotted. "You didn't have to stay there," I said. "I doubt I would have woken."

"I like being inside you," he said softly. The expression on his face softened. "Just like this. Connected."

He began to pull back, and I stopped him. "Stay."

"Yeah?"

"Yeah."

He pushed his hips closer, turning us so he was a little more on top of me, pressing me back into the pillows. I saw the appeal. Being filled with the softness of his cock like this was completely different from being fucked. It simply felt like being full, and it was comfortable. The closeness filled something in me I couldn't name. "I never thought of this."

"I'm glad you like it, because I know for a fact I'm not the only one of us who does."

I imagined being in their beds, and them taking the time to slip inside me before we fell asleep, connected, even though we were unconscious.

My fingers found Emery's hair and I pulled him down to kiss me. Soft and slow. "Thank you," I finally said. "For showing me what you were feeling, and giving me what I needed."

"That was fucking fun," he said. "I'll happily do it again. Maybe pull out the toy in the closet and tie you to it while I fuck your throat."

I moaned. "You can't say things like that now. I'm too tired to go again."

"Sure about that?" He teased.

Sighing, I nodded. "I'm done."

He kissed the center of my forehead. "Anytime you like, we'll do it again," he said. "And as much as I wish we could stay here just like this, your phone rang while you were out. Don't worry, you were only out for about an hour. But given what happened, we should both check our phones."

"I'd rather throw it out the window," I muttered.

Gently, we came apart. I wasn't sore like after the heat, but my body was making sure I knew it had gone through something.

I picked up Emery's t-shirt off the floor and slipped it on. It fell to the middle of my thighs, and I couldn't ignore the heat in his gaze.

"What will I do for a shirt?" He finished buckling his jeans.

"I think I prefer you without." I winked before finding my phone in the living room where I left it. Several missed calls from my father. "Better get this over with."

I placed a finger to my lips and the phone on speaker. Emery nodded and came to sit next to me on the couch.

"Petra? Where have you been? Thank god," my dad's voice came over the speaker.

"Sorry," I said, my voice croaking. "After everything, I took a nap. Didn't mean to scare you."

"But you're all right?"

Was I? "A little shaken, but I'm okay."

Emery put his arm around my waist, and I leaned on his shoulder.

"Well, I've spoken to Mr. Atwood. They're tracking the culprit now. Looks like the school has shut down for the next couple of days as well."

My eyebrows rose into my hairline. I hadn't known that. "Oh. I didn't know. I guess they probably emailed me."

"I imagine so." He sighed heavily through the phone. "I'm very glad you're safe."

"Me too." But everything else was still fucked.

Dad's voice was a little softer now, like he wished he didn't have to say what he was. But it was still his choice. "I've had Ezra email you a copy of the file I showed you last night and the details of the meeting. It's set for Thursday."

"Dad." I huffed out a breath. "No."

A long silence stretched the air like taffy. I inhaled, focusing on Emery's scent and wishing he could purr right now. Already the tension was creeping back into my body at the thought of even considering another pack.

I was that far gone already?

Yes. Yes, I was.

"Petra." Dad sounded sterner now. "I'm sorry you had the misfortune of being born into a family where appearance matters, but it does. For you, for me, for Carmen... all of us. I know it's not the life you wanted, but it's the life you were given. We've been very lenient with you, given everything—"

"You won't even listen," I hissed. "You're being lied to."

"Which is lying to me? My wife? Or the test results that prove you're not telling the truth about the conservatory incident *or* the charity ball?"

"Test results—Dad what are you talking about? I haven't been to the doctor in months. And my test results were fucking *clear* when I was in college."

Emery turned and pulled me into his lap, giving me all the comfort he could without sound. The same panic I felt at dinner was rising. How could I make him believe me if there was evidence to the contrary?

"Why won't you believe me?" I asked, voice breaking.

When he spoke again, I heard the decision he'd made, and it wasn't in my favor. "You are a Merriton," he said. "That means something, whether you care about it or not. I know you, Petra. You will find joy. So you're going to follow the plan that's been laid out for you, and there will be no more drugs. No more acting out. No more headlines about you being out of control. You're going to go to the meeting on Thursday, and accept that ninety-four percent compatibility is the best you're ever going to get.

"Ezra will be there to make sure everything goes smoothly, since I need to go back to the capital. And once you wrap your head around your new pack, you'll go on to be one of the best lawyers Slate City has ever seen. Maybe you'll even follow in my footsteps one day."

Tears ran down my face, and Emery wiped them away gently. "I won't do it," I whispered. I wasn't sure who I was telling. My father or Emery.

"Yes, you will. Because I need you to. And someday, you'll see that I was right, and this was the best course. You're careening off course, and I'm *pulling you back* because I love you."

I wanted to throw the phone across the room and make him hear it shatter. But that would prove his point about me being out of control. There was no way to change his mind. Dad was a man who relied on facts. As a politician, he had to. Because everyone in his life was trying to spin something one way or another. And he'd been presented with facts about me I had no way to refute.

"I met them briefly," he said. "I talked to them. They're a good pack. Good Alphas and Betas. You need this as much as I do, Petra. You need to be protected. After today? I hoped you'd see that."

My throat froze, and I couldn't speak. Why had he hired bodyguards if he just wanted to sell me off to a pack? What the hell were the test results he was talking about, and where did he get them? Was there any way out of this that would still leave me with a father?

"Now stay safe and stay home while we find the person who's after you. Mr. Atwood is going to take care of you. You're going to have everything you ever wanted, Petra. I promise. A bonding ceremony fit for a queen, a pack that will take care of you and make sure you stay sober. A validating career. You're getting what most people would kill for."

Most people would kill for it, and yet it was going to kill me. Being the dutiful, silent Omega he wanted would wither me until there was nothing left. And looking around, the world was drying up because I didn't know how to stop it.

The words slipped out before I could stop them. "Do you regret Mom?"

A sharp intake of breath came across the line. Emery held me tighter, bending to press soothing kisses against my neck. He was the only reason I was holding on.

"Thursday, Petra. Be at the meeting. This is not optional."

The call died, and I stared at the phone.

Emery leaned his head against mine. "If that was anything close to what dinner was like last night, I'm so sorry."

"That was a little worse," I said honestly, feeling entirely blank. "But I don't know what to do. The test results? I have no idea. And the pack? I didn't think they wanted me, but what if the guy was just being polite? Anything I do that's not what he wants makes me look *exactly* like he's making me out to be."

"We'll figure something out," he said. "Because we're not letting you go."

I looked at him and found no lies on his face. "Not even if they make you?"

"Not even if they put a gun to my head, sunshine."

Shuddering, I leaned closer. "Yeah, let's try to avoid that, okay?"

"Sorry. Probably not the best day to make a joke like that."

"No." Outside it was getting dark. "It doesn't sound like he wants to come over here, so we can go to the penthouse now, right?"

"Yes."

I didn't want to move, but I did, standing up off his lap. "Let me grab some things."

I went back to the bedroom, which smelled overwhelmingly like the two of us. It was good no one had come over. Even putting Emery in the closet, there would have been no question.

"I chose everything in this apartment," I said when he came and stood in the doorway. "It was supposed to be this..." I didn't finish the sentence. "Now it just feels empty and sad."

"I'm sorry."

"It's not your fault."

"No? We practically dragged you out of your apartment on your first day here."

I laughed without humor as I tossed my suitcase on the part of the bed that wasn't damp from Emery making my body into a literal fountain. "That, and what we did in here, are the only good things that have happened in this place. I got told someone was trying to kill me. My stepmother attacked me, and my father just confirmed that he thinks I've been lying to him for a decade. So..." My throat went tight. "Yeah. I'd rather be in the penthouse."

Tossing in clothes and other things, Emery watched me carefully. "Petra."

My name startled me. The nicknames they used had already become more normal.

"You know we want you to stay, right?"

"It's only been a week."

"And?"

I looked up at him. "You can't know if you want to spend the rest of your life with me after a week."

"That's bullshit and you know it." His eyes blazed. "I'm fully aware that your parents are a sensitive subject right now, but they're a good example of knowing right away. I also know plenty of other examples. When *this*," he gestured between the two of us, "happens, it's not an accident. If you need time to choose us, fine. But I don't. I—"

He cut himself off and looked away. The absence of the words he almost spoke was *visceral*.

"Come home with me," he said finally. "We want you there, and we won't pressure you. I understand why we can't tell everyone else, but I want *you* to know exactly where I stand."

I didn't know what to say to that. Warmth filled my chest, and simple relief, even though it didn't solve everything in front of us.

"Now let's get what you need because Blake is losing his *mind* that he's the only one who hasn't seen you since the incident this afternoon. I checked with Harrison. It's fine to go straight up with me."

"Okay." The weight on my shoulders was lighter, and I packed faster.

CHAPTER THIRTY-ONE

BLAKE

"*Y*ou need to learn patience," I said to our new pet. She was practically climbing me, trying to get to the food I was setting out for her. "Down."

I stared at her until she relented. Alpha tendencies were good for more than one thing. Still, Stormy slithered around my legs, rubbing all over my sweats and tapping her front feet in anticipation. "We're going to need to do some training with you, huh?"

She chuffed at me, and it turned into a low growl. Like she was agreeing, but please give her the fucking food. She was *hungry*. I laughed. "Okay."

Setting down her food, she settled instantly, tucking into the bowl of raw meat happily. Emery's instinct was spot on. Of all the animals we could have chosen, this one was a little ball of light. I loved her already, and Harrison's grumpy ass did too, no matter what he said.

Crouching down, I stroked my hand along her back. "You're a good girl," I told her. "We're going to take good care of you."

Footsteps came into the kitchen, and I looked up to see Cole heading straight for the coffee. He was already dressed in a suit like he was ready to go. But I knew for a fact the Omega he was protecting was still passed out in her nest. Naked.

"Morning."

"Morning."

"Where are you headed?"

He took a travel mug from the cupboard and filled it with coffee. "I'm going to Atwood headquarters to do some more in-depth analysis on the results from yesterday. And we have some new people I need to evaluate."

I frowned. "What about Petra?"

He looked at me. "What do you mean?"

"If you're not here? I thought about taking her somewhere today."

"Oh. Sean will lead her detail. We have four people for her at all times."

I studied him. He was tense, and he hadn't slept in the nest last night. Neither had Harrison, but the latter had come to say goodnight. Petra felt Cole's absence. "What's going on, Cole?"

"Nothing."

"Yeah, okay."

He hung his head. "I'm fine. I just need some time."

"Are you having second thoughts about her?"

"*Never.*" The snarl tore through the room and had Stormy skittering backward, away from him. She crouched behind the corner of the counter, looking at him, terrified. "Fuck. I'm sorry." He bent down and held out a hand. "That wasn't at you."

Stormy came out from her hiding place and sniffed his fingers before lifting her head into his palm for pets. He smiled. The little leopard had that effect on people. Just like someone else I knew.

"No, of course not," Cole said, still focused on Stormy.

"Then why are you avoiding her?"

I caught the wince before he hid it. "I'm not."

"Cole."

"I fucked up." It was a whisper. "I got distracted, and it could have been so much worse than it was."

Turning, I grabbed two more mugs from the cupboard and began pouring coffee into them. I let the silence hang.

"I'm the one who's supposed to be protecting her, and because I was so wrapped up in *her*, I could have gotten her hurt or worse."

Cream and sugar in one of the coffees. Only cream in the other. "I'm sure Harrison has already set you straight about this, so I'm not going to give you another lecture. But you did what you had to, and she's safe. That's all that matters."

The silence was so tense I had to turn around. Cole stared at the floor. "What if she's not next time?"

"So that's why you're going to the office? To try to track the guy down faster?"

"That's one of the reasons, yeah."

I nodded. "All right. But you can't avoid her forever."

"I'm not—" he took a breath. "No. I couldn't, even if I wanted to. Which I don't. I just can't get the what-ifs out of my head. Figured maybe if I beat on some newbies, it would help."

"Can't argue with that," I chuckled. "What do you want me to tell her? Because she's going to ask."

"What I told you. It's true. I want to look at what we have of the flash bang and the photos and see if I can do anything with them, and I need to meet the new recruits." He laughed and ran a hand through his hair. "Sometimes I have to act like I'm the co-owner."

"All right. But sort it out, Cole. She has enough to worry about without thinking you're upset with her."

Fear flashed in his eyes. "Does she—"

"She hasn't said anything. But you didn't even say goodnight to her, and you're not going to see her today. So just... do what you need to do, then come home and fix it."

He sighed and headed for the door. "Yeah. I will."

"Hey," I called, stopping him before he disappeared. "It's all new. We're figuring it out. But let's figure it out together like we always do."

Cole nodded, and it was clear he still wasn't fully with me. At this point, we'd known each other for so long we didn't need all the words to communicate. It would be even easier once we were bonded.

I stopped the thought before it went too far. We were heading in that direction with Petra, and more than anything, I wanted it. I was all in. The others were too. All we needed was our little Omega to be there.

Deep down I thought she was, but she had perfectly legitimate reasons to be nervous, and a hell of a lot going on at the moment. I didn't care how long it took for her to get where she needed to be. I would happily hitch along for the ride.

Grabbing the mugs of coffee, I left Stormy to finish her breakfast and took the elevator up to the nest floor. Petra was just where I left her. Beneath her favorite blanket—a pale blue-violet, like the center of the flame that was her nest—laying like a goddess fallen to earth.

I set the coffee mugs on the low wall of the nest and snapped a picture of her, wanting to preserve the peace and beauty of the moment.

She stirred a little when I crawled closer, carefully fitting myself next to her. "Blake?"

"That's right, baby."

"Mm." She turned and snuggled against my chest, curling one arm around me. "Hi."

Fuck, this woman. I didn't need to know anything more about her to know I was falling in love with this Omega hard and fast. I didn't care that it was fast, and I didn't care that we didn't know everything about each other. I knew she was mine—I'd spend the rest of my life learning all her curves and edges. Discovering her secrets.

"I brought you some coffee if you want it."

"Where?" Her voice was still sleepy.

"Over there. I wasn't sure if you wanted food in the nest. During the heat is one thing, because we don't have that kind of time."

She blinked open her eyes and looked up at me. There was no way to resist. I kissed her, savoring the little sound of surprise she made. After yesterday, I wouldn't take any chances *not* to kiss her. We would keep her safe. I knew that. And still, not seeing her right away had driven me out of my mind.

"I don't think I want food in the nest," she said. "But coffee's okay. Tea too."

"Perfect."

She sat up while I brought our cups back. "Where did Emery go?"

"The Clinic. I think he had some early appointments to make up for the ones he canceled during the heat. Just like yesterday."

"Oh."

I handed her the cup. "And don't for a second think it's an inconvenience or that it wasn't worth it. He would cancel more if he had to, for you."

The expression on her face wasn't easy to read. Somewhere between embarrassment and sadness. I wished we were bonded so I could feel what she felt and there wouldn't be any questions.

234

Petra took a sip of the coffee and closed her eyes, humming her approval. "This is good."

"I stopped just short of adding chocolate. Wasn't sure how you felt about mocha for breakfast. Also didn't know if you'd had enough coffee and chocolate for the time being."

She blushed, and I laughed.

"It's good."

Now for the surprise. The last few days I'd been sending out orders to some of my employees, and they would be ready today. Even if they weren't, I couldn't wait to show her. "Since you don't have school, I wondered if you wanted to come with me."

"Oh my god, I don't have school today." Her eyes lit up. "Where are we going?"

"My test kitchen," I said. "The rest of it is a surprise once we get there."

"I'm allowed to go?"

I frowned, shifting my mug to my other hand so I could take hers. "You're not a prisoner, baby."

"Yeah, I just wasn't sure how the security would work now."

Weaving our fingers together, I lifted her hand and kissed the back of it. "You have a team of four today, and I make sure all my facilities and restaurants have top-notch security."

That made her smile. "Okay. Are we cooking?"

"It's a surprise."

She looked at me, eyes narrowed, but she couldn't keep the smile off her face. "When do we leave?"

"Whenever you're ready."

In my life, I'd never seen anyone down an entire cup of coffee that quickly. And she was holding the blanket to her body as she ran through the bathroom and into the room where she left her suitcase.

If we were moving in this direction, we needed to start getting her furniture for the suite. I loved the nest, and Petra did, too. But sometimes you wanted to sleep in bed, and there wasn't anything wrong with that.

I grabbed Petra's mug from where she left it and went to change my clothes. She was in for the surprise of her life, and about to find out that I kept my promises.

Four men stood in our foyer. Sean and Richard I knew well, given they often staffed the building. The others, Casey and John, I didn't, but if both Harrison and Cole put them on Petra's detail, they were trustworthy.

"Thanks for doing this," I said quietly.

"Oh," Petra's voice came from the stairs. She was dressed casually, jeans and what looked like an incredibly soft shirt sliding off one shoulder. And suddenly my dick was standing up and waving for attention. But he thankfully stood down when I saw exactly what I'd predicted to Cole. Petra searched the faces of her team and didn't find her Alpha. "Where's Cole?"

"He went to the Atwood offices to help with training some new employees, and he also said he wants to look more closely at the remains of the explosive from yesterday."

She bit her lip, looking at the four men again. "But it's okay to leave?"

"It's fine, baby. They picked these guys."

She shook her head a little, like she was clearing it or beating herself up for questioning. "Right. Let's go."

If Cole didn't get his head on straight by tomorrow, I was going to kick his ass.

Petra was quiet in the elevator and even in the car. I kept her hand in mine, never letting her more than a foot away from me. Not only because I wanted her close in case anything happened, but I wanted her to know I was here.

The test kitchen was a little way from downtown, in a more industrial neighborhood where the space you could find was more customizable. On the outside, the warehouse looked completely blank. On the inside were multiple kitchens where staff from all my restaurants learned how to prepare the dishes, my chefs could experiment with dishes to pitch to me, I could play, and also instruct them to come up with things.

In this case, my dessert and pastry chefs had been busy.

"I'm not sure what I expected it to look like," Petra said, peering out the car window. "But not this."

"Wait till you see inside."

We moved quickly, three men flanking us into the building while one stayed with the car. "Through here." I brought her down to my personal kitchen, where, just like I'd instructed, everything was ready.

"Okay, this seems more like it."

The kitchen itself was a work of art. All pale gray walls and stainless steel appliances. It was a chef's wet dream. I knew, because when I'd finally seen the thing in person, I might have come in my pants.

Not that I would be saying that out loud anytime soon.

And set up on one of the long, silver work tables was everything I'd asked my chefs to prepare. The first round of new desserts for my most experimental restaurant, Bitter After Dark.

All under sterling, so Petra couldn't see what they were.

"What are those?"

"Are you guys okay to wait outside this door?" I asked her detail.

After checking the kitchen, they were. And I closed the door firmly behind them. "Okay, go ahead."

"What am I doing?"

"Take a look."

She went over to the first platter and pulled off the top. Beneath it was a bowl of ice cream. Perfect. Petra looked at it suspiciously, and I grabbed a spoon. She glanced at me. "It looks like vanilla ice cream."

"It's not. Promise."

I watched her take a hesitant bite, and she gasped. "You did not."

"I absolutely did." The ice cream she was currently tasting was honey and cinnamon. All the desserts on the table were. Based on *her*. "I told you I was going to."

"It was the *heat*. I thought you were just saying that to get me off."

I laughed. "I was. But I also thought it sounded like an excellent idea." Grabbing another spoon, I also grabbed a notepad. It was incredible. But the sweetness was just a touch too much. That could happen with honey. Once they pulled it back just a touch? It would be perfect.

"Oh my god." Petra pulled the cover off the next dish. A crème brûlée. She tried it and made a face. "Honestly, crème brûlée has never been a favorite of mine, and I'm not sure I love that."

She wasn't wrong. The flavors didn't match the texture of the dessert. "You're right. We'll cancel that one. I'll think of something else to fill the spot. But I think you'll like the next one."

Honey cake with cinnamon frosting. Petra's eyes rolled back in her head. "I should feel weird about eating something that's based on the flavor of my pussy, but this is way too good to care."

"Not *just* your pussy," I said, placing my hand on my chest, dramatically playing up my pretend offense. "Your gorgeous scent, too."

She smirked and stole another bite of the cake. "That's my favorite so far."

"Noted."

We worked our way down the length of the table, tasting everything. A milkshake, again a touch too sweet. A cannoli, which needed to be switched. Cinnamon filling with honey drizzle was the right call there.

Petra watched me make my notes. "You just *know* how things need to be better. That's crazy to me. My one trick is the cookies I baked. I'm terrible at everything else."

"I highly doubt that."

"It's true." She hopped up and sat on the work table, and I brought her samples of the last two deserts. Honey cinnamon hard candy, and a honey doughnut with cinnamon cream filling. "How did you get to be here? This is... it's so much. And you're incredible at it."

Filling clung to the edge of her mouth, and I pulled her in to catch it before I kissed her. Fuck, she was so sweet. She tasted better than *all* the desserts combined. "My Dad," I said. "He's a male Omega. And he always loved cooking. Baking. I spent a lot of time with him in the kitchen as a kid, and I just fell in love with it. There's never been a time when I didn't want to be a chef. I went after it with everything I had."

"You know the saying never trust a skinny chef?"

"I'm not skinny, baby. I'm all muscle."

She laughed. "Exactly. You don't look like you've eaten sugar a day in your life."

I winked. "I'm lucky. And I wish my story was more interesting. But really, I just fucking love food. After culinary school, I took out a loan to start my first restaurant, and I got lucky again. Plenty of restaurants go under."

"Not with the kind of food you make."

"I appreciate that, baby. Now you have to tell me what your favorite is."

Petra shook her head. "No way I can choose a favorite from things based on me."

My grin was so wide it hurt. I stepped between her legs, and Petra wrapped her arms around my neck. "Is it okay that I did it? Is it too weird?"

"It is weird," she said quietly. "But it's also amazing. No one's ever done anything like this for me, Blake. It probably seems like my life should have been perfect. Living in a mansion, with famous parents, never wanting for anything. But—"

"But not everything is what it seems," I finished for her. There was a difference between having everything and only having things. Life was so much more than possessions and situations. Yes, those things helped. I was so grateful Petra hadn't wanted for anything material. But she'd been starved of other things, and I wanted to give them all to her.

"Yeah," she said. "It's not always as shiny and perfect as it looks from the outside."

"I get that. Which is why I'm going to keep doing things to make your life—our life—exactly as amazing as it should be."

Petra slumped over and rested her head on my shoulder. "When are you guys going to stop being perfect?"

"Baby," I snorted. "I am far from perfect. None of us are perfect. Harrison can be a grumpy bastard, I'm a perfectionist,

Cole avoids things that make him uncomfortable or anxious, and Emery reacts before thinking sometimes. Just a few of our many flaws. If we have our way, you'll see all of them. But like my dad always says, your flaws are boulders in a river. It's up to you whether you let them sink your boat."

"Your dad sounds like a smart man."

"He is." I tightened my arms around her, pulling our bodies as close as they could be like this. "And he'll love you."

"I want to meet him. And your other family."

"Absolutely," I whispered. "My biological mother is an Alpha, my other mom is a Beta, and I have another dad who's also an Alpha. They live closer to the capital, actually, in a little town called Vellara Hills."

"When can we—"

"And now," I slipped my hand behind her neck and interrupted her. "We're going to stop talking about my family. Because I need to come up with a dessert to replace the crème brûlée. And to do that, I need to sample the flavors from the source."

"Blake."

"Petra."

She stared at me with her mouth open before bursting out laughing. "This is a *kitchen*."

I shrugged. "It's my kitchen."

"But aren't there like... sanitary rules about stuff like that?"

"I'll tell them to burn it," I said. "Clean every surface with fire. I don't care. But my tongue is about to be inside you."

"I—"

The look I gave her stopped her short, and I grinned, pulling her shirt up over her head and tossing it on the floor. "You never told me your favorite."

"They're all too good. I can't choose."

I stripped her bra off. It joined her shirt on the floor. Even though she was protesting, Petra helped me get her pants off by lifting her hips. "Let me put it this way, baby. I love food. I *love* food. I'm going to compare all these desserts to the taste of your cunt. So choose a favorite, because that's the one I'm going to lick off you first."

Petra looked along the table and considered. Very seriously considered. "It's a tie between the cake and the cannoli."

"Good to know."

Suddenly she grinned, laying back on the table, back arched, legs open. "Am *I* still your favorite?"

"Fuck yes you are." I dove face first into her pussy and *consumed* her.

CHAPTER THIRTY-TWO

PETRA

*B*lake was a man dying of thirst in the desert and my body was the first water he'd seen in a week. His fingers dug into my thighs, pushing them wider even as he pulled me closer to ravage me with his tongue.

And *god*, what a tongue it was.

"Fuck," he breathed out the word against my clit. "Nothing tastes as good as you do, baby. Not a thing in the goddamn world."

He dragged the flat of his tongue up and over my clit, lazily tasting me. "Just keep me between your legs forever," he whispered. "I'll live off you for the rest of my life."

For half a second I forgot the kind of mouth Blake had. Now I remembered, and my body flamed with enough heat to melt every dessert on the table.

Suddenly he was up and moving, grabbing the cake and swiping his fingers through the frosting, coming around the table to where my head lay. One finger dragged across my throat, leaving sugar behind for him to lick away.

Slowly. Deliberately.

"These desserts are great," he said, putting a dab of the frosting on my lips for me to taste before painting my nipples with it and sucking them clean.

"Fuck, Blake."

"Don't worry, baby. That's up next. But I was saying these desserts are great, and I still think you've ruined sugar for me. In the best way. You will always be my favorite treat." He drew a line down to my belly button with the last of the frosting on his fingers and leaned over the table to kiss it away. Every touch had me sinking deeper into this dance with him.

"Do I get to eat anything off you?" My voice was lower than it normally sounded.

"Anything you want. Hell, baby, I'll make you a lollipop

shaped like my cock if you want it. Watching you lick that?" He moaned. "I can't even think about it."

"Or I could just lick the real thing." I slid off the table before he could catch me, sinking to my knees in front of him and undoing his belt. His cock was so hard it strained through his underwear. Not bothering to take him out fully, I licked him through the fabric, making him hiss.

"God, Petra."

"Make me the lollipop." I pulled down his underwear. "I want it to taste like you." One brush of my tongue underneath his head. "And the same size."

His hand curled into my hair, not moving, just holding on. I sank down onto his shaft, savoring the sharp citrus flavor of him that was strong today. If all champagne tasted the way he did? I would fucking love it.

"Then," I caught my breath and looked up, locking eyes with Blake while I drew my tongue down the length of him. "You can fuck my throat with your candy cock and fuck *me* with your real one."

He swore, eyes closing, leaning back against the table. I didn't think this was what he had in mind when he stripped me down, but that was the fun. They could surprise me, but I could surprise them too. Wrapping my hands around the back of his legs, I pulled myself onto his cock.

All the way.

Until the metal of his zipper brushed under my chin and I could nearly reach his balls with my tongue. They were all my favorite treats. That was the truth.

Blake's voice was ragged. "This wasn't what I had planned."

I hummed, pulling back and releasing him. "Too bad."

His eyes were wild, and he let his head fall back. His fingers jerked in my hair, like he was itching to sink his hands the rest of the way in and take control, and he was resisting. There weren't even any dirty words.

"Cat got your tongue?" I licked up underneath him, kissing the head of his cock gently, teasing.

"Omega's got my cock," he growled.

"I do." My grin made it hard to do what I wanted, which

was to drive him fucking crazy. Until he couldn't hold back anymore. I wanted his control to snap. "But the last time I had it, Emery was controlling it. I want to know what *you* like, Alpha."

Blake's head snapped back up from where he'd let it fall. Eyes blazing with lust and power. The Alpha energy made me wet. It dripped down my thighs and we both fucking knew it.

He moved his hand, slipping his thumb into my mouth. I closed my lips around it and sucked instinctually. "What I like?" He asked softly. "Baby, I don't think there's anything you could do I wouldn't like." Before I could open my mouth to say anything, he kept going. "But, if you want me to tell you..."

"I don't want you to tell me. I want you to *instruct* me."

His whole body stiffened, including his cock, twitching with need. "Wrap those pretty lips around my cock, baby. But just the head."

I did as he asked, sealing my mouth around him at the same time I let my fingers slip between my legs. I couldn't remember the last time I got myself off with nothing but my fingers, but I was so turned on it didn't matter. One stroke of my fingers and I was gasping around Blake's hard length.

"Use your tongue," he said, fingers tightening in my hair. "Swirl it around. Tease me. Suck as hard as you want to. It's never too hard. *Fuck*, baby." He moaned as I followed his instructions.

His hips moved in time with my suction, thrusting shallowly into the movements of my tongue. Already I could taste the deep flavor of him, the appetizer to the main meal. Orange. A little lime. Grapefruit. The *good* flavor of champagne.

"Take me deeper," he said. "But never stop sucking. I want your cheeks to be fucking hollowed out. Oh my *god*. Don't you dare take my cock out of your mouth, Omega. Your lips don't leave my skin until I come."

He didn't ask me if I understood—the command was laced through the words. "Up and down. Fuck me with your mouth."

I pulled back, obeying, and dove back onto him. Nearly all the way. Blake's fingers stopped me. "Not in your throat. Not this time. This is as far as I want you to go. Don't stop."

The strangled sound of his instructions lit me on fire. I

couldn't even touch myself, unable to focus on both at once. All I wanted was him. And whatever came after.

"That's it." He helped guide my rhythm up and down, eyes closed, his free hand gripping the edge of the worktable so hard his knuckles turned white. "That's so fucking good, baby. Oh my —Fuck. I'm so close. Squeeze my balls."

Cupping them in one hand, I squeezed gently, drawing a shudder and a moan from Blake. I loved hearing him. I loved giving him exactly what he needed. I loved feeling so fucking powerful. Blake's body might be standing, but he was the one truly on his knees. Because I put him there.

"Don't stop," he said. "I'm going to come in that sinful mouth of yours. All over your tongue. And you're not going to stop sucking my cock until you've drained it dry. Not even then. Not until I tell you to."

I dragged my lips up his shaft, flicking him with my tongue, and watched him fall apart. "Holy fucking—"

Heat flooded my mouth. The rich taste of him. I sucked his shaft like a good Omega, swallowing everything he gave me and fucking reveling in it. Maybe I was out of my mind, but I wasn't going to apologize for it. I understood Blake's obsession with me, because I craved them just as much. Give me a cushion for my knees and I would stay here as long as any of them would let me, basking in the incredible gift of each other.

So much more than scent-sympathy. It was... everything.

Looking up at Blake, I sucked, just like he wanted me to, even after there was no more cum. The way his chest moved, heaving up and down, told me all I needed to know. "If heaven doesn't feel like your mouth, I'm not fucking interested."

I wrapped my hand around his swollen knot, feeling the stiff heat, and Blake growled. The kind of growl that had arousal rushing down my legs in response.

He pulled me off my knees and switched us, pressing me against the table. Cold metal met my back. Except where his cock jutted away from his body, he was still fully clothed, and I had nothing on me. Why the fuck did I love that? It didn't matter, but I did.

Blake lifted one leg. "How flexible is my Omega?"

"Not as flexible as I should be."

His mouth slammed against mine, Alpha dominance and power cascading into me. What was left of my awareness faded in the face of desire. "I'll be the judge of that. You want this knot, don't you? Even though it's already swollen."

A whine worked its way out of me. I desperately wanted him inside me, but—

He tossed one leg over his elbow and fit his cock against me, thrusting up until his knot pushed against me, huge, hot, and taunting. "How badly, Petra?"

"Please." My pussy squeezed down on him, feeling empty in spite of the size of what was already inside me. "Please, I need it."

Blake thrust up at the same time he pulled my body down, the knot slamming into me and locking. An Omega could take a knot even if it was already swollen, but once it was in, there was no way to get it out until it eased. Blake's knot pressed against all the delicious places inside me, priming me.

Now wherever my skin was touched felt like pure pleasure. Where the metal of the table dug into my back, I wanted to press harder. The back of my knee where he held my leg.

"It's unfortunate I can't knot you and tongue fuck you at the same time," Blake said, winking. "But I'm still going to taste you."

The heel of his hand met my clit—

White hot inferno burst through my body, every bit of built up arousal expanding outward and holding me at the center of the storm. "*Blake*." I called his name, and he kissed me, wrapping me up in his arms and keeping me together while the orgasm broke me apart. I came on his cock, gripping his knot, sinking into his kiss like I was falling and he was gravity.

"Mm." He dragged his fingers around my clit and down near my entrance and lifted them to his mouth. "I'm thinking baklava to replace the crème brûlée. Or maybe cinnamon swirl bread with honey butter. Maybe both."

I started laughing, my chest and soul feeling far lighter than they had earlier this morning. "What are you going to say when you launch these? You can't say 'this is what my Omega tastes like.'"

"Why not?"

Gripping his shoulders, I looked him straight in the eye. Our noses brushed. "Please don't do that. This is amazing, and they're too delicious not to serve. But please don't actually tell the world they're based on me." My cheeks felt hot, the sweat from the sex cooled on my skin.

Blake curled my lifted leg around his hip. There was no teasing in his face. "To be clear, I have no problem admitting to the inspiration. But I would never embarrass you, Petra. I was actually thinking of adding it as a dessert rotation at Bitter After Dark called 'Nights of Sweetness and Spice.'"

My fear eased. "That sounds really nice."

"I'll take you when it's ready."

Blake lifted me off the ground and carried me to the corner where there was a chair, and we could rest until his knot eased. "I will say one thing. If I were going to say anything about the inspiration, I would one-hundred percent say it was inspired *by* my Omega. But not specifically how."

"Emery said something like that. It's hard for me to believe."

"Why?"

I couldn't answer that. It wasn't like I felt unworthy or that I didn't deserve them. I wanted them more than I could make myself say out loud. But there was still an undercurrent of fear which made me tense up when I thought about forever.

But the real question was if the fear was because of them, or because of me and everything I'd already been through.

"I don't know."

Blake took my face in his hands. "It's okay," he said. "And it's still okay to be scared. Something this big *is* scary. That said, I want you to know where I stand. You are my Omega, Petra DeWitt-Merriton. There is no question in my mind. I don't need more time, because the very core of who I am already knows you belong to me, and I belong to you."

My breath caught in my throat, and I waited for him to offer a caveat. But he didn't.

"I'm falling for you, baby." He pulled my face closer and kissed me softly. Every aching word was reflected in this kiss. It hit me in the chest and left me with no doubt.

Breaking the kiss, I tucked my face into his shoulder. It was easier to say without him seeing me. Seeing me was too vulnerable, even though he was currently inside me. "I want to stay with you. But they might not let me. They're trying to take me away."

"We won't let it happen." He made it sound so simple.

I wanted to believe him. I did. But at the same time, I know how determined Carmen and my father were. Really Carmen. If Dad knew the truth...

I had to make him believe me. I needed proof. Somehow.

Blake held me until his knot eased, and then he helped me dress. "Is this room soundproof?"

He chuckled. "No. Sorry, baby."

I pressed my lips together. They were bodyguards. I was sure it wasn't the first time they'd heard a client having sex. In fact, one of the ones on today's team was outside my door last night. There was no way he hadn't heard my time with Emery.

Blake grabbed the pad he'd scribbled notes on. "Just a few changes, but I think this will go over well."

"You made the recipes, right?" I asked. "It's incredible. I know you've been doing it a long time, but you're really talented, Blake."

"Thank you." He searched my face. "Can I ask you something?"

"If you're going to ask for another taste, I want to go home first."

Chuckling, he shook his head. "No, not that. You just reminded me of something." It seemed like he had difficulty finding the words, and nerves jangled in my gut. "Cole mentioned where he found you. Before the flashbang."

My stomach plummeted. "Did he?"

"You didn't want to talk about school. Is that why? Because he said you were incredible."

"It was a moment of weakness," I said. "With everything happening, I've been thinking about Mom. But I don't imagine we'll be going through that building again anytime soon. So no more pianos for me."

"But—"

I shook my head. "I can't, Blake. I'm sure I'll tell you, but I can't right now."

Blake searched me from head to toe and back. Finally, he held out a hand. "Okay. Let's go."

He didn't push, just kissed the back of my hand when he took it. And if I hadn't already been falling in love with him, too, that would have pushed me over the edge.

Too late.

Even if I couldn't say it out loud, I'd stepped off that cliff the second I went into that closet. No turning back now.

CHAPTER THIRTY-THREE

PETRA

When I woke up in the morning, Harrison's arm was around my hips, his naked body pressed to my back. He was so big his chin fit over my head. When I'd gone to bed, he hadn't been in the nest. Now the scent of whiskey, cedar and the light, shivery notes of frost infused the air around me.

I stretched, and his arm tightened. A kiss brushed my ear. "Good morning, little one."

"When did you get here?"

"Late."

Turning over, I burrowed into him. "Missed you."

Yesterday he'd been gone at the Atwood Security office, just like Cole. Then locked in his office until we'd gone to bed. "I missed you too. And I request a nest rule."

"Oh?"

A rumbling purr started beneath my ear. "No clothes."

I had a large t-shirt on with a set of underwear, but nothing else. "Ever?"

"We have regular beds for clothes," he noted. "Here I want to be able to feel your skin."

"Why didn't you undress me?"

Harrison kissed the top of my head. "You weren't awake for me to ask, and you were sleeping so deeply, I didn't want to bother you."

I wouldn't have minded if he had, but I loved that he didn't and wanted my permission. I loved... all of them. Just like Blake said, I was falling in love with these men, and I had no desire to turn back. "What would you have done if I were naked?"

A soft laugh rose behind me, and suddenly another warm body pressed against my back. "I bet I can guess," Emery said. "Because Harrison and I are a lot alike."

My breath went short. I knew now, but I wanted to hear him say it. I looked up at him, and Harrison smirked, eyes alive with

251

mischief. A hand crept between my legs, touching me through the fabric of my panties. "I would have slid my cock inside you and kept you close. Then, when we woke, and I was already hard because of the morning, I would have fucked you slowly, teasing you until you came quietly. Nobody else even would have known."

"Wow." I swallowed. "I've never... slept with someone inside me. Except for the quick nap with Emery."

The Alpha in question kissed my neck, inhaling deeply. "Our cocks get cold," he sounded like he was teasing, but I didn't think he was. "We need to keep them warm somehow."

A shiver worked its way through me. "Two of you like that. Is that all?"

"Nope," Blake called from where he was, out of sight. "Definitely not just them."

"What about Cole?" There wasn't any answer, and my heart fell. "He didn't sleep here again?"

"Honestly, I'm not sure he slept much at all," Harrison said. "Your stalker sent a message after the flash bang, and yesterday we were working to track it down. We got closer, but he's clever."

"What did it say?"

"It doesn't matter."

"The hell it doesn't." I sat up between them. "Tell me."

Harrison didn't want to. It was crystal clear on his face. But he nodded. "All right, but I need you to come back here." I stared at him until he blew out a breath. "Petra, I can't tell you what it said unless you're in my arms and my instincts understand you're safe. Please."

Was it really that bad?

I laid down again, curling against him, Emery behind me. Harrison's hand drifted down my side, finding the hem of my shirt and pushing up beneath it so he could feel my skin. "It was sent to the campaign. This person—we assume it's a man—has a vehement hatred of your father. Because of that, he's fixated on you. He keeps referring to you as various things. Single. Unbonded. Pure. Beautiful. Defenseless. Ripe for the taking. I'll spare you the manifesto. It's delusional at best."

Something clicked into place. "I'm guessing whoever they are is leaning heavily into the single, unbonded, and defenseless?"

"Yes. How did you know?"

"Because it's one of the reasons my father is pushing me towards the Gidwitz pack. He thinks if I'm bonded to them, with their bullshit compatibility, I'll be safe."

"And I've informed the Senator that nothing but catching the man will keep you safe. But that's the last thing I plan on telling him until we do catch him. I've stopped taking payment from him." I looked up, startled, and he tightened his hold on me. "We don't need money to protect you, Petra. And if I'm taking his money, I have to report to him. Given everything between the two of you, and everything between us, I don't want to do that. You're my priority, little one."

I pulled myself up his body and kissed him. "Thank you."

"The message detailed what he wants to do. Which is take you, have his way with you, and for each day your father doesn't resign and make a public statement announcing his retirement from politics, he will..." Harrison cleared his throat. "Send pieces of you. But he intends on keeping you alive."

I blinked, staring straight into Harrison's chest. "Well. That's fun."

Emery burst out with a laugh, burying the sound in the back of my shirt. "I'm sorry. It's not funny. I just didn't expect you to say that."

I smiled, but Harrison could see it wasn't real. It wasn't every day you got told someone wanted to systematically dismember you. Just like everything else, it didn't seem real. Because being killed wasn't a problem people dealt with every day. And why me? Why not Carmen? Pretty sure my dad liked her more than me right now, anyway.

"Are you all right?" Harrison asked.

"Is it bad if I say I don't know? I don't even know how to process that."

He yanked me hard against his chest, purring fiercely. "I don't know how either. All I know is I want to keep you in this nest forever."

That didn't sound like a bad option. "I'm supposed to meet Sloane and Eva today. Is it safe?"

"Cole will have the team around you, and he said he gave the owners of Nautilus a heads up. You'll go in the back. But other than that, and the meeting on Thursday, we'll be very careful with where you go."

Taking a breath, I tried to sound neutral. "Where is Cole?" I hadn't seen him since he left me with Emery in my apartment.

"Probably in the gym," Emery said. "You should go see him."

"It doesn't seem like he wants to see me."

Blake appeared at my feet. "He does, baby. I promise. He's just in his own head about a couple of things."

I looked back at Harrison. "I'll agree to no underwear in the nest, but I want comfort clothes sometimes. So I don't want a *complete* no clothes rule. But also, for the record, you have my permission to undress me when I'm asleep. Or to wake me up."

"I look forward to all of those things," he said with a grin.

Sitting up, I looked at Blake. "Anything I should say to Cole?"

He smiled wickedly. "Tell him that I'm going to take matters into my own hands if he doesn't get his head out of his ass."

I blinked. "Okay then."

They all laughed, and I picked my way through the pillows and blankets to the edge of the nest. "Where's Stormy?"

"In my office," Emery said. "Thought it might be good for her to have a couple nights to get used to things before she had free rein all day and night. She's got water and a litter box in there."

"Oh. Well, don't keep her locked up on my account."

Emery stood and stretched. "I'm sure she'll be sleeping in here in no time."

I didn't bother to put on any more clothes, creeping down the stairs to the second floor. Music blared from the gym. I heard it now, but the soundproofing was great. Even on the third floor, there was no sign of the sound.

I peeked through the door and froze. Cole wore no shirt and low slung joggers which looked like they could slip off at a moment's notice. I caught him in the middle of jumping up before going to the floor and stretching out to a plank and repeating the motion over and over.

He leapt up, still not seeing me, and jumped for a long, straight bar above his head. My jaw dropped as he swung fully over the bar and made it look *easy*. He released, spinning twice in the air before catching the bar and swinging over it again. There now was no doubt in my mind he was a gymnast. Especially when he released the bar, did a backflip, and caught the bar like his hands were magnetized.

It was then, in his next whirling release, that he saw me standing in the door and dropped from the bar to the floor. His bare chest glistened with sweat, and as I crossed the room toward him, there was nothing but the rich scent of caramel and salt. I could drown in it.

Cole turned down the music to a manageable level and looked. Guilt swam in his eyes. I twisted my hands in the fabric of the big t-shirt, feeling suddenly awkward. They said I didn't have anything to worry about, and I believed them. But there was still tension in the space between Cole and I. "Hi."

"Hey," he said, taking a step forward and stopping.

I whined, my heart breaking a little at his hesitation. "I—" I cleared my throat. "I haven't seen you. Did I do something?"

Panic entered his gaze, and he crossed the rest of the distance between us, hauling me up into his arms and pressing me into the wall. My legs curled around his hips, and I couldn't even hear the music over the purr meant to soothe me. "Fuck, Petra, no. You didn't do anything, honeybee. I'm sorry." He kissed my forehead. "Blake warned me you would think that, and I should have listened."

"You didn't sleep in the nest." I hated how small my voice sounded. "Which is fine. I would never force you or anything. I just don't know why."

"Because I've spent the last day and a half dealing with my guilt. And every time I looked at you, all I saw was how badly I fucked up and how much worse it could have been."

I frowned. "Cole, what are you talking about?"

The way his body pinned me against the wall, his hands were free, and he sank them into my hair, tilting my face to kiss me that much deeper. "He never should have been able to get that close," Cole whispered. "We should have seen him coming from a mile away. You shouldn't have even known there was someone there, let alone almost be hurt by something like that.

"And Harrison might disagree, but I'm not sure if I can be your bodyguard if that's going to happen. You need to be guarded by someone who *will* see monsters coming, not watching you, scenting you, wishing you were underneath them and coming on their knot."

I sucked in a breath, but didn't speak yet. It didn't feel like he was finished.

"You were so fucking beautiful," he murmured. "The way you played. You were all I could see. And I fucking *love* you, Petra. I love you so goddamn much and you could have been hurt —could have been taken—because I didn't pay close enough attention."

Staring up at him, his eyes were so close. The gray in them like storm clouds gathering. The guilt poured off him in waves. I felt it even beneath the purr, in the way he pressed me harder into the wall and the way his fingers gripped wherever he touched me.

I waited for the protests to come from my mind. That it was too soon and too fast for any one of us to say we were in love, but they didn't come. Yesterday, after Blake told me, the truth hit me. I'd already known I was falling for them, and I was refusing to admit it.

All I felt was warmth and emotion. *Joy.*

Cole telling me he loved me felt like a key slipping into a lock only he could open. It was *right*. Not too soon, because how could anything like what the five of us felt be put on a timeline?

Was I scared? Yes. Fuck yes. Terror swam beneath my skin, ready to spawn monsters and drag me down. But if I let that fear win, I would have nothing. And it would be me *choosing* to have nothing because I'd already fallen so far I didn't know if I could ever go back. "You love me," I whispered.

"Yes."

"I love you," I said. "And it terrifies me. But I do. You didn't fail, Cole. You protected me."

"It could have—"

"It *didn't*." I grabbed his face and made him look at me. "It could have, but it didn't. You realized in time. You protected me. You brought me home and made sure I was safe. Please don't beat yourself up over a hypothetical situation."

He kissed me, desperation leaking through. "I know. I know. But you are everything, Petra. And when I close my eyes, I see his words and I see the fucking blackened, burned remnants of that homemade flash bang, and it makes me so fucking angry I can't breathe. He'll never touch you."

I ran a hand through his hair. "Harrison told me what the threat said. Are you any closer to finding him?"

"Yes. The police have some leads. He wasn't as careful this time with the threats. They think they'll have him soon."

"Good. Then I'll try not to worry, and you should come back to being my guard. I don't like being away from you."

Cole grinned. "Because you love me?"

I flushed pink. "You said it first."

"I did." This kiss was softer. Gentle and teasing. Asking forgiveness without the words. "I'm sorry I stayed away."

"Don't do it again without talking to me."

"I won't. But," he raised an eyebrow. "Fair is fair in that department. You have some things to share."

A different kind of dread pushed down on my chest. "So do you, Mr. Gymnast."

He shook his head. "I honestly wasn't very good."

"What I saw when I walked in here says otherwise."

Setting me on my own two feet, Cole went back to the bar and hung from it, all his lean muscles on display. I was covered in his scent now, like he was holding me without touching me.

"I loved it, and I competed. But there's only so far you can go, and I wasn't good enough to be in the best of the top tier. I wanted a career doing something active after I retired, and I took a job as a security guard just to pay the bills. But I got assigned as a bodyguard pretty quickly, and I found that I loved it. The analytical side of it—figuring out where people need to be and where the most danger is—it's almost like planning a routine.

"I like fitting all the puzzle pieces together, and I like knowing whoever I'm protecting feels better knowing our team has their back."

"I do feel better." I held on to the pole that supported his bar. "Was that how you met Harrison?"

He swung back and forth lazily. "In a roundabout way, yes. He worked for another company at the time, and our firms worked together on a big event. It was... a disaster. No one was hurt or anything like that, but what was clear was no one really knew what they were doing as far as organization. Harrison and I hit it off immediately, and we both quit our firms the next day. Harrison's family is richer than god, so it wasn't a problem."

He spun over the top of the bar, stalling on the top with his foot before changing direction and doing another complete circle. Show off. Then again, I was greatly enjoying the show.

I watched him drop back down to the floor again. "Why hadn't he already started one?"

"Even he doesn't know. We like to think something made him wait until we met. But he hadn't. I need to shower before we go to Nautilus."

"I do too, since you got your sweat all over me." I put my hands on my hips, daring him to do it again.

"Well," he took a step toward me, a silly grin. "We *could* shower together. Since you love me and all."

Tapping my chin with my finger, I made a big show of thinking it over. "Well, since you love *me*... you'll have to catch me first." I sprint out of the room and toward the stairs, Cole's footsteps thundering behind me.

CHAPTER THIRTY-FOUR

PETRA

"I think I should have been less worried about this trip," I said, looking out the windows of the car. The outside of the tattoo shop was *swarmed* with photographers because Eva was inside. But because she was inside, her security was everywhere, and she had a whole hell of a lot more of it than I did.

The car turned down an alley by the building and pulled into a tiny back lot, miraculously clear of people. "The owners have made it clear that if anyone unauthorized is ever caught back here, they'll be dealt with in the harshest of ways," Cole said, laughing. "Which is good for us."

He held my hand on the seat between us, and I squeezed. There were two other Alphas with us, so I couldn't turn and straddle his lap and continue the very *very* thorough make-out session we had in the shower. But Cole stroked his thumb over the back of my hand, and I knew his thoughts matched mine.

The others got out of the car first, making sure it was clear, and Cole reached for my hand. We didn't make it very far before Sloane slammed through the back door and tackled me. "You're *here*. God, I'm absolutely going to kill you for being in danger."

Cole guided us inside, and I smiled at her. "You know that kind of defeats the purpose, right?"

"I'm aware."

We stood in what seemed to be a very comfortable office space. A couple of comfortable couches, some drafting tables, and a kitchenette. "This is Bennet Gray," Sloane said, gesturing to the man standing by the door. He was tall and handsome, t-shirt showing off arms covered in tattoos. "He's one of the owners, and one of Esme's Alphas."

Bennett came forward and shook my hand. "Call me Ben. It's nice to meet you. Eva says great things about you, and Esme is very excited to meet you."

259

"I'm excited to meet her," I said honestly. To meet *two* Omegas who'd gone through this process? This was a gold mine.

Cole extended a hand and Ben shook it. "How's Emery?"

"You know Emery?" The words blurted out of me before I could stop them.

"I do. Got a few of my pieces in that tangle of work he's got all over him."

Sloane grabbed my hand. "Come on. Eva's almost done with her session, and she's going to want massive girl time to make up for the pain."

I glanced back at Cole. Even in this place which was already safe, I didn't want to take any chances. But he smiled and nodded. Sloane pulled me away, and I heard him talk to Ben. "Thanks for keeping security so tight."

Ben laughed. "Believe me. We're no strangers to keeping the press and everyone else out if we need to."

That was all I heard before Sloane pulled me into the main shop. A few people were getting tattoos.

A giant of a man with a beard was inking some kind of script on a man's calf, a blonde worked on a woman's shoulder, inking a thick black line which looked like it would hurt like hell. Eva's security lined the windows, and I saw a couple of her Alphas lounging on seats in the waiting area.

"Back here," Sloane said, knocking quickly and listening for the okay.

"That camera better be off," Eva said, and I heard a man's laugh. "Yeah, we have what we need for this session."

"Okay." Her voice sounded weaker now. "See you next time."

Sloane and I pushed ourselves against the wall as a man with a giant camera and someone with a clipboard slipped out of the room past us. "Seems like it's a busy day," I said.

Eva's head whipped around from where she was lying chest down on an angled chair, a burly redhead inking her back. "Bee!"

"Hey."

"I would get up and hug you, but, you know, tattooing."

I smirked. "I'll hug you later, and you'll regret it."

"Bet your ass I will. Because, unlike *someone*, I can't get fucked into oblivion while I'm getting tattooed."

A piece of popcorn flew at Eva, and I suddenly saw who must be Esme sitting on the other side of her, lounging in a chair. "Don't hate because you're jealous, Va-va. I'm sure they would if they could."

"Yes," Jack, Eva's Alpha said. "Absolutely."

"When you get your own tattoo studio, feel free," the redhead chuckled. He put the needles to her skin again and Eva winced.

"Petra, this is my sister Esme. And the meanie torturing me is her Alpha Avery."

Avery lifted his head and smiled. "Nice to meet you."

"Hi." I looked over at Esme. "We might have met a long time ago."

She laughed. "Probably. But at the same time, I rarely went to anything Eva went to, so maybe not."

"I'm almost done here," Avery said. "Baby girl, why don't you take your guests into the office and Eva will be in shortly."

"And no one else," Sloane said. "There are things we will be discussing not for Alpha ears."

Both Avery and Jack laughed. Esme stood, and Avery caught her by the hips before she could make it past him. "Come here." He tugged her down and kissed her. And not only kissed her— kissed her like they were alone in their bedroom. I swore the temperature in the room went up.

When he let her go, her cheeks were pink. "Go have fun. But not too much fun. You know why."

Esme tried to keep the smile off her face and couldn't. "Yes, I know why." She looked at us. "Let's go."

The shirt she wore showed off her sleeve of tattoos, one of which was a cupcake so realistic it looked like I could reach into her arm and grab it.

Cole and Ben still stood talking, my other guards lining the outside windows like a line of toy soldiers. Esme walked up to Ben, and he pulled her into his side like it was second nature, pausing to kiss her head. I wanted that.

The thought stopped me in my tracks, and I blinked.

I *had* that.

Sloane was already halfway to the couches, and I was pinned

to the spot by Cole's gaze. He always managed to see so much, including this. Tilting his head so slightly no one would catch it, he called me to his side, and he pulled me to him in just the same way.

Esme grinned. "So he's one of yours?"

"Cole," I said. "And yeah, he is."

Ben pulled his phone out of his pocket. "My next appointment is about to be here. Cole, wherever you want to hang out is fine." He looked down at Esme. "Have fun."

"I will." Her eyes closed as he kissed her forehead.

"I'll be out in the front keeping an eye on things, if you need me," Cole said before nodding to the windows. "And they're there."

"Yeah."

Esme watched them go. "You guys want drinks? We've got soda and water. I keep trying to get them to let me set up a bar in here, but so far the answer has been no."

"I'll take a water. Why aren't you allowed to have too much fun?"

She flushed bright red as she opened the fridge. "My Alpha Kade and I have plans later. He likes to chase me and I... like to be chased. So I need to save my energy if I actually have a shot at getting away." She laughed. "I mean, I won't either way. He'll catch me, and I'll love every second of it."

I shuddered, knowing exactly what she meant. Being chased wasn't my thing, but given how much I liked Emery holding me down, I got it completely.

"God," Sloane flopped down onto the couch across from me. "It's so unfair. I'm *surrounded* by happiness. Makes me want to hurl."

I laughed. "It'll happen, Lo."

"When you least expect it," Esme added, handing each of us a bottle of water before sitting down. "Mine sure was."

"Eva mentioned something about that while I was in the middle of finding Cole. In a ballroom full of people."

She burst out laughing. "Fuck, that's familiar. I met Ben at one of Eva's studio parties. I smelled what I would have sworn on my life were cupcakes. Turns out it was him all along. It was pretty much over after that, but I resisted for a long time."

"That's... familiar," I admitted.

Sloane looked at me, everything in her face and body saying '*I told you so.*'

"So my sister said you had questions about being scent-sympathetic?"

I took a sip of my water. "I do, but they sound weird to say out loud."

"Everything about it is a little weird," she said. "I'm grateful there are no pictures of me charging across the room at Ben."

Sighing, I winced. "Unfortunately, there *are* pictures of me right after I met Cole. That one," I pointed at Sloane. "Locked me in a closet with him. For not nearly long enough, by the way."

"You're welcome, bitch," she smirked.

I flipped her off, and we all laughed. "But I looked wrecked, and the picture someone took is all over the papers now, and they're saying I was high."

Esme shook her head and went back to the kitchen, grabbing a box and coming back. She set the box on the coffee table and flipped it open. It was filled with cupcakes. "Have one if you want. They never let the house or studio go without them now."

"The cupcake tattoo makes sense now."

Sloane grabbed one and immediately broke off the bottom of the cake and flipped it over, crushing the frosting beneath it and making a sandwich. I rolled my eyes, and she looked at me. "What? It's the only way to eat a cupcake."

"That's brilliant, actually," Esme said. "But trust me. I've had my share of bad press because of Eva. It's never really about you. It's best to just ignore it."

"I would if I could. Unfortunately, that's not an option."

She frowned. "Why not?"

"Because her stepmother is the Wicked Witch of the East, but *before* she got crushed by the house. I could try to make that happen, by the way." Eva said on her way in. She was pulling on a sweater over her thin camisole, wincing. "It never gets less painful."

Esme rolled her eyes and grabbed a cupcake. "I'm sure the

guys are *more* than happy to rub the lotion on it and make you feel good."

"This is true," Eva said. "They've made a schedule for which one gets which appointment. It's Jack's turn. That's why he was in the room with me."

"We're not quite to turns yet," I said. "It's been a kind of free for all."

"That never stops," Esme said. "And I don't want it to."

I was blushing hot, but at the same time it was nice. Because they knew exactly what I was going through.

"So spill," Eva said. "How's it going?"

"Other than the press?"

"Yeah, fuck them. And those stories? Bullshit."

Sighing again, I pulled my legs up onto the couch. "It's a lot worse than that, but that's not the fun part of the conversation."

"Oooh, yes." Eva beamed at me. "Let's do the fun part. Ask away."

Rubbing my lips together, I thought of a way to phrase it delicately, and there was no fucking way to do it. "Okay, I'll just say it. Is it normal for them to taste so good? Like, it's going to sound really fucking weird, but I literally crave the taste of their... you know."

Both Esme and Eva cackled with laughter, and Esme had to wipe away a tear. "God, that's hysterical. I asked Eva the same question. Yes, it's normal, and yes, it doesn't get less weird. You just have to go with it, because let me tell you, the craving doesn't get weaker."

Relief swirled through my chest. "Oh, thank fuck. I don't know what I thought, I just... this is all so *fast*, and I wanted to talk to you guys because I don't have anyone else I know who's scent-sympathetic except my mom, and she died a long time ago."

They hesitated, and Eva reached out to put her hand on mine.

"I'm sorry," Esme said. "Our dad passed almost three years ago."

"I know there are plenty of scent-sympathetic packs. But it's not like I can just walk up to strangers and ask, 'is it normal to be completely in love in two weeks or less?' Because that's what it feels like, and it scares the hell out of me."

"What?" Sloane sat up straight. "Really?"

I shrugged. "Yeah. I don't know how to explain it, Lo."

"That's normal too," Eva said. "Hell, my pack and I bonded... what was it, like three months after we met?" She looked at Esme.

Her twin nodded, swiping her finger through the frosting of her cupcake. "Yeah, seems about right."

"Honestly?" Eva looked at me and leaned in. "If everyone hadn't made us wait to plan a big public thing, we would have bonded within a month, and I would have had no regrets. Esme bonded that fast."

My eyebrows rose. "Really?"

"Yes. Once we knew, there wasn't a point in waiting. Because why not?"

"I'll tell you why not," Sloane said, leaning forward and slamming her water bottle down on the table. "Do you mind, Bee? Even the stuff from forever ago?"

At this point, it didn't matter. "Be my guest."

Sloane launched into my story, outlining everything from the incident at the conservatory and the fallout, to the present with the charity ball and my pack, and everything Carmen and Dad were forcing on me.

Eva held out a hand. "Wait a second. Do you have a copy of that report?"

"Yeah. Why?"

"Can I see it?"

Esme sat up. "You think it's Katarina?"

"Maybe."

I handed Eva my phone with the report pulled up. She shook her head. "Yup. If it's not her, it's someone at her agency."

"Who's Katarina?"

Eva snorted. "A bitch of epic proportions. She's a matchmaker. Our mom used her to try to find a pack for Esme, but she was ludicrously bad at her job, and I'm pretty sure she liked the money from her clients more than actual matchmaking."

"Meaning," Esme said, "she's the kind of person who wouldn't hesitate to fake compatibility if she were paid enough.

But that must be new. I never had anything like that in the files they gave me. How would they even calculate that?"

"No idea. But it's the same pack from the charity thing. I'm meeting with them tomorrow."

"You shouldn't go," Sloane said. "Just blow it off."

I threw up my hands and stood. "And how do you think that would go? I'd end up with Carmen at my door again, or my father coming back from the capital to drag me off to fucking rehab. George, the one I danced with, was reasonable enough. We'll just agree, once again, that we don't actually want to bond, and that will be the end of it."

Eva set my phone down on the coffee table. "Petra, this is all a lot, and it doesn't all add up. I don't get why this is being pushed so hard."

"I thought you'd recognize someone trying to fix a scandal," Sloane teased.

"I do, but..." Her forehead creased as she frowned. "I'm sorry. It all sucks."

"Yes, it does."

The door to the office slammed open. "Petra?" Cole came in heading straight for me. "Away from the windows. All of you."

Suddenly the room was flooded with Alphas, the Nautilus pack drawing Esme to their center, and Eva's Alphas doing the same. Cole had me behind him, and his gun was in his hand. Sloane stood with me. "Cole, what's going on?"

"He sent pictures of the studio. He knows we're here. So we're locked down until we clear everyone outside the building. Harrison is sending everyone we have."

Since the pictures had come to my phone, the threats had gone back to being sent to the campaign. I closed my eyes, pressing my head to the back of his suit. Dread flowed over me. "What if that's what he wants?"

"No other choice, honeybee."

Turning, I looked at everyone, especially my friends. "I'm sorry. I shouldn't have come."

A low growl ripped through the air from one of Esme's Alphas. It was the huge bearded one, covered in tattoos. But his gaze was surprisingly gentle. "You're not responsible for some

266

asshole coming after you, and you certainly shouldn't let that stop you from seeing your friends."

Sloane wrapped an arm around my shoulders. "He's right."

"Yeah."

But it didn't change the fact that everyone was in danger because of me. If he—

No. I wasn't going to dwell on hypotheticals like I scolded Cole for this morning. We would make it through this and then take the next step. "Thank you," I said to both Eva and Esme. "I do feel better about everything. Scent wise, at least."

"No problem, girl, and you need to be less of a stranger. I never see you anymore."

Raising one eyebrow. "Says the movie star whose schedule is ten times busier than mine."

She laughed. "Fair point. But I'll at least see you next week, right?"

Fuck. I completely forgot about it. "Oh my god."

The Slate Gala. It happened every year, hosted by the Mayor and the city, another fundraiser and another excuse for the rich and famous to rub shoulders. It was a chance to see and be seen. If you were invited, you *were* someone.

And announcements were made there. I couldn't remember a time when the night after the gala the news wasn't filled with some kind of story. This one? My father was planning to officially announce his run for chancellor. "You're going to that?"

Of course she was. She was Eva May Williams.

"If you'll be there, I'll go," she said with a shrug. "Hell, I can get Esme and her guys in too. We'll make it a much better party. It's usually boring."

"And," Sloane said. "We can all get ready together."

Eva pointed at her, grinning, and Tyler wrapped his arms around her like he thought she was going to go running. "I like the way you think, Lo."

Cole lifted a hand to his earpiece. "You're sure?" He listened. "Thanks. We're clear," he said to the rest of us. Everyone outside had press badges and surrendered their memory cards. "If anyone matches the photos, we'll have them. But they all pretty much scattered like rats at the suggestion of stalking and threats."

Ben laughed. "That's probably because of me, and I say good riddance."

"I should probably exile myself back to my tower so you guys can get on with your lives without all of this."

Sloane wrapped me in a hug. "A four-story penthouse. I would kill for that tower."

"You'll see it soon."

I hugged Eva and Esme as well.

"I've been where you are," Esme said. "Trust your instincts. We have them for a reason."

"Thank you."

Cole said goodbye to some of the Alphas, and we went. I wasn't outside for more than a few seconds, the Atwood team getting me into the car in record time.

Unlike on the way to the studio, Cole didn't let me out of his arms.

CHAPTER THIRTY-FIVE

―――――――

PETRA

I didn't want to do this.

And there were four very unhappy Alphas who also didn't want me to do it. But here I was, walking into The Feldman's lobby.

The irony wasn't lost on me. This was where I met Cole and everything changed, and now I was meeting the pack I was being thrown at. Again.

The Feldman had a lot of comfortable meeting rooms on the lower floors. Its central location made it convenient for anyone who needed to gather downtown. Something I knew because my father and his campaign used them regularly. Ezra directed me upstairs to the correct room, but was wise enough to back off when I gave him the death glare of the century. Like hell was I going to have a spy in this meeting with me.

Cole was at my back, distinctively silent. All of them already knew how much I didn't want to do this, so I appreciated him allowing me the space to think.

Three-forty-three.

I turned to Cole. "After you check the room, I need you to wait outside."

"Petra."

"Cole." I glanced down the hallway. The rest of the team was spread out in various positions, and no one else. "Please. Trust me."

His hand came up to cup my face. "I do trust you, honeybee. It's everyone else I don't trust."

"You'll be right outside. The door won't be locked. You can be with me in a second. Besides, I really don't think this is going to take that long."

I could tell he struggled not to pull me back down the hallway and all the way home. But he nodded. "Let me go in first."

He knocked and entered, doing his sweep. Before I went in, he caught my arm. "I love you."

I let the words warm me and carry me into the space where the pack was waiting. God, this room smelled awful. They seemed nice enough, but whatever person said we were compatible was a fucking liar. "Hi."

They stood at various places in the room, one getting water from the pitcher provided. No one spoke.

"First, I just want to apologize for my behavior at the charity ball. You caught me at a strange moment. In the middle of being introduced to you, I got hit with a scent so strong it blew everything else away. I couldn't even think straight."

An Alpha on my left laughed. "That makes so much sense." He shook his head and held out his hand. "I'm Terry."

"Hi, Terry."

George was here again, and there was Terry, Roger, Ethan, and Stuart. Three Alphas, two Betas. I looked at all of them once we'd been properly introduced.

I looked at George. "So, did you guys change your mind? Or were you only being polite when we danced?"

He cupped the back of his neck, groaning. "No, we didn't change our minds. You seem nice, but we really are happy as we are. It's my dad who's really pushing this. He's... so eager. I don't understand it."

I tried to throw my memory back to the moments before Cole's scent carried me away. "He was there too, right? My dad introduced him right before you?"

"Yeah," George said. He sat down next to Ethan and took his hand. "He's a big fan of your father's."

I sat down in one of the chairs near them. At least this was less awkward than I expected. "So what's his reason?"

George winced. "He didn't give one. But, unfortunately, even though we haven't changed our mind, we're not in a position to say no."

Staring at them one at a time, I shook my head. "I don't understand. You said you're happy."

Roger cleared his throat and leaned forward on his knees. "We *are* happy. But—"

"But what?" I asked. "None of us want this. As much as they're trying to push it, they can't make us if we all shut it down."

They looked at each other, communicating silently. It irritated me. They weren't bonded, clearly, but they were a pack who knew each other inside and out. That much was clear. "What aren't you saying?"

"My father is wealthy," George said.

I fought the urge to roll my eyes. "Yeah, not shocking. Most people who were at that fundraiser are rich as fuck. What does it have to do with anything?"

The Alpha scrubbed his hand over his face, and I was starting to wish Cole was in here with me. I needed them to just fucking say it. This was our lives we were talking about. There wasn't room to be delicate.

"Respectfully," I kept my voice even. "Russell Merriton is my father. I'm not made of glass. Whatever it is, please just say it."

A hardness entered the Alpha's gaze. *There you are*. I pushed him. Good. Because this was going to take forever if every sentence was something he had to ponder for minutes on end.

"My father didn't get to where he is by giving things away. He's ruthless, even with me. Everything my father is giving to me is wrapped up in trust until I turn thirty. And up until then, he can change his mind at any moment and leave me with nothing. I have to stay in his good graces."

I stared at him, mouth falling open. Then I looked at the rest of them. None of them contradicted him or looked the least bit phased. "Money?" I asked, standing because I couldn't possibly sit still a second longer. "You're doing this for money?"

"It's not just money," Stuart said. "It's pieces of Mr. Bower's companies. He owns half the media in the country. Maybe more than half. It's pharmaceuticals. It's real estate. It's finance and insurance. And yes, a lot of fucking money."

"So you're ruining *all* our lives because of money. Don't you all have jobs? If you're really that happy together, how could you expect me to sacrifice that?" My voice cracked in spite of myself. "Because if you're happy without me, you know where that leaves me? Alone. Living with a pack who doesn't

271

want me, and cared more about money than they cared about a person."

"Look," George said. "I meant what I said at that night. It wasn't until after my father made it clear if we wanted anything, I needed to abide by his decision on this. And if it were you, I doubt you'd walk away from everything you'd had and known."

Except that was exactly what I was about to do. If I somehow managed to solve this, my father might not ever forgive me. I might lose the only family I had left because I wanted my happiness more than anything else. The penthouse was beautiful, but I knew to my core I would still be with them, sleeping in their arms, even if they'd had to make me a nest out of cardboard boxes.

"Your life won't be ruined," Ethan said with an encouraging smile. "We'll make sure you're taken care of and happy. Hell, we don't even have to bond. We can fake it until the heat is off, and then you can do what you want."

I leveled him with a glare. "So you expect the man who controls everything and has you all by the balls to not want iron-clad proof of a bond? Of course he will."

They were silent, confirming my suspicion.

"I came here expecting to find allies," I told them, and pointed at George. "Because when you told me you were happy and didn't care that much, I thought we could solve this together. But I guess that's not going to be the case."

"We're sorry," he didn't sound it. "Truly. But I have to think about the pack as a whole, and our lives. Once I have my inheritance, not only will we be taken care of for life, but any children we have and their children as well."

Rage and revolt slammed through my veins. "Fuck you for prioritizing people who don't exist over someone who's living and breathing. But thank you for making yourself clear. I just have one last question."

Terry cleared his throat. "What's that?"

"Since you're so unwilling, if I find a way out of this in a way that protects us both, would you support it?"

"Of course." George's answer was instant. "But how do you

expect to do that? From what I gather, you have even less leverage than we do."

As soon as he spoke the words, I saw the glimmer of regret in his eyes. Too little too late. "I don't know," I said. "But I'm going to try. Just give me some time. Hold off the announcement for a few days. My side won't care if it comes from you. And it's the least you can do."

All of them looked supremely uncomfortable, and I didn't feel remotely sorry for them. Let them be uncomfortable and get used to it if they wanted this to be the rest of our fucking lives.

"We will," Ethan said.

I spun on my heel and stalked to the door, not bothering to say goodbye. Cole was by my side the second I walked out the door, but I said nothing. If I opened my mouth now, I would explode.

They were right. I had even less leverage than they did, and an explosion in public wasn't going to help that. So I kept my mouth shut, and we drove toward home.

CHAPTER THIRTY-SIX

HARRISON

"*Y*ou're sure?" I asked again. "Because this isn't something we can fuck up."

Nick laughed on the other end of the phone. "I know, boss. We're pulling up to the place now, and the police are on their way. Won't be long until we have him."

I breathed out a sigh of relief, and the knot of tension between my shoulders eased just a little. "Good. Call me when it's done, and he's in handcuffs. Then tell me who to call to press maximum charges and inform the Senator the situation is resolved." If I could avoid speaking to him, I would. Until everything with Petra was settled.

"Will do," Nick said.

He ended the call, and I sat back in my chair. Thank *fuck*. The person stalking Petra made the mistake we were waiting for. For once, the pictures he sent could be traced. It was a lucky break. One little misstep that he hadn't made before which led us straight to him. After the explosion at the university, the president of the school was salivating for an arrest. I was too, because it meant Petra would finally be safe, and I wouldn't be worrying every time she and Cole left the penthouse.

Out in the hallway, the front door opened, and two sets of footsteps entered. "Petra," Cole said, "Slow down, honeybee."

I stood and went to the door. My Omega was beelining for the stairs, and she looked devastated. Her scent was darker and more bitter than normal—a sure sign something was wrong. Cole looked at me and shook his head. She hadn't said anything to him.

He caught her at the edge of the stairs and spun her around, pressing his forehead to hers. "Whatever happened in there, I love you," he said. "We'll figure it out."

She shook her head silently, and my heart broke for her. Petra had spent most of her life without anyone to truly rely on, and I knew from experience it was a hard habit to break. She knew we were here, but her first instinct was to shut everything out, because that was the only way she'd managed to survive. And now, even with us to help her, she was facing more than she ever had.

"I have good news," I said to both of them.

Petra startled and looked at me. "Really? I could use some right now."

Letting my smile appear, I slid my hands into my suit pockets. "We found him."

Petra gasped. "*What*?"

"We found him, and he's being arrested as we speak."

"Oh, fuck." She sagged, and Cole caught her. I was by her side in a second. "I hadn't realized how much I needed that."

I took her gently from Cole and held her. "You're safe, little one."

"I'm going to miss following you around," Cole said, smiling.

Petra buried her face in my chest. "You can still follow me around. I don't know what good it will do, but I wouldn't mind."

Frowning, I glanced at Cole, and he smirked. He clearly didn't want to leave her, but the way Petra clung to me, she needed something from me. He leaned in and kissed her on the shoulder. "I'll be back."

She nodded into my shirt. This was part of the dance of being a pack. We all wanted to comfort our Omega, but there would always be times when her instincts craved one thing more than another. At the moment it could be as simple as not wanting to talk to Cole about the meeting because he was there and too close to it.

Maybe it was something else entirely.

"It's real?" She asked, looking up at me. "He's gone?"

"It is real," I said. "We tracked the photos he sent of you, along with the threat from yesterday. More of the same."

She shuddered, and I held her tighter. "God, that's such good news."

"It is." I picked her up and carried her into my office, kicking the door shut behind us. "I'm glad I can give you some good news, little one. Now tell me the bad news."

Petra stiffened in my arms. "I never said there was bad news."

"You didn't have to. It's written all over your face and body. In your scent."

I sat us down in my chair together, and she shifted, straddling my lap just like she had in the car on the way back from building her nest. My cock hardened, because I had a soft, sexy Omega in my lap and I wasn't made of stone. Her honeyed scent got sweeter as she moved, and the bitter note of cinnamon lifted along with her mood.

"I know I need to tell all of you." There was a tiny break in her voice, and she cleared her throat. "But what if I don't want to think for a little while? Would that be okay?"

Raising an eyebrow, I ran my hands up her ribs. "What did you have in mind?"

She was hiding from whatever happened. I wasn't going to force it out of her. But I already knew from experience my Omega was more likely to talk when she'd had a few orgasms. And since we'd been tracking this asshole, I hadn't fucked her in days.

I was only so strong.

"First, I want you to tell me something," she said.

"I'm listening."

Her fingers trailed up the back of my neck and into my hair. "You always hold back with me. There's never been a time when you didn't. I just want to know why."

I smiled. She asked me this before, and it wasn't the time to answer, but I always knew she'd come back to it. "It's not anything sinister, I promise." I brushed a piece of hair behind her ear. "I haven't wanted to overwhelm you."

Alphas, Betas, and Omegas came in every flavor and personality. Along with that, there were variations in the level of instincts we carried with us. Some Alphas were stronger than others, and it could be a powerful thing. It could also be terrifying to some.

Petra wasn't someone I wanted to frighten. I let myself out of the box a little with her heat, and I knew I would again. But unleashing the full power of my Alpha? It wasn't something I did often.

"What if I want to be overwhelmed?" The hope in her eyes shook me. "I think it's exactly what I need. Between you and Emery, I'm learning I like to let go sometimes, the same way I like to take over and tease Blake. But I don't want to take over. I want *you*." She leaned in and brushed her lips over mine. "Show me who you really are, Harrison. Because I'm falling in love with you, and I want every part of you."

The words snapped the rubber band inside of me that always held me back. One hand slid behind her neck and the other pulled her ass down onto my lap, grinding her on my cock. "I love you, little one." My voice sounded raw. "And if this is what you want, I'll give you everything. If it's too much—"

"You're not too much, Harrison. If you were, you wouldn't drive me mad with your scent, and every part of me wouldn't *crave* what you're hiding." A tiny whine slipped out. "Show me."

"One condition. If—for any reason—you need to stop, tell me."

"Yes."

I wove my fingers into her hair and gripped it, thrusting up with my hips so she felt the hard ridge of my cock. Then I let myself free. Her scent tantalized me, swirling around me and drawing out my deepest instincts. Already I felt the way her body shifted, melting into submission as I released that energy.

"When I let go, this is what's going to happen, Omega." She shook when I said the word. "You're going to stand up and strip off every piece of clothing you have on. Because my Omega doesn't get to hide from me."

"Fuck," she muttered under her breath, a wave of perfume surrounding us.

"Then you're going to get on your knees beneath this desk and wrap your pretty lips around my cock. I haven't decided whether I want you to suck me slowly or if I'll fuck your throat until you're desperate for breath. Guess you'll find out."

"Yes."

"But Petra," I pull her closer until I'm speaking softly in her ear. "I *will* knot your mouth. When I wrap my hand around this throat that's begging me to bite it, I want to feel it stuffed full of me. And you're going to be my good girl and wait, not knowing if I'm going to bend you over the desk and fuck you when it's done, or take your throat again and keep you knotted on my cock all fucking day while I work."

Her breath hitched, and I laughed softly, kissing the skin beneath her ear. "I think my Omega likes the sound of that."

"No." She breathed the word. "Of course not."

"Really?" I lifted her and sat her on the edge of my desk, spreading her legs apart. "The wet spot tells me differently, little one. Now strip."

I sat back and watched her stand off the desk and begin to pull her shirt over her head. Her hands shook, but it wasn't from fear. It was from arousal and adrenaline. The amount of heat in her eyes told me that.

Every inch of her was fucking stunning. I couldn't take my eyes off her, and each piece of clothing that hit the floor made me question my plan and tempted me to bend her over the desk and fuck her till she screamed.

But the way she sank to her knees in front of me told me I made the right choice. My cock was so hard it ached. It wasn't going to take long for me to come. Just the *thought* of her lips around me was almost enough.

I undid my belt and zipper, freeing my cock. During the heat I didn't have enough of her mouth. And I was impatient. "Don't touch yourself," I said, watching her hand creep toward her pussy. "Wait, and I will make it worth it."

Petra curled both of her hands behind her back, locking eyes with me while she took me into her mouth. "Good girl." My purr was loud and rough, and fuck me, her mouth was heaven. The way she used her tongue undid me.

She moaned, and I saw white. "You taste so fucking good."

I reached for her hair again. "Another day I want to enjoy the slow luxury that is your mouth and tongue, little one. And once you're done, I want to lick you slowly until you're shaking so badly you're begging me to let you come. Today I don't have that kind of time."

Petra smirked at me, and sucked a little harder, teasing me. She knew exactly how much power she held even on her knees: absolutely fucking all of it.

Sinking my hands into her hair, Petra yielded. We faded together into our instincts. Alpha and Omega. Dominance and submission. Yielding and control.

I thrust deeper into her mouth, Petra taking every stroke. Everything I gave she accepted and wanted more, leaning in, meeting every movement with eager joy and arousal.

Heat and pleasure spiraled through my body. It had been too long without her. This would be fast and messy, and deep down, I knew it was what we both needed.

Pulling Petra down on my cock, she swallowed me like it was easy. My eyes rolled back in my head, the feeling of being sheathed inside perfect warmth enough to undo me. Lightning blazed down my spine, but I held it back. I fought the pleasure rising like a tide, giving Petra a chance to breathe before I pulled her onto my shaft again.

"I can't last." My words escaped through my gritted teeth.

Petra brought her hands forward and grabbed my legs, pulling herself more firmly onto my cock, ready for me to knot her gorgeous mouth, and I fell a little more in love with her.

She swallowed, and I was done for. The tide took me, electric bliss sizzling through my cock and balls, cum gushing down Petra's throat in waves. I fought my eyes open to see the way she drank me down, eyes closed in pleasure.

I held her against my body, making sure her mouth was sealed around the base of my cock as my knot swelled, locking behind her teeth. The gentled scrape of her tongue against it, the way she swallowed around my shaft. "Fuck, little one."

She laughed around my dick, what parts of her lips not stretched trying to smile.

"I'm not sure if I can explain how good this feels."

Instantly, she sucked hard, and my whole body jerked, thrusting deeper into her throat. My hand shot out, and I curled it around her throat, feeling my thickness there just like I promised her. A growl came out of me, her perfume suddenly drenching the room. "Be careful, Petra. I'm off my leash."

Her eyes told me she didn't care. She was going to push me, and there was every chance I would break. The urge to take her swept through me, overruling everything. As soon as my knot released, I was going to spread her out on this desk and fucking consume her. Fuck her. Until I was knotted so deeply it would take hours to release.

The phone on my desk rang, and I sent it to voicemail. Now was not the time. I stroked Petra's hair, savoring the way she leaned into my hand. Even in this position, there was such trust between us.

Hearing her say she was in love with me made me want to prove it. Mark her. Show the world she was *mine*.

The phone rang again, and I sent it to voicemail. Nick could fucking wait.

Petra shifted on her knees, and I stroked her shoulders. "Such a good girl."

My Omega whined, drawing my Alpha to the surface. I'd never wanted my knot to dissipate like this. Because I needed her pussy more than I needed anything else.

The door opened and Cole came in, phone to his ear. "Yes, Sir. Yes, he's right here." He suddenly stopped short, scenting the perfume in the room and seeing Petra's clothes scattered by my desk. His eyes dropped to my desk, as if he could see her kneeling. "Of course."

He handed me the phone, looking guilty.

"Harrison Atwood."

Petra sucked and swallowed, and I gripped the edge of my desk with my free hand. *Fuck,* I was going to come again if she kept doing that.

"Harrison, I'm just calling to thank you for catching the bastard threatening Petra. I knew you were the right man for the job."

"Senator." One single strangled word that made Petra freeze, and then she moved more deliberately, fucking herself further onto my shaft, sucking around my knot while I spoke to her fucking father. "Thank you. We're very relieved he's been found."

"We'll charge him to the fullest extent. But while I have you, I wanted to ask about continuing my daughter's protection through my campaign. Maybe with a wider perimeter. But it would put me more at ease."

I reached below the desk, sinking my hand into Petra's hair, unsure if I wanted to stop her or fuck her mouth harder. "Of course," I managed. What were words? What the hell was a conversation when the love of my life was making me see fucking stars with her mouth and tongue and sassy determination? "But Senator, I'm about to leave for a meeting. Can I schedule a call with you next week?"

"That's fine. I'll have one of my aides reach out."

"That's perfect, thank you. And thank you for trusting me with your daughter." He had no idea how true that statement was.

I heard him say something to someone on the other end of the phone. "You were the first person I thought of. I'll speak with you next week. Thank you again."

Ending the call, I dropped the phone on my desk. Cole winced. "Sorry."

Possession flared through me. *My* Omega on her knees for me. *My* good girl. *My* little one. I needed to take her and make her mine. Pin her down and fuck her. I tried to keep my voice even, but it didn't work. "Leave, Cole. I'm going into rut."

He grabbed his phone and held up his hands in surrender, smirking. "Have fun."

As soon as the door closed, I looked down at her. "Naughty Omega, teasing me like that."

My knot began to ease, and as soon as it was small enough, I pulled her off my cock and hauled her into my arms. "*Mine.*"

"Yours." Her breath came in short gasps, and I didn't remember crossing the room to the door, but we were here and Petra was in my arms. "You going to rut me, Alpha?"

I took the stairs two at a time. It was faster than waiting for the elevator. Straight into the nest where I dropped her on the cushions and tore my clothes off. I couldn't be naked fast enough, and as soon as I was, my body covered hers, my cock filling her pussy until she couldn't take more of me.

"I knotted your mouth, and I'm going to knot this pussy." I barely knew what I was saying. All I knew was her. Her scent and her breath and the way she moaned as I drove myself deep. Hard. Merciless.

I grabbed her wrists and pinned them to the cushions. "And I'll knot your ass too, Omega. You're *mine*." My growl tore through the space between us, Petra arching off the cushions into me. "All your holes are mine. Your body is mine. Made for my knot."

"Yes."

My teeth found her neck. Her heart raced beneath my tongue. I could bite her so easily, and the one single shred of my mind that was left kept me from breaking her skin. I wasn't going to bond Petra in the middle of rut. But I would fuck her like our lives depended on it.

"You teased me," I growled. "How should I punish you?"

My hips never stopped moving, fucking, burying my cock all the way into my Omega over and over and over. She would be filled up with my cum until it spilled out of her and I would make her clean it up before starting all over again.

Lifting her legs, I pushed them up and out and used them to hold her down while I took her. Owned her. She was mine.

Mine.

Mine.

"Alpha." A sultry whisper.

Ripping my cock out of her, I knelt back. "Present," I growled. "Show me who you belong to. Who your cunt belongs to."

Petra scrambled to turn over on the cushions, shoving her perfect ass in the air and baring her soaking pussy to me. I spanked her, enjoying the moan which met the sound and the handprint warming on her skin.

She spread her hands in front of her, flattening every part of her except for her glistening cunt. Her body writhed, wiggling and calling for me. "Rut me, Alpha. *Please*."

The last of my conscious mind slipped away. *Omega*. I leaned forward and licked that sweet honey out of her slit, tasting what was mine. I liked this cunt. It took my cock perfectly. And it was about to. Over and over.

Grabbing her hips, I sank balls deep in one brutal thrust. My Omega's body softened beneath mine, surrendering. Yielding. She would take everything I gave and more.

"*Mine.*"

I unleashed myself.

CHAPTER THIRTY-SEVEN

PETRA

I groaned at the delicious sensation, Harrison's thumbs pressing into my shoulder blades, massaging deeply and firmly. "I don't understand how something that hurts can feel good like that."

His low chuckle warmed me. "I don't either, but it does. But I am sorry you're in any pain at all."

"Worth it."

There was no way to deny I was sore. Harrison's rut lasted nearly an entire day. Even now, as he straddled my back, easing my aching muscles, he was hard. "Do your ruts usually last that long?"

"I have no idea," he said. "It's the first time I've had one. But I'm guessing not. Probably because it was my first, and also because my Alpha instincts want you so fucking badly, there was no way to stop."

"Really? You've never?"

"Some Alphas never do. It takes a lot to push us over the edge."

I turned beneath him, and he let me, shifting to massage my shoulders and collarbone instead. "What pushed you over?"

Harrison smirked. "You and that infernal mouth of yours. The combination of that, Cole walking in, and having to be on the phone with your *father* while you were deep-throating my dick."

"I'm not apologizing for that," meaning teasing him while he was on the phone. "It was fun."

"I'm not asking you to. But if I'm going to follow through on that little fantasy you seemed to like and keep you under my desk all day, I need to be careful who I take calls from."

Unbridled desire whirled through me. It didn't make any sense. Neither of us would last an entire work day in those positions, but the *idea* of it was impossibly hot.

Harrison stared down at me. All lean muscle, relaxed and sexy. There wasn't any doubt how fit he was, but I loved the softness of him as well. A dusting of hair on his chest matched the stubble which grew because we'd spent an entire day in the nest.

"When you look at me like that, I don't know what to do with myself," he said.

"Why not?"

"Because it feels impossible, after this long, to have you here and looking at me like I'm the only person in the world. And it feels equally impossible that you're here, and *mine*."

I grinned. He'd said it a lot during his rut, and I didn't mind in the slightest.

"But you're here, and I am so fucking in love with you." He bent, leaning down to kiss me. "And now that I have you where I want you—"

"Uh-oh."

"Not this second, because I don't want to ask you to put yourself through something more than once if it's hard, but I'd like to know what happened. Cole is probably beside himself with wanting to know what made you look like and smell like that."

All the joy immediately drained out of me.

"Exactly like that," Harrison said.

"It's not fair to any of you. I don't want to tell you about the other pack who I'm being forced on. Even talking about it feels like admitting it's a possibility."

Harrison rolled off me and pulled to his side, covering us with a blanket. "Not talking about it doesn't make it go away."

"Says you," I muttered, and Harrison laughed.

"Listen. We're all finding our way in this, and you've been dealing with things on your own for years. But you're not alone anymore, little one. You can trust us."

"I know." I inhaled. The sweet top notes of whiskey and the full lower notes of cedar. A dash of coldness and frost. "And I do trust you. I will tell you everything. Just... in the same way I'm learning to share, I'll ask you give me the space *to* share. I'll get better, but I need time to wrap my own head around things before I talk them out."

"Sounds fair enough. However, I reserve the right to pin you down and fuck answers out of you if you take too long."

I laughed. "Promises, promises." Then, "Harrison?"

"Yeah?"

"Thank you for catching him."

He tightened his embrace. "You're welcome. He didn't stand a chance. Because we were never going to let him touch you."

It was still unsettling that anyone had come after me at all. But the relief told me I'd been pretending to be less worried about it than I actually was.

"I suppose we should emerge from the nest at some point. Eat something. Shower."

"Probably."

I pressed my palm to my forehead. "I've probably got a dozen missed calls about the guy getting caught."

"I'm sure I've missed something." Harrison sat up and pulled me with him. "Think we can convince Blake to cook something delicious even though we left him out?"

"I hope so." My stomach growled. "I'm going to have to start eating three times as much if there's this much sex. You guys might have to use the gym, but I'm not sure I'll have to, with the four of you."

He pulled me to my feet. "I don't know. There are a lot of interesting things in the gym. Not to mention the pool. We could have fun in there."

God, I hadn't even had time to try the pool yet. When I had some real time off I was going to go swimming. I deflated. "I guess since he's caught, I'll have to go back to classes on Monday."

Harrison watched me, remaining carefully neutral. "I guess so."

I looked at him. "This is one of those things you're going to fuck out of me, aren't you." Not a question.

He shrugged. "I'll give you a little more time. But the others are going to want to help me on that one. You'll enjoy the interrogation, but it will still be one."

Tossing a look over my shoulder, I raised an eyebrow. "Guess I'll have to make a decision about that."

His laugh followed me. I showered quickly, and I *did* think about it. Honestly, it wasn't the most dramatic thing about me, it was just the thing which hurt the most. I don't think Dad even remembered it.

I, on the other hand, would never forget.

My suitcase was almost empty. I needed to do laundry *and* go back to my apartment to get more clothes. At some point I needed to make the decision to just stay here. The big empty space the men had created for their Omega was begging to be made into something truly beautiful.

Fear gripped my chest.

Until all of this bullshit was worked out with the Gidwitz pack, I didn't want to make the call. Moving in here and having to move back out would be ten times more painful than never moving in at all.

I would find a way out. *That* was what I needed to talk to Harrison about. Finding whoever falsified my drug tests and made that bullshit compatibility report. If I had proof, Dad would listen.

He had to.

The house was quiet as I went downstairs. There was some conversation on the second floor in the living room. But I needed to grab some things first. My clothes were right where I left them on Harrison's office floor, along with everything else. I gathered them all and fished my phone out of the pocket of my pants.

I was probably going to have to apologize to Dad for missing his calls.

My entire body froze when I tapped on the screen to wake it up. I had nearly a hundred missed calls. Some were from my dad and Carmen. Others from Eva and Sloane. And the rest were from numbers I didn't know.

The texts were the same. The ones from my friends grew increasingly more frantic. I felt sick to my stomach.

Sloane in particular.

> I heard they caught the guy who attacked you at the school, or at least I think it's him, since they never mentioned your name. That's amazing!

> Let me know how the meeting went, okay? I'm worried about you.

> Uhh... Petra? What the hell is going on? I thought you were going to work something out?

> What happened???

> PLEASE call me. I am FREAKING OUT right now!

Terror ripped through me. What the hell happened? I was petrified to open the internet. Instead, I flipped to my phone app, clicking on the first voicemail of many.

> "HI, I'M LOOKING FOR PETRA MERRITON. MY NAME IS DONOVAN KANE. I'M A REPORTER FOR THE SLATE CITY STAR. CONGRATULATIONS ON YOUR ENGAGEMENT. WE WANT TO OFFER YOU AN EXCL—"

That was all I heard of the voicemail because I dropped the phone. It clattered on the stairs, and I stared at it like it had suddenly become a poisonous snake.

"Petra?"

Emery's voice came from above me, and then he was there, scooping me up into his arms and holding me. I still stared at the phone.

"I'm so sorry," he said. "I'm so fucking sorry."

"They announced it." I sounded dead.

"Yeah, sunshine, they did."

How could they have done that? They promised to hold off the announcement for a few days. "They said they would wait. I—"

Panic pulled me down into a whirlpool of spiraling thoughts, each one worse than the last. Did they lie? Did George tell his father I agreed? Tears pricked my eyes.

289

"Come upstairs," Emery said. "We have something for you, and you can tell us what happened."

I shook my head. "No."

He went stiff. "Why not?"

Because I wanted to run and scream, not sit and talk. Because I was falling into a pit of despair, and they didn't deserve to feel that. Because somehow, for the third time in my life, I might have just lost everything. I wasn't sure I would survive it another time. None of that came out of my mouth. "I can't. I can't talk about it right now. I need—" I pulled out of his arms. "I need some space to think about how to get out of this."

He was looking at me with worry in his eyes. And my heart hurt because he was hurt. "We can figure it out together."

"He's right, baby." Blake spoke from the top of the stairs. Harrison and Cole appeared beside him. "You're a part of a pack. That means everyone."

"I just need to be alone for a bit." My throat felt like it was closing up. I needed to get the hell out of here. Where no one could see me and it was safe.

"Petra," Harrison said, taking a step down, and I backed up.

I pointed at him before I grabbed my phone. "I just told you this is what I need. I'm not going to do anything stupid, just going to my apartment. I love you, I—" I turned away from them. "Don't follow me."

None of them did, but the silence I left behind me was fucking deafening. Tears started to fall before I even got all the way to my apartment.

I wanted to turn around and go back. Fall into their arms and let them comfort me. But I couldn't. Because if I was about to be ripped away from them, it would only hurt more. So I shut the door to my apartment behind me and collapsed into tears the way I always did.

Alone.

CHAPTER THIRTY-EIGHT

COLE

I couldn't breathe. A giant hand had reached down from heaven and was squeezing the life from my lungs.

Blake looked the way I felt. Wrecked. Destroyed. Terrified. "Did she just break up with us?" He asked.

"No." Harrison's word was definitive. "Absolutely not."

"Then why is she running?" Emery asked.

He sighed. "Because we've only been together for a couple of weeks, and that's not much time to change a lifetime of habits. She told me not even an hour ago that she needed space to process things before she spoke about them. I told her that we would allow her that, but there was only so much time we would give before pleasuring it out of her.

"She's scared." He crossed his arms. "Her worst nightmare just happened. Let's give her a couple hours to breathe. She's safe in her apartment. But we won't let her be alone too long."

I closed my eyes. It hurt to watch her walk away. It hurt even more to see the devastation on her face. Worse than yesterday. Not even an expression, just... utter and complete blankness. Like her soul had been decimated.

"I hoped we could take the edge off with..." I trailed off. There was a brand new grand piano in our living room. Petra had been cagey about it so far, but she looked so happy when she stood up from the piano at the university.

Peaceful, too. I had the idea yesterday, and as soon as Harrison saw it he started laughing. We all thought it was a good idea.

I sat down on the stairs and leaned my elbows on my knees, and Blake sat with me. Emery leaned against the railing, and all of us stared at the front door like we wanted it to open and reveal our Omega coming back.

That was why it hurt. Because my every instinct was telling

291

me to comfort her. Protect her. And she'd turned and left. I knew doing what she asked was protecting her, but fuck me, I hated it.

"Don't sit here and wait for her," Harrison said. "You'll start climbing the walls."

"If she lived here, she could just go to her room," Blake said. "Then at least she'd be here."

Harrison chuckled. "And could you say you'd leave her alone?"

Blake said nothing. We would learn to. It would help if we were bonded and could feel her. Even if we needed to keep our distance, we'd know how she was doing, when she truly needed space, and when she was ready for us to come back. Right now there was only aching emptiness in my chest.

She loved us, and that was real. I needed to trust that and breathe through the instinct to follow her, haul her into my arms and purr until she knew nothing bad would ever happen to her again.

"I'll be in the kitchen," Blake said, standing.

He loved cooking more than anything, but it was also his place of safety. It was the way he handled the world. Whatever he was making, Petra would be at the center of it.

"I'll be in my office, seeing if there are any fires I need to put out."

"You should be fine," I said. "A couple messages to return, but you're good."

"Thank you." He put a hand on my shoulder as he passed.

I nodded. Rut wasn't a thing you controlled. It just happened. So I made sure to check and see if Harrison had any appointments or meetings. We needed to hire him a secretary, and I was going to put my foot down about it soon.

A small scratching sound came from Emery's office, and he smiled fondly. Stormy came out of the door as soon as he opened it, looking around, and instantly looking at the front door.

"Here, girl." I held out my hand, and she padded over, rubbing into my hand and flopping down on the stair next to me for pets.

"I think she's adjusted enough now to let her out permanently."

"I agree."

Emery stood at the bottom of the stairs. Finally, he spoke. "I'm the only one she hasn't told she loves yet."

"It'll happen. She said it to all of us just now."

He blew out a slow breath. "Let me get this girl some exercise. Take my mind off it. Stormy."

The cat looked up from her place, and he jogged up the stairs past her. She jumped up and followed him without question, eager to match his playful energy.

I couldn't move. There was nothing for me to do except punish myself in the gym, and I'd already done that once today. Pulling out my phone, I gave in to the temptation of looking at the coverage everywhere.

Senator's Daughter Engaged to Influential Pack.

Party Petra Finally Settling Down?

How Will the Bonding of Senator Merriton's Daughter Affect His Political Future?

Arranged? Petra Merriton's Partying Finally Landed Her a Pack.

Will Petra Merriton's Bonding Put an End to Childish Antics?

Is She Okay? Why We Think Miss Merriton's New Pack Isn't Ideal.

If the Senator weren't about to announce his run for chancellor, I didn't think there would be quite as many stories. As it was, the campaign made a huge deal out of it. I saw the official press release. Which meant that media outlets *had* to cover it if they didn't want it to look like they snubbed the Senator.

I shook my head. He always seemed like a decent guy when I was on his detail, but the way he treated Petra had me questioning everything I thought I knew. We still protected him, but I didn't think I would ever volunteer again.

Most of the pictures of Petra were the ones she hated. The one from her time in college, and the one when she'd been with me. I saw one with the Senator and his wife from that night, and another where she danced with George, one of the Alphas of this pack.

But other than that... there was very little. Petra wasn't in the public eye unless she was dragged there. It dawned on me that these were the only photos they had of her. No doubt she'd been instructed to keep out of the spotlight after what happened all those years ago. But why? Temporarily, yeah. But if the media never had anything else to report on when it came to Petra, the same narrative would have to do: she was an addict and a party animal who needed to be contained.

Something hard and ugly hardened in my chest. It felt intentional. For all these years, my Omega did what she could to preserve the only family she had left, be respectful of her father's grief, and make him proud.

He hadn't done the same.

From my view, there was the expectation that Petra would fall in line like she always had, no matter how she felt about it. End of story. I nearly lost my shit when Emery told me what he said to her on the phone.

But you would never know from the outside.

Whoever the Merritons had running their PR was damn good at their job, and either had it out for Petra, or had been instructed to do this. If it were true, there would be hell to pay.

I sat on the stairs for more than an hour, hoping Petra would come back. But she didn't. The whole downstairs smelled incredible because of whatever Blake was cooking, and Emery had long since tired Stormy out. Finally, I stood and went to the door of Harrison's office. "Have we waited long enough?"

He glanced at the clock. "I think so."

"Good." I spun on my heel, and he called after me. "Cole."

"Yeah?"

Sighing, he stood. "I don't know how to break her shell. She's holding back the last piece she needs to fully trust us. Be gentle."

As if I could be anything else with her. "I will."

Everything felt better. I headed for the door, ready to bring our Omega home.

It was strange seeing her door without anyone guarding it. But in a way I was glad. Our employees had already seen enough without adding this to it. I knocked, and Petra didn't answer.

"Petra? Are you okay?"

There were no sounds from inside. Not even the telltale shuffling of someone intentionally *not* opening the door. Dread and instinct had me pulling up the door logs on my phone. We didn't collect much data, but every time one of our locks was opened, there was a record.

Sure enough, her door opened when she'd left us. Half an hour later, it opened again. I called Harrison, barely waiting until he picked up. "She's gone."

CHAPTER THIRTY-NINE

PETRA

*A*n unknown number rang on my phone, and I declined it, wiping my tears on my sleeve. Probably another reporter looking for a comment about the engagement.

The same number called again, and I declined it again. "Fucking stop it," I hissed.

Then a text.

> It's George. Please pick up.

This time when the call came through, I answered. "You fucking screwed me."

"We didn't, I swear."

I flipped the phone to speaker and stalked to my bedroom, anger overcoming my grief for the moment. "Yeah, well, if you didn't, why is the whole world talking about our engagement? You promised me you'd ask them to hold off for a few days."

"Petra," George said. "We did. I swear, we said we wanted the announcement to wait. We're just as surprised as you are about it."

"I haven't even been able to dig into everything. Who released it first?"

A long silence stretched out over the call. "Your father's office did," another voice finally said. Maybe Stuart. "We're really sorry, Petra. But we promise we'll make the best of it."

"I'm still looking for a way out of this bullshit arrangement," I said. "So you better keep your phone on. If you don't, and I figure out something, it'll be you who's getting the unpleasant surprise."

I hit the end button on the call and sank onto my bed. It still smelled like the combination of Emery and me. Enough to make me cry all over again.

Fuck this.

Fuck all of this.

I glanced at a few of the headlines while I was sobbing in the hallway. They were predictable. But fine. If they wanted Petra the party girl? They'd fucking get her.

Part of me hated the impulse, but what else could I do? Sitting here in this apartment was fucking impossible. It felt like there was no air in here. Going back upstairs, I would be in tears because all of them would be perfect and understanding. I needed mindless. I needed fun. I needed something else all together.

Sloane picked up on the first ring. "Oh my *god*, I am going to kill you. Where the hell have you been?"

"I'll tell you everything, but first, question."

"Sure."

"Feel like getting drunk tonight?"

No hesitation. "Fuck yes."

"Preferably somewhere where the press won't be on my tail. But I can't stay in my apartment."

"Not a problem," she sounded like she was moving around. "I can get us in the back door of Pavilion. So if you can get there under the radar, we're golden."

"Good."

I spilled all the details to her while I stripped and shoved my way through all the clothes in my closet, looking for something that was very much *not* appropriate according to Carmen and her PR brigade.

There. A strapless dress which started black at the top and faded into shimmering gold. It was short enough I would need to be careful getting in and out of the car.

"That's awful," Sloane said. "But it'll be good to get your mind off it."

"If you have any ideas, I'm open to hearing them."

She laughed. "Yeah, I know you, Bee. You're actually not ready for them. Why the hell do you think you're getting ready to go to a club with me right now? If you actually wanted to talk about a plan we'd be curling up with ice cream and a movie we've seen twenty times."

"Fuck." She wasn't wrong. There was a reason I wasn't upstairs being held. Because I needed something else. I needed to *not think*. Exactly like what I asked Harrison for yesterday. "I feel attacked."

"Sorry, Bumble. It's the truth."

I took glittery gold eyeshadow and brushed it on. "Am I running away?"

That made her laugh even harder. "Oh, one-hundred percent. But it's okay. Run away for one night, get the anger, fear, and shock out of your system, and make sure you don't get so drunk you have to deal with all of this while hungover."

"And I'm not being a total idiot?"

"No." She snorted. "You and I both know I've done dumber shit than this over less important things. I'm surprised the pack doesn't at least want to come with you to the club, even if they're not dancing with you."

I said nothing.

"You haven't told them you wanted to go out?"

"I told them I needed space to get my head around it. The stalker is gone. I'm not their property."

Sloane's voice was soft. "Bee, you know that's not what I meant. But those guys? I know I haven't met them all, but if they all look at you the way Cole does? They care about you."

They loved me.

And I loved them.

Tonight, when I wasn't this person I hated, I would tell them all again how much I wanted them. How much I loved them. If I couldn't get us out of this mess, I didn't want them to see this version of me. The messy, angry, scared, *broken* Omega who couldn't seem to get ahold of herself. If I needed to say goodbye, I wanted their memories of me to be of someone brave and collected.

I couldn't help but imagine it the other way. If I had to say goodbye and let them see everything, it would hurt them so much more.

"I know," I said softly, finally answering her. Wiggling the dress over my head, I straightened it and used some dry shampoo and fished some dangly earrings out of my jewelry box.

"I'm ready," I told her. "I'll have Brian drop me off behind the club."

"Okay. Be careful please. That guy is in jail, but you just got blasted all over the news. So..."

I grabbed a clutch for my phone and wallet and slipped into my black heels, which were *definitely* more than two inches tall. "It'll be fine," I said. "I'll go out the back entrance of the tower."

"All right. See you soon!"

Hanging up, I looked at myself in the mirror one last time and called Brian.

Pavilion was incredible. I wasn't normally a club person, but this place was so cool I wanted to come here when I wasn't trying to forget the rest of my life.

Above our heads, a giant circus tent was suspended from the ceiling. It seemed to shift colors in all the lights, but in the rare flash of white, it was crimson and gold. Haze hung in the air, catching the spinning lights in their whirling patterns and making the aerialists above us seem like ghosts or angels.

Music pounded through my ears and swirled around me. The hard, electric rhythm was so far from what the scene of the club portrayed, and yet it fit perfectly at the same time.

Sloane and I danced near a pedestal where a woman juggled balls made of glass, never making a mistake. My best friend was true to her word. We'd slipped in the back of the club past the security guard with him only tipping his hat.

"How is it you can just walk in here?" I asked. "Isn't this club super exclusive?"

She shrugged. "I dance here sometimes."

"So do a lot of people."

Grabbing my wrist, she guided me down a darkened hallway toward where music was thumping. "I mean as an employee."

"What? You didn't tell me that."

"I... didn't tell anyone that. Not exactly a good thing for a ballet dancer to moonlight as a club dancer."

I frowned. "Why not?"

We dodged past a club employee coming out of a supply closet. "They just don't like it. Now, what are we drinking tonight?" She laughed when I winced. "Something that doesn't taste like alcohol. Got it."

The drinks she ordered were delicious. Sweet apple, nearly like a caramel apple. Which made sense as a treat for a circus. But it also made me think of Cole. So I downed the drink and Sloane got me another one.

Now two drinks in, my dancing was easier, and the tightness in my chest was finally easing. Here in the middle of this crowd, I could be anonymous, and just *move*. *Breathe*. Be someone whose only worry was how long her feet would last in her high heels and not whether she was going to be forced into an arranged bond.

I shook my head. Stop it, Petra. You're trying to *not* think about it, remember?

Sloane spun me under her arm, and then I spun her under mine, her wild blonde hair catching the lights and turning into a rainbow.

She grinned at me, and let me go, stepping a little away. The scent of salt and caramel wrapped around me like a caress a second before hands skimmed my waist and pulled me back against a body I knew too well.

The music was too loud to hear the purr I *felt*, but it was no less effective. "I wish this was the dress you were wearing when I met you," he said into my ear. "Because it's fucking stunning, honeybee."

Sloane winked and blew me a kiss. My mouth dropped open. "You called him?"

Stepping forward, she grabbed my hand. "I did. Because you were running away, and whether or not you can see it, you need them as much as they need you. Don't be mad."

Part of me felt like I should be, but I wasn't. It was like she'd popped a hole in the shield which had risen around me the moment I found out everything had been announced. I couldn't let anyone near me because I was alone. It was how it had been since Mom and the others died. Now felt no different.

Except it *was* different. Because there was an Alpha wrapped around me, and all he wanted was to comfort me. "I'm not mad."

"Call me later," she said, stepping closer. "And do me a favor."

"What's that?"

"For your sake, and everyone else... *stop giving a fuck*."

She disappeared into the crowd before I could say anything else, and I turned to face Cole.

We weren't dancing, not really, and I couldn't interpret the look on his face. "I don't know whether to kiss you or spank you," he said. "Do you have any idea how terrifying it was to find you *gone*? A day after we caught the guy trying to kill you? If Sloane hadn't called when she did, all of us would be a fucking wreck."

I couldn't help but look at him. Dark jeans and a t-shirt that stretched over his chest and biceps. "I'm sorry."

He took my face in his hands, pressing his forehead to mine. I barely heard him through the music. "You don't have to be. We're not your jailers, Petra. I—" One hand shifted to grip my hair. "I won't lie. The bodyguard in me is pissed. But the rest of me is just relieved to see you're safe."

My heart ached. I held his forearms like an anchor. "I thought I was safe. He's gone, right?"

"Honeybee, I can't feel you," he said. "The minute you walk out of my sight, I can't fucking breathe, not knowing how you feel or if you're really okay. After weeks of thinking about every way someone could come after you? It's not your fault I feel that way, but I do."

Slowly, I slid my hands up his arms and wove them around his neck. "Are the others here?"

"Just me. We didn't want to overwhelm you even more."

Pressing my body against his, I moved my hips back and forth. "Dance with me."

Cole's hands fell to my waist, and we moved together, surrendering to the music. He was right. I was so fucking overwhelmed that it had felt like too much. I'd removed myself from the situation. But I didn't stop to think how they would feel when I left.

Like he could sense the direction of my thoughts, his hands tightened on my ribs. "Petra, stop."

"Stop what?"

He pinned me with a stare that had me relenting. "You know exactly what. I didn't come after you to make you think you did anything wrong. Or to make you feel guilty. I came because my Omega is in *pain*, and I can't fucking stand it."

I held onto him so tightly I had to be hurting him, but he didn't move at all. Cole only held me back.

There were two options in front of me. I could fall apart in the arms of my Alpha, the way my entire being was screaming to, or I could push it aside until we were home and have some fun.

"Come with me." I grabbed his hand and pulled him through the crowd of dancers back the way Sloane and I had entered.

Please don't be locked.

The closet the employee had come out was right there, and I grinned when the handle turned. Fuck yes.

"A closet?" The smile was obvious in Cole's voice. "Seems appropriate."

"I thought so."

The door barely closed before his hands were on me, pushing me back against the door so he could lock it. "This dress has me conflicted too," his mouth collided with mine, both of us falling into a place where it was just us. Just our scents. Just two people finding each other in the darkness, like it had been the night we met.

Sloane wasn't going to drag me away this time.

"Why?"

Cole lifted me, holding me against the door and wrapping my legs around his hips. His body made sure I didn't fall as he slid his hands up my thighs to find my lace thong beneath the tiny hem of the dress. "Because it's so fucking hot. I only ever want you to wear things like this." He yanked my thong down around my thighs. "And at the same time, I want to tear it off you and burn it so no other Alpha gets to see you in it."

His mouth met my neck, teeth and tongue scraping over my pulse. "You turn me into a fucking animal." Cole made a sound, one low grunt of effort, and the thong ripped apart.

"Fuck." I arched between him and the wall. "I didn't think people did that in real life."

"Most people fuck in beds instead of closets too, honeybee.

Guess we're not normal." He moved between us, slipping my ruined thong into the pocket of his jeans and undoing his belt.

I grabbed his shoulders, holding him to me and inhaling the salty sweetness that was him. The salt grew stronger when he was like this, adding spice to his caramel. I knew exactly what he meant when he said he turned into an animal, because I felt it too.

Cole lined his cock up and sheathed himself inside me in one smooth movement. Sparkles and stars swam across my vision. "Promise me," I begged him. "Promise me we'll never be normal."

There was so much more to the words I hoped he heard. Promise we'll be together for there to be a *never*. Promise you'll stay even though it was all fucked right now. Promise me everything.

His mouth came down hard on mine, everything between us slamming together. Tangling. Combining. There was no denying this thing between us. Maybe the papers were right. Maybe I was high when I left that charity ball—but it was because I was high on him.

"I promise." His words scraped along my skin, rough and powerful. Every thrust punctuated the simple phrase. My back scraped against the door, the hinges creaking like a headboard.

Cole's fingers gripped my ass, yanking me against him, and that tiny change in angle sent me through the roof. I was floating up with the aerial dancers and falling back down through a symphony.

"Cole, please." I had no idea what I was begging for. More of him and this? For him to remind me of what they were and how we all got here. The length and the curve of him made this so good. So *fucking* good. Like my orgasm didn't end, it was one long dive into pleasure and shining and glittery as the gold on my dress.

I loved the sounds of him about to come. As long as I lived, nothing would ever make me feel more powerful. That being with me could unravel an Alpha and make him feral. Drive him mad. Make him rut.

He slammed deep, dropping his head onto my shoulder as he

shuddered, pulling back just far enough that his knot wasn't inside me. "Wait—"

"I think that's the hardest thing I've ever done," he groaned. "And don't worry, honeybee, I want to be knotted inside your cunt for hours. Don't ever doubt it. But while I'll fuck you in a closet, I don't want to knot you here. Neither of us would be comfortable."

Even now, in the middle of his own pleasure, he was only thinking about me. I held onto him while he slipped out of me and zipped up his jeans. He tilted my chin up so I was looking at him. "You okay?"

"Are they going to be angry with me?"

Cole shook his head and kissed me. "Not even a little, honeybee. We were worried—" He cut himself off.

"What?"

He sighed. "For a second it felt like you were leaving for good. Harrison killed that idea before it even had a chance to take root. But *that* was our first thought. Not fear."

"I'm sorry. I—" My voice broke.

"Shh." He held me close. "You're okay. We have you, Petra. I promise we have you."

Sighing, I reached down and unlocked the door. "Take me home?"

Cole smiled. "Yes, ma'am."

CHAPTER FORTY

PETRA

Cole kept his arm around me all the way home. It was a little weird to be in a car with him while just a couple, not a bodyguard and protectee. He called one of their drivers, and I sent Brian home.

We pulled up to the back of Starling Tower, and he got out first, still keeping his arm around me. "I need to stop at my apartment first," I said.

"You sure? I kind of want them to see you in this dress."

I smirked. "I'll keep it on, but I need more clothes. And panties."

There was a silence. He wanted to ask me to move in—it was spinning in the air between us. That would be part of everything I was sure we were about to talk about.

"Unless you plan on giving that pair back?"

Cole's hand crept down to my ass and squeezed. "Not sure what you'd do with them now. They are *thoroughly* ruined."

I held out my hand. "I'll throw them away."

"Maybe I'll keep them." He pressed the elevator button for my floor.

"Why on earth would you do that?"

He pulled them out of his pocket and held them up to his nose, inhaling so deeply I blushed. Cole never looked away. "No reason."

For once, I had no response. He laughed and followed me out of the elevator. I tapped my keycard, and the door unlocked. The door stuck a little when I pressed it open, and a scrape under my foot made me freeze. "Cole."

He pulled me behind him immediately, putting a finger to his lips. We listened, but there was no sound. He opened the door silently, and I looked around the corner.

My apartment was destroyed.

"Stay here," he said.

Somehow he managed to be silent, even on the broken glass on the floor. He wasn't armed. What if there was someone in the apartment? I didn't dare speak in case. Fear rooted me to the spot.

He disappeared around the corner toward my bedroom. A minute later he came back. "It's clear."

I stepped inside, taking in the wreckage of the apartment. There wasn't anything that wasn't touched. Even the couch was ripped open in multiple places. Glass crunched under my shoes.

Everything I chose to make this place home was ruined. The oven door was cracked. My television tipped onto the glass coffee table, shattering it. One of my lamps was the source of glass and porcelain beneath our feet.

And somehow, despite the pain of seeing this place destroyed, it still hurt less than everything else.

"I guess I really need to grab things, huh?" I stepped toward the bedroom, and Cole stopped me, wrapping his arms around me from behind. "Hold on." He sounded like he'd just run a hundred miles. "I need a fucking minute."

It all slammed into me at once. I'd been gone maybe three hours. What if I'd been here and not at the club? What if I'd had Sloane come over for a girl's night like she suggested? What would they have done?

The entire apartment was painted with blatant violence.

I could be dead right now.

How did they get in? *Who?*

"Oh, fuck." My knees went soft, Cole still holding me upright. He was holding me so hard it hurt.

Cole made sure I was steady as he stood me up and turned me around. Raw devastation shone through his gaze. "Whatever made you go to the club, I'll thank it every single day for the rest of my life." He crushed me against his chest.

"I don't understand." My mind couldn't wrap my head around it. "You caught him. They arrested him. Who?"

His mouth firmed into a line. "I don't know. But we're going to find out. I can't let you get anything right now. We have to leave everything the way it is, okay? We'll get you your things after."

I turned and went to my bedroom, understanding and still needing to see it. "Oh."

It was no better. In fact, it was worse. The drawers were turned out—including the sex toys—and the bed was destroyed. Long tears through the comforter, with what could have been a knife. Through the crack in the door, I saw my bathroom mirror was shattered.

Cole's arm curled around my shoulder. "Let's go, honeybee. We'll save whatever we can. We need to get the police here as quickly as possible."

"Wait." I pulled away. "Just one thing."

There, on the floor, was the red scarf. It looked mostly unscathed. I picked it up, relieved to feel the jagged pieces of wood still inside it. The scarf, too, miraculously survived the destruction.

"Okay."

I let Cole lead me away and to the elevator. How could I feel this blank? It was like there was a window between me and the rest of the world.

He opened the door to the penthouse, and it smelled incredible. Both sweet and savory. Low voices resonated in the kitchen and stopped as soon as we entered.

"Harrison," Cole called, walking me to the kitchen. "We have a problem."

My three other Alphas were around the island, and Blake was the first to move, crossing the distance in seconds and holding me. "Hey, baby," he whispered.

"Hey." I choked back a sob.

They weren't angry. Cole said it, but I had needed to see it.

"A security breach," Cole said. "Petra's apartment was vandalized."

The air in the kitchen was deadly still, and Harrison's voice was deadlier. "What the fuck did you just say?"

Cole spoke in clipped words, telling them what happened. "We need to deal with this right now. Starting with checking the penthouse security."

"We've been all over the house," Emery said. "There's definitely no one here. But I'll check the systems."

Harrison tilted my head to him, though I was still in Blake's arms. He kissed me. "I'm glad you're safe, little one. We have a lot to talk about once this is taken care of, don't we?"

"Yeah."

"Okay," he said.

I shifted. "Is it okay for me to go upstairs? I'd like to change."

"It is," Emery said. "But I'll go with you."

Blake kissed my cheek. "I made all kinds of food if you're hungry. And I love the fuck out of this dress, even if you're changing."

My smile was there, but I didn't feel it. "Thanks."

Emery took my hand as we went to the elevator. It would be good to take the shoes off. My feet hurt.

"Do you want your clothes or our clothes? There's no right answer."

"Your clothes."

"Okay. Do you want to wait in your nest?"

I nodded, wishing I could express some kind of emotion. But I felt flat and lifeless.

"I'll be right up." He got off on the bedroom floor, and I went up to the nest. I kicked my shoes off in the bedroom near my own suitcase and wandered through the bathroom. Finally, a real smile broke out on my face.

Stormy was curled up in the nest. She blinked sleepily at me when I turned the low lights on. "Oh, you think this is your nest now?"

She chuffed at me, shifting herself to be more comfortable. I climbed in next to her and leaned my head on her like a pillow. "I guess we can share."

Emery knelt next to me when he arrived. "Snuggling?"

"She's a very good snuggler."

"Yes, she is."

He started to pull the dress up over my head, freezing when he reached my hips. "Sunshine, did you go to the club with no underwear on?"

I laughed. "No, that was Cole."

Smirking, he stripped me the rest of the way, and I let him. He put me into a giant long-sleeved t-shirt and a pair of boxers.

310

They smelled like him. Tonight it was a warm scent, like hot chocolate with a splash of espresso.

Emery laid next to me, squishing me between him and Stormy. "The others have all told you. I haven't had the chance, but I think tonight it's more important than ever. I love you, Petra."

I whined and curled in on myself. Emery came with me, not letting me go. "I love you," I whispered. "I'm sorry I hurt you. I didn't mean to. I wasn't thinking."

He moved so I was entirely the little spoon. All of me was enveloped by him and his scent. "You know what I think?" A kiss on the back of my neck. "You've spent a long time trying to be perfect. Trying to not make anyone angry, staying under the radar, keeping yourself safe the only way you knew how. Of course watching you leave hurt, but because I wanted to help, not because I'm angry with you.

"I'll promise you this, sunshine. I'll never get angry with you for trying to protect yourself. Do I hope you'll feel safe enough with us not to have to? Of course. But it will take time. None of us are perfect, and even though I love you, I'm going to fuck up. We're all going to fuck up. That's okay."

He turned me over to face him, stroking his knuckles down my cheek. "To be clear, tonight you didn't do anything wrong. You *did not* fuck up. I don't want you to think we're going to get angry with you over everything. I'm sure we're going to fight and have fabulous makeup sex, but tonight? You were trying to protect yourself. Nothing more."

His words slowly sank in. Because he'd put into words something I'd always known but had never truly risen to the surface. I was trying to be perfect and stay under the radar. Because when I didn't, bad things happened. They always had, and I'd always had to deal with it alone.

Maybe I didn't have to anymore.

"I love you," I said again, reaching out to trace the lines of his face. "I don't want to leave."

"You don't have to."

"Maybe..."

Emery kissed me hard. "Definitely."

311

A few more kisses and Stormy protested where we pressed up against her. We broke apart laughing.

"I'd like to go see if I can help make anything go faster," Emery said. "Are you okay to stay here with Stormy?"

"Yeah." My whole soul felt a thousand times lighter.

Emery kissed my temple and grabbed a blanket while I curled up next to Stormy. When they all came home, we would figure it out.

CHAPTER FORTY-ONE

BLAKE

*T*he wreckage was devastating. The police weren't here yet, and I would clear out when they came, but I had to see it for myself. There was almost nothing left. Looking at the bedroom, we would be lucky if anything was salvageable.

"Who the fuck did this?" I asked. "I thought you caught the guy. What was his name?"

Harrison stood in the center of the living room, arms crossed, staring at the wreckage. "The man who was arrested was named Greg Winters. We traced the photos and the last message back to his personal computer. He swore he had nothing to do with it, but that's pretty standard when someone's being arrested. But now? I might believe him."

"At the moment I care less about the who and more about the how," Cole said. "Whoever did this came into the building and bypassed every security measure we had. The logs say her door *opened*. It wasn't broken into, it was opened. Which meant they either copied her keycard, made a skeleton card, or stole the Senators. And it allowed them to slip right past her security system."

"You can't tell whose it was?" I asked.

"No." Harrison's mouth was a grim line. "We had to walk the line between security and privacy. When the building was being designed, it was decided that collecting data on individuals going in and out was one step too far. Not to mention hard to regulate, as cards can be borrowed. And guest cards are available."

I understood it, and it made sense. Not everyone wanted fingerprinted locks on their doors. But I sure as hell wished we had the information now.

"Security cameras?" I asked. The look on his face told me everything I needed to know. That footage was gone. "Fuck. This looks bad, doesn't it? And not only for Petra."

"It doesn't look good," Cole said.

"There will be an entire review of the building's security," Harrison said. "Everyone will be issued new keycards, and I will approach the owners once again about giving people tagged ones, but I don't expect it to go well."

I scrubbed my hands over my face. "Do we think there was a mistake? Is this the same person?"

Cole looked like he was about to punch a hole through the wall. "I think so. It's too convenient. We catch the guy and then *boom*. This happens? Petra isn't a big enough player on the public stage to draw murderous attention from multiple people so close together."

"God, I hope not," I said.

We looked around the wreckage, and Cole shook his head. "I was pissed she left, but what if she'd been here? The way the bed looked? I didn't even want her to see it."

"Every resource we have that's not in another active contract is going toward this," Harrison said. "I don't like being toyed with, and I like even less that I threw everything at him before and this still fucking happened."

He rarely sounded like this. Of all of us, Harrison was the most calm and collected, his recent rut aside. So much of what he did was behind the scenes. I didn't doubt he'd tried to find this man with everything he had. They were just more stealthy or luckier.

"Fucking hell," Cole said. "Can we keep this out of the press? Petra's already dealing with enough."

"Oh god." Emery stood at the door.

"Where—"

He held out a hand. "She's in the nest with Stormy. All the alarms and systems are armed. Is there anything left in here?"

I shook my head. "Not much. Maybe some clothes, but they were thorough."

"They're going to want to talk to her," Cole said. "Interview her."

"Not tonight," Emery said, voice final. "She's settled and needs us to be with her. Not the police."

Harrison pulled his phone out of his pocket. "It won't be a

problem. But they're almost here. Cole and I will stay. You guys need to go back to the penthouse."

We didn't need any extra questions. It would be hard enough for Harrison to keep it out of the press entirely without extra pack members hanging around.

"Let us know if you need anything."

Emery and I walked back to the elevator. "Puts a bit of a damper on the surprise."

I shook my head. "No kidding."

This feeling of helplessness was awful. There wasn't anything we could do except wait, and I hated waiting. I'd already made more food and desserts than we could eat for the next few days. *And* put them away.

"I'll feed Stormy," he said. "I think everything else needs to wait until tomorrow."

"Yeah."

We walked into the nest to find Petra and Stormy curled up together, fast asleep. "Stormy," Emery called softly before making the sound cats loved. She opened her eyes sleepily and looked over at us. "Come eat dinner."

Clearly she was conflicted, looking back at Petra before standing and coming to Emery. "Good girl. Let's go. You can snuggle later."

The lights were still on in here, and I turned them as low as possible before stripping down and climbing in next to her. I loved Petra soft and sleepy. "I'm awake," she said. "Promise."

"You don't have to be."

"Mmmk."

I kissed her softly. She was awake enough to respond and wrap her arms around my neck. "Want to keep my cock warm while you sleep, baby?"

The softest whine reached my ears. "Yeah."

It wasn't about warmth. Not really. It was about the fact that she'd been in danger and we hadn't known. And now I wanted to be as close to her as possible, including inside her.

Easing her out of the boxers Emery gave her, I pulled her leg over my hip and eased into her. All the way, as far as I could go. She was heat incarnate. Being inside her was sweet fucking heaven, and her cinnamon scent lifted as we came together. Pure, delicious sugar. My girl was happy, even if everything around her was falling apart.

"You feel good," I told her softly.

Petra smiled and nestled in closer, relaxing into sleep.

When Emery came back he just smirked, seeing the way we were arranged. But he said nothing, simply joining us, taking Petra's other side.

Whatever remained of the tension in her body disappeared between the two of us. Her unconscious mind and body trusted us completely. In the morning, we'd make sure the rest of her did too.

CHAPTER FORTY-TWO

PETRA

*W*aking up with a cock inside me was oddly soothing.

I giggled to myself. That wasn't a sentence I ever thought I'd say. I squeezed down on it and Blake moaned in my ear.

"I didn't think waking up with you could get any better, but hearing you laugh and your pussy gripping me just changed my mind."

His hand gently cupped the back of my head, holding me against him. My body was sprawled across his chest, legs falling to either side. "Morning."

"Morning, baby."

Lifting my head, I looked at the nest. Emery was still asleep, and Stormy was lying next to Blake and I, stretched out, belly exposed. "Someone's a happy girl." I buried my hand in the fur of her stomach, and she turned even further into the stretch, rolling on her back.

"Where are Cole and Harrison?"

"They're in their rooms," Blake said. "It took a while downstairs, and they didn't want to wake you. They checked in when they got back."

"I should go see them," I said. Then I grinned. "Is your cock going to survive without me?"

He sighed dramatically. "If it must, I'll make it a burden I must bear."

Pushing up off him, we both groaned when we came apart. "I liked it, though. Definitely want to try it again."

Blake's eyes were dark with promise. "Good. But be warned, we all like it. Be careful what you wish for."

I stopped in the bathroom on my way out and went down a floor. It struck me that I'd never been in the guys' bedrooms. There hadn't been a need. With everything spinning out of control, it hadn't crossed any of our minds. But I knew which door belonged to which. The first door on my left was Harrison's.

Of my many good qualities, stealth wasn't one of them. I tried to be quiet while opening the door, but it creaked. "Traitor," I breathed the word.

I looked around the room and smiled. It was very much my Alpha. Rich, warm earth tones and rough textures. A big leather armchair sat near the big window, and his bed was big, wood, and felt exactly like him. Dark sage walls made it feel like the woods I sometimes imagined with his scent.

Harrison slept on his back, one arm thrown over his face and a sheet covering his hips. What I could see was all bare skin, and I liked it. If he'd been up all night fixing things, I didn't want to wake him. But I did want to be near him.

"Little one, how long are you going to stare at me before you get your ass in my bed?"

A gasp startled out of me. "You're awake?"

"I am."

I crossed the room and slid onto the bed. Harrison met me halfway. "I'm sorry. I didn't want to wake you up."

"If the door hadn't, your scent would have. Don't worry."

"Still. You were up late because of me. Why would that wake you?"

"Just the way I am," he said, stroking one big hand down my side until he reached my bare hip. "I was in the military for a while. The training from it sticks deep. Even more so when you protect people for a living. Sometimes you have to wake up and be alert at a moment's notice."

The military made so much sense. It just reminded me I had so much to learn about them. "The military, then security. That's a long way from practically owning a building in downtown Slate City along with the best security firm there is."

He chuckled. "I suppose so. The military and Atwood Security were all on my own. The latter with Cole. As far as this place?" A sly smirk played on his face. "The Atwood name might not be well known, but we're well off."

"No kidding."

"But I wanted to do something other than invest my family's

318

money. I wanted to experience life in a different way, so I joined. When I... left, I still wanted to protect people."

I rolled on my back and stared at the ceiling. This bed was so big we were both in it and I could still starfish to the fullest extent. "You say you left like something bad happened."

"It did. I didn't protect someone the way I should have, and they were killed."

My stomach swooped. "So you protect people to make up for it?"

"Something like that."

"I'm sure you did everything you could."

"Yeah." He looked away. "I did. And it didn't matter. I won't let that happen again."

He looked so sad. It reminded me the way I felt whenever I thought about mom. Harrison didn't deserve to have that look on his face, or any of those emotions. I turned and climbed over until I was on top of him looking down.

The tattoo on his shoulder drew my eyes. It was an incredible piece. The outline of a roaring lion, the image fading into what looked like a map from above. The piece that curved down over the front of his shoulder was a military braid woven with symbols. I saw a date, what looked like military ribbons, and some coordinates. "How long ago was this?"

"A decade."

"How many lives have you saved since then?"

Harrison grabbed my ribs, his hands wide enough to nearly span my whole body with them together. "Saving lives doesn't negate lives lost. I wish it did, but I'll always carry it with me."

"You're a good Alpha," I whispered. "If I'm not allowed to beat myself up over stuff I can't control, then neither can any of you. Do you want to talk about it?"

He chuckled, lifting me up and lowering me like he was using me to work out. "I'll remember that. It's closer to the surface today, given last night. And no. Not right now."

"Someday I'm going to get stories about you. I can only imagine the kinds of things younger Harrison got into. Especially somewhere like bootcamp."

"Deal," he said. "But only if you give me a story for each of mine."

"This is a trap, isn't it?"

Lowering me down close enough to kiss me, he grinned. "And you walked right into it."

"Seems like I'm missing something in here." Cole stood in the door, hair mussed, nothing on but boxers. "Harrison?"

The Alpha beneath me nodded and smirked at my raised eyebrows. "Because we're all so close, we ask before we go into each other's private space."

"That makes sense."

"It goes for you too," Cole said, joining us on the bed. "With upstairs."

I rolled my eyes, and for the moment imagined this was normal and permanent. "I can't keep you guys away from an entire floor."

"If that's what you need, then yes, you can," Harrison said, bringing me to the mattress between him and Cole.

Pulling the neck of the shirt aside to kiss my shoulder, Cole took his time. "Good morning. I know it's probably not what you want to think about right now, but the police will need to speak to you later."

Fuck. "Yeah, I guess I saw that coming."

"They're going to keep it quiet," Harrison said. "And I hope it's okay, but until the Mayor's party, I want to keep you here. Where you're safe. I fucked up finding him once—I don't plan on doing it again."

I closed my eyes. "No arguments from me. I just want it to stop. Does it even have anything to do with me? I'm just something he's using to get at my father."

"The destruction last night was very personal," Harrison said. "It's possible he's become attached to you through his threats. But we're going to find him. Everyone I have is working on it, and I'm going to call in all the favors until something breaks."

"Thank you."

He only kissed my forehead in response.

"And now," Cole said. "The five of us need to have a talk, honeybee. I saw Blake. He's getting you tea, and I think he might even give you a slice of the cake he baked last night for breakfast. Plus, we have a surprise for you."

My stomach twisted. "What kind of surprise?" All the surprises lately were awful, and I wasn't really looking forward to another one.

"It was Cole's idea. I think you're going to like it."

"Okay."

"Do you want to do anything first? Shower or change?"

I sat up. "I guess I should put underwear on."

"No one will mind if you don't," Harrison said with a laugh.

No, they wouldn't. But given what we were talking about, clothing was probably good. At least to start. It wasn't exactly a barrier when they were determined.

"Meet us in the living room, little one."

"Okay."

I didn't want to have this conversation. Instead, I would rather pretend the world outside of this penthouse didn't exist. But they were right. It needed to happen.

Changing into comfy clothes, I cleaned up some of the ones left on the floor. Stormy lunged after a pair of my leggings dragging on the ground. "You like that?"

I pulled them again, and she chased them. Her claws dug in, but then she let them go. She was used to playing like this. The space on this floor was huge. "You want to play?"

Stormy lowered her body to the ground, focusing on me and the leggings. Her butt wiggled like she was getting ready to pounce. My smile couldn't be stopped.

I ran.

Leggings flew behind me like a flag. They were the only reason she didn't tackle me because she was trying to catch the leggings out of the air. She almost had them, but I ripped them away, zigzagging them across the ground and watching her smack her paws on the carpet trying to stop them.

We went another two circuits of the room before I let her catch them. I was out of breath, but I was smiling. I never imagined having any kind of leopard as a pet, but Stormy was one of the sweetest animals ever.

Thinking about having her as a pet dragged me back. I was procrastinating. Time to get it over with.

I took the elevator down to the second floor and stopped the second I stepped into the living room. At the other end, framed against the city visible through the wall of windows, was a grand piano. Morning light fell on it like a spotlight. This hadn't been here the last time I was in the room.

The four of them were here, all looking at me. It felt like we were all collectively holding our breath.

Every emotion under the damn sun poured over me. Shock, grief, awe, joy, and a jumble of so many things I couldn't take a full breath.

"You bought me a piano?"

"Yes," Cole said simply.

I burst into tears. All the emotions boiling up and over. Ragged, jerking sobs which nearly put me on the floor.

Arms came around me. "I'm sorry," Cole said. "I thought you would like it."

"I do." If I weren't already crying I would have laughed from how different my sentiment was to my tone. "I love it. I love it."

He released me so I could go to it. I lifted the cover to expose the keys. *Steinway*, painted in gold lettering across it. It was a full concert grand too. I hit middle C, the note floating purely and crisply through the air. "This is—" I shook my head. "I'm sorry for crying. I just don't know what to say."

"You don't have to say anything. But I know what I saw in that room, Petra. Not only are you gifted, you *love* this."

Since we met, this was the thing we'd been dancing around. I hated talking about it, and thinking about it, but it was time. They had to know. "I do."

"Then why?" Emery asked. "Why are you going to law school and not... playing?"

"Before you answer," Harrison said with a smile. "Will you play something?"

Nerves swirled in my gut. It was different playing for people so close to you. Vulnerable in a way you couldn't explain to those who didn't perform. But it was *them*. And I wanted to play.

Turning, I found my place. E minor. A soft and echoing

beginning. I pressed the damper pedal down, allowing the ethereal notes to blend together.

This song was simple, but beautiful. It used discordance to its advantage, putting together notes you wouldn't quite guess, but resolved into something that made you feel wistful and emotional.

It moved from the high registers to the lower, resonating deeply and growing stronger before fading once more. The song ended at the opposite end of the piano from where I started, the bass notes lingering in the air as I lifted my hands from the keys.

Four Alphas stared at me, spellbound. "For the love of everything, please don't clap," I begged, my face already flushing red.

Emery was on his feet and suddenly next to me. He didn't even make me stand before pulling me to him, holding me against his body. "You are incredible," he whispered. "That was so fucking beautiful."

"It's a simple song."

"Just because something is simple doesn't make it easy," Blake said. "The same is true in food."

Emery held me close a moment more before leaning down and kissing my hair. "You don't have to be modest with us, sunshine. We see all of you, and we know the truth."

My face flushed with embarrassment at the same time as my chest filled with joy and peace. It was one thing to perform, and another to have someone connect with it.

I sat on the piano bench and pulled my feet up, cross-legged. This was a pose my body recognized. Feeling keys beneath my fingers—even just dragging the tips across them—was pure comfort.

"You okay for this?" Cole asked.

"I have to be. You need to hear it. First, I didn't go to college. I went to conservatory to study piano when everything happened. It didn't matter much when I had to pull out. I was already good." The one thing I wouldn't do anymore was hide my talent from them.

I *was* talented. I was damn fucking good.

"And this is hard to talk about." There were still tears on my face. I wiped them on my sleeve. "Everything seemed fine until a couple of years ago. My dad was home from the capital, and I don't know where Carmen was. It was the anniversary of the accident, so not a great day for him.

"Up until then, I practiced pretty much every day. I didn't know where I wanted to play, only that I wanted to. Secretly, I hoped to be part of an orchestra, or even be like Mom and play on my own. That part did, and does, make me nervous because I genuinely don't like being in the spotlight."

Blake smirked. "Could have fooled me."

I raised my middle finger, drawing laughs from all of them.

"I woke up in the middle of the night to huge crashing noises. Our house is a fortress like this place, so I wasn't worried about anyone being in the house. And there wasn't. I found my father blackout drunk, destroying my mother's piano."

Instant growls came from all around me. "Did he hurt you?" Harrison's voice promised violence.

"No. No, it wasn't like that. Dad doesn't drink that much, with the rare exception of the anniversary. And it was never that bad before. I tried to stop him, but he was too far gone and too far along in breaking it apart." Emotion rose in my chest. "When he stopped... he was on the floor, sobbing. I'll never forget the look in his eyes."

"I can't, Petra. I can't do it. Every time you play I hear her and it tears me open all over again. I can't listen to it anymore. It'll break me more than I'm already broken. I had to make it stop, do you understand? I had to make it stop."

He sobbed, the cries wracking his body in the middle of the wreckage. "All you do is play. You look so much like her. You play just like her, and it's always a new knife in the heart."

I cleared my throat. "I got him in bed and cleaned up what I could. In the morning I called our cleaning service. They took the wreckage away, but I kept a couple of keys. Middle C, a D, and one of the flats. It always got stuck and sounded plunky. But my mom never fixed it. Said it gave the piano character."

Cole sank down to the ground from where he'd been standing, mirroring my pose on the floor. "The scarf?"

"Yeah. The pieces are okay. Even if nothing else is, at least I have those."

"Sunshine—"

I shook my head, barely keeping my voice from breaking. "Let me finish or I'll never get through it."

Emery watched me with such love in his eyes, it hurt. All of them looked at me like I was precious. I wasn't used to it. "The next day, Dad asked me what happened to the piano. He didn't remember anything. It hurt him so much that I told him I'd had it moved into storage because it was painful to have it around. I shouldn't have lied, I know, but I couldn't bear making him feel any of that again. Or telling him he'd destroyed it.

"It was such an act of grief, I knew he'd regret it. And it wasn't just the piano, it was me. I was the one thing causing him pain. Giving him flashbacks. Bringing up pain. Like he said, a dagger to the heart over and over again."

"Petra—"

I forged ahead. "A few days later I asked what he thought about me following in his footsteps by going to law school. Part of me hoped he'd say no and tell me to keep going with music, but I don't think I've ever seen him so happy. And *proud*.

"My dad... my dad loves me so much," I said. "But I never had that. Especially after the conservatory thing. Before the accident, maybe, but I don't really remember. I don't know if it was selfish or naïve, but I couldn't let that go. So I studied for LSATs. Took me a while to get it right, because I'm smart, but my mind isn't made for it. And by the time I wanted to tell him I couldn't do it, it was too late. He'd been telling everyone I was accepted to the school. He paid my tuition up front even though he didn't have to. And for once, I wanted him to look at me and be proud of a real accomplishment."

I shrugged and ran a finger down the keys again. "So now I'm here. Stuck."

"If you could do anything," Blake asked. "What would you do?"

How long had it been since I thought about that? Years, probably. "It will sound silly."

"I very much doubt that," Harrison said.

"I would just... exist. And play music. Write it. Learn it. Play it for people."

Emery leaned forward. "That doesn't sound silly at all."

"For as long as I can remember I wanted something quieter than the rest of the world seemed to want. When Mom was alive it was one thing. We traveled with her and Dad, but it was always just the five of us. It never felt like more."

Blake stood. "If that's what you want, I think you should do it."

I opened my mouth, and he shook his head. "Let me talk, baby. Because I know what you're going to say. That the tuition is already paid. It will make your father upset. People already know about you going to the school and they expect it. The media will go after you for dropping out. Right?"

"Yeah."

His gaze turned me to stone. I couldn't move even if I wanted to. Passion radiated from him in both form and breath. "You know what's missing from every one of those reasons? *You*. Absolutely none of those reasons have to do with you. They're all about making someone else happy or keeping the peace. And please hear me when I say this. It is *bullshit*."

I stared at him, speechless.

"Tell me this. What happens if you drop out of school? Truly? What happens?"

"I'll be disappointing people."

Blake came and knelt in front of me, taking my hands. "And what about that is different from your relationships now?" I winced, and he squeezed my hands. It was true. Everything I did seemed to disappoint someone, no matter how hard I tried. "I know, baby, and I'm sorry. God knows I hate that you have to feel it. But if they're going to think of you one way no matter what, what do you have to lose? You are destroying yourself for everyone else. You deserve to be happy, too."

"So just don't go back? What about the money?"

Harrison snorted, and I smiled in spite of myself. It was so inelegant for him it took me by surprise. "You were attacked on school grounds. You could sue them and get five times the tuition money. I'm guessing they'll fall over their feet to give it back if you promise not to sue them."

I shook my head. "I don't have any music connections

anymore. No one knows who I am. If I wanted to do anything in that world, it would be entirely from scratch."

Blake came up higher on his knees and slid a hand behind my neck, pulling me closer so our foreheads touched. "Baby, *listen* to yourself. You're bending over backward trying to get away from what you really want. Yes, people's feelings might get hurt if you choose a different path. But no one is *harmed* by that. The only person who's harmed by going to law school is you."

Air rushed into my lungs on a gasp.

Every moment of dread studying for those fucking tests and the times I failed. All the days I forced a smile when someone congratulated me. The idea of being in school for years learning something I hated. It was a bleak landscape.

Blake was right.

They were all right.

But the stubborn, selfless part of me clung to the idea that it was better this way. I would be in pain, but everyone else wouldn't be.

Sloane disappearing into the crowd last night crashed into my mind.

For your sake, and everyone else... stop giving a fuck.

It didn't stop there. If I was going to take that step, the world unfolded at my feet, and everything became a possibility.

Why did it take someone else saying something out loud for you to fully understand it? Everything I'd done in years hadn't been for me. I hadn't wanted it, and I did it anyway. Because it was the way things were. No change allowed. No other options possible.

Head down, in control, just keep going.

"Oh my god."

"There you are," he whispered. "We've seen the real you. Here. With us. You let go, and you're free. It's everywhere else you paint yourself into a box that's too small for everything you are."

"I feel so..."

"Don't," Cole said. "Please. Don't spend time harassing yourself for believing the world that was built around you."

Emery came and sat behind me on the bench. "They're right.

327

What else didn't those people do?" He asked quietly. "No one else questioned what was best for you. No one asked what you wanted. And I don't care. Someone would need to be blind not to see how little you wanted to do with law school. Or politics. Anything in that sphere."

Things unraveled in my mind, one after another.

Stop giving a fuck.

It felt like taking my first full breath in years.

Stop giving a fuck.

This was terrifying, but the kind of fear that bordered anticipation. The same kind you had when going up a really tall roller coaster knowing what was at the top.

Stop giving a fuck.

The world froze. Everything came together at once. There was a way out of this. Staring me in the face, and I ignored it because it was outside the lines. No more.

Strength and energy had me almost vibrating. "Where's my phone?" I asked. "I need my phone."

"Upstairs I think—"

I was up and running before Blake finished speaking. It was on the wall of the nest. I didn't remember putting it there, and it didn't matter. Scrolling through the missed calls, I found the number I needed.

One ring. Two. Three.

"Hello?"

"George," I said. "I know what we need to do."

CHAPTER FORTY-THREE

COLE

FIVE DAYS LATER

*T*he cameras flashing made the crowd along the stairs look like they were made of glitter. More photographers than I'd ever seen, all stacked together along the stairs of the red carpet which descended into the massive, decked out courtyard of the Slate City Mansion. Or, what used to be City Hall until it was turned into a museum and tourist attraction.

Gorgeous architecture, priceless history, and a rotating selection of exhibits from all over the country. The Slate Gala kept the museum funded, along with a charitable cause, which changed every year. This year it was raising money to create greenspace in underprivileged areas around Slate City.

Or rather, the money was already raised. You needed to be invited to come to The Slate Gala, but once you were, the price for entry and the amazing dinner provided was through the roof.

I glanced around, feeling bare without my earpiece. Still on duty for the moment, waiting for Petra to enter with the Gidwitz pack. Annoyance burned in my throat at the mention of their names.

Nick was taking point outside the ball, and the entire Gala was sewn up so tight I wasn't worried for Petra's safety here. If someone managed to penetrate the net, she—or any of the guests —would never be more than ten feet from security.

A five story arch dominated the front of the mansion, opening to stairs which cascaded down into the courtyard. A suspended fabric roof made the whole place seem like it was inside and outside at the same time. Dark blue fabric with tiny sparkles which glittered more than the real stars.

I stood on one of the landings, tucked away near a television camera and a reporter. As each one came down, she interviewed them about the over the top outfits they wore, and any anything else which might be on her mind.

A roar came from outside the building, which made sense when Eva and her pack appeared at the top of the stairs. Her sister too, and her Alphas, though Eva's twin looked far more uncomfortable than the movie star who was used to the spotlight.

Eva's poofy white dress looked like she was wrapped in clouds. Esme's violet dress was equally soft. Together, they complimented each other.

"Oh my god, it's Eva May Williams," the reporter said. "It's been a while since I've seen you. How are you?"

Eva laughed. "Hi, Shelly. I'm doing great."

"That's so good to hear. *Love* the dress."

"Thank you." Eva twisted so she peered over her shoulder at the cameras and did a little curtsey. The woman knew exactly what she was doing, and it was a beautiful thing to watch. "It's an Iris Alexander. As is Esme's." She reached out and Esme joined her. Their packs were arranged behind them, and covered a smile. I hoped we looked like that standing behind Petra. No question about who the beautiful Omegas belonged with, and no question that if anyone touched them, they'd lose a hand.

"And you look gorgeous as well. Along with your packs, of course." The two women smiled at that. Even Kade, Esme's Alpha I met at Nautilus, was dressed to the nines in a tuxedo. He wore it well, despite what people's impression of him might be.

"We tried to leave them at home," Eva joked, "but they weren't having it."

"Aww," Shelly the reporter, put on a mock frown. "No girls' night out?"

"Oh, I think we're going to have fun," Esme said.

Eva nodded. "Keep an eye out for more Iris Alexander, because I know a couple more people wearing her tonight."

The reporter took the cue. "Thank you so much for your time, ladies. I hope we'll see you soon!"

Eva and Esme saw me and smiled. They couldn't stop here to talk, and I didn't want to attract attention to myself.

Sloane came down the stairs too, in a silver dress with a train long enough to trip her. All the photographers took the opportunity, but she didn't do an interview.

I resisted the urge to pull out my phone and check the time. Because of the tux, my phone was pressed right against my chest. If they called me, I would feel it. Still, I was growing anxious standing and waiting. Normally, doing my job didn't agitate me this much.

A group appeared at the top of the stairs, drawing my gaze.

Time froze, and the world went quiet. Like someone took the volume on everything and turned it down to nothing. Petra stood at the top of the stairs, and I couldn't take my fucking eyes off her.

A black, shimmering dress that shrugged off her shoulders like the entire thing was about to fall into a puddle on the ground. It didn't just sparkle, it sparkled like the goddamn rainbow. Every color flickered and flared in the fabric, painting her with color.

I shifted my stance, making it less obvious that I was hard as a rock. Petra's dress had a slit up above her thigh, and there was nothing underneath it but skin. Every step was a nearly indecent, tempting taste of her.

Black heels high enough she was almost as tall as I was. My mind was filled with visions of her in those heels and absolutely nothing else.

Hair that fell around her in curling waves, and a necklace of so many diamonds it almost sparkled more than the dress. A gold band wrapped around her arm, and the final piece of jewelry to catch my eye was the ring.

It sparkled on her hand, a beacon for all the photographers calling her name. The stories hadn't stopped or died down. There was no point in trying. The press wanted what it wanted, and they smelled a story. They wouldn't stop until they got it.

The only thing that soured the image was that she was on George Bower's arm.

"Petra DeWitt-Merriton," Shelly said, holding her arm out for Petra to join her in front of the camera. "I was hoping to see you tonight. You've certainly been the talk of the town for the last few days, haven't you?"

Petra smiled. "I'd rather I wasn't, but you know how it is."

"I do, I do. And I think you're wearing Iris Alexander? Eva Williams gave me a heads up."

"I am," she beamed. "Iris was such a sweetheart doing it for all of us last minute."

"Everyone is looking forward to your father's announcement later. How do you feel about it?"

"I'm excited, like everyone else," Petra said. "I support my father in all his ambitions."

Shelly took a step back and looked at the Gidwitz pack arrayed behind Petra. "Okay, I know everyone and their *mother* will be doing this tonight, but you look stunning and you arrived on the arm of some very handsome Alphas. Congratulations on your engagement! Can we see the ring?"

"You absolutely can," Petra said. "But we do have an announcement on that front. And Shelly, you'll be the very first one to hear it."

"An exclusive?" The reporter gasped dramatically in a way the audience watching would love. "You're making me blush."

"We thought it was a good time to tell everyone."

Shelly leaned in. "Well, we're all dying to know your secrets."

Petra leaned in too, like she was only sharing a secret with one person and not thousands. "I'm not only engaged. I'm bonded."

"*Oh my god,*" Shelly said. "That's incredible."

"There is more," Petra said, looking at the men standing behind her. "The Gidwitz pack is incredible, and they are all gentlemen. Anyone would be lucky to have them as their partner. But I am not bonded to them."

Petra's eyes fell on me, and I smiled, anxiety fading. Fuck I needed to get used to that. The anxiety which had been so loud in my chest wasn't mine—it was hers. Through the bond which now sang between us. Beneath the gorgeous waves of her hair, I could just see the healing marks of my bite on her neck.

Around us, everything had gone quiet except for the click of cameras. It was out there now, for better or worse. Petra DeWitt-Merriton was our Omega. Forever.

"Wait a second," Shelly said. "You're telling me this pack behind you *isn't* your pack?"

"They are not."

They stepped up next to Petra, and one of them spoke. His name might have been Scott. Or Stuart. I didn't remember. We only met them briefly today, and they were nice enough. But I still wanted them as far away from Petra as humanly possible.

As soon as possible.

"When Petra told us she'd found scent-sympathy, who were we to stand in her way? We're very happy for her, and we'll stay friends. Plus, she's right." He took the hand of the Beta next to him. "We are happy. In the end, it works out for everyone."

The reporter blinked for a second, shocked. This wasn't what she'd expected or planned for. We made sure to keep it that way. The only way to make sure we controlled the story *and* the fallout was to give it to them in the most direct and splashy way possible.

"Then I guess we wish you well," Shelly said. "Enjoy the Gala, gentlemen." They moved on, touching Petra on the shoulder, but she stayed where she was. "Then the question on everyone's minds right now, Petra, is who your real pack is?"

My Omega smiled so brightly she rivaled every bit of glitter and shine in the room. I loved seeing her so happy. *Feeling* her so happy. Our bond swirled with sweetness and spice, just like she did. Like an echo of her scent, even when she wasn't close.

"I'm happy to say I'm now bonded to the Atwood Pack."

"Are they here?" Shelly asked, looking at the camera. "I'm sure everyone is dying to meet them. I know I am."

"They are."

That was my cue, and everyone else's. We'd all secured invites thanks to Eva and paid for tickets. But thankfully being security, I brought the others inside early. They'd waited at the top of the stairs this whole time, blending in with the Gala's security.

Except for Harrison, who was so tall he rarely blended in anywhere. They came down the stairs in a line, and I stepped out from my corner and around the back of the camera to join Petra. There was no way to help myself. I wrapped my arms around her from behind and leaned around to kiss her cheek.

She melted against me, and if we weren't standing in front of both a camera and a microphone, there were dirty words I wanted to say to her about the high heels and this dress.

"Wait," Shelly said. "We've seen you before. Isn't he your bodyguard?"

Petra looked up at me with such love in her eyes, and I felt the weight of it in my chest. We'd agreed to keep our closet rendezvous out of the main story. "That's how we met," she said. "The minute we scented each other, that was pretty much it. I met the rest of his pack and we just knew."

Shelly looked behind us as we were joined by the others. Emery put his arm around Petra, pulling her close. I could barely hear him speak. "You look fucking stunning, sunshine."

"Introductions, *please*," Shelly begged. Her eyes were bright. This had the possibility to be one of the biggest moments of her career.

"This is Cole," Petra said. "Emery, Blake, and Harrison. Harrison owns and runs Atwood security. So I guess it was kind of fate from the beginning." Her cheeks were pink, not only with excitement, but from feeling all four of us and the emotions pouring into her. The others were present too, as an echo. But an echo was all I needed to know. We were all on the same page.

"And since you asked, here's the ring."

It was really two rings. The first was a pale violet stone with a vine of diamond leaves curling around one side. The other was a much smaller band with diamonds and came together at a delicate point.

"That is absolutely stunning," Shelly said. "I'm still practically speechless. You've certainly shaken things up, Petra."

"Exactly what I was hoping to do."

A line of people was starting to form behind us for their interviews and time in front of the cameras.

"One more question, and I'll let you guys go. I need to see a kiss. From just one of you. But you know it's what the people want."

To my surprise—and Petra's—Harrison stepped forward with a gleam in his eyes. "Well," he said. "If it's what the people want."

Taking our Omega in his arms, he dipped her back in front of the cameras, and the world exploded with light. A thousand flashes at once. The way he held her, her dress was showing enough skin to be just on the legal side of decency. Her hand was on his shoulder, showing her ring, and her hair fell back, exposing my bite marks.

It was the perfect photograph. It left no questions or doubts.

He kissed her, and we all felt it. The surge of desire and need. Pure animal craving from both of them. Fuck, this night was going to last an eternity before we could get her home and strip that gorgeous, glittering confection of a dress off her.

The cameras still clicked away when he lifted her back up, and I smirked. There would certainly be more pictures of her now for the press to use. *Good* ones.

"Thank you so much for your time and your *bombshell*," Shelly said. "I hope you guys have a great time."

"We will," Petra said, hand still linked with Harrison's.

We all moved past the camera together, the three of us naturally arranging ourselves around her. I waited until we got to the bottom of the stairs to direct everyone to the side and into one of the small alcoves on the side of the courtyard. We'd just announced ourselves to the world, and everyone here would want a piece.

But before that, we needed a minute with our Omega.

CHAPTER FORTY-FOUR

PETRA

*M*y whole body shook with adrenaline. Not to mention the height of these heels was a hazard. At any time, I could fall flat on my face, and that would be the story instead of the bomb we just lobbed at the media, my family, and everyone in general.

"You did so good, baby." Blake pulled me into a hug. "And god you are beautiful."

He meant every word. His genuine emotions floated in my chest, with a hint of citrus that reminded me of his scent. So much fucking love and happiness from all four of them. It was overwhelming.

"I have to say, I like the position of this." Blake's hand slid under the slit in my dress, across the few inches to where his bond mark was hidden from view. His fingers stroked over the place on my hip and my knees buckled.

Heat and pleasure whirled through me. Arousal. Love. Lust. Fuck me. I leaned into him and moaned softly. "I love you, but if any of you want me to survive the night, you're going to need to stop that."

"You sure, sunshine?" Emery lifted my wrist and kissed the inside where his mark rested.

I shivered. "Yes. Please."

Emery winked. "Once we're home then."

"Hell, you can start in the car on the way home."

"I'm all for that," Cole said. "But I get it."

I placed a hand against my chest and took a breath. Which was difficult with the weight of the necklace. It wasn't mine—I needed to give it back to Vernier later—but I loved it.

"That was the easy part," I said. "It's the rest of the night that will be hard."

"How quickly do you think your father will know?" Blake asked.

I looked past him to the main room where everyone mingled. "I'd be surprised if he didn't know already."

"We won't leave you alone unless you ask us to, little one." Harrison's steady calm in my chest, alongside the depth of his feelings, grounded me. All of my Alphas felt different. I could call them into the forefront, and if I didn't, their emotions were a pleasant hum together.

"Anyone want to take bets on which they'll be more upset about? The bonding or school?"

Cole chuckled. "Depends on who we're talking about."

As of yesterday, I was no longer enrolled in law school. The tuition money would be returned by the end of the week. Harrison was right. They practically tripped over themselves to make sure I was happy and didn't have a lawsuit in my back pocket.

A law school getting sued wasn't exactly great for recruitment.

"Okay," I said. "Let's go."

Our friends were here, and they were fully on board with this. Eva had been incredible, orchestrating everything from the tickets to the dress—the same dress I'd been eyeing that day in Bergman's.

A few people eyed us with interest when we came out of the alcove, but thankfully it was clear we hadn't been doing anything more than talking.

No matter how much we all wished otherwise.

Eva spotted me and headed across the room, her cottonball cloud puff of a dress impossible to miss. "That was fucking epic," she said, hugging me.

"Thanks. I feel a little like I'm going to throw up."

"Well, throwing up is a handy excuse if you need to get out of here at any point."

I glanced across the courtyard. It was beautiful. The theme seemed like the night sky. Glimmering fabric hung above us, moving in the gentle breeze, and tiny, shining stars hung on invisible strings. Every table had glitter strewn across it and a twisting centerpiece that exploded upward in an explosion of silver flowers, jewels, and more stars.

The dress on me matched as much as it stood apart

"Have you seen Sloane?"

Eva looped her arm through mine and began to navigate me through the room. "She's at our tables."

I looked over at her. "You managed to get us seated at the same tables?"

"Yup." Her eyes sparkled. "And it was easy."

Sloane stood up when she saw me, beaming. "Girl, you are already blowing up all over everything."

"What?"

"Right now, you're all anyone is talking about when you look at things about the Gala. Everything from loving your look to being happy for you."

Pride, pleasure, and satisfaction radiated from my Alphas. "Anything bad?"

She made a face. "There are always bad things. But way more good than bad right now. And there are *plenty* of people lining up to love the Gidwitz pack. If they ever decide they need another member, you just put them on the national map. They can have their pick."

I laughed. "Good. But I don't think they'll want it." They were on the other side of the room, and we were all on perfect terms now. When I called, they were surprised, but more than happy to go along with the stunt. George could blame it on me entirely, and he would still get his inheritance.

"Petra," Emery said. "Incoming."

Carmen and my father were coming toward us, determined. He got caught by someone saying hello, but Carmen didn't. She was on a mission, but we knew she would be.

"Where do you want us?" Blake asked.

"Give us some space," I said. "If I need you, you'll know now."

"Damn right," he whispered before leaning in to kiss my hair. "Remember, you're doing all this for you. Your choices."

Eva and Sloane faded away too, keeping their eyes on me. Hell, the entire ballroom looked in this direction, monitoring the potential explosion.

Tonight, if anyone exploded, it would be Carmen. Not me.

As soon as I snapped out of the box I'd locked myself in, everything changed. I wasn't afraid of her, and I didn't care what she thought. Dad would be more difficult.

Anger burned in her eyes. "What the fuck are you doing?"

I smiled. "Exactly what you wanted. An engagement and a bonding ceremony to coincide with Dad's campaign." I feigned shock. "I thought you'd be happy."

"Do you have *any idea* what you've done?"

"Yes." I stood my ground. "I'm living my life the way I want to live it. Not the way you want me to, or the way the campaign wants to."

Carmen stepped closer. She wanted to hit me. I felt it. All my Alpha's tensed, ready to spring. I sent calm back to them. I looked down at her hands. There were scratches on them, like she'd gotten into a fight with a cat. Or a pile of papers had decided she needed to be taught a lesson. I didn't care.

"You are so fucking selfish," she hissed. "If Russell doesn't win, it will fall entirely at your feet."

"No. I think that falls at the feet of the campaign and the voters. If Dad's position is so fragile that me bonding to Alphas I love ruins his chances? He was never going to win."

Her face contorted with rage. "You'll see, Petra. You're one person. Compared to the countless lives which would be helped by your father? All you had to do was say yes. One sacrifice."

"But it hasn't been one sacrifice, has it?" I asked, looking around to make sure we weren't becoming the center of attention. I wanted any pictures of the two of us to look civil. "I've made one sacrifice after another. For *years*. I left conservatory."

"Because your little *incident* nearly destroyed your father's career."

"You mean the incident that was a lie? Where did you get the fake test results? Because all this time I thought Dad knew I wasn't high. The only person who would have told him otherwise? Was you."

She stiffened and rose up to her full height. "I don't know what you're talking about. We did everything we could to help you."

"Sure. You did a good job burying the evidence. But I'll find it eventually. In the meantime, I'm going to have a conversation with my father. Excuse me."

I pushed past her, struggling not to smile. The fact that every single one of my Alphas was bursting with pride didn't help.

Dad and I approached each other, and he slowed, looking unsure. "Petra."

"Hey, Dad."

We hugged awkwardly. Hopefully, any photos of it would look all right. But he didn't look pleased. "Was this really the way you needed to lash out? Here? Tonight? Pretending to have found a pack just like your mothers?"

His gaze fell on my necklace, and he stiffened. I reached up and touched the cool stones, closing my eyes and gathering my strength.

My shoulders fell. "I'm not lashing out, Dad. I *did* find a pack like *ours*. And I have you to thank for it."

"Yes. I'll be speaking with Harrison about it. Taking my money to protect you while—"

"He hasn't been," I cut him off. "He stopped taking your money. Harrison is the same man you respect, only now he's mine. Nothing else has changed."

Dad's face hardened. "I doubt that."

"Why?"

"Taking advantage of someone who needs help isn't honorable. Especially not the kind of help you need and are refusing to get."

I nodded slowly. "Okay, Dad. I hoped this would go differently, and I hoped I wouldn't have to do this. But I have to." My heels allowed me to look him straight in the eye. "I'm sorry you're disappointed, and I'm sorry you think I'm this out-of-control woman you believe exists. But that's not me. I've never been high. Not even once. The picture at the charity ball was after I met Cole. And you can't tell me you don't understand what that's like.

"Yes, I met him before you introduced me, and I didn't even know who he was until he walked into my apartment. I love him. And Harrison, and Blake, and Emery."

"Petra—"

"I'm not finished." I kept my voice gentle and firm. "I've withdrawn from law school. Your money will be returned to you by the end of the week. I have the dean's personal assurance about that. Going forward, I will be pursuing music."

Pain flashed across his face. I hated seeing it there, but I wasn't responsible for his pain. I'd taken care of it long enough, and I needed to tend to my own now.

"I don't know how that will look, but for now, it won't look like anything. Because I'm still being stalked by someone who wants *you* to drop out of this campaign before it even starts. My apartment was destroyed last week."

"*What*?" Shock, horror, and anger rolled across his features. "How come I didn't know? Why didn't you tell me?"

Wrapping my arms around myself, I took a shaky breath. "Because we wanted to keep it out of the press. An addict loses her drugs and destroys her apartment, right? That's what they would have said? And you might have believed it. Or if we'd told you about it, and told you it was because of this person attacking me, you would have tried to move me home. I didn't want that. But I'm lucky to be alive."

I could count on one hand the number of times I'd seen my father speechless. This was one of them.

"I love you, Dad. And someday I hope you'll realize your part in all of this. You can believe whatever you want about me, but it won't make it true. So until you can have an open mind about my past and the truth, and accept my pack? You won't be hearing from me."

"Petra..."

Emotion rose, and I swallowed it down. "Good luck with the campaign, Dad. I hope my bonding boosts your numbers the way you wanted it to."

Turning, I walked back to my pack, now sitting at our table. Emery wrapped an arm around my hip while I stood by his chair. "You okay?"

They knew I wasn't. It was so much easier now, feeling the sympathy flowing through them. "No, but I have to be."

Dad still stood in the middle of the room, staring in my direction. I hoped everything I said sank in. Probably not tonight, but someday.

Esme smiled at me from the other table. Her red-haired Alpha who'd been tattooing Eva sat with his arm around her, fingers absently stroking her shoulder. The little gestures of love made all the difference. Like the way Emery held me now, the tips of his fingers pressing into my hip and releasing, almost squeezing me softly.

He smirked and looked up at me. "You like that?"

"I like you." I kissed him, loving that we didn't have to hide it. They were mine, and I was theirs.

Harrison stood. "I think I'll get us some drinks. And maybe get an awkward conversation over with."

I shrugged. "You don't have to."

"But I will anyway," he said with a wink before heading toward my father.

"Glad I'm not over there for that conversation."

"I want to make a toast," Eva said. "But we need champagne."

I groaned. "Or literally anything else."

"Why don't the girls go to the ladies' room while the boys get us drinks?" Sloane said. "It's about time we touched up our makeup."

Blake stood behind me and stretched. "What would you like?"

I told him I was sorry through our bond. "Something that doesn't taste remotely like alcohol."

"It'll be as sweet as you," he said. "Promise."

Sloane grabbed my hand. "Let's go, lover girl."

Eva and Esme joined us. "Is there a reason you're taking us away from the boys?"

"No. Except for maybe some selfies together because we look *fabulous*."

"Ooh," Eva pointed to a pillar draped in the starry fabric. "Over there."

I allowed myself to breathe, and it felt amazing. Laughing with my friends. Sensing happiness and peace in my chest, *this* was what I needed. Nothing else.

About a hundred selfies later, we actually headed to the bathroom.

"Well, you got what you wanted, I guess."

I turned toward the voice. A tall man stood near the edge of the courtyard, a glass of something dark in his hand. "Excuse me?"

He looked vaguely familiar, but I couldn't place him.

"Petra?"

"I'll be right there."

The man looked me up and down before extending his hand. "My name is Charles Bower."

Recognition clicked into place. We met at the charity ball for half of a second. "You're George's father."

"I am. Or who should have been your father-in-law."

"Don't blame George for this," I said. "It was my idea. None of them knew or had anything to do with it, and I didn't give them a choice."

He took a sip of his drink. "I find that hard to believe."

"I don't particularly care what you believe. It's true. George was more than willing to do what you wanted, and I wasn't. He's very loyal."

"Time will tell if you made the right decision."

"I did."

All he did was smile. "I hope you're right. I myself like playing the long game. As for George, we'll see what he has to say for himself. The rest of his... pack, too."

If he was expecting me to apologize or take it back, it was a little late for that. Exactly why we'd made it permanent immediately. Nothing could undo it.

Not bothering to say goodbye, I pushed into the bathroom. Sloane looked up from touching up her mascara. "Who was that?"

"George's father. Seems like a Class-A prick. But we already knew that."

"When are we eating?" Eva asked, flouncing down on one of the fancy seats. "I'm starving."

I made a face at her. "We told you to eat more."

"You did. And Blake's cooking is probably better than what we're eating here."

"If it is, I'm never going to hear the end of it," I said. "He'll be trying to cater the Gala until it happens."

Eva laughed. "It's not a terrible idea."

Leaning against the sink, Esme looked at me. "How did the talk with your dad go?"

I winced. "About as well as I expected. So not great, and it sucks, but I feel good about it."

"Good."

"Hell yes, it's good," Sloane said. "Someone should get what they finally want without people trying to get in the way."

Her tone had me looking over at her. With everything happening in my life, Sloane hadn't told me much about what was happening with hers. And when I did ask, she was cagey. "You okay, Lo?"

"Fine. Just... work drama."

"You know we love a little drama," Eva said. "Maybe it's time for me to become a patron of the arts so I can kick some asses."

Sloane smiled and put her makeup back in her clutch. It wasn't her real smile, but I didn't call it on her here. "I've got it handled. But believe me, I'll let you know if I need you to."

"Good." Eva rose and brushed invisible dirt from her dress. "Let's go have a toast and eat some food and celebrate Bee's bonding, because I'm still salty I didn't get to throw a party for it."

"Nothing saying you can't still throw a party," Sloane pointed out.

Esme and I made eye contact, understanding passing between us. Neither of us were the real partiers in this room. "If you throw a party, at least wait until I'm not being stalked," I said. "Please."

"Will do."

People were making their way to their seats when we exited the bathroom, and Mr. Bower was thankfully gone. However, Ezra, my father's PR manager, was lying in wait.

"Petra."

Eva and Sloane closed ranks in front of me, Esme behind. I

smiled. "It's okay, I've got this." I looked at the man. "You and I are not on a first name basis."

His smile turned sickly sweet and deadly. "Miss Merriton."

"Miss *DeWitt*-Merriton. My mother might be dead, but her name is not. And going forward, any communication the campaign or my father's office has with me, or puts out about me —of which I expect there to be *none*—without my full name will be dealt with appropriately." I let him imagine what I meant by that. "Dinner is about to start. How can I help you?"

Ezra hesitated. Both fury and annoyance bled through, but he managed to hold on to his customer service smile. "The Senator feels that given the size and importance of his announcement, and the contrast with your... news, your continued presence at the Gala will only cause confusion and dilute the coverage."

My friends gasped, but I smiled. "Did my father tell you that? Or did Carmen?"

He said nothing, which answered the question just as clearly.

"I thought so. You can tell 'the Senator,' that unless The Slate Institute itself is revoking our invitations and the tickets we paid for, my pack and I will be at our table enjoying dinner. And I would hurry, because if I recall correctly, any support staff will be dismissed before the food arrives."

Eva walked beside me, covering her mouth to disguise the giggles. "I need to introduce you to Jasmine. My manager," she said. "And can I call you when an asshole director needs to be shot down? Because that was incredible."

"Living with Carmen all this time taught me a few things."

I felt when they saw me coming toward them. Heat crept under my skin, their attention intoxicating. They loved teasing me, though no one could see it. A glass with a pink drink in it waited at my seat, and Harrison was back.

"Everything okay?" I asked him.

From him I felt calm and resignation. Not relief. "Everything is fine, little one."

"Just fine?"

He helped me sit and scoot in my chair between Cole and Emery. "Just fine. You?"

"I met Charles Bower. He's a peach," I let my sarcasm drip. They laughed along with me.

A chime sounded through the room, calling everyone to their seats for the meal. Sloane and Eva joined us at the table, one of Esme's Alphas switching places so she could join us as well.

Emery took my hand and lifted it to his lips, kissing my ring before quickly turning my hand over and kissing his mark. "Love you, sunshine. No matter what."

"I love you."

No matter what. Tonight was going to be an amazing night.

CHAPTER FORTY-FIVE

PETRA

FIVE DAYS EARLIER

"*Y*ou're serious?" George asked. "You're going to bond with a different pack just to avoid us?"

I rolled my eyes, wishing he could see me and my expression. "You want to rethink that sentence?"

In the background, I heard other low voices. "Yeah," he said. "Sorry."

"To be clear, I'm not bonding with a pack to avoid you. I'm bonding with a pack because they are *mine*. For obvious reasons, I've kept our courtship quiet. Your father can't come at you for this, because it's my decision. I'm not giving you an option to say no to this. What I'm giving you a choice about is whether you want to be involved in the announcement."

Silence stretched out so long I wondered if they'd muted the phone. Finally, Terry's voice came through. "What do you have in mind?"

I blew out a breath. "Thank you. This is better for all of us. Promise." I told them what we needed if we didn't want our families breathing down our necks, and they agreed. Once I hung up, I only had to convince my real pack. But I knew they would say yes.

Shaking my head, I went slowly back downstairs. Stormy heard me talking and came with me, rubbing against my leg while we walked.

It seemed simple and obvious now. Why hadn't I thought of it before?

Because I'd been so tangled up in the idea of what I had to do and who I needed to be, I hadn't seen the solution staring in front of me. On top of that, my lingering fears about being a repeat of my parents.

I was still scared, but I no longer cared. The more Dad

pushed me away from anything close to our old life, the less I felt he cared about my happiness.

He loved me. But love and care didn't always walk hand in hand.

They were all where I'd left them. Cole still lounged on the floor, Emery on the piano bench. Stormy trotted into a spot of morning sun and flopped, rolling onto her back. "I love her."

"I think she loves you too," Emery said. "You're her new Omega."

Harrison looked at my phone. "You found it, I see."

"I did." I set it on the nearby side table, flexing my fingers in and out. This was nerve-wracking despite being sure of their answer. "I'm going to do my best not to dwell on how... blind I've been. I feel embarrassed and ashamed, and more than a little foolish, but I will try. And I think I have a way to fix everything."

"What's that, little one?"

My mouth went dry. Terror of both the unknown and the permanence of my question froze my breath. "Will you—" My fingers flared and curled into fists. "Will you bond with me?"

In a flash, I was on the floor, pulled down by Cole. His lips covered mine, body pressing me into the ground. The purr resonating from him was echoed four times. He growled—the kind of growl that sent a heat-seeking missile between my legs. "I'm willing to bite you right here, honeybee. There's nothing I want more in the world than to make you mine."

Emotion welled up, blocking my voice.

"You're going to need to share, Cole," Harrison's amused voice reached me. Cole didn't want to let me go, but he smirked as he pulled away, satisfied with my boneless body and the perfume now spinning around us.

Blake got me up and held me close. "Yes, baby. My Alpha has wanted to claim you since I met you in the kitchen. And I'm going to do everything I can to make sure you *don't* feel embarrassed. Because I got to help you see the truth, and I don't take it for granted."

"I'm going to be a puddle if all of you say things like this," I whispered.

He kissed me, coaxing my lips open and tangling his tongue with mine. The kiss created a very different kind of puddle.

"Then be a puddle, baby. You're going to be ours, and nice things come with the territory. Get used to it."

Coffee and chocolate swirled around me, Blake surrendering me to Emery's arms. They wrapped around me from behind. "I'd given up before you," he said, so quietly I was the only one who heard. "I didn't think it would ever happen, and I was devastated. I couldn't admit it felt like being abandoned. I love these guys, and we were happy enough, but it wasn't the same. And the second—the *second*—I met you, it was like the world got brighter." He laughed, turning me around so I could see him. "It's why I call you sunshine."

I bunched my fingers in his shirt, blinking away tears. "I love you. I knew you'd say yes, but I was nervous."

"But you did it," he said. "And to be clear, if you hadn't, we would have. We weren't ever going to let you go without a fight, Petra."

"And we never will." Harrison still sat where he'd been, gaze burning into me. The power in his eyes pulled me to him like a moth to a flame. He pulled me between his knees, hands settling on my hips. My stoic Alpha.

"Come here." He pulled me onto his lap, one hand tangling in my hair. "If I'd known going down to your apartment that day would change my life so completely, I would have run there and not walked. Standing there and pretending like your scent wasn't setting my lungs on fire is still one of the hardest things I've ever had to do."

"I had no idea."

One side of his mouth tilted into a smile. "I hope you know now."

I flushed, remembering every breathless moment between the two of us. "Yes."

The hand in my hair made sure I didn't look away. "We waited to ask this because we knew you were overwhelmed, little one. But we've belonged to you just as much as you belong to us. I hope you know we're going to show it."

"More than you already have?" I asked, laughing. "Hard to believe."

"Oh yes," he said. "Because we've been holding ourselves back from spoiling the fuck out of you. Now that you're ours forever? We're going to make a habit of it."

"Harrison."

"Starting with rings," he said quietly, purr rising steadily in his chest. "I know not all packs exchange them, but if you're willing to wear one, I want to see our ring on your finger. After that, we'll start with upstairs, creating whatever the hell you want. And finally, when I catch the fucker who's after you, and I will, I think we should turn your apartment downstairs into a studio for you."

I stared at him, speechless. Finally, I found my voice, gripping his shoulders. "You don't have to buy me things to make me love you, you know."

He grinned. "I know. But I happen to enjoy spoiling good girls."

"Fuck."

His laugh made me smile as much as his praise made me *want* him. "So you're saying yes?" Growls came from everywhere. I tried to keep my voice even and failed. "They can't force me with the other pack if I'm already bonded to you. I don't want to wait. I don't need a ceremony."

"You don't need a ceremony, but I want you to have the ring," Harrison said and stood me on my feet. "Let me call Howard."

He was halfway out of the room before I could even ask, "Who the fuck is Howard?"

Blake laughed. "You're going to love Howard."

"But who is he?"

"He's the man who can get anything." Cole finally stood up. "You need a rare mushroom for a dish you're making and you need it now because your supplies dried up and you have VIPs scheduled to come to your restaurant?" He looked at Blake pointedly. "Howard is your guy."

"That was one time," Blake said.

Emery stretched. "Basically, Howard knows everyone and can

get anything. Or, as I think in this case, contact jewelers and have them come here instead of us going to them. Not only for your safety, but because I'm guessing you don't want everyone to know about the rings until we tell them."

"Correct," I said. "But we don't have to—"

Blake took my hand and spun me under his arm. I ended up against his chest as he danced with me slowly around the room. "No," he said quietly. "We don't have to. But we will." He lowered his voice even further. "Listen to me, Petra. We're lucky. We understand the privilege we have and where we come from, and we try to do good things as well. Harrison's roster of charities will knock you on your ass. But the truth is, we have enough money to last for lifetimes, and now it's going to belong to you, too. You don't have to worry about us spending some of it on you."

I had my own money. Mom left me plenty.

Emery cut in. "Another truth bomb for you, sweet girl. Your life and your boundaries aren't the only thing you've been depriving yourself of. Your apartment, may it rest in peace, was lovely. But I think you and I both know it was far simpler and stark than it could have, or even should have been." He leaned his head against mine. "You're so used to having nothing emotionally, it translated to everything around you. I can't wait to see what you create upstairs."

I whined. "All of you have to *stop* being so sweet to me."

"With your scent?" Cole said. "Unlikely, honeybee."

"Speaking of honey," Blake said. "I made the cake."

My head snapped in his direction. "Really?"

"Really."

Emery moved, sweeping me up into his arms, and before we moved, I snatched my phone from the table. "I was going to say we should eat a normal breakfast. But now I think cake is called for. Stormy," he called behind us, and I loved the padded thumps of her running footsteps behind us. She beat us down the stairs.

"When do we do this?" I asked. "Are you going to bite me over cake?"

Emery chuckled. "Let's see what Howard says. Because I'm

with Harrison. I like the idea of you having our ring on your finger. And nothing else."

I liked that idea too.

Emery didn't carry me into the kitchen, he took me into the breakfast room with the lovely windows and couches overlooking the city. It was still early enough that the view was warm and soft, the sun slanting onto the downtown buildings.

"You want tea?" He asked.

"Only if you're not going to use me to sweeten it."

He winked. "Not this morning. But no promises in the future."

Stormy hopped up on the couch beside me and laid her head in my lap, huffing out a breath. "It's hard to be a leopard isn't it?" I asked, stroking her side. "So hard."

She pushed firmly into my leg, exposing her belly. "You're so sweet. I'm amazed anyone could give you up. But I'm glad they did. Guess I'm sticking around, so you really are mine."

Stormy couldn't purr. Not the way smaller cats or my Alphas could, but sometimes I caught rough sounds that felt like she was trying to. In the end, it didn't matter. She made it clear how happy she was.

Cole sat across from me, and I couldn't help but notice he never put on a shirt. With hair still a little messy, and the morning light casting shadows on his body, he looked like a painting. Or one of those ads with beautiful people that weren't really selling anything but the dream of being so beautiful.

I lifted my phone and took a sneaky photo before he noticed.

"I have one of those." Blake set my cake and tea down on the table next to the couch. "I forgot to show you." He retrieved his phone. I was the first thing you saw when he unlocked it. Me, asleep in the nest, hair wild and dressed in nothing but a blanket.

"When was that?"

"The day we went to the test kitchen."

I couldn't even be embarrassed. It was a nice photo, and it made me want to take more pictures of them. *With* them. "I wonder if Howard knows any good photographers who take pictures only packs are meant to see."

Cole smirked. "He will. But if he doesn't, then Eva definitely will."

Calling Sloane was high on my list. Because she was the one who gave me the first push. Truthfully, she'd been pushing me for years and never gave up on me. Eva too. She was busy, and we'd grown apart the last few years, but she'd been amazing, and I wanted to keep us closer. Esme too, if she wanted to get to know me.

I sliced off a piece of the cake with my fork. *Fuck,* it was so good. The subtleness of the honey flavor contrasting with the cinnamon frosting's warmth and sharpness was perfect.

"Baby, if you want to finish that cake, you can't make sounds like that. Especially when it's something I made."

I froze, with the fork halfway to my lips. "What sound was I making?"

Cole's voice sounded far deeper. "Like that bite of cake made you come."

"It almost did."

Blake swore and went back into the kitchen. I smirked, enjoying my victory, and never taking my eyes off Cole while I took the next bite. "I'm going to remember all the teasing later," he said. "Just a warning."

"And you don't think I'm doing it on purpose?"

"Oh, I know you are. I'm just not sure you're ready to take all the teasing you have coming in return."

I blushed, taking a sip of my tea, but was saved from responding by Harrison coming in. "All settled. Raphael Vernier will be here in an hour."

My teacup clattered as I tried not to choke. Never in my life had I come so close to spitting out a drink. I hauled in a ragged breath, coughing. "Are you serious?"

Harrison frowned. "Of course. Why wouldn't I be?"

"Because it's Raphael Vernier," I said. "Like, the actual *person*?"

"Yes, little one."

I sat back, stunned. Raphael Verier made jewelry for royalty. And the richest people in the world. Even buying something from a Vernier store, the waitlist could take months or years. And he was going to be here in an *hour*.

Staring at Harrison, I swallowed. "When you said the Atwood name wasn't well known but was well off, you weren't kidding, were you?"

"No, I wasn't."

Taking another sip of tea to soothe the ache in my throat, I thought about it more. "And when you said 'not well known,' did you mean in general? At all? Because someone like that coming so quickly means something."

Blake carried in a tray and set it on the coffee table, filled with everything from more cake to coffee. "She's learning how filthy rich you are?"

I stared at Harrison until he leaned down and kissed me. "We are known in circles most people don't know about, little one. And I don't talk about it much. Not to hide it or because I'm ashamed, but because like most people who come from wealth, I prefer people see me and not my money.

"That being said, I will absolutely use every advantage it gives me when it comes to you, and my family is going to love you."

"So is mine," Blake said.

Emery didn't have any family. Cole's never came up. I looked at him and he nodded. "My father passed, but I have two moms alive and well. I'm sure they're going to fall all over themselves when they find out."

A whole mixture of emotions washed over me. I was going to have more family than I knew what to do with. But of course, it threw my own family—or lack thereof—into sharp contrast. "When will we do that? Meeting them."

Harrison stroked my hair. "When you're ready. And when you're safe."

I made a face. "Yeah."

It didn't seem possible the break-in was last night. Even stranger that I didn't miss my apartment. If I was honest with myself, I'd mentally moved in here a long time ago.

I was being honest with myself a lot today, and it was exhausting. The cake was delicious, and the tea calming. "I feel weird," I finally said. "What do I do until he gets here?"

"I've got an idea," Blake said.

Raising an eyebrow, I stood. Stormy stayed where she was, languidly sleeping. Cats were liquid, and she was no exception, draped over the edge of the couch like she'd melted there. "We have less than an hour. You and I both know we can't start that."

Because if we went down the road to sex, we would be bonding. Me and everyone.

"You could play," Cole said softly.

The leggings Stormy liked were upstairs, but she looked peaceful. "I don't want to wake her."

He looked at me until it hit me in the chest. *He wasn't talking about playing with Stormy. He was talking about the piano.*

I sprinted up the stairs.

CHAPTER FORTY-SIX

EMERY

*M*y Omega was fucking adorable.

She practically bounced on her toes waiting for the door to open. It was from more nerves than excitement, but we would take care of that soon enough. Stormy sat by my side, tail flicking back and forth.

Harrison pushed the front door open, and I caught sight of both our security and Vernier's. Who knew how many carats of diamonds and other gems he was carting around in the rolling bag which came behind him?

Petra froze, seeing him. We'd never met, but I knew of him. He was an older Alpha, silver-haired and dignified. His face had laugh lines so deep it seemed a wonder he wasn't always smiling.

He had a French accent. "You sat on my knee when you were a baby. You don't need Howard to call me, Harrison."

Our Alpha smiled. "It's been a long time, Raphael. I didn't want to assume."

Vernier's gaze fell on Petra. "And this is your lovely Omega?"

"This is Petra DeWitt-Merriton," Harrison stood beside her. "And yes, she is our Omega."

The amount of love and devotion in those words made my chest ache. It didn't feel real, and yet it was. Raphael suddenly looked at Petra differently. Almost reverently. He took her hand in both of his. "It is an honor to meet you."

Petra turned about as red as her nest. "Thank you. I still can't quite believe you're here. In person."

Harrison gestured to the elevator. I would meet them upstairs.

"Why not?" Raphael asked. "I would not accept anything less than my own work for anyone in the Atwood family."

"Come on, girl," I whispered to Stormy, and took the stairs.

The Atwood fortune wasn't entirely Harrison's, though that would change in the future. Still, he was right. We didn't talk about it because most of the time we didn't think about it, and it was hard to know if someone truly wanted you with millions of dollars between you.

Still, we would have known Petra was ours, regardless.

Cole and Blake sat near the fireplace. We were trying not to overwhelm our girl, and also not make Raphael feel like he was being watched. He was, but none of us were worried. The man had a reputation among those who knew him for being unfailingly kind and respectful.

Raphael laid out black velvet trays on the coffee table, and Petra sat across from him. She would try to minimize this.

Not allowing herself to accept what she deserved was a habit we would do our best to break.

Stormy crept toward Raphael, seemingly shy. She moved slowly. His eyes fell on her. "Oh hello." He held out a hand, and she cautiously pushed her head into it. Harder when he stroked her head. "You are very sweet. Much like your Omega."

"Stormy," I called her back to me so he could focus. Now satisfied, she flopped down at my feet.

Raphael looked at both Petra and Harrison. "We are looking for rings, yes?"

"Two," Harrison said. "An engagement ring, and a bond ring."

The man nodded, then smiled at Petra. "Before I ask what you like, I have a special skill, if you'll let me try."

"What's that?"

He shrugged. "I choose options based on scent. This is why I am who I am. Because I give people jewelry they didn't know to want." The man was utterly unapologetic. It was simply fact. "If I am wrong, we will choose something else."

"That sounds fun."

Raphael reached across the table. "May I?"

She extended her hand, and he held it delicately, scenting her wrist. And then he let her go. "Yes, I see. I have something for you, I think."

The front of his cart zipped off, revealing thin drawers. He began pulling them out, and setting things on the coffee table. Loose stones of various colors and different styles of bands. Petra clasped her hands in her lap, and Harrison put an arm around her shoulders.

Spoiling her would be a blast. Especially if it continued to turn her cheeks that shade of pink. I *craved* that shade of pink. It looked amazing when it spread to the rest of her body.

She wasn't perfuming now, but where I stood, I scented the remains of it from earlier. Sweet as sugar, warmed with cinnamon, and that bit of spice took you back to the sweetness, drawing you in a circle.

My need to mark her was growing. We might not be able to wait until these rings were ready, because now that I knew? My instincts to *claim* were screaming at me. I wasn't alone in that either. Soon we would need to bond her or start climbing the walls.

"I think this color for you," Raphael said, pointing to a line of stones. They sparkled from here. I went a little closer to see. Various shades of blue and purple. Petra leaned toward warmer colors, but the purples Raphael chose would look incredible with her eyes.

He picked up a band. "For the engagement ring. With one of these around it." Small decorations lay on the mat as well, too small for me to see what they were. "And for the bonding ring, these will rest against it."

"They're beautiful," Petra said, reaching out to touch a stone reverently.

"If you don't like these, I will make you something else. Whatever you like." He glanced at Harrison. "Your Alphas will accept nothing less."

"No," she said. "I do like it. Am I allowed to touch them?"

"Of course."

She picked up a couple of stones, and I went to lean on the back of the couch. "What do you think, sunshine?"

"I think I probably shouldn't be holding something worth this much."

I laughed softly and kissed the back of her hair. "Of the stones. What do you think of the stones?"

"They're all so beautiful."

Raphael lifted a finger and pointed between the five of us.

"You are not bonded yet, but you have a bond." His accent was stronger now. "I've seen this many times. You knew," he snapped his fingers. "Like that, no?"

Petra nodded. "Yes."

"Jewelry is like that. You know, or you don't know. If you must think, it is not for you."

She put the stones she held back on the velvet and reached for a different one. Round and a lovely violet. "This one."

Raphael smiled. "See?" He said to Harrison. "She has good instincts."

"Yes, she does," he murmured.

Then she looked through the ornaments. "I can't explain why I like this one."

I spotted tiny leaves made of diamonds which would curl around one side of the stone.

"You don't have to explain," Raphael waved a hand. "All you have to do is love."

Wandering toward the others near the fireplace, I gave her some space. They couldn't take their eyes off her, either. At least Cole put a shirt on before the jeweler arrived.

"Anyone else picturing her naked and rolling in diamonds?" Cole asked under his breath. "Because that's what I've got in my head."

Blake shook his head and groaned. "Cole, I'm about to strap myself to this chair because I need her so fucking badly. Don't make it worse."

"There's nothing about that image that makes anything worse. Only better," I said. "But yeah, we're not going to make it much longer."

"Yes," Raphael said behind us. "That will be lovely."

"You're happy?" Harrison asked.

"Yes." Petra was quiet, but in that single word was awe and love and acceptance. Fuck, I wanted to *feel* those emotions with her.

Raphael began to measure Petra's finger, and Harrison spoke. "We need these rings as quickly as possible, Raphael. Wednesday afternoon at the absolute latest."

"Of course. I will deliver them personally."

362

"There's one more thing. Would you be willing to open the safe for Petra and her friends? They are attending the Slate Gala."

Raphael noted her ring size and began quickly putting away the jewels and bands. "It would be my pleasure. Make sure my assistant knows the details of where and when." He zipped up his bag, and it was like there had never been enough jewels to buy this building spread out minutes before. Once again he took Petra's hand in both of his. "Your rings will be beautiful, miss Petra. It is my honor to make them, and I offer my congratulations to all of you."

"Thank you."

He shook Harrison's hand, and the rest of ours, on the way to the door. Harrison followed him. "I'll see you out."

My little Omega sagged back on the couch and looked at the ceiling. "That really just happened."

"Yes, it did." I sat down next to her. "How are you about all of this?"

"Which part?"

"Harrison's family and their fortune. I don't want you to think we hid it on purpose."

She shook her head. "He didn't hide it. Not really. I knew. Cole told me and he told me. I just didn't realize it was at that level." Then she smiled. "It's intense."

"But you're okay with it?" I pressed.

Petra looked at me, reaching out to touch my face. "What aren't you saying?" I didn't need to tell her. "Someone else either had a problem with it or took advantage of it."

It wasn't the only thing which contributed, but it had happened. Now, I was grateful. "I'm glad now, but..."

"But the scar is still there."

It was. I shook my head. "Sorry, sunshine, I didn't think you would care." But all the same, sweet relief washed through me.

"But you needed to ask," she said quietly. "I understand."

Petra pulled me down to her, stretching us out on the couch. I smiled, pressing my face into her neck. "Dangerous game, Omega. When all of us want you this badly."

"I know, but look at me." I did, watching the golden flecks in her eyes. "I love *you*. I would love you even if you lived under a bridge. I'm sorry anyone ever made you feel like you weren't worth that."

All the breath rushed out of me. "I love you so fucking much, Petra."

"I'm not going to pretend it's not weird," she whispered. "Raphael fucking Vernier just somehow picked the perfect rings out of my head. He was *here*, and that's so..." her breath hiccuped. "I don't know if I'll ever get used to it. I know you guys want to spoil me, but I don't know if it will ever feel normal."

"I hope it will." I kissed her neck again. Being this close to her was intoxicating. *Bite. Claim. Mine.* Pushing up on my arms, I pulled back. "Unless you want me to bite you right this second..."

Petra's eyes went dark, perfume exploding around the two of us. "Fuck, sunshine."

"Sorry."

"No, you're not."

"You're right," she said with a smirk. "I'm not."

The door opened, and Harrison came back in. "He's off. He's going to make a special exception for us. We'll have the rings on Monday."

Today was Saturday. Two days.

"That's amazing." Petra sat up and looked at Harrison. "Thank you."

He smiled and leaned over the back of the couch. "Do you like them, little one?"

"Yes. Very much."

Tilting her face up to his, he kissed her. "Good."

"For the record, I would have taken a ring from a quarter dispenser if it was from any of you."

Harrison's eyes crinkled in the corners when he smiled. That only happened with the biggest and purest smiles. "I know. But my Omega will only ever have the best."

The flash of true emotion on Petra's face broke my heart and warmed my soul at the same time. She still didn't believe she was worth it, and my relief about the money gave way to desire. Not only for her, but to show her she was worth absolutely everything.

Petra stood up, and as soon as she did, Blake and Emery were on their feet too. "I know you wanted to wait for the rings," she said quietly, "but I don't think I can last till Monday." Looking at Harrison, she asked. "If I said you can fuck me for the rest of our lives with nothing on but the ring—"

Harrison reached out with one arm and pulled her against him, mouth coming down on hers. Hard. "Little one, I never said we had to wait. I said I wanted our ring on your finger, and I want it there for the entire world to see at the Gala. But waiting? No part of me is capable of that."

He lifted her up, hands planted on her ass. Already Petra's perfume was thickening and swirling into a cloud around us. "One of these days," Harrison said, "I'm going to take you in my bed. Slowly."

"I think I'm going to like that. But yeah. Nest right now."

"Nest. Right now."

I only glanced back to make sure Stormy was settled, because this could take a while.

CHAPTER FORTY-SEVEN

PETRA

*B*reathless.

I was breathless, and they were my oxygen. The way I needed them, it almost felt like heat. Harrison's hands on me while we were in the elevator burned through my clothes. He was hard between us, straining through his pants.

"Four Alphas with the need to claim you, little one. Are you prepared for this?" The frosty side of his scent wrapped around me, bringing an edge.

"Fuck yes I am."

I peeled my shirt off over my head and tossed it on the floor on the way out of the elevator. My bra went the same way. When he set me down, hands were waiting to strip my pants off me. I was touched from every direction, and I immediately understood what Harrison meant.

The energy was different. Intentional. Charged. Their instincts sang to mine. I let them undress me and touch me. We were coming out of this nest bonded together as a pack.

No going back.

Blake sank to his knees and took my panties with him. "We can't knot you yet," he said, kissing my stomach. "Not until we've all bitten you."

I wasn't in heat, and waiting for the knots to ease would drive the other Alphas mad.

"But as long as I live, Petra, I'm never going to get tired of fucking your cunt with my tongue." He pulled my thighs apart and ran his tongue over my clit. I had to brace myself on his shoulders so I didn't fall over.

"Oh my god," I panted the words. It felt like so much longer than last night since I'd been fucked. I didn't just need them to take me, I needed them to wreck me. Ruin me. Mark me with more than just their bites, but with everything. Show me that every inch of my body and soul belonged to them.

Emery turned my head to him and kissed me, his hand on my throat. "We're going to replace all the toys from your apartment," he said. "I have so many ideas, sunshine."

I couldn't focus on his words with Blake's mouth on me. His fingers dug into my ass, holding me against his face and rendering me utterly speechless.

He released me for a fraction of a second. "Get her down."

Emery moved, gently shifting my balance, but I never fell. They lowered me to the cushions together, Blake pulling my knees wide and licking me like I was made of ice cream.

"Blake," I tried to reach for his hair and drag him closer, but there were hands holding me back. My Alphas, only adding to my pleasure with their touch.

"That's right, baby. Say my name. Scream it if you have to, because I'm the one who's going to make you come right now."

Need *shook* my body. I arched off the cushions in the nest, desperate to get closer. Blake slipped two fingers into me, and then a third. "You're not wet enough," he said, sucking my clit between his lips. "If my face isn't dripping with your cum, you're not fucking wet enough."

How he had the ability to say exactly what I needed, I didn't know. Moving his hand along with his tongue, I shuddered, the first taste of real pleasure rushing through me. A small orgasm, and the first of what I was sure would be many.

All the other hands disappeared, and it was him and me. When Blake lifted his head, his chin *was* dripping with me. But he didn't stop moving his fingers, keeping me on the edge of shaking pleasure. "I wanted you to come first," he said. "Nice and warmed up before I make you mine."

His eyes locked on mine. Those infernal fingers never stopped moving. Blake smiled, knowing he had me exactly where he wanted me. "I love you, baby."

He lowered his mouth to the side of my hip and bit down. *Pain* ripped through me, followed by heat. Like I'd been torn in half and knitted together in the same breath. And suddenly Blake was there. In the center of my chest, bright and shining. His thoughts and emotions were sharp like his scent. They *felt* like him. And the truth of his love crashed down on me.

I gasped. This couldn't be real. It couldn't be this deep and true. It couldn't...

Blake's mouth found mine, cock thrusting inside me in the same motion. "It is real, Petra. So fucking real." His pleasure fed my pleasure. I was dizzy and dazed, lost in the feeling of him. Every movement amplified because I felt it twice.

We didn't hold back. My nails scraped across his skin, he lifted one of my legs and fucked me harder. We tried to consume each other, two flames at war, but burning together. I wasn't even sure who came first. It was simply a firestorm of pleasure whirling and carrying me away.

Pulling back, Blake came across my chest. I felt the surge of lust and desire at the sight. Never in my life had I felt sexier than with his eyes on me, covered in *him*.

He pressed his palm to my chest, directly between my breasts. The sounds he made somewhere between a purr and a growl. "*Mine*."

"Mine." I said it back, a soft echo before he kissed me.

No part of me wanted him to go. I wanted him knotted inside me so I could know what it felt like. I wanted to stay wrapped up in his arms forever. "I'm not going anywhere, baby. You're stuck with me now."

One more soft kiss, and he was pulling away, replaced by Cole. My caramel Alpha slid into me with aching slowness, gathering me up so his arms were beneath me. Cradled and held. Slowly fucked as he rocked his hips. I moaned, allowing my head to fall back.

Every one of them was so different, and they never ceased to surprise me.

Cole rocked into me, peppering kisses across my bare neck. "I've never been so happy to be assigned to a charity ball," he whispered.

I laughed, but it didn't last, every movement of his cock stealing what little voice I had. Gripping his shoulders, I lifted my head until ours were pressed together. The way he moved his hips, grinding down on my clit, electric sparks worked their way through me, leading me to the edge of orgasm like a path of fireflies.

"Alpha," my voice sounded strangled. "Please."

He growled, my eyes closing as I bared my neck. Please, please, *please*. I needed him. More. Faster. Everything.

Cole bit where my neck met my shoulder, pain ripping through me and disappearing, taking me down over the edge into pure fucking light. My voice filled the nest. Somewhere close was a purr, and pleasure so deep I couldn't see or breathe.

Inside me, our bond flared to life. I felt him remember those first moments scenting me. The realization that everything was going to be different. Forever. He slowed down the memories, the emotions so fucking clear I could almost see them. Feel the way he did when we came together in the closet, or the joy when he walked into my apartment the next day.

"Don't cry, honeybee."

My eyes fluttered open and closed again. He kissed away my tears, still moving. Still rocking into me and bathing us both in sweet, delicious pleasure. The tears were happy, and I couldn't stop them. This was everything.

He pulled back too, seconds before he came all over me. Another claim and another mark. The deepest, most feral part of the Alpha which needed to see me covered in cum, scented only like them and no one else.

Pride and satisfaction echoed through my chest.

Cole kissed where he'd bitten, the result instantaneous. I moaned, writhing on the cushions. One touch felt like his tongue was between my legs. "Is that always going to happen?"

"Yes," he said, licking over his mark again. "And I get to feel everything you feel when I touch this mark. What makes you hot and bothered. What makes you *wet*. Exactly what you need, Petra. Every day."

I pulled his face down to mine, devouring his mouth, crushing us together until we were both laughing. Two Alphas rested within my chest, and it felt so fucking right I couldn't breathe.

"Love you, honeybee. You're mine."

Emery didn't give me a chance to miss him, pulling me onto his chest and lining up his cock with deliberate ease. "Come here, sweet girl," he said, bringing our mouths together. "Your mouth is the sweetest fucking thing," he murmured. "Almost as sweet as this pussy." A thrust up, and I moaned into his mouth.

"Emery." I breathed his name. My mind was untethered from the world, lost in the feelings of them. Blake and Cole, happy and content. Fucking proud I was their Omega. Loving watching me with Emery.

"Give me your hand," he said, an order I absolutely wanted to obey. I gave it to him. He held it, free hand gripping my hair and holding me close, all while driving himself so deep I saw stars.

God, the sounds he made had me on the edge. Sounds of masculine pleasure and effort. All because of me. "Don't look away, sunshine," he growled. "Not for one second. Don't close your eyes."

I drowned in the blue of his gaze. Pure fire. The hottest part of the flame. Pleasure spiraled up between us, his thrusts hitting me exactly where I needed.

Right. Fucking. There.

Holy *shit*. "Oh, fuck." The words ripped out of me. "Oh fuck. I can't. I can't. I'm—" My eyes closed, savoring the bliss on the edge of the explosion. A moth daring to fly too close to the flame and secretly hoping to get burned.

"*Look at me*." The urgency in his voice drew my eyes to his. I came watching him fuck me into oblivion.

Emery lifted the wrist he held and bit. Pain merged with the pleasure of my orgasm and blew outward, pulling me tighter into the coil of golden, glittering light. Shuddery breaths and desperate moans.

I felt him. Relief and joy and himself on the edge of his own orgasm. He was so fucking *happy*. I laughed, my own joy leaking through. "Hi." I kissed him, holding his face. "I feel you. I can feel you."

He deepened our kiss as he pulled out of me, the orgasm crashing through him and spilling over into me. Cum splashed across my thighs, marking me as his all over again.

"I fucking love you. You're all mine now."

Our kiss turned raw and feral, biting and pulling, need and

lust and desire. Emery pulled back, panting. "I'm never going to have enough of you, sweet girl. Not even now. Don't move. Just enjoy it."

He shifted beneath me, turning, mouth reaching my pussy as Harrison's hands landed on my hips. One tongue stroked over my clit, and the other glided over the bud of my ass. "Oh my god." I gripped the cushions beneath me, trying not to move, which was nearly impossible trapped between two sides of heaven.

They didn't stop, teasing me, pulling my attention between their two mouths until I was so close I ground my hips down into Emery's mouth. One final lick over my clit, and he pulled away.

"Noooo," I begged. "Don't stop."

Harrison dragged his tongue up my spine, making me pant. "Don't worry, little one. I've got you."

He took me from behind. One thrust was all it took for fireworks to flare behind my eyes. The size of him stretching me open, the way he wrapped himself around me entirely, the heel of his hand scraping over my clit. I was a rupturing nova only for him.

Pain shattered me as he bit, below where neck met shoulder and opposite to Cole's bite. Our bond locked into place, and I came all over again. The four of them together felt like something clicking which hadn't been aligned, and suddenly it was. All of them were there, and they could feel each other through me.

Harrison was a calm, steady presence in my bond. But beneath the surface, all that power rumbled, ready to erupt.

"*Mine*," he said the word into my neck, fucking me into the cushions without any mercy. I wanted none. My mind floated in a glittering haze of sweet bliss and vast emotion. All of us together. Love and acceptance I never knew was possible.

Harrison roared his pleasure, pulling back and coming across my back. Lowering himself on top of me, his purr was the loudest thing in the world. I loved the pressure of him pinning me down. Keeping me safe. Making me his.

Theirs.

I was theirs.

The way all of them blended together and stood out... It was going to take time to get used to it. But I belonged to them, and they belonged to me, and no matter what, no one could take it away from us.

A laugh bubbled up through my chest. Pure happiness and joy.

"Petra?"

I buried my face in the cushions, unable to stop the laughter and giggles. Harrison turned me over, and I smiled so wide it hurt my face. He looked at me like he was trying to figure out what was wrong until he registered what I really felt through our bond. Then he smiled too, collapsing back down to kiss me and tangle us together.

Somehow, I ended up in Cole's arms, and then Blake's. Finally, Emery. He kissed me slowly, smoothing my hair back from my face. This giddy euphoria singing through all of us was almost too much. And one single thought would turn it over into desire all over again. I wanted to experience their pleasure. Get fucked by them and *feel* them fuck me.

"Something we'll all have to adjust to, sunshine, is how much our thoughts affect each other. Because all four of us want you at all times. And as much as I wish we could spend eternity in this nest, we can't."

"We can today though," I said. "Right?"

"Yeah, baby," Blake said. "Today we can."

"I might need a shower before we continue this," I said. "I'm covered in all of you."

Four growls met the statement, along with a flood of possessive pride through their bonds. Emery rolled fully on top of me and pinned my wrists to the floor of the nest, running his thumb over his bite. Need erupted, perfume exploded, and I whined.

"No fucking way," Emery said, mouth brushing mine. "We want you like this."

The quadruple dose of lust injected into me would have put me on the floor if I hadn't already been there. My moan wasn't voluntary. "If you're going to make me feel like that, you need to follow through. Otherwise, your Omega will be very, very, sad."

Emery chuckled. "As you wish, sunshine."

A hand gripped my ankle and yanked me out from underneath Emery and into the center of them again. I laughed, not quite believing I could be this happy. But as Blake kissed me and Cole slid inside me to the hilt, I vowed to remember this and try to savor every second.

CHAPTER FORTY-EIGHT

PETRA

"*Y*ou know, when you mentioned getting ready together, I wasn't sure if you were serious."

"Of course we were serious," Eva said, keeping her eyes closed as her makeup artist perfected her eye shadow.

My currently blank Omega suite had been transformed into a dressing room and salon. Tonight we would make our move and announce to the world I was bonded.

I glanced down at my ring. Raphael couldn't have done a better job, and I couldn't stop staring at it.

"With that ring I *almost* wish I got you a different dress," Eva said. "But I don't. This one will be perfect."

The girl doing my hair smiled and fluffed it out. We were almost ready, and my stomach had a cloud of butterflies inside it.

"Can I look?"

"Yeah."

I went over to the rack where all our dresses hung in garment bags. Downstairs, the guys were already gone. I felt them in my chest and wished they were here. But for this to work, they needed to be at the venue. The only reason they left me at all was because Eva's security had us locked down tight, and both her and Esme's security had more than proven themselves.

Harrison made it clear he would hire any of them.

Unzipping the black bag, I froze. It was the dress. The one I'd stared at in Bergman's when Eva ran into me. "You didn't."

"I told you. You will look killer in that dress, and considering you're going to give a bunch of people a heart attack, I thought it was appropriate."

I laughed and pulled it out of the bag. The black, shimmering fabric draped down to the floor, the slit so high Carmen would probably faint.

"Thank you," I said. "Seriously."

"Iris and I know each other," she said. "She wanted to come and help us herself, but was already booked."

Esme was in the bathroom changing, and Sloane was finishing up hair. My best friend had been quiet all day. Subdued. It wasn't like her. "Lo, you okay?"

She met my eyes in the mirror and gave me an unconvincing smile. "Yeah, I'm fine. Just work things."

I narrowed my eyes.

"You've been busy, Bee. I'm okay."

She didn't seem okay, but one thing I knew about Sloane—if she wasn't ready to talk, she wasn't ready to talk. When she was, I would be here for her. "Okay," I touched her on the shoulder. "Love you."

"Love you."

The dress fit perfectly. I felt like I was going to flash the world, but I also felt powerful. Like this was going to work. If anything, this was exactly the *take back my life* dress I'd been looking for.

For the last three days, my Alphas and I hadn't left the apartment. They helped me drop out of classes, recover the few unbroken things in my apartment and talk to the police about the break-in, set up a preliminary interview with the director of the Slate City Orchestra, and at the same time, showered me with love. I think one or another had taken me on every surface of the apartment. We even finally made it into the pool, though it didn't last long when they decided the tile floor beside the pool was another place which hadn't been christened.

My whole body was sore, and I liked it. It reminded me what we had, and every aching muscle brought me joy, strange as it was.

"Holy fucking shit," Sloane said when I came out of the bathroom. "That is incredible."

Eva turned and began to clap. "Yes, Petra. This is what we want. God, if you'd been wearing something like this at the charity ball, we never would have been able to get you *out* of the closet."

I laughed. "I really love it."

"Miss Williams," a voice said from the hallway.

"Yes?"

Neil, Eva's head of security, poked his head in the door and spotted me. "Ah, Miss Dewitt. There's a visitor for you downstairs. Mr. Atwood approved him before he left."

I blinked. "Really?"

"Yes."

"I'll be right down. Escort them to the living room?"

"Of course."

The fact that he cut off Dad's name didn't bother me nearly as much as the reverse. Because he was still around. It wasn't nearly as much of an erasure.

"Do you know who it is?" Esme asked.

"No," I admitted. "But if Harrison approved them, it's fine. Visitors have to jump through about ten hoops to get past the lobby right now."

One of the assistants Eva brought set out the shoes she chose for me. Matching black with gold glitter spangled across them, they were tall and made the dress just barely trail on the floor. "I'll go see who it is."

The elevator ride down, I wondered if I could send a question to my Alphas. Their emotions were more distant than when they were close by, and I couldn't feel exactly where they were. But the bonds were with me, and comforting.

Raphael Vernier was in our living room, once again setting out *gorgeous*, sparkling gems. But these weren't raw stones. These were pieces that looked like they belonged to royalty. "Mr. Vernier," I stared at him. "What are you doing here?"

He looked up and clasped his hands. "Mademoiselle Petra. You look stunning." In the way he had, he took my left hand in both of his and kissed the back briefly. "Harrison asked me to open my vault for you and your friends, and of course I said yes."

I remembered him asking that, but I'd been too overwhelmed with the rings and jewels in front of me for the words to sink in. "You can choose what you like. But," he held up a finger. "I think I have what you need."

"First, this." He chose a golden cuff which had small filigree designs carved into the metal. "It goes here," he gestured to his upper arm. "May I?"

I turned, offering him my arm. The cuff opened and closed seamlessly, a little tight so it didn't move, but not so it was painful.

"And maybe this."

The necklace he showed me made my mouth drop open. A cascading galaxy of diamonds set in gold. They dropped artfully, like stars had been flung to earth and caught in a sparkling net. "That's too much," I said. "I can't wear that."

"Why not?"

I didn't have an answer for him.

"Petra," he said, turning to me and putting his hands lightly on my shoulders. "When Harrison called me to make your rings, I didn't know who you were. But as soon as I heard your name, I knew. Your mother made the most beautiful music. Given the piano behind you, I will assume you do as well."

Raphael sighed, but smiled. "I am an old man. I have seen much of the world, and though I am old, I am not foolish. Perhaps I see too much." He shrugged. "But do not diminish yourself out of fear. You mean to shock the world tonight, yes?"

I gasped. "How do you know?"

Only a wink in response. "Like I said, I see too much. And there is one thing I have not told you."

"What's that?"

He picked up the black mannequin bust which held the necklace and turned it to me. A label ran down the back with a list of names. "We know who has worn each of my pieces. It adds to the mystery and the allure." We both laughed. "Please look."

I scanned the names, and froze, my lungs no longer capable of drawing breath.

Mallory DeWitt.

"Many years ago, when Mallory DeWitt was welcomed into the International Hall of Music, she wore this necklace. Of course you should wear it, and when you yourself are welcomed into it, I hope you will wear it again."

Blinking back tears, I reached out and touched her name. "Thank you."

"Turn."

He placed the necklace on me, and it was *heavy*. But when it was in place, before he could even show me a mirror, I caught a half-light glimpse of myself in the window.

Mom stared back at me.

It was me when I looked in Raphael's mirror, but the peace of her image remained. I tried not to think about her that much, because it hurt. But it also hurt to forget her. This, tonight, my pack, my path to music...

It was the right one.

She would be happy for me.

She would be proud of me.

That was all that mattered.

"We wondered if you'd left without us," Sloane said, coming in and stopping short. "Holy crap."

I laughed, my spirits lifting. "Lo, this is Raphael Vernier. He's here to let us borrow some jewelry."

She came closer slowly, looking at the mass of shine on the coffee table and Raphael like they were about to dissolve into smoke. "Seriously?"

"Seriously."

Eva and Esme swept into the room, and we were all taken by laughter and the sheer delight of trying on jewelry that was worth more than all of us combined. Finally, when each of us was dripping in diamonds, we were ready.

"Is the Gidwitz Pack here?" I asked Neil.

"They are. Waiting downstairs."

Sloane pulled me into a hug. "I wish we could all go together. But it might ruin the surprise."

"Yeah," I breathed. Nerves popped up in my stomach, and through the bonds in my chest, my Alphas sent me calm and love. They were ready for this, and I could be too.

"See you on the other side," Eva waved, and Esme gave me a thumbs up.

They left first, and when I was given the all clear, I went downstairs, ready to change everything.

CHAPTER FORTY-NINE

HARRISON

*M*y phone rang, dragging me from sleep instantly. I rolled and grabbed the phone from the nightstand, answering it before Petra woke.

Looking over, my Omega was still passed out, hair wild. The curls from the Gala hadn't faded, and she looked like a beautiful sea monster. I smiled to myself as I slipped from the bed and into the hall. "Hello?"

"Boss," Nick said. "You need to check your email."

"Why?"

"It's better if you see it."

Never a good sign. "Hold on."

I checked my phone. It was later in the morning. We had a late night. The email was there at the top, forwarded by Nick from the main Atwood Security account.

The same format as the others. This time with pictures of all of us at the Gala.

HAVING ALPHAS WON'T SAVE HER EITHER.

Cold rolled down my spine. I hadn't expected him to give up, but part of me had hoped he might, given the emphasis on her being alone and unprotected. Clearly not. If anything, the description that followed was worse and more detailed.

I held the phone up to my ear. "I see it."

"No trace. Sorry, boss."

Where our bond was, there was nothing but a gentle haze that felt like Petra. She was still sound asleep. Good. Because the anger and terror in me right now would alarm her.

But Cole was awake. I felt him like an echo through my bond, and his door opened. He frowned, staring at me. "I don't care what you have to do, Nick. Expense isn't a concern. Scrape the data we have until we can find *something*. He's good, but he can't be perfect."

"You got it."

"I'll probably be in later to help."

Cole raised his eyebrows and disappeared into his room for a second, reappearing with his phone.

"Keep me posted if there's anything else."

I watched Cole's face as he saw the email. "This doesn't make sense, Harrison."

"Why not?"

"Because it doesn't. You can't tell me this follows a normal pattern of stalking. It hasn't. He hasn't escalated beyond the flash bang. It's pictures and threats, pictures and threats. For something vague and immaterial."

I slid my hands into the pockets of my sweatpants. "We haven't exactly given him opportunities to escalate."

Petra had been with a secure bubble since the flashbang, and every time we had to leave the perimeter, we made sure every angle was covered three times over. For the Senator as well. To say he'd been unhappy with the situation was an understatement. But he couldn't argue with me when he'd met Petra's mother in the same way. He knew the power of a scent bond, and in spite of his anger, I sensed there was also relief.

For the time being, we were still in charge of his security.

"Something isn't right," Cole said. "This whole time the threat has been 'don't run for chancellor.' Well, the Senator announced last night. I understand this," he held up the phone. "This feels like a natural escalation. But the rest of it?" Cole shook his head slowly. "You and I both know there are easier ways to destroy someone's career than death threats. This is either deeply personal or they don't want what they're saying."

I looked back toward my bedroom. "I don't disagree, but I don't see another clear motive. Petra has been so under the radar, it doesn't feel like the motive can be her. The threats came before the press coverage."

"She has her interview today," Cole said. "Should we move it?"

"Not yet." I shook my head. Petra was looking forward to it. "Do me a favor and call Nick. Tell him to send a team to clear the

382

location and secure it. We'll make sure it's good to go. If there's even a flicker of uncertainty from the team, *then* we move it."

"Yeah." He hesitated. "What do we do, Harrison? What do we tell her? We can't keep her under lock and key forever. And I don't understand why this guy is a fucking ghost."

"You and me both," I said, the same anger building up under my ribs. "As for the rest of it? I'll go to the office today. I still have favors I can call in. I've kept everything on the right side of legal to shield her. But now that she's ours? All bets are off."

Cole nodded. "I'll make the call. Maybe I'll go help them check it. Don't know that I'll be able to sleep after that."

Me either.

I slipped back into my room and closed the door. Petra hadn't moved. The sparkly black dress she wore last night was carefully spread over the back of my chair. The diamonds and cuff lay on the table. All my Omega had on was what she wore beneath it. Which was almost nothing. It was still too much for me, but I would take it. Especially now that I had her permission to undress her while she slept.

Now more than ever, I needed to feel her.

I put my phone back on the nightstand and my pants hit the floor before I slipped back into bed. She didn't stir as I turned her toward me and slid her bra off and tossed it aside. That dress didn't allow panties.

It was a lot yesterday, and she was exhausted. Waking up to find she was still in danger wasn't what I wanted for her.

Pulling her leg over my hip, I used my hand to guide my cock inside her. Even asleep, the heat of her body was incredible. I pushed in far as I could go before I stroked my hand down her bare spine.

Being inside her like this satisfied a nameless desire inside me. To keep her whole and safe and by my side.

Cole was right. Not all of it made sense. There was a puzzle piece missing. But it wasn't a jigsaw with a neatly made hole where you saw the shape of absence. No, these were pieces that were floating. You didn't know how many there were, or how many there were supposed to be. You could only try to connect them as best you could and hope the picture came into focus.

Petra sighed in her sleep, snuggling closer to my chest. I covered us both with the comforter and held her as tight as I dared. I didn't think I would be able to fall back asleep, but as long as I could hold my Omega, I was content.

CHAPTER FIFTY

PETRA

A deep, rumbling purr vibrated in my ear. Harrison's delight at me waking up tumbled through our bond, making his purr stronger. I wasn't wearing anything anymore, and he was inside me, holding me close.

I lifted my face without opening my eyes, searching for him with my lips. Too short to make it all the way to his lips while his cock was buried in me, I found his neck and inhaled the rich combination of whiskey and cedar. The frosty edge of his scent was nearly absent.

"Does the no underwear rule apply in your bed, too?" My bra was gone. Not that I objected.

His deep chuckle warmed me from the inside. "No. I needed to feel you, and since you gave me permission..."

"I did." I sighed and finally opened my eyes. "Morning."

"Good morning, little one."

The delight of waking up with me faded and was replaced by apprehension. His face hadn't changed at all. Our bonds were going to come in handy. "What's wrong?"

His mouth formed a grim line. "I'm really sorry, Petra, but I need you to reschedule your interview with the orchestra."

"Why?"

Harrison sighed, moving us both so he sat up, leaning against the headboard and I was on his lap, stuffed full of his cock. "Another threat came this morning. Cole went with a team to check it out, and we can't secure it. Not the way we need to with something like this. Will the director understand?"

"Given that it's life and death, yeah, she will. It sucks, but there's not much we can do about it, right?"

"Right." Unhappiness rang between us. "I'm going to find him, Petra. We're going to catch him and stop him, no matter what I have to do."

I leaned forward and laid my head on his shoulder. "As long as you're safe, too."

"Always."

My phone chirped from somewhere in the room. Over where I left my dress and everything. I'd been so tired I'd basically stripped and fallen asleep. "I guess I should cancel it early enough to save her trouble."

Lifting myself off Harrison, I felt the flash of lust through our bond and smirked. My body missed him as soon as he was gone. I found my phone on the floor near my shoes. There were a couple of missed calls and texts, a voicemail from Carmen. I rolled my eyes. "I can only imagine what she wants right now."

"Who?"

"The Wicked Witch of the East," I said under my breath.

Harrison laughed. "Carmen?"

I sat cross-legged on the bed and put the phone on speaker before I played the voicemail.

"PETRA. YOUR FATHER AND I FEEL WE MAY HAVE GONE ABOUT THIS THE WRONG WAY. WE'D LIKE TO SIT DOWN AND TALK TO YOU ABOUT YOUR FUTURE AND THE CHOICES YOU'VE MADE. JUST FOR A LATE LUNCH. AT YOUR FATHER'S CAMPAIGN HEADQUARTERS. WE'VE ALREADY RESERVED A CONFERENCE ROOM AND ORDERED LUNCH FROM THE SAFFRON MARKET. ONE OF YOUR ALPHAS OWNS THAT RESTAURANT, RIGHT? PLEASE LET ME KNOW. I'LL PICK YOU UP AT NOON."

"I'm glad you gave me a reason to get out of it."

Harrison put his hand on mine. "Don't hate me, little one."

"I'm stuck with you for life. I better not hate you."

Reaching out, he sank a hand into my hair and hauled me across the bed to kiss me. "It's not the same as the interview," he said. "Because we provide the Senator's security, his campaign headquarters are secure at all times. If you think it's a good idea to go, you'll be safe while you're there."

I sighed, going boneless and flopping down on the bed. "You could have lied and told me it was wildly dangerous. Technically, it *is* because whatever the hell they have to say to me is probably going to piss me off."

"True. And you can get out of it if you want to. But that's

not going to stop them from trying to talk to you. If you say no to lunch, they'll try to come here. If you say no to that, they'll want a video call."

I made a face. "So this is how it's going to be? You're just going to *be right* all the time?"

"Better listen to your Alpha," he whispered in my ear.

"Fine," I sighed. "I'll go. But I want Cole with me."

He laughed. "There was never any chance of him staying behind, little one. You're still under our protection. Besides, all the cars are Atwood staff. You'll be there and back in no time. Maybe you can start shopping for your suite later."

"Do we get to go back to Nest Inc.?"

Harrison stood and pulled on a pair of sweatpants, which was a pity because they disguised his absolutely magnificent ass. "If you want. But you can also pick whatever you like and have them bring it to you."

I had no idea what I wanted. There was so much *space*. The whole floor could be divided into different zones. "I'm going to need the world's biggest cat tree for Stormy."

"We'll have to make sure it's industrial," Harrison said. "She's no house cat."

Grabbing my phone, I texted Carmen that noon would be fine. "I can't believe you're making me do this."

Harrison raised a single eyebrow. "Making you?"

I rolled my eyes. "Not providing an adequate excuse."

"Little one," coming around the bed, he leaned over me, giving me a very nice distraction with all his skin and muscle, the scruff of his beard and the hair on his chest. "I know you want to make up with your father. If this is the moment he chooses to come to his senses, you would be upset about missing it."

He was right, but it didn't make the idea of lunch any more fun. "Fine. But if they try to send me to rehab or any other crap, I'm walking the hell out."

His eyes crinkled at the corners when he smiled. "Good girl."

Heat shot straight between my legs, and I felt his attention turn toward my body in our bond. "Nope." I scrambled out of the bed and grabbed my phone. "No, sir. You can't do that, or I'll be late and she'll be pissed at me and make it even worse."

"I can be fast." He caught me around the waist, pressing a kiss below my ear and dragging his mouth down to his mark. "Promise. And I thought you wanted an excuse?"

I moaned, but gently pulled away. "I promise I'll let you have your way with me later. My head needs to be clear for this."

"Fair enough." The feelings in our bond were beautiful and strange. Peace and comfort, and the deep knowledge that we had forever. We didn't have to rush anything.

Less than an hour later, I was leaning against Cole in the lobby, waiting for the Atwood car carrying my stepmother.

"You should have worn the diamonds again," Cole said. "Just to make a point."

"What point would that be?"

He laughed. "I don't know. Maybe I just like seeing you sparkle. Think Raphael would mind if I fucked you in them before we gave them back?"

A blush rose to my cheeks. "I would mind," I said. "He's too kind to do that. But buy me a sparkly necklace, and I'll wear it anytime you want."

"You think I won't?" He pressed his lips to my ear. "I absolutely will. Then I'll press you up against the windows in the living room and take you from behind, so the city can see you in diamonds and nothing else, and know who you belong to."

"I'm going to spend the rest of my life turned on, aren't I?"

"If I have my way? Yes."

Three cars pulled up outside. Now that my father was a candidate for chancellor, they put more security protocols in place. "Well then, you better tell Harrison to buy stock in panties if the four of you are so intent on ruining them."

"I will."

I headed for the door and stopped. Carmen got out and came inside. She had a sickly smile on her face. "Petra." She looked beside me and her distaste was visible. "Cole."

"I thought we were meeting you in the car?"

She sighed. "I wanted to ask for some privacy. Cole, if you would ride in a different part of the motorcade, Petra and I have things to discuss."

"Cole is my Alpha," I said, pulling my hair over one shoulder to expose his still-healing bite. "We are bonded. Whatever you say to me, you can say to him."

"Please, Petra. I... There are things I want to keep between us."

Never in my life had Carmen said please to me. Not only that, but she looked strange. Not quite sad, but contrite. Suspicion rose, but I held it back. Maybe Dad had a change of heart and it spread to her.

I looked over at Cole. "It's all Atwood, right? The security?"

"It is."

"So is that okay?"

He hesitated and scanned the motorcade. Then he pulled me a few steps away. "Are you sure? Not for your safety. I trust our men. But for you. It's not a short ride." My father's headquarters were clear on the other side of the city. With traffic, it could be an hour. "You'll have no buffer."

"If she's offering a hand, I have to take it." I pressed my lips together. "If something goes wrong, you'll feel it. Or I can text you and you can come charging in while we're stopped at a light."

Cole grinned. "I like the sound of that. It's fine with me, but only if you're sure."

"No," I said. "I'm not sure. But I think I have to."

"Okay." He kissed me softly, deepening it until it bordered on inappropriate, and winked when he pulled back. "Just have to stake my claim."

"To my stepmother?"

"To everyone, honeybee."

I pressed my hand to his chest where our bond was, feeling the depth of what he saw when he looked at me. "I love you."

He grinned. "Keep talking dirty to me and I won't ride in the other car."

I smacked his arm before going back to Carmen. "Let's go."

Cole kept his hand on my lower back all the way to the car door and shut it behind me before going to the car behind us.

In the limo with darkened windows, we were very enclosed. Cole was correct, no buffer between Carmen and I. We sat on opposite sides of the limo, and she stared down at her phone, typing. None of the contrition she'd shown in the lobby was present now.

That was fast.

"Well," I said. "You've got me where you want me. You can start talking any time."

Carmen made a face. "We have plenty of time, Petra. Let me finish this."

I slumped back against the seat. This was probably a stupid idea. But there were worse things than being stuck in a car with my stepmother for an hour. Except maybe her scent.

My own phone buzzed with a text message. Cole.

> You okay?

> Do I feel that annoyed already?

> Yes.

> It's fine. Remind me to tell Blake to put green apple on the 'never' flavor list.

In my chest, I felt his amusement.

I set my phone down on the seat and found Carmen staring at me. "Based on that kiss, I can only imagine what they're texting you."

"Really? That's where you're going to start? Shaming me for being affectionate with my pack?"

She rolled her eyes. "Your *pack*. You mean the men who ruined everything? Yes, I'm familiar. And I'd rather not watch them stick their tongues down your throat."

I locked eyes with her. "Last time I checked, you weren't invited into my bedroom, but next time they want to fuck me, I'll check who's on the audience list."

"You expect me to talk to you when you say stuff like this? We can't have a conversation when you don't even show the barest amount of respect."

"Respect?" I shook my head. "Carmen, you've been my step-mother for what... ten years? Tell me when in those ten years you've ever shown me any respect, and I'll tell you why you deserve any in return. Go on, I'll wait."

She didn't say anything.

"The only thing you've ever done is push me into doing exactly what you wanted me to do. And I went along with it because I love my father and I felt guilty. But I refuse to let you control my life anymore. You want to talk about *respect*? How about respecting when someone says 'no.' Like all the times I informed you that myself and the Gidwitz Pack were *not interested* in bonding with each other?"

Carmen opened her mouth, and I stopped her.

"If you're going to say anything about duty and sacrifice and all that ridiculous bullshit, save it. I did what I needed to do in order to protect myself. I am scent-sympathetic with my pack. You know when I met Cole? The night of the charity ball, when you claim I was high. I wasn't. I was finding out what it's like to be so deeply in tune with someone you know instantly they're meant for you."

"You're living in a fucking fairytale world, Petra."

"You're right. I am. It's great. Thank you for noticing."

She glared at me. "That's not what I meant, and I think you know it. I mean that as much as everyone likes to think they can do whatever they want, they can't. You don't have any idea what I've done to protect you and your father."

"Then why don't you explain it to me?" I snapped. "Since you have such a habit of being honest with people."

The car stopped briefly at a light, and I glanced out the windows. There was less traffic than I expected. That was good. It meant the ride and this torture would be over sooner.

She leaned forward on her knees. "Let's start with your little incident at the conservatory."

"Yes, let's." I mirrored her position. "You mean when I was going through my first heat and the Alpha I chose to help me got so fucking high he couldn't actually do his job, and then left his drugs in my room when I kicked him out? So I was left going through everything alone and in pain because I wasn't used to it? Or when someone heard me and thought it was *funny* to take a picture of me like that and release it? Let's talk about how somehow the media and my *father* got positive test results when I've never used drugs in my life."

"I did what I had to," she said. "We needed to save face."

"Why didn't you just tell the truth?" My voice rose. "One fucking blood test would have done it. All you had to do—"

"Because it was *too late*, Petra." She shouted. "The damage was already done. Your father's numbers were crumbling, and he would have lost. Lost his senate run because of you. Because the picture had already done too much damage. Russell was soft on drugs, soft on his daughter, unable to control a *teenager*. The numbers were going in only one direction, and there wasn't enough time to recover. So yes, I did what I had to in order to save his career and turn the tide of the press.

"You were given a comeback story. A recovery. And Russell was given a chance to take a stance on drugs. A mea culpa starting at home. And it was still a close race."

She wasn't wrong there. The first time my dad won his senate seat, there had been maybe a couple of percentage points in between him and his opponent. The second time? He won in a landslide.

"Are you expecting me to thank you?"

Carmen laughed and threw her head back. "No, Petra. I already know that will never happen."

"Good. It won't."

I still didn't understand what any of this had to do with me or her trying to give me to the Gidwitz pack. There was something missing.

You were given a comeback story. Carmen didn't say that *she* gave me one. I looked at her suddenly, wondering exactly how far Carmen was willing to go to help Dad. "Do you love my father?" I asked.

A question I never let myself ask all these years because she and I already struggled, and if the answer was no, I knew I would never be able to look at her the same.

"I can't believe you would ask me that."

"Well I am asking, Carmen. Do you love my father?"

"Of course I love him. I wouldn't have done everything I've done if I didn't love him. Because that's what you do. You do anything and everything for the people you love, even if it destroys you."

I wanted to tell her she was wrong, but I couldn't. Every single one of my Alphas would say the same about me, and I couldn't pretend otherwise. But her answer told me enough.

"What did you do?" I asked, my voice far calmer than I felt. "Because you know that none of this makes sense. And I know you hate me, but if you love my father, you wouldn't have tried to hurt me unless you had no other choice. So what did you do?"

Carmen stared at me, assessing. It felt like an eternity, her deciding if she was going to tell me the truth. Given we were about to have lunch with my father, I understood her hesitation.

When she finally looked away, still silent, I sighed. It was too much to hope for the truth. "So you wanted to spend time alone in the car for some good old fashioned stepmother and daughter bonding time? I can't believe I thought you might apologize."

She didn't say anything, and neither did I. There was nothing but the sound of the road and cars around us, and buildings passing. Carmen occasionally checked her phone, but didn't acknowledge my presence again.

Until she crossed her arms and looked at the roof of the car. "I'm not a bad person," she said quietly. "I know you think I am, but I'm not."

Given there was no evidence to the contrary, I took a pass on responding.

"Sometimes things get out of control, and you're just trying to do the right thing and make everything better. But it's hard." She almost sounded emotional. The car pulled to a stop. I didn't recognize the buildings outside, but I'd never been to my father's new campaign headquarters. On purpose.

I cracked the door open, and Carmen stopped me with a hand on my arm. "You want to know what I did?"

"Yes."

"I asked for help," she said simply. For the first time, the way she looked at me wasn't filled with disdain. It was closer to something like pity. "But sometimes, help comes at a price, Petra. And this time the price was you."

Confusion hit me. "What?"

The car door ripped the rest of the way open, pulling me with it. I nearly fell onto the pavement and barely recovered. Not fast enough. Someone had me—someone was dragging me—hard and fast away from the car. I couldn't even be afraid. The thought which sliced through me like a blade was that Carmen was in so much deeper than I realized.

I fought, and it didn't matter. I wasn't strong enough.

Brief, sudden pain in my neck, and everything faded to gray.

CHAPTER FIFTY-ONE

COLE

*T*he emotions coming from Petra had me unsettled. Pretty much expected being trapped in a car with her stepmother, but I wished I could be with her to act as a shield.

Instead, I was in the back of the third car with four Atwood Security staff. I tried to take my mind off it and texted Harrison at the office.

> Anything?

> Unfortunately not.

I checked my anger, aware that my own emotions could affect Petra's mental state.

We got caught in the daily traffic, the motorcade cars separating a bit in the fray. Until Senator Merriton was the chancellor, the motorcades didn't get to clear traffic. He had to live with it like everyone else.

Finally, we pulled up to the campaign, and my car was in front of Petra's. She felt blank. Frustration and shock had been there too, now a calm nothing that felt like she'd shut down her thoughts. Whatever Carmen said to her, I needed to kiss the hell out of my Omega when she got out of the car.

I pushed out of my car first, scanning the block for anything out of the ordinary. The big building in front of me was a nondescript office building, but it certainly had enough space for a campaign the size of this one.

The door opened, and the Senator himself came out. He paused when he saw me, and frowned. "Cole? What are you doing here?"

My entire body tingled. "I'm escorting Petra," I said. "For your lunch with Carmen. She asked me to ride in the other car so she and Petra could speak. We agreed."

He went pale faster than I'd ever seen. "I'm not having lunch with Petra today. I came down when I saw the car because Carmen is late, and she's never late."

I swallowed, trying to keep a level head and not react with fear. "Is there any reason to believe Carmen would surprise you with your daughter at lunch?"

"No," he said, clear grief in his voice. "After last night, Petra and I both need time."

Pulling my earpiece out of my pocket, I put it in. "This is Cole Kennedy. Everyone on our lines shut the fuck up. Someone get me Harrison. He's at headquarters."

There was a commotion, and I swore, grabbing my phone and dialing. I'd go with whatever was faster.

"Cole," Harrison said into the phone. "Nick just sprinted into my office and told me to get on the radio. What's going on?"

"I'm at the campaign headquarters." I whirled at the sound of tires, the last car of the motorcade pulling up to the curb. I sprinted to the car and ripped it open. Empty. No sign that Petra or Carmen were ever present. "Petra never made it here. Carmen is gone too."

Dead silence over the line. Then, "I'm keeping the private channel open. You need your hands more than the phone."

I ended the call and tuned back in to the chaos. "Carl Jennings, come back," I said. He was the driver assigned to Carmen. "Carl, man, I need to hear from you, okay?"

Approaching the door to the car, I unclipped my gun. Our security from the building was already backing me up, getting orders from Harrison and headquarters.

The guy saw me coming and paled. He wasn't one of ours. We employed a lot of people, but one of the things Harrison and I prided ourselves on was the seamlessness of our team and the way we worked. Which meant we knew everyone who worked for us personally.

I pointed my gun at the window, fighting dread. "Put your hands on the wheel," I said.

He obeyed.

Nodding to my right, I kept my gun trained on the guy as

they got the door open. "Get out of the car, and I swear to god if you make a wrong move..."

"Hey," the guy looked panicked. "I'm sorry. I don't know what's going on. I don't know anything."

One of our guards grabbed his hands and got them behind his back. "Who are you?" I asked. "And why are you here? Where's the man supposed to be driving this car and where are the passengers?"

"I never had any passengers, I swear. Some guy offered me a thousand dollars if I would drive this car, replace the other limo when it broke off, and that's it. I figured it was some kind of covert thing, so I didn't ask questions."

"Could you identify the man?"

He shook his head. "It was all digital. I guess it could have been a woman. I'm sorry."

"Take him," I said. My staff surged forward, putting him in cuffs. We would deal with him later. Holstering my gun, I flipped my frequency and looked at the license plate. Also not one of ours. "Harrison, this car isn't ours. Carl isn't answering." I looked at the Senator. "Where was Carmen picked up?"

"Our house."

Fuck. Fuck. I flipped back. "Who's on detail at the Senator's mansion?"

"I am. It's Richard Emerson."

"Rich," I said. "How long has it been since you heard from Carl?"

"Since he left to take the Senator's wife."

Cold fear crept along my limbs. "Go to the garage, please. Right now. I'll be back in a second."

I flipped back. "Harrison."

"The car detoured before the traffic. Went in the opposite direction. GPS places it in an industrial area on the west side."

"What about her phone?"

"Same location. It's off now."

"Fuck, Harrison." My voice was ragged. "How did this happen?"

He growled. "Worry about that later. Getting her and Carmen back is the priority."

"Call them, Harrison. They're going to feel us, anyway. They need to know."

"I will."

Flipping back, I felt like I was being pulled in a hundred directions at once. "Rich?"

"Cole. Mr. Kennedy. Carl is dead. Double tap to the back of the head. It must have been silenced, or we would have heard it."

"Fuck." The garage at the Senator's mansion was a separate building. No reason they would have checked it after the car was gone.

"We'll keep everything as it is. Do we want the police here?"

I hate that I hesitated even for a second. "Hold on." Turning, I went to the Senator and stepped way, way too close. He stepped back, and I went with him. "You're going to tell me the fucking truth. Carmen's driver is dead at your home, your wife and daughter are missing. Did you have anything to do with this?"

"*No.*" The man was white as death. "God, no. I would never. After Mallory? I couldn't—I can't—"

I placed my hand on his shoulder. A guilty man didn't look like that. "If I send the police to your home to look at the crime scene, this is going to leak. I hate that I have to, but I need to ask you if you're okay with that."

"You think I fucking care about the press when they're missing? Would you?"

"If it were me, they'd already be on their way."

"Then get them there," he snarled. "And find them. Do whatever you need to. If it's the same man—"

"I know." I turned away. "Get the police there, Richard. Keep the mansion locked down and wait for further instructions."

"Yes, sir."

"Harrison." I flipped my channel. "Carl's dead."

He swore. And swore again. A crash came through my earpiece. God, I wished there was something I could smash, but the second I let in the panic strangling me like vines, it was all over.

"Harrison."

"*What?*" he snapped.

"Carl is dead at the mansion. He never left the garage."

Harrison heard what I meant, and what the Senator didn't seem to realize. I saw Carmen, and she didn't appear under duress. We couldn't be sure, but the chances of her being involved just went up to nearly one-hundred percent.

"We have nothing." Harrison's voice was ragged. "We have nothing, Cole."

"I'm moving the Senator inside, and I have some questions for him. Keep working the problem."

The bond between Petra and me still lay quiet and hazy. Suddenly I understood. The shock and confusion and fading. She was unconscious. Whatever happened had occurred so quickly she hadn't even been afraid. Nothing that would have alerted us there was a problem.

"Get the Senator inside," I said. It felt like an hour had passed when it was only minutes.

For one brief moment, I caved in and gave way to fear. So strong I choked and couldn't breathe. We said we'd protect her, and we didn't. Someone who knew us so well he used our well-oiled machine against us. Terror turned every cell in my body to ice.

And then I forced it back.

Fear couldn't control me. Not now. I had work to do.

We just found our Omega.

Like hell was I going to lose her.

CHAPTER FIFTY-TWO

***

PETRA

*M*y head ached.

Pounding like I'd drunk too much and had one hell of a hangover, but I hadn't been drinking. I was drugged.

Voices were muffled around me, like they were in a room nearby. A man and a woman.

Fear—true fear—crushed down on my chest. I hadn't even opened my eyes, but I didn't want to. Because what if what was on the other side was the man waiting to kill me?

My bonds lit up inside me. Relief and anger. Desperation. Determination. So they knew I was gone. Good. That was good. God, I wished it would help more than just letting them know I was alive.

Carmen did this. Why?

The threats were all her?

It made my head ache more.

"I need to leave. Now," Carmen said, voice coming into clear focus. "This wasn't the plan. You were only supposed to drug *her*. If I don't show up when Russell expects me, there are going to be more questions than you're prepared for."

"You'll stay until it's done," a male voice said. Vaguely familiar. "Plans change."

I took stock of myself. I was sitting upright in some kind of chair, my arms behind it. Something was around my wrists—handcuffs maybe?—But I didn't dare move or stretch my hands to confirm. Other than the pounding in my head, I felt okay. No other part of my body hurt. So if I could find a way to run...

"I have *paid my debt*," Carmen said, voice low. "You have her. Now let me the fuck out of here so we can make it go as planned, Charles."

A low laugh that skittered across my skin and gave me chills. "Don't be naïve, Carmen. If you showed up now? Without her?

401

While her fucking bodyguard is in the other car? How exactly do you think that would go over with her pack and your husband?"

No other sounds. Carmen didn't protest.

"This way is better. This way, you get to be the *survivor*. It takes the story we're trying to tell and elevates it. The grieving stepmother of a deeply troubled young woman. You tried to get her clean and failed. And she got mixed up with the wrong people. You managed to get away, she didn't, but you'll always carry her in your heart.

"Russell gets a boost to his platform about drugs and violence, and I'll be the man who rescued his wife once I 'use my network' and hear what I need to hear. And finally, the thing I've wanted from the beginning is there. A chancellor who owes me everything."

Carmen swore under her breath. "Fine. All right. But I don't want to see you kill her."

"I'm not going to kill her. This entire time, I've kept my hands clean. You think I'm going to get them dirty now?"

"How long until she wakes up? They're not stupid. They'll figure out a way to track her."

Something stark and metal clanged. "Not too long. It's fast acting. Pity, really. She didn't make the right choice."

The voice clicked, and I opened my eyes. Charles Bower stood across the room, leaning against the wall. Carmen had her back to me, but Charles saw I was awake instantly.

"In fact, I think she'll be awake right about now."

I did a quick scan. There was nothing in this room to tell me anything. Basic cinder blocks and a concrete floor. We could be anywhere by now. Clearly, I hadn't been unconscious for long, but it didn't matter. I didn't even know where we'd been when I'd been taken. Even an hour unconscious could put me anywhere in Slate City, or a good distance outside of it.

My stepmother turned and saw me. For a flash, I imagined I saw regret there. But it was only a flash before her face hardened with determination. "Ah. I see."

Charles Bower. He wasn't who I expected, and yet it made a perverse kind of sense. "This is who you asked for help?"

"Charles and I have known each other for a long time," Carmen said. "Our families have always been close."

The man smiled like a snake, looking at me like I was prey. Exactly how he wanted me to feel. "So when my good friend came to me for help to save her husband's career, who was I to say no?"

I blinked. "You fixed the election?"

Charles scoffed. "I didn't get to where I am now doing things sure to get me sent to prison. No, I didn't rig the election. Your father won fair and square, helped along by public perception. *That* is what I corrected."

When George and the others told me about what they were in line for, they said he owned half the media. My father had mentioned it too. "They'll say what you want them to," I was half thinking out loud.

"They will, and do." He pushed off the wall and walked toward me, slowly and casually, like he had all the time in the world to mock me before he killed me. "I told you, Petra. I like to play the long game. Unfortunately, you forced my hand. Now I have to adapt to get what I want, but that's all right. Things always go my way. And I plan for everything."

The puzzle pieces were coming together in my mind. Why Carmen was so desperately pushing me toward the Gidwitz pack. I stared at her. "You sold me? That's what you did? You gave me away?"

"If it makes you feel better, she didn't want to," Charles said. "She even cried about it. But in the end, she needed what I had, and I wanted an alliance."

I shook my head and regretted it immediately, the pain spiking. "If you wanted an alliance, why wait so long? It's been years."

"Because Russell wasn't ready to be chancellor. He needed time to develop into the politician he is now. With some guidance, of course."

Carmen had the grace to look ashamed. So she'd been pushing him in the direction Charles wanted all this time. My only relief there was my knowledge my father didn't play those games. If he didn't agree with something, he wouldn't do it, no matter what.

It was why his solid belief in Carmen's lies over my truth hurt so much. He made up his mind.

"You played your role perfectly, by the way," he said. "Stayed out of the spotlight until I needed you. But *you* needed a push." He leaned down in front of me. "I read people. I figure out what makes them tick, and you needed a reason to bond with my son. I have to say, I'm impressed. You're one of the few people I've failed to read correctly."

Mouth dry, I wet my lips before speaking. "Am I supposed to say thank you?"

He laughed. "No, I don't imagine so. But you're stronger than I thought. Everything said at the first sign of danger you'd fold and do what they wanted in order to be safe. After all, you'd kept your head down so long, I didn't think you had it in you."

So everything had been him. The threats and the fear. The attack. "Was there ever a person threatening me? Or was it just you?"

"Oh, never me. I would never do such a thing. I don't know how you could think that." He smiled. "I'm just a businessman, Miss Merriton."

"*DeWitt*-Merriton, asshole. If you're going to kill me, get my fucking name right."

Charles chuckled. "I would have enjoyed having you as a daughter-in-law. You certainly have more spark than my son does. No, it wasn't me. I never sent any emails about you, or photos. I couldn't possibly have been threatening you."

So he paid people—more than one—to do it for him. Enough money that they didn't care if what they were sending was horrific death threats. And enough money they didn't mind risking jail time, like the one they caught.

"But I'm sure your stepmother's fingerprints will be found on the key card she borrowed from the Senator before destroying your apartment, which is one of the many reasons why she'll do what I say. Couldn't let you get too comfortable. It was the most willing I'd ever seen her to do anything I asked."

Carmen paled, and I just closed my eyes. Of course. That was the reason her hands were all scratched up. Probably from all the broken glass and damage she did. After all the frustration I caused her, because *she* chose to give me away like an object, she wanted to hurt me with the only thing I had—my freedom and my sanctuary.

Anger burned in my chest, caution flying to the wind. "Wow. I expected more from someone like you. More money than god, but you still can't get it up to threaten someone yourself? Kind of pathetic if you ask me."

Then it hit me. It wasn't just pushing me toward the pack. A laugh burst out of me, and even Charles looked surprised. "You really do play the long game. The threats, the photos, they were for this. In case Carmen couldn't convince me to go through with the bond. You can kill me free and clear, and pin it on one of the ones you used as puppets. And if the danger happened to help things along, so be it."

Pride shone in the man's eyes. "See how beautiful things are when they work out exactly like you predict? It's the biggest high you can have, bending the world to your will."

I locked eyes with him. "Fuck you."

Charles turned and stalked to the back of the room and picked up a gun on the table. Now I knew what the metallic sound was earlier. He didn't hesitate, cracking the butt of the weapon across my face.

Pain blinded me, the momentum of the strike taking both me and the chair to the ground. Carmen screamed, and I couldn't breathe.

My bonds were on *fire*. They could feel my pain. I tried to think soothing thoughts and project any sense of calm, but I couldn't. I was faking it. All I wanted—

I squeezed my eyes closed, willing my tears to go away. If he saw me cry, I lost. Whatever power I had lay in strength, whether or not that strength was real.

"Shut up," Charles barked at Carmen. "If I have to listen to you regret things after all these years, I might just kill you both."

I kept my eyes closed. Maybe he would think he knocked me out, though I wasn't sure that was better. My arms were twisted, one pinned under the back of the chair, handcuffs digging into my wrists. They would be asleep in minutes.

"Did you just kill her?" Carmen whispered.

Rough footsteps approached, and I fought not to move. Fingers pressed against my throat. "No. Not yet. She's still breathing. I haven't quite decided if I need her for a ransom video yet. But I do need you for one. There needs to be a few hours for the story to take off and Russell to be the grieving, desperate father. Go."

Footsteps shuffled, and a door shut. I blew out a shaky breath. All of this was for power. One mistake, trusting the wrong person all those years ago during my heat, and suddenly I was a pawn in a game I never meant to play.

I let the tears out.

Charles was so careful. There had only been one mistake when that reporter was arrested, and I wasn't even sure it was a mistake, or yet another false trail he orchestrated on purpose. The man was a puppet master, and he held all the strings. With that much money and that much power... that was what he chose to do with it.

Never was there a clearer comparison between what money could do to a person. Harrison took it and tried to protect people. Lift people up. Bring them joy, safety, and peace. This man used it to manipulate, murder, and consolidate power.

I listened to the bonds in my chest. All four of them were terrified and desperate to get to me. But I didn't know how they were going to find me. When he had infinite resources and could bury any trail under a mountain of *nothing*?

Tears kept leaking out of my eyes, dripping down onto the floor. I loved my Alphas, and if this was the last of everything, they were going to know it and feel it from me until the end.

It wasn't their fault. No one could see a plan this long and this intricate coming. Maybe we would get lucky. But if we didn't...

I thought the words and willed them into the hollow space they filled inside me. I love you. I love you.

I love you.

CHAPTER FIFTY-THREE

BLAKE

*H*elplessness wasn't my strong suit.

With Petra's bond filled with grief, pain, and love, it was all I felt. The entire world knew my Omega was gone, along with her stepmother.

I didn't often come to the Atwood Security headquarters. A couple of times when Harrison and Cole taught Emery and me how to fire a gun and care for one. They wouldn't keep guns in the penthouse unless we were all properly trained.

The headquarters were different than I'd ever seen them. Thank fuck for Harrison's reputation, because the authorities were using this as their base instead of setting up a new one, since Harrison had already been tracking whoever was threatening Petra.

We currently sat in Harrison's private office, which branched off to a conference room that was full of Atwood staff, police, and other government agencies. Given the political ramifications of this, it was a nightmare.

I was numb.

My only way to keep from sinking into a black hole of grief I wasn't sure I'd ever come back from. I locked it away and kept myself as even as possible. If there was even a fraction of a chance, Petra needed me to function.

Every minute felt like an hour. It had been at least two. Maybe more. Emery was engrossed in his phone, scrolling through the coverage of their disappearance, hopeful someone would know something we didn't.

The door to the conference room opened, and Cole came out. "Harrison, please."

"Cole," his voice was low. "I know. I know, okay? But I need you to take a lap. Now."

The door closed in Cole's face, and I looked up at my pack mate. Through the distant bond with him, his devastation was clear. He was raw. Turning away from the door, he sank into a crouch and dropped his face into his hands.

"Cole," I said. "This isn't your fault."

"I should have told Carmen no," he said. "I should have insisted we be in the same car."

"So then you'd be missing too?" Emery said.

"We don't know that."

"Nor do we know that you could have stopped it," I pointed out. Ragged pain tore through my chest again. "I feel what you're feeling, and I have no idea what to fucking do about it. But I have to believe you being here is a good thing. You can help find her faster."

He sprung to his feet and slammed the flat of his hand against the wall so hard I was surprised it didn't crack. "We don't have anything. They've been so fucking careful. She disappeared into thin fucking air, and all I can think about is that fear and pain."

Petra was quiet in our chests now. Awake, but steady. Occasionally, there was a pang of grief, quickly covered with love and calm. Tears pricked at my eyes and I swiped them away. Those feelings didn't take away her fear—we still felt that too—but she was trying to project love and peace for our sake.

Petra knew as well as we did how dire the situation was. If they could have found him by now, they would have.

Finally, Cole took a breath, and his voice shook. "What I say next doesn't leave this room. But we have people working on it who shouldn't necessarily be. Hackers. People who can try to dig into the trail in a way we legally can't."

"And?" I pressed.

"And even they're saying that it's stunning work. Meticulous and careful. Data bounced through so many channels and re-encrypted so many times that the only person who could trace it is the person who performed the exact sequence. And that there are multiple sequences from multiple sources."

Emery stood and began to pace, his phone in his hand. He hadn't stopped monitoring the news since it broke. Because of who Petra and Carmen were, the story consumed everything. We were in them too because of our announcement. Thankfully, we weren't being bombarded with calls *yet*. It would come sooner or later.

"And have your people told you who they think is capable of doing those things?"

"Yeah," Cole said, slumping against the same wall. "But we'll never find them in time. Not if they're that good."

"Cole," Emery said. His voice had changed, and he was frozen. We both went to him and looked over his shoulder. Carmen was on the screen, tears running down her face. "We are alive. That's all I'm allowed to say. We're alive, and we'll stay that way if you give them what they want. Senator Russell Merriton must drop out of the race for chancellor and resign from politics." She listed money and immunity too, but my mind was already spinning toward anything we could use. Ransoms were almost always useless, or so I'd been told.

Harrison and Cole had dealt with kidnappings and negotiations before, but it had never been so close to home. "Where is she?" I asked. It looked like a blank cinder block room. Not anything you could use to pinpoint it. This wasn't the movies.

"Wait, no," Carmen said, her voice rising in panic. "You have to show them her. You have to show she's alive, *please*."

The camera moved roughly, bouncing up and down as whoever held the phone moved. A plain gray door was shoved open, and she was there. On her side on the ground, hands behind her back. A mark on her face told me she'd been struck.

I shoved down the rising growl. Whoever put hands on her was going to die. The stiffness in my pack mates and the echo of their emotions told me they felt the same.

Petra looked unconscious. We knew she wasn't, but if pretending she was kept her safer, I willed her to keep her eyes closed.

"Petra," Emery said quietly before the video cut off.

"Where is this video?" Cole asked. "Where did you see it?"

"It's everywhere," Harrison said behind us. The door to the conference room was open again, and he nodded inside. We filed in, though it was already crowded. Senator Merriton sat at the table, his head in his hands. "This was sent, anonymously of course, to every news station in the country. It's going wild across social media. There's no way to pinpoint it, but it's everywhere."

Cole pulled his phone out of his pocket and glanced at it before putting it away again. "Unknown. The press must have found our numbers." He pulled it out again and set it on the table, where it rang.

"Anything we can use to identify the location?" A guy in a uniform asked. "Let's watch it again."

The door from the outer hallway opened and one of the staff I kind of recognized stuck his head in. "Mr. Atwood, you have a call."

"It'll have to wait."

"No," the man said. "You want to take this."

The console in the center of the table had a light blinking, and Harrison pressed it. "Hello?"

"I need to speak to Petra DeWitt-Merriton's pack *immediately*."

Every head in the room turned and stared at the invisible voice. The four of us and Petra's father froze.

"This is Harrison Atwood speaking. You are on speakerphone with the rest of her pack, her father, and members of law enforcement. Who are you?"

A brief hesitation. "This is George Bower."

I looked at the others, confused. Why the hell would George need to talk to us right now?

"George," Cole said. "If you had anything to do with this…"

"I didn't," the man said. "But I know where she is."

The Senator stood up so fast the chair he sat in fell over. "How? How do you know that?"

"Because my father is an asshole," George said. "When I was younger, as punishment, he sent me and my brothers to do physical labor on any of his construction sites that were active. While we were there, we always found a way to leave a mark so something wouldn't be quite perfect, since that was his benchmark. Our small way of rebelling."

"Get to the point," Emery growled next to me. He vibrated with energy, coiled and ready to spring.

"Right." There was a shuffling noise, like something moved

410

on the other end of the line. "Play the video again. The part where he goes through the door. Look at the wall on the left."

The video was already projected onto the wall, and whoever controlled the display scrolled it forward and froze it just before the cameraman slammed the door open. "Okay, we have it," Harrison said.

"I know it's hard to see," George said. "But look at the mortar between the cinder blocks."

Every eye in the room strained to see what he meant, and I did see it. "There's a pattern."

"I was a teenager," George said. "If I had my way, I would have drawn a dick or something. But I needed something that could have been anyone."

In the crevices between the bricks, someone had drawn Xs in the mortar before it dried. It wasn't something you'd notice unless you were looking for it... or you already knew it was there. Your eyes skipped right over it.

Relief flooded my system. There was a chance. If George was lying or somehow in on it, as revenge for not giving in, we were fucked. But it was also the only lead we had.

"Where is it?" The Senator asked.

"A warehouse on the south edge of the city." He rattled off an address.

Everyone began to move, and I reached for the center console to hang up, and George spoke again. "Harrison."

"Yes?"

"I don't know if my father is involved with this. But if he is? He might be a gambler, but he never bluffs."

A warning not to delay, because he would kill her if he had the chance.

"Thank you, George," Cole said.

"Just find them." The call ended.

This time, everyone paused. "We need a plan," the man in the uniform said.

"My team will pull satellite on the way to see what we're dealing with," Harrison said. "We can coordinate by radio. But I won't stand here debating while my Omega is in danger."

It was the final word on the subject. We all poured out into the central hallway and people broke in every direction, gathering with their group. Cole turned to Emery and me, and I already felt what he was going to say. "No fucking way, Cole. You don't have to give us guns if you don't want to, and I'll wear a vest. But I am *not* staying here."

Emery simply crossed his arms, backing me up with a silent glare.

"Get them vests," Harrison said. "I want to be in the car in less than two minutes."

The four of us moved as a unit, grabbing what supplies we needed and sliding into the car together. For the first time since we heard the news, there was a sense of confidence and purpose between all four of us. Our Omega had already gone through hell, so if we had to go into hell to get her back?

So be it.

I tried to push hope toward Petra. Anything to let her know we were on our way to her.

Hang on, baby. We're coming.

CHAPTER FIFTY-FOUR

PETRA

*M*y arms were asleep. They hurt for a while, being on the floor like this, but they faded into numbness a while ago. I stayed still and breathed. Those were my two jobs, and I could do them. I listened to my bonds, trying to figure out all the emotions coursing through my pack. Some of them were moving too quickly for me to understand.

A while ago, Charles came storming back into the room, but said nothing. I didn't move, and he left. But it had been long enough I was starting to wonder if they just left me here.

The feeling in my bonds changed all at once. Now all four of my Alphas were brimming with determination. What did that mean?

Footsteps pounded, and I forced myself to go limp before the door opened again. "Time to get up, Sleeping Beauty. You think I don't know you're faking it?"

Charles grabbed my arm and hauled me upright. My arms screamed with the sudden movement, and I staggered when he lifted me to my feet. The world spun around me because I was moving too quickly after so much time on the floor. "Where are we going?"

"Does it matter?" He asked. "It's the last place you'll ever see."

Fear cracked my chest open. No. This couldn't be real yet. This wasn't the way this was supposed to work. There was supposed to be more resistance than this. The good guys were supposed to come through and save the day.

I pulled on his hold, still dizzy, still off balance, with my arms tingling and blood flowing again. There was no way for me to get away from him. Even if I managed to break away, I didn't know where I was. With my hands bound, was there any way for me to escape?

We went through another door, this time into a space that

really did look like a warehouse, big and empty except for the batch of tables Charles was dragging me to. I stumbled, seeing what was there. Drugs. Neatly stacked packages of it, scales, syringes, and a faint white dusting everywhere.

Carmen was tied in another chair, gagged, her hands behind her like mine. Her makeup ran down her face like she'd been crying, but I knew better. This was all her, too. She'd watch me die and be fucking happy about it.

"Don't do this," I begged him. "My father will owe you just as much if he gets me back alive. I won't say anything, I promise. You can just walk away and still be the guy who saved everything."

He threw me down in another chair. I barely kept this one from tipping. "A little late for that, Petra. You were given a chance to live, and you chose not to take the gift in front of you."

I shook my head. Like bonding with the men I loved was in any way equivalent to *choosing* to be murdered.

Charles gave a cheeky little salute to Carmen. "Pleasure doing business with you."

"Wait," I called after him. "You can still change your mind. *Charles.*" My voice echoed in the big empty space. The door to the outside opened and closed, and he was gone.

Carmen spit out the gag as soon as the door closed behind him. I stared at her. "This whole time..." I laughed once. "I knew you hated me, Carmen. I didn't know you hated me enough to kill me."

"Shut the fuck up," she snapped. "I don't want to kill you. It was never the plan, and I'd rather not. But you made the choices you made, and here you are. Did you ever stop to think there was a reason why I was pushing you at that pack so hard? You could have had a perfectly good life with them."

"Yeah, pushing me toward people I have *no* compatibility with whatsoever. Good call. Even as low as you stoop, you should have known that wouldn't work."

"Why?" Her eyes glittered. "You were always the perfect, obedient princess before then. I thought you would do it for your father."

I straightened my shoulders and attempted to stand. Looking

414

around, the only doors were the one Charles left through, a giant loading bay door I would never get open, and back the way we came. So Carmen had misjudged me? Good.

Would Charles already be gone? The door was a push bar. I could get out easily. Carmen was tied to her chair. He hadn't bothered with me.

"I wouldn't do that if I were you," Carmen called.

"Yeah, I'm done taking advice from you."

I shoved my hip into the door and tasted the cool freedom of evening air, and found myself staring down the barrel of a gun.

Three men—three Alphas—in masks stood in front of me. "I don't think so. Back you go." I backed up slowly, keeping my eyes on all three of them. Their scents nearly made me gag. Burned fruit, garlic, and chalk.

"We have them," the one on the left said into a phone.

A voice spoke. Altered through a voice changer, but I could still tell it was Charles. "Good. The older one stays alive. The younger one you can't kill for another hour. I gave them a deadline. But you can do whatever you want to her in the meantime."

"Perfect." They looked at me like I was their next meal. What were the odds I could get back around them and to the door without getting shot? Slim to none.

"If you fuck this up, none of you will get your money. So don't fuck it up."

"Yeah, yeah." The man said. "We've got it."

The one with the gun jerked it back toward the chair. "Sit."

I ground my teeth together, obeying. Why the hell was I following their instructions? They were going to kill me either way. But I had an hour. Maybe it would be enough.

"What the hell did you do to make him kill you?" The third man asked. "Seemed like you really pissed him off."

No way I was rising to that bait.

They explored the drugs on the table, syringes and everything else which was laid out. It was artful, staged, I was sure, to make it look like I was here to get high. A junkie desperate for a fix, and was killed for it. Too bad they didn't realize Charles was setting them up too. Now their fingerprints were on everything.

"Well, if you're not going to talk, we can have some other fun."

I looked over at Carmen. She sat still, eyes straight ahead. Was she going to sit here while they played with me like a toy? They could do anything they wanted. Chop pieces off me like Charles's threats said he wanted to. Or worse. There were any number of violent things they could do in an hour.

"But I get the feeling," the one who'd held the phone said, "this one is more feisty than she's letting on. But we can take care of that." He held up a syringe, and my entire body went cold.

"No."

"So she *does* speak."

I glared at him. "Keep that fucking thing away from me."

"You don't want to get high before you die? Most people would love for that to be the way they went."

"No, I don't fucking want that," I spat the words out like the bullets I wish I had. "Take it yourself, if that's what you want."

For ten years, I fought against this idea. Like hell would my last hours alive make it come true.

"No," the gun Alpha said. "This will be more fun."

He came around the table, and I bolted. I sprinted for the door back into the depths of the warehouse. If I could make it through some of the doors, maybe I could find *somewhere* to hide.

Swearing rose behind me, and pounding footsteps. I didn't stop, lungs burning, forcing myself through the door and spinning to the side. A body collided with mine and took me to the floor.

Pain shattered through me, nausea following. The weight on me, the overwhelming scent of burnt fruit—I gagged, retching.

"Fucking bitch," the man grabbed my hair and slammed my face into the floor. I saw light, for a second, liquid trickling from my forehead. "Help me get her up."

"See? I told you she was fiery."

They each had one of my arms, dragging me back through the warehouse to that fucking chair. "No," I screamed them. "*No.*"

They weren't letting me use my legs, anyway. I kicked at

them, thrashing, trying to get loose or hurt them. Anything to make this stop or take longer. I didn't want this. Terror overtook me, giving way to sheer instinct. If they injected me, it was over. I wouldn't even be fully conscious for my last moments.

Until this moment, I didn't know how much I needed that.

I screamed at them, strength and adrenaline allowing me to take them off balance. They held me that much harder. But I wasn't going to stop. Never.

"Hold her still."

The two Alphas put me in the chair and held me there, twisting me so my arm and elbow were exposed. Right where they needed it. "*No.* No no no no, don't do this." My voice was a scream and a sob. "*Please.*" I arched against their hold and I saw stars. Someone hit me. I still fought them.

"God *damn it.* Hold her so I can actually get a vein, or this will be no fun."

"Please." Tears poured down my face. "Don't."

"Sorry, not sorry, sweetheart. Don't worry. After this, you won't feel a thing."

Wet splattered across my face. My ears rang. The Alpha with the needle slumped over onto me, dead. Blood seeped through the ski mask.

And standing in the doorway with his gun pointed where the Alpha's head had been, was Cole.

The other two reached for weapons, and two more gunshots rang out. One from Cole, and the other from Harrison stepping in behind him. They fell heavily, sickening thuds of dead weight.

It was all chaos then, people pouring into the room. I burst into tears, struggling to get the dead man off me. "Get him off. Get him off. *Get him off.*" I fell off the chair, and Cole was there hauling the body off me and bringing me up to my knees.

"I've got you," he whispered. "I'm so sorry, Petra. I've got you."

I sobbed into his shoulder, finally letting every bit of pain and fear free. One hand sank into my hair, the other locking behind me and keeping me against him. "I need handcuff keys," he called. "*Now.*"

There was no way to contain it. Horror and pain, thinking I might never see them again.

Gentle hands touched my wrists, unlocking the handcuffs. They stuck to me where I'd been cut by the metal and bled, but they were gone.

Cole turned me. Other arms touched me, and I fought back, my voice tearing through the air. "*No.* Don't touch me. *I won't let you fucking touch me.*" No one would take me again.

The arms wrapped around me more firmly. "It's me, little one. It's me."

Harrison.

Cedar and whiskey and snow.

I sagged in his hold, Cole finally releasing me. His eyes were glassy before Harrison turned me fully toward him. There were too many emotions for me to feel the bonds. Mine were too strong to feel anything else.

My feet weren't touching the ground. Harrison had lifted me, and I clung to him like he was the only thing left in the world. "You're safe," he said quietly, but there was emotion he was holding back. "You're safe now."

Running footsteps and familiar voices. "Thank god."

I couldn't even look up from where my face was buried in Harrison's neck. My hands held his shirt so tightly they hurt. If I let go, I would unravel. Every breath was a ragged sob.

Harrison's hand ran up and down my back. "You're safe, Petra. And little one, we're not leaving you. Not even for one second. But I need you to talk to me, okay? It's important."

"Charles," I said, already knowing what he wanted. "Charles Bower."

"Good girl," he whispered. "You're doing so good, little one. Now, can Emery and Blake hold you? We need to get to Charles before he figures it out."

I nodded into his neck.

Gently, he set me down on my feet. Emery swept me up, and Blake stepped in behind me, pressing against me from every angle. My breath hitched, sobs not leaving me. But he needed to know. "Harrison."

He turned. "It was Charles... and Carmen."

Harrison's face hardened, and my Alpha's stiffened around me. Leaning down, Harrison cupped my face. "I need you to know the only reason I'm walking away from you right now is because we need to find him. If it were any less important than your life, you would still be in my arms. Do you understand?"

"Yes."

His lips brushed my forehead and his thumbs swept away some of the tears. "I love you. I'll be with you as soon as I can."

He stalked away, and I turned my face into Emery's shirt. His bullet-proof vest. They all wore them. The thought of them getting shot trying to save me had me crying all over again.

Blake set his chin on my shoulder. "We've got you, baby, okay? Whatever you need, you can let it go."

Outside, I heard sirens. All kinds of voices now echoed in the warehouse, but I didn't move. I let my Alphas hold me.

A voice rose, echoing across the warehouse. "This was *you*? All this time?"

Emery turned so I could see without moving. My father stood in front of Carmen. Even after the accident, I never saw him look like that.

She was being untied from the chair. "Russell, please," she begged. "I did this for you. For us. I did *all of this* for *you*."

My father's face turned cold. "You lied to me for almost our entire marriage and tried to have my daughter murdered, and now you're trying to tell me you did it for me?"

"I was desperate." She began to cry. "You were going to lose, and you were devastated. I didn't want any more bad things to happen to you."

He glared at her. "So you sacrificed Petra?"

"I promise, Russell, if you just let me tell you everything from the beginning, it will all make sense."

Turning, my father walked out the big loading bay door that was now open, and Carmen ran after him. Should I feel something? I didn't. He still didn't believe me when I needed him to. He still chose her.

Always chose her.

Blake kissed the back of my neck and ran his hands down my

arms. Our bonds were lit with love, but all I could feel was terror and blankness.

"Hey, sweet girl," Emery said. "Can you walk?"

"Don't go."

"We're not going anywhere, sunshine. The EMTs need to look at you, all right? I'm going to carry you to the ambulance and sit with you while they do, okay? You're not going to be alone."

I couldn't stop the fear shoving through my chest like an ice pick. Screwing my eyes shut, I fought panic, and more tears came. "Okay."

Blake didn't let me go until Emery had me firmly in his arms. He walked me out the door. Bright lights were everywhere. Red and blue flashing lights. Police. People in suits. Three bodies covered in sheets.

Ahead of us at the ambulance, Blake was already speaking to the paramedic. A woman with dark skin and a kind smile. Emery sat on the tail of the ambulance with me in his lap. "Hi Petra," she said. "I'm Dani. I want to check some things to make sure you're not hurt, okay?"

"Okay." I sounded small.

Blake stood nearby, blocking me from the view of everyone. Behind him, I saw Harrison and Cole directing people. But they looked in my direction every chance they could.

Dani took all my vitals and flashed a light in my eyes. "Did you hit your head, Petra?"

I stared straight. "They hit my head."

Emery tensed underneath me.

"She needs to get checked at the hospital," she said quietly. "Everything else is surface."

"Okay," Emery said. "Sunshine, we're going to get into the ambulance now. I'm going to set you on the stretcher, but Blake and I are going to hold your hands while Dani gives you some fluids."

I was shutting down now. Everything felt distant, and I needed to just...

I didn't know.

He lifted me into the back of the ambulance and did exactly what he said he would. They held my hands.

"*Petra*. Petra, oh my god." My father's voice.

He was running across the pavement toward us.

"Do you want to see him?" Emery asked.

I shook my head no.

Without another word, Emery got up and shut the doors to the ambulance.

"Petra," my father said outside the doors, words muffled. "Please."

I laid down, my Alphas by my side, and we drove away.

CHAPTER FIFTY-FIVE

PETRA

*B*lake smoothed the hair back from my face and kissed my temple, lingering. One or the other had been touching me the entire time in the hospital. Which was good, because I didn't want them anywhere else. What I really wanted was all my Alphas with me so I could feel safe.

But I knew they were needed elsewhere.

Because if Charles got away, he wouldn't stop. He'd try to kill me again, this time for revenge.

Now we were in a hospital room, waiting for the results of my scans. Bandages laced my wrists, more on my cheek and forehead.

"What do you need, baby?" Blake whispered.

"I don't know."

Emery sat at the foot of the bed, smoothing his hand up and down over the blanket on my legs.

"That's okay. You don't have to do anything but be here."

"Did they arrest Carmen?"

"Yes," Emery said.

"Does my dad know?"

Blake nodded. "Yes, he does."

"Okay." Then I had a thought. "Can one of you call Sloane? Eva? They're going to be losing their minds."

"Already done," Emery said. "They were about to bust down the doors to the hospital, but they agreed to wait until you're ready. But they know you're safe."

I turned on my side, facing away from Blake. They both still had their hands on me, but I needed—

"I thought I was going to die."

Two sounds. His shoes falling to the floor. And suddenly Blake was sliding into the bed behind me, slipping an arm underneath me. He held me like I would disappear if he let go. It felt a little like that.

Emery blinked away the shine in his eyes before moving his

chair closer. "I'm so sorry, Petra. I'm sorry you ever had to know what that feels like."

I hadn't had the chance to ask. "He was so careful. How did you find me?"

A brief flicker of a smile. "George."

"George *knew*?" Rage burned and had me ready to go rip his throat out. I struggled to stand.

Blake held me tighter, keeping me still. "No, baby. He didn't know. He saw something in the ransom video he recognized and called us because he knew where you were. Without him—"

He didn't finish the sentence because we knew the end of it. Without him, I would be dead. I eased back into Blake's body and was rewarded with the rich sound of his purr. The sound allowed some of the tension to fall away.

Emery pulled out his phone. It vibrated in his hand, and he answered it. "Yeah?" A pause. "Okay, hold on."

He turned and grabbed the remote for the television and turned it on, flicking it to the closest news channel.

Night had fallen, and in both the darkness and stark brightness of police lights, Charles Bower was being arrested.

"In a stunning turn of events this evening, billionaire businessman and media mogul Charles Bower, has been arrested for a litany of crimes, including stalking, harassment, kidnapping, and attempted murder.

"The target of the murder was Senator Russell Merriton's daughter, Petra DeWitt-Merriton, and it was originally thought his wife was a victim as well. However, Carmen Merriton has been charged with crimes of her own, having been involved in a years-long plot to put the Senator in Bower's debt."

I watched while the cops put him in the back of the car. My relief was short-lived. "He has so much money," I said. "He'll be out in no time."

"No, he won't," a voice spoke from the door. Harrison stood there, Cole right behind him. "He will be held without bail until the charges proceed. And though I would never intentionally wish anyone harm, a man with so many skeletons in his closet can have a lot to fear in prison."

Cole came straight around the bed and leaned over to kiss me and breathe in my scent. Harrison was on his heels. They were here, and I finally felt complete. "You think they'll kill him?" I asked.

"I have no idea," Harrison said. "But I would be lying if I said I hoped they didn't. I want nothing more than to put my hands on that man and rip his head from his body."

I shivered at the violence in his tone. It didn't frighten me—it made me feel safer. There was a simplicity in it. "If it had been him in the warehouse?"

"I would have shot him too," Cole said. "He touched you. I don't know if it makes me evil, but I won't mourn him if something happens."

Reaching out, I put my hand on the back of Harrison's. "I don't want you to go to jail either, so I'm glad you didn't kill him."

"That's the only reason why I'm glad," Harrison said under his breath. It brought a small smile to my face.

Cole switched places with him and knelt, taking my hand in his and kissing the back. "I'm so sorry, Petra. I shouldn't have let you get in that car alone. God, I'm sorry."

"You couldn't have known. I didn't even know until it was too late."

"They planned it well," Harrison said. "I'll give them that."

Cole still stared at me, and I felt his anguish firsthand in our bond. Tears washed the world into a blurry mess, and he pulled me far enough from Blake to embrace me. "I thought I lost you," he whispered. "I love you. More than you can ever know."

He was wrong about that. I did know. I could feel it through him. "I love you."

He gave me one flicker of a smile. "I apologize in advance for the overbearing ass I'm probably going to be for a while. The thought of you being... anywhere other than near me is unbearable."

"No complaints from me," I said. "At the moment I don't ever want to leave the penthouse again."

Harrison squeezed my foot. "We'll keep you safe, little one. And when you're ready, we'll help you get back to the world. But none of us are going to mind you being home for a while."

Home.

They were my home.

"Yes, we are, baby," Blake said, sensing my thoughts.

"There's something else I need to tell you," Cole said. I cringed away from his tone, but he didn't let me. "Your father is here."

Emery stood and went to the door, looking both ways down the hallway. "Petra said she didn't want to talk to him."

"I know," Cole said, never taking his eyes off me. "He told us about the ambulance."

"Are you going to make me?" I asked.

He shook his head. "Never, honeybee. Of course not. But I'll ask you to think about it. He knows he fucked up, and he knows he may not be able to fix it. But he doesn't want to lose you either."

Anxious nausea swam in my stomach. "It shouldn't take this," I said. "It shouldn't take someone trying to kill me to make him believe me."

"I know." Cole kissed my hand again. "I know. Just think about it. Doesn't have to be now, or ever. I know you love your father, and if there's a chance you guys can come back from this, then that's good. But it's your choice, always."

Whatever prompted me to open my mouth and just start telling them, I didn't know. It just bubbled up. "Charles told them they could do whatever they wanted to me. They just had to wait until the deadline to kill me. That's why they tried to drug me. So I wouldn't fight."

Their rage resonated through me, followed by grief, because of everything it could have meant.

"I ran," I whispered. "I promise I tried. I fought, and I wasn't strong enough. But I tried."

Cole pressed his fingers to his eyes. "Fuck."

Emery came around and gave Cole a moment. "Of course you tried," he whispered, gently turning me on my back once more so he could lie with Blake and me. "Of course you did. We never would have thought differently."

The news still played on mute. There was a photo of me on the screen. But it wasn't one of the bad ones. This was of

Harrison and I at the Gala, when he dipped me back and kissed me, the others beaming like it was the best thing they'd ever seen.

It felt like a lifetime ago. I was so far away from that girl. "What if I'm broken?" I asked quietly. "What if I'm never the same?" Because those moments branded me in a way I wouldn't be able to forget.

When you touched true despair, it left a mark.

"Look at me, baby," Blake said.

I turned my head, not quite able to meet his eyes.

"You're not going to be the same. No one ever is after going through something like this. You weren't the same person after your mom and dads died. You weren't the same person after that fucking photo at the conservatory. Hell, you aren't the same person you were before you met us. But you are *not* broken."

"Can I..." I stared at the ceiling. "Can I sleep?"

"Yes, baby. You can sleep. We're not going anywhere."

I closed my eyes and breathed in the scent of home and safety. They weren't going anywhere.

CHAPTER FIFTY-SIX

PETRA

*W*hen I woke, we were home. The nightmares I had left me almost more tired than when I fell asleep, but at home I felt better. I spent the next two days resting with my Alphas. Lying on their chests while we watched movies. Snuggling with Stormy. Being fed the most incredible food in Slate City because Blake was working his ass off. Waking up screaming for the men in masks to *stop*.

I said almost nothing.

The third morning, I felt different. I had no idea what day of the week it was, but I felt *better*. Blake was right—I wasn't going to be the same. But I was still me, nightmares and all.

Blake's room was one of my favorites. The walls were a burnt orange that made everything feel warm, with lighter furnishings. It almost felt like it could be a beachside cabana.

Rolling over, I found him already awake and watching me. "How long have you been awake?"

"A while," he said, smirking. "You feel better?"

"Yeah."

"I'm glad." He pulled me in, resting his lips against my forehead. "Your bond feels brighter. Easier."

"Sorry."

He chuckled. "You know that's not what I meant, baby. There's no shame in taking time. We needed it too. We still need it."

There was no doubt in my mind it *would* take time. But my subconscious finally understood I was home and safe, and my Alphas were never letting me go. It was enough.

"I need to take a shower."

Our bond turned deeper, the feelings between us more sensual. "Want me to come with you?"

A smile broke over my face, and I laughed. God, that was a

good feeling. "How about we see if I don't immediately panic when you're not in the room with me first?"

"Fair enough." His gaze swept down my body. My body was painfully aware it hadn't had them in days. And I wanted them just as much. But there were a few things I needed to get out of my head before we did that. Kissing my cheek, Blake got out of bed. "I'm going to make some breakfast."

Stormy came flying out of the nest when I got into the bathroom and played in the shower with me. She loved trying to catch the water droplets, even though it was impossible.

I dried her off too and sat on the floor. She pushed her head into my shoulder. It was easy to hug her. "We're going to have so much fun," I told her. "I'm going to build you the biggest cat tree ever. Maybe we'll even get you a hammock. Would you like that?"

Stormy chuffed, and I laughed.

Fuck, I needed to go shopping. I barely had any clothes left after Carmen destroyed my apartment. And I needed to start decorating this *room*.

By the time I'd found a pair of leggings and put on one of Emery's stolen hoodies, the aching pressure had lifted from my chest. I was alive. I was healthy. I was loved.

I was okay.

A smile came to my face, and I sat down on the stairs. I was okay. It hit me like a freight train—everything was *good*. The danger was gone. I didn't have to go to fucking law school, and I was bonded to a pack who loved me. Now I couldn't wipe the smile off my face.

It didn't change things. The thought of stepping outside the penthouse still terrified me right now, and I doubted the nightmares would disappear for a long time. Harrison had already found someone for me to talk to, and I looked forward to it. My first appointment was in a few days.

Still, there was far more for me to look forward to than there was before all of this.

The scent of eggs and bacon wafted from the kitchen, but I turned right and went to Harrison's office. The sight of him in comfortable sweats and a t-shirt instead of a suit undid me. He looked up when I appeared, a smile taking over his face. "Hello there."

"Hey." I went to him and slid onto his lap.

"My little Omega found herself again?"

"I think so. Not perfectly."

His hands squeezed my hips. "Perfect is overrated."

Biting down on my lip, I hesitated. Harrison didn't prod me. Just waited until I figured out what I wanted to say. If we ever got into a fight with the silent treatment, he would be the one to win. One-hundred percent. "Can you do something for me?"

"You know I will."

Blowing out a sigh, I looked out the window over the city. "I need to see my dad."

Harrison didn't speak right away. "You're sure?"

"Yeah. I need to hear what he has to say, at least. And now that I'm feeling better, I don't feel like I can... do anything else until I do. Does that make sense?"

"Yes. Absolutely. I'll call his office and bring him over here."

"What if he's in the capital?"

Harrison smiled. "Petra, your father has been calling me every couple of hours to make sure you're okay. I think he has a car waiting on standby in case you made this exact decision."

My mouth popped open. "Really?"

"Yeah. I actually asked him to call me *less* because if you wanted to talk to him you would, and if something happened, like you going back to the hospital, I would let him know."

I frowned. "But everything was fine on my scans."

"I needed to use something." A devious smirk took over his face. "If I made him worry about his daughter a bit more and think about his actions, then so be it."

"You're a little ruthless," I said, grinning.

"When it calls for it. And it did."

I sighed. "Yeah, call him. I'll be in the breakfast room."

Emery at work—though I swore he was becoming annoyed he was the only one who truly had to work outside the penthouse. Cole went to headquarters to continue training the new employees, and Blake would have to do the rounds at his restaurants after this kind of absence.

The eggs and bacon were so fucking good. The noises I made while eating them had Blake staring at me like he wanted to eat *me*. And based on our bond, he did.

I took a slow sip of orange juice while he watched me.

"Baby, don't tease me when I can't follow through on what we both want."

"But it's fun."

He groaned and threw his head back. "God, I love you." Then he stood and leaned over me, as close as we could be without touching. "Are you feeling well enough for tonight?"

For sex. I shivered. Yes. What I wanted most was to get back to some kind of normal. Or as normal as we could be. Like I'd made Cole promise, we were never going to be the boring normal. But I wanted them to take me and fuck me and make me think about nothing but them. "Yeah," I said.

"Good. Because my tongue has a date with your pussy. My life hasn't been nearly sweet enough without it."

Heat sank through me, drawing familiar and welcome arousal. "Maybe we won't have to wait till tonight." Wrapping my arms around his neck, I let him kiss me until we were both breathless.

The sound of the front door broke us apart. Blake laughed softly. "Sorry, baby. Shouldn't have turned you on before this kind of conversation."

"Gives me something to look forward to."

Harrison's voice and my father's echoed softly in the entryway. But I didn't move yet. I wanted him to be in the living room when I got there.

"Do you think I should forgive him?" I asked.

Blake shrugged and sat down with me. "I don't know."

"That's not an answer."

"It's the only one I've got. This is between you and him. Whatever you decide, we'll respect it and support you."

I turned and pulled my legs up. "But if you were me, what would you do?"

He sighed, looking out over the city. "I would listen to everything he had to say before I made a decision, and that's the truth.

432

But Petra," Blake's hand landed on my knee. "Remember that this isn't *your* problem to fix. It's not your job to repair the damage he created. If you want to let him close that gap, then he has to be the one to build the bridge."

The words hit me in the chest. Yeah, I was going to have to remember that. A lifetime of habits made me want to make sure he was okay. Blake was right. "Thanks."

Harrison appeared. "He's up there whenever you're ready."

I smirked at him. "Is he still mad at you?"

"No, I think the 'I saved your daughter's life' outweighs the 'I fucked and bonded your daughter behind your back.'"

Blake fought a smile. I didn't fight mine. "Good. He didn't have a right to be mad at you, anyway." I stood and stretched. "Wish me luck."

"If you need us, we're here. And I will throw him out anytime you want. If you need me to."

"I'll remember that too."

Harrison kissed my hair as I passed and took the longest walk up a flight of stairs ever. The living room door was cracked open, and I peeked through it. Dad stood facing away from me, staring down at my piano. From here, he looked defeated, shoulders slumped and head bowed.

It was weird seeing him in casual clothes. I couldn't remember the last time I saw him relaxed instead of in a polished suit worthy of being chancellor.

Finally, I stepped into the room. "Dad."

He startled and turned. "Sweetheart." Immediately, he took a step forward and stopped. I nodded, and he closed the distance to hug me.

The familiarity—

I missed this.

It felt real and simple, and absent of everything really between us.

Dad finally stepped back. "I've been beside myself the last couple of days, hoping you'd call."

"Harrison told me. I only just felt up to it."

He blew out a breath and ran a hand through his hair. "Petra,

I am so sorry. I know it's not enough. No apology will ever be big enough, but you need to know that I am."

I swallowed. "For what?"

"For everything. All the way back to the conservatory. Before that. It sounds like an excuse to say I was so blinded by my grief and my work to see anything but what was in front of me, but it's true. I hate that it took something like this to make me see it."

My hands curled into fists. "I am so... *fucking* pissed at you."

My father stood there, acceptance in his gaze.

"You could have asked me, Dad. You could have talked to me. Instead, you believed her over me. Every time. Do you realize that? When I told you I'd never done drugs in my life, you *didn't believe me*. And you made it so no matter what I did, there was nothing I could say to convince you."

Now that the words were flowing, they came in a rushing torrent.

"For years, I did everything for you. I kept you going after Mom died. And Levi. And Garrett. And I was happy to do it because they were your pack, but you never seemed to notice that *I LOST THEM TOO*." Angry tears spilled over, and I wasn't fucking done, because this had been a long time coming, and it felt good.

"And I tried. I tried to make sure you were okay. You married Carmen and things were good. Then the whole thing with the photo happened, and again, I tried to do what was best for *you*. I dropped out. I stayed out of the spotlight, because if I did, then you were okay. No matter that it was my first heat, I didn't know what I was doing, and I was nervous, alone, and taken advantage of. I still did it for you."

"Petra—"

"I swear to god, Dad, you will let me finish. You owe me that much."

He nodded slowly.

"Did you know that it was your key card? Carmen was the one who destroyed my apartment, and she used your card to get in. Did they tell you that? Did she tell you that she slapped me so hard after the charity ball photos that I saw stars?" I shook my head, and my voice cracked. "Everything I have done in my entire fucking life has been for you, Dad. And I am done. From making sure you got out of bed in the morning to Mom's piano. I can't do it anymore. I need to have something for myself."

Dad was white as death. "What about Mallory's piano? You said you put it in storage."

I swiped tears off my face, frustrated that I couldn't stop. "You destroyed it," I whispered. "On the anniversary of the accident you got blackout drunk and broke it into pieces. I told you I sent it away because I knew seeing it broken would wreck you. You told me you could barely look at me or listen to me play because I was too much like her. That it was a knife in your heart. And then you lit up like a fucking Christmas tree when I asked about law school, and it was the first time..." I swallowed, trying to get it out. "It was the first time you'd ever been proud of me. So I did it, even though I hated it."

Tears streamed down my father's face as he looked at me. "Can I hug you, sweetheart? Please?"

I nodded.

He carefully wrapped me in his arms and hugged me. It was comforting to be surrounded by his scent. That elusive smell of paper and ink, old books. It reminded me of playing in his office when I was young.

"You are so much like your mother," he said. "I won't pretend it doesn't hurt. It does. But I welcome the pain, because with you I get a little tiny piece of her. I can't even tell you how sorry I am that I said something like that. Regardless of anything else, I have always been proud of you."

My tears didn't stop, a different kind of dam broken. "And the rest of it. God, I'm so sorry, Petra. I wish there were better words to say it."

I finally stepped back, scrubbing my face with the sleeve of Emery's hoodie. "I'm not going to tell you it's okay. It's not. I know you're sorry, but right now, I'm not sure if it's enough. I need time, and I need you to fix it."

"I will," he said. "I will do whatever it takes."

Stormy came into the room, and my dad froze. She came to me and curled around my leg, sensing my distress. "This is

Stormy. She's a clouded leopard. Her Omega died, so Emery brought her home."

"She's beautiful."

I knelt down next to her and scratched behind her ears. "I don't know what it will take, Dad. I really don't. But I meant it when I said I'm done. I don't want to lose you, but if you're going to be in my life, you will take the lead in repairing the damage."

Stormy crept forward, and my father held out a hand for her to sniff. She rubbed against it, but not nearly as enthusiastically as with some others. "I promise, Petra. I will."

We fell into silence for a moment, Stormy pushing me down to climb into my lap, even though she was far too big to fit there.

"I want to say a couple things, okay?"

"Okay."

"First, I would hope it's obvious that Carmen and I are done. I imagine she'll plead to a lower charge because Charles masterminded so much of this, but she will go to prison, and as soon as my lawyer finishes them, she will be served with divorce papers."

"Good."

"Second, Charles Bower will never leave prison. If there's one thing I do in my life, it will be to make sure of it. He still has power, but I will do everything I can to limit it and strip him of anything he can use inside."

I only nodded. Thinking about him still drove a spike of fear through my chest.

"And third, I'm considering stepping down."

"What?"

Dad turned and went to the windows by the piano. "Charles helped me win. If he did that, I shouldn't even be where I am now, let alone running for chancellor."

"He told me he didn't change the votes. Only the media."

"Does it matter?"

Setting Stormy on her feet, I stood back up. "To me it does, yeah. Because anyone can play with the media. It was just easier for him. But more importantly, everything I've gone through has been specifically so you could be here. If you just give it up, then what the hell was the point?"

436

He looked hopeful. "You would be all right with that?"

"Yes," I said. "Carmen wasn't wrong about one thing. You do what you do because you care about people and making their lives better. So try to do something good to make it worth it. Please."

Dad slid his hands into the pockets of his jeans. "I... thank you. I honestly didn't expect that."

"I'm not trying to punish you, Dad. It's just time for me to live my life for me."

"You said you're going to pursue music?"

I tried to smile. "Yeah. I don't know how, really, or how it will turn out. But I'm going to try."

"It will turn out great," he said. "You've always been incredible."

"Thank you."

He looked over his shoulder at the piano. "I know now isn't the right time, but in the spirit of trying to make amends, I'd like to meet your pack. On your terms. I wish I'd known you were scent-sympathetic."

"I don't know if it would have changed things."

"Maybe not. But I'd still like to meet them."

Reaching down to scratch Stormy's ears, I nodded. "All right. We'll figure something out. Either here, or one of Blake's restaurants."

"That would be nice."

We stared at each other awkwardly. Dad scratched the back of his neck. "I guess I should go. I'm relieved to see you safe... and happy."

"Thanks, Dad."

No hugs this time. It didn't feel right. But he paused at the door and looked back. "I miss her, you know. Every day."

"Me too. I—" Emotion closed my throat. "I saved a couple of keys from her piano. I'll give you one next time, if you want it."

Dad's eyes went glassy. "I would like that. Very much."

"Okay."

"Okay," he whispered. "I love you."

He didn't wait for me to say it back, slipping out the door to the elevator. "I love you too."

Stormy leaned against my shoulder, flopping down onto the floor and rolling for belly pats. "Thank you, girl."

I felt them before they appeared, even Emery. "You're home?"

"The nice thing about being a vet for exotic animals, you're not booked to the gills every day. I only had one appointment." His smile was welcome.

"And you?" I asked Cole.

"I came home as soon as Harrison said your dad was on the way."

"Didn't think I could handle it?"

An eye roll. "You're more than capable of handling your dad. More like I was already looking for an excuse to come back."

Emery was in blue scrubs like the day I first met him, and he sat down on the floor on the other side of Stormy. "How'd it go?"

"About as well as it could have. He's going to try, and I'll let him. But I made myself clear." I looked at each of them. "He also wants to meet all of you, this time as my pack and not anything else."

Cole leaned against the wall. "We can make that happen."

"Not for a little while, though."

He smirked. "Noted, honeybee."

"What do you feel like doing?" Blake asked. "We have all the time in the world."

I knew exactly where his thoughts were heading, but after that conversation, I needed to breathe for a bit. "I've been keeping you all from working. Don't you have to make sure your restaurants aren't on fire?" I looked at Blake. "And I know you were looking for an excuse, but I'm sure both you and Harrison have things to do."

"There's nothing that can't wait until tomorrow, little one. We decided we want one more day. One more day with our Omega before we let the real world back in."

The words *our Omega* made my heart pound and my skin flush. I really was their Omega. "Well, I'm not going to say *no*."

We all laughed. It felt easy and light. The way I wanted it to be.

"I vote we order pizza and soda and ice cream and turn the

living room into half a nest," Emery said. That sounded amazing. Blake groaned, and Emery pinned him with a stare. "We can order from one of the like... two pizza places you like. For once, you don't have to be a foodie."

Blake laughed. "I could just make the pizza."

"Or you could relax with me." I held out my hands like scales and tipped one hand down. "You can survive some fast food pizza."

He shook his head, but he was laughing. "Fine. I will endure the pizza."

"He won't tell you, but he secretly loves it. We'll need to order an entire pizza just for him."

Blake didn't disagree.

"I thought you all would be tired of watching movies by now," I said. It was half of what we'd done the last couple of days.

"Oh, I think we can handle some more. Besides, we haven't even touched what any of our favorite movies are," Harrison said. "And we don't know yours."

All the love and comfort pouring through their bonds was everything. For a glorious flash I was back when we bonded, living in the moment. I loved these men with everything I had.

"And maybe later," I said softly. "We could go to the arcade?" Leaving still felt like terror, but with them? I could do anything. "I need to see Harrison dance again."

Emery stood and lifted me up before sweeping me off my feet and over to the couch. "I think we can do that, sunshine." He set me down. "I need to change."

"I'll grab blankets and pillows," Blake said, jogging out of the room.

Cole pulled out his phone. "I'll order the pizza and change."

"I guess I'll set up the movie." Harrison found the remotes and started flicking through menus.

In minutes, they were all back, dressed in comfy clothes, with enough pillows and blankets for all of us. Harrison claimed a seat beside me, Emery on my other side. Blake and Cole sat on the floor where they could still touch me. I was sure they would all switch at some point.

I leaned over onto Harrison's chest, sinking into pillows and blankets and soft touches. "I love you."

Suddenly I was surrounded by purrs, and there was no doubt that every single one of them thought it. Sent it through the bond. Stamped it on my heart.

Harrison held me closer to his chest. "We love you too, little one."

EPILOGUE I

PETRA

TWO WEEKS LATER

"Oh, fuck," I nearly screamed the words, pleasure overtaking me like a tidal wave laced with starlight. My whole body moved, writhing in pleasure only to be held where I was.

"I told you I would replace all the toys," Emery said in my ear. The vibration lowered enough for me to breathe. "I know."

He had said that, and decided to start with the one we never made it to—the one I hid in the closet. They decided it was a good idea to illustrate how that session with Emery had gone first thing on a Sunday morning.

My legs came down on either side of the seat, my clit *right* where the center of the vibrations were. Emery held my hands behind my back. I couldn't even hold on. The machine and cushions and my legs were soaked after what must have been the tenth orgasm they wrung from me.

"That's right, little Omega." Harrison knelt in front of me, hand around my throat, casually stroking his cock like I wasn't wrecked, breathless, and dazed with pleasure. "We're looking forward to all of them. But I think this one will become a favorite." He leaned in and bit the sensitive skin beneath my ear before using his tongue to soothe the skin. My Alpha loved those tiny sparks of pain that somehow made everything sharper and clearer.

I did too, though I would never admit it.

"I hate all of you." My voice sounded like I'd been screaming for an hour.

Which, I guess, I had.

"You guys have had nothing this whole time. It's your turn."

Blake knelt on my left and put his lips to my ear. "I don't think you understand how *delicious* feeling you come is, baby. My

441

cock is so ready for you, I'm not going to last for shit by the time I fuck you, and every single orgasm is worth it."

"Speaking of orgasms," Cole spoke from where he knelt on my right, controlling the vibrations. "I think we can get one more out of her, don't you?"

I whined, desperate for something. Whether it was more or if it was for it to end, I had no idea. The vibrations rose, and I moaned. "I can't."

"We already know you can, sunshine. And you love it. But I have something that will make it even better."

He lifted one of my hands to the side. I didn't know what he was doing until they all did it, moving in sync, biting down on their bond marks all at the same time.

I exploded. A galaxy of glitter caught me in the middle of breaking apart. It ripped me into pieces, covered me with shine, and put me back together again. So this was what true fireworks meant.

The toy disappeared. Harrison slid beneath me and lowered me onto his cock. I was already so sensitive I nearly came from the friction of the single movement. Emery was there next, easing into my ass so they could share me the way they loved.

"Oh my god," I murmured, head lolling back on Emery's shoulder. "The only thing better than this would be taking all of you together."

"There's a way to do that, sweet girl," Emery growled, thrusting deep. "During your next heat, we'll try it."

Three of them inside me, and the other in my mouth... I shuddered.

Blake tilted my chin up to look at him, his hand moving over his cock. "Let me paint those pretty tits, baby."

My eyes rolled back in my head and closed. The way they brought me to the edge and wrapped my mind in a golden fog where there was nothing but bliss.

Heat splashed on my skin, and the base, raw part of me reveled in being marked. Owned. Loved. Treasured. His orgasm through our bond was incredible. Sharp and electric, and I knew what he meant when he said feeling it was delicious.

Blake's mouth slammed down on mine a second before

Cole's hand gathered my hair and turned me toward him and his waiting cock. It had been too long since I had the taste of caramel.

"I'm there too," he said, thrusting deeper. Not far enough to knot. He came, pleasure spiraling between us as sweetness burst across my tongue. "God, Petra, *yes.*"

I swallowed him like candy.

The Alphas inside me were close. I felt the tension and power building inside them and yielded, letting them take me and enjoying every fucking second. All those orgasms they gave me had affected them, too. One after another they came, taking me with them, knots pushing together.

White flashed behind my eyes, and this time I couldn't even scream. I simply melted into bliss.

It felt like ages later when I realized I'd collapsed on Harrison's chest. Emery's hands were on my ass as his knot eased and he pulled back. "So I think this toy is a keeper."

I laughed, breathless and exhausted. "I'm going to start hiding them from you."

"Oh, do it, sunshine. It'll make it so much more fun when I find them and surprise you."

A little thrill ran through me. Harrison's knot let me go, and I slid to the side, sprawling on the cushions. "That's it for the day," I said. "I'm done."

Harrison laughed. "Nope. We have a guest, remember?"

"Right. When is he getting here?"

"I don't have my phone, but probably an hour?" Cole said.

"Okay, I should shower. And no," I said before they could ask. "You can't come with me. Yes, I want you to, but you know why."

Our bonds sang with their amusement.

I showered and dressed, enjoying the beginning stages of my new bedroom. It was painted now, a rich shade of burgundy that matched the nest, but not quite. I had a bed too, a big four-poster with dark, carved wood. Not much else yet, but we were working on it.

And across the room, there was the beginnings of Stormy's castle, as I liked to call it. She was currently passed out in the hammock we'd hung from the ceiling. When she wasn't trying to steal my nest, I could usually find her there.

Checking my phone, I found another article featuring George and his pack. Since Charles went to prison, he stepped up into his father's shoes, and it seemed like every day there was some new horror to uncover about the man who tried to kill me.

Every time something new was found, I felt better. Everything added to him being in prison for the rest of his life, and George was just as determined as my father to strip him of anything he had left.

There was also a text from Sloane planning our lunch in a couple of days, and Eva, lamenting she couldn't make it because of her filming schedule. Esme told us she could be there, which sent the two sisters into an emoji battle the likes of which I'd never seen.

"Petra," Blake called. "It's time."

"Be right there." I took the elevator down and met the rest of them in the entryway. "He's here?"

"Coming up now."

Harrison opened the door after the soft knock, revealing an older Alpha with a cane. Emery stepped forward. "Hi, Dennis."

"Hello." The older man took off his hat. "It's good to see you again." Then his eyes fell on me, and where Cole had rested his hand around my hip. Unmistakable grief shone in his eyes. "I very much appreciate this."

"Any time," I said. "Really. I'm sure she's going to be so excited to see you."

Dennis chuckled. "She might not even remember me."

I went to the stairs. "Stormy," I raised my voice. Even with the four floors, the cat had supernatural hearing. It wouldn't be a problem. "Here, girl."

A few seconds later I heard the telltale thumps we'd all gotten used to. Stormy trotted around down the stairs and straight over to me. "Hi there," I scratched behind her ears. "Someone is here to see you."

I pointed to Dennis, and Stormy followed where I pointed. And she *ran*. Up on her two back legs, she nearly knocked Dennis over. He managed to hold on to her, but in the end, they were both on the floor with him holding her, and her making every happy noise she could.

Using my sleeve, I dabbed the corners of my eyes. The older man wept. It was both hard and beautiful to watch. Finally, he looked up at us. "Thank you."

Harrison gave him a hand to help him up.

"Would you like some coffee?" Blake asked.

Dennis looked down at Stormy. "I think I would like it."

In the breakfast room, she curled up beside Dennis with her head in his lap, and we listened to stories about her first year of life. The crazy things she'd done when she was still a kitten, like climbing the drapes all the way to the ceiling and falling asleep in the empty washing machine.

"We're building her a castle upstairs," I told him. "She already has a hammock, and we're working on a big cat tree she can play on."

He stroked her side. "She'll love that."

"I hope so."

Slowly, he scratched behind her ears. "I don't want to take up your whole day. It was good to see her."

"You don't have to leave," Cole said. "Truly."

Still looking down at Stormy, he nodded. "Yes, I do. I—" His voice broke off, and he didn't have to say anything else. I understood. Not only was seeing Stormy painful, but we reminded him of everything he lost.

When he stood, Stormy rose and followed him. We all did. But he turned at the door and set his hand on her head. "Love you, wild one. You have a new Omega to take care of now, don't you?"

She leaned into his hand and brushed against his leg before turning and trotting to my feet. She sat right in front of me and looked back at Dennis like she was telling him *yes*.

I put my hand on my chest to fight the ache.

"You're a beautiful pack," Dennis said. "I'm grateful she has you."

"You're welcome to visit her when you please, Dennis," Harrison said. "Our door is open."

"Thank you." But I didn't feel like he was going to take us up on the offer. Something about this felt like a true goodbye.

One more time petting Stormy, and he was out the door.

"Wow," Blake said. "That was…"

"Brutal," Cole finished for him. "Beautiful, but brutal."

"Hang on just a second." I dashed out the door after him and down to the elevator. "Dennis," I called.

He was waiting for the elevator to arrive, and smiled when he saw me. "Miss Petra."

"I just needed to ask you." I caught my breath. "Was it worth it? Even now?"

Dennis's eyes shifted. Not looking away, but seeing things I couldn't. Memories and love I couldn't imagine. I didn't have to tell him what I meant.

The elevator doors opened, and he went inside. "Yes," he said, the doors closing. "It was more than worth it."

I slid to my knees inside the front door and hugged Stormy, who still looked after the older Alpha. "He loves you," I whispered. "So much."

Cole lifted me to my feet. "Why?"

I wrapped my arms around him. "I asked him if it was worth it."

"Was what worth it?" Blake asked.

I looked at each of my Alphas. "This."

Being a pack. Loving and being loved, despite knowing it would eventually end in loss.

Harrison stepped closer. "What did he say?"

Emery was already smiling, because he knew the answer. I closed my eyes. "He said yes."

I wasn't sure if the tears in my eyes were happy or sad. Maybe both. But as each of my Alphas held me, I knew it was the truth.

This would always be more than worth it.

EPILOGUE II

PETRA

ONE YEAR LATER

"*I*'m going to throw up."

"No, you're not," Sloane scolded me. "You're going to be fantastic. Seriously."

Eva stood from where she'd been lounging in my dressing room. "She's right. You look fucking *fabulous*, and you're going to kill it out there."

Someone knocked at the door.

"Okay," Sloane said. "Everyone out. It's Alpha time. Break a leg, Bee."

"Thank you."

My Alphas entered, and it was hard not to stare, because they all looked absolutely incredible in tuxedos, and the last time we'd all been this dressed up was when we announced our bond to the world.

As their scents filled the room, I felt the appreciation they had for me in this dress just as much as I had for them. The black silk was long in the back, short in the front, so I could reach the pedals without any issues.

"You nervous?" Cole asked.

"Don't ask her that," Blake elbowed him in the side. "That's just going to make it worse."

I laughed. "Yes, I'm nervous. But I'm also ready."

It was the truth. There was no more rehearsing I could do unless I wanted to beat the pieces I was playing tonight to death.

My first solo concert was sold out. If I closed my eyes, I could hear the faint hum of the audience.

"And didn't you hear?" Emery asked. "The *Chancellor* is here."

I smiled. "You know, I actually did hear that."

Dad won the election in a landslide, and even though the two of us weren't where we wanted to be, we were getting better. He was making the effort I needed him to, but slowly, given he now had to run the country.

Harrison reached out and touched the necklace I wore. "Your mother would be proud, Petra."

A flood of emotion hit me in the face. It was going to happen anyway, considering what I was playing tonight. But putting on the necklace from the Gala, the one she wore too, she was close to the surface. And for once, it wasn't all pain in the memories.

"Don't make me cry," I said.

"Never on purpose, little one." Harrison pulled me close. "We love you."

Emery was next. "I'm so fucking proud of you, you know that?"

"I do know that," I said, grinning. They told me nearly every day.

Blake spun me under his arm before dancing me around the space quickly. "You're going to be incredible."

"Don't jinx it."

"You can't jinx talent."

Cole caught me and steadied me. He smiled down at me, enveloping me in salted caramel. "Should I find a closet for us to sneak off to? Just for good luck."

"Maybe after."

He kissed my forehead. "You have this."

The stage manager knocked. "We need you, Petra."

"I guess it's time."

They headed for the door, and Harrison winked. "We'll see you after."

I shook my hands out after they left, taking a few deep breaths before I went to the stage. The hum of the crowd went straight to my gut. So many people. In the darkness behind the curtain, the piano waited. The few musicians accompanying me were already in place.

Tonight, I played the same concert my mother did the night she died. Some people wondered if I was a glutton for punishment, but it calmed me. It felt like closure to know I was continuing where she left off.

The lights in the house faded to nothing, and the curtain opened. I walked out. As soon as the spotlight hit me, a wave of sound crashed forward. Thunderous applause, so much the stage vibrated under my feet. Bowing, I went to the piano and sat.

The first piece was just me.

A slow and delicate start, the same song which had played in the living room a year ago. A song burned in my memory. And I was entirely swept away.

Now I didn't have to hold anything back or check my emotions. I gave into them, letting the music take me down into memories I'd nearly forgotten.

Dancing with Mom in our sunroom. Baking those cookies with Levi and Garrett. Singing silly songs on the road when we traveled with her. The bedtime stories she would make up so I could fall asleep in strange hotel rooms.

One song into the next, I barely felt time passing.

Instead, it felt like peace.

A single, echoing note ended the last piece. There were tears on my face, and I didn't remember crying. I barely remembered any of it. But the knot in my chest which had been there since the accident?

It was gone.

"Thanks, Mom," I whispered.

The audience was on their feet. I couldn't see them through the brightness of the lights, only that they were standing, and cheering, for me.

This was the moment I had dreaded. The final moments of being in the spotlight, where I'd never wanted to be. But it was so different than I imagined.

The bonds in my chest were bursting with pride and awe. When we got home, my pack would shower me with love.

I took my bow and slowly breathed.

The applause was thunder and rain, and the spotlight was the eye of the storm. A true sense of calm and purpose I never believed until this moment.

One more bow as the curtain closed, and I looked up at the ceiling, letting it wash over me. It was so easy to regret and wish things were different, but I didn't. All of the missteps and all of the pain, they all brought me here. To this moment.

And finally, I was exactly where I was supposed to be.

The End

There will be more in the Slate City world soon!

*H*ello beautiful readers!

Thank you so much for joining in Petra's story! She was *so* fun to write with so many ups and downs. I'm a little in love with the Slate City world, and I can't wait to dive into more stories there!

In the meantime, I'd love to meet you! Sign up for my newsletter for updates and sneak peeks, and the occasional dessert recipe!

I also have a Facebook group where we share memes, I share snippets of works in progress, and everything in between. Come join the Court of Fantasy! I hope to see you there, and there will be more books very soon!

Devlyn Sinclair

PLAYLIST

This is a playlist of some of the songs I listened to while writing *Knot All That Glitters*.

This playlist is available on Spotify

**Songs used for inspiration within certain scenes while Petra plays the Piano

- **687 Days** — David Maxim Micic
- **After All** — Culture Code, ARAYA, RUNN
- **Already Numb** — Dayseeker
- **Altar** — Kehlani
- **Amène-moi** — Gísli Gunnarsson
- **Ascension** — Berlinist
- **Bagatelle En Mineur** — Franz Gordon
- **Beauty of Kura** — Vusal Zeinalov
- **Collateral** — Gustavo Santaolalla
- **Dance For Me Wallis** — Abel Korzeniowski
- **Don't Let Me Go** — Roniit
- **Duck Shoot** — Rupert Gregson-Williams
- **Elegy For The Arctic** — Ludovico Einaudi
- **The Encounter** — ABBOTT, 2WEI
- **Experience** — Ludovico Einaudi
- **Face My Fears** — Wind Walkers

- **Fever** — Sunsleep
- **Fire** — Fabrizio Paterlini
- **For Granted** — Lauren Spencer Smith
- **Fractions** — Gabriel Parker
- **Frost** — SayWeCanFly
- ****Gnossienne: No. 1** — Erik Satie, Alexandre Tharaud
- **Gnossienne: n° 4** — Erik Satie, Alexandre Tharaud
- **Godless** — BANKS
- **Gris, Pt. 1** — Berlinist
- **Hard to Forget** Jane XØ
- **The Home We Made Pt. II (Bonus Version)** — Crywolf, Dylan Owen
- **Hundreds** — Lissom
- **Idea 10 (Slowed & Reverb)** — Gibran Alcocer
- **If I Had an Airplane** — SayWeCanFly
- **If You Don't** — IMERIKA
- **Just Pretend** — Bad Omens
- **Lenitivo** — Jeanelle Bolduc
- **Le Papillon Solitaire** — Franz Gordon
- **Limbo** —Lissom
- **Lonely** — Skyfall Beats
- **Low Mist Var. 2 - Day 1** — Ludovico Einaudi
- **Low Mist Var. 2 - Day 7** — Ludovico Einaudi
- ****Main Theme in F#/Poème in F#** — Re ut Ben-Ze, Nicholas Britell
- **Mascaron** — Lissom
- **Minefields** — Faouzia, John Legend
- **Miracle** — Hazy
- **Moncage** — Berlinist
- **Music Box** — Andrew James Johnson
- **My Father Said** — Hurtwave
- **Nagorno Mist** — Vusal Zeinalov
- **The Night We Met** — Lord Huron
- **Peace In Emptiness** — Blanke
- **Please Don't Go** — Barcelona
- **The Remedy** — Ana Olgica
- **Renegade** — Aaryan Shah

- **Savagery - Hahlweg Remix** — Lissom
- ****Silence** — Jannik Haverland
- **Silent Messenger** — Desiderii Marginis
- **Suffocate** — Nathan Wagner
- **Tempest Sonata 3rd Movement** — Beethoven, Kassia
- **Three Worlds: Music From Woolf Works/Mrs. Dalloway: War Anthem** — Max Richter
- **Tides** — Crywolf, Skrux
- **Varúð** — Sigur Ros
- **Walking Disaster** — SayWeCanFly
- **What if I took it off for you?** — Nemahsis
- **Where the Light Fades** — PALESKIN
- **wRoNg (feat. Kehlani)** — ZAYN, Kehlani
- **You Are a Memory** — Message To Bears

ABOUT THE AUTHOR

Devyn Sinclair writes steamy Reverse Harem romances for your wildest fantasies. Every sexy story is packed with the right amount of steam, hot men, and delicious happy endings.

She lives in the wilds of Montana in a small red house with a crazy orange cat. When Devyn's not writing, she spends time outside in big sky country, continues her quest to find the best lemon pastry there is, and buys too many books. (Of course!)

To connect with Devyn:

ALSO BY DEVYN SINCLAIR

For a complete list of Devyn's books, content warnings, bonuses and extras, please visit her website.

https://www.devynsinclair.com/

Made in the USA
Las Vegas, NV
21 June 2023

73670782R00270